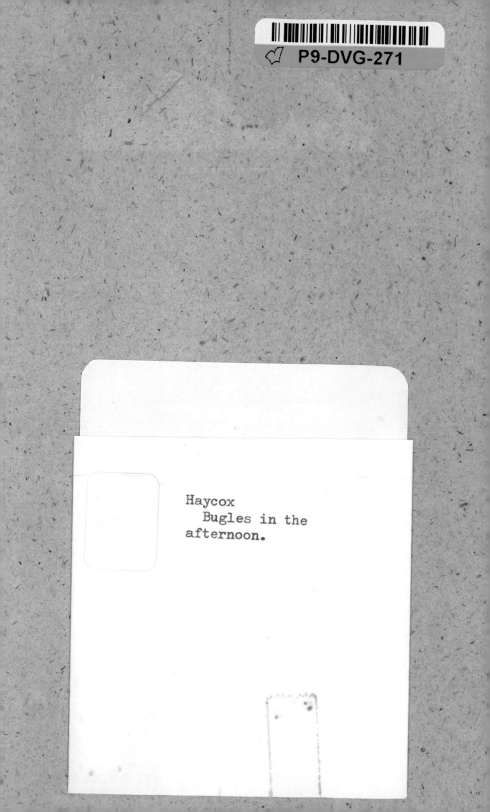

Haycox
  Bugles in the
afternoon.

Bugles in the Afternoon

The Gregg Press Western Fiction Series
Priscilla Oaks, Editor

Bugles in the Afternoon

Ernest Haycox _1899-1950_

with a new introduction by
Ernest Haycox, Jr.

Gregg Press

A division of G. K. Hall & Co., Boston, 1978

Republished in 1978 by Gregg Press, A Division of G. K. Hall & Co.,
70 Lincoln Street, Boston, Massachusetts 02111.

First Printing, October 1978

Library of Congress Cataloging in Publication Data

Haycox, Ernest, 1899–1950.
  Bugles in the afternoon.

  (The Gregg Press western fiction series)
  Reprint of the ed. published by Little,
Brown, Boston.
  1. Custer, George Armstrong, 1839–1876—
Fiction. I. Title. II. Series.
PZ3.H3237Bu 1978 [PS3515.A9327] 813'.5'2
ISBN 0-8398-2473-4   78-14278

Gregg 12/78 6343

Introduction

There are many characters in my father's works whose backgrounds contain some possible reflection of the writer's own life. The hero of *Bugles in the Afternoon*, Kern Shafter, is one of them in his dark and doubting moments and his remembrance of loneliness and disappointment in times past.

Ernest Haycox came from a poor and early-broken family and, by his 12th birthday, perhaps earlier, was on his own. He would tell me of some of these early times, and how he supported himself by selling newspapers on marginal streetcorners (in those days, you fought for the good locations and he was a small boy), vending peanuts and candy on the railroad and, finally, supporting himself through high school as a bellhop.

He lied about his age to join the Oregon National Guard and, at 16, was on the Mexican border with his unit during Pershing's fruitless expedition against Pancho Villa. He went with them again to France where he served as a rifle instructor and military policeman. One assumes, therefore, that he could handle a gun even though, in later life, his only treasured weapon was the frontier army's stock in trade, the Spencer repeating rifle.

He never seriously considered any other profession and started writing early, for high school and college newspapers. He produced fiction at every opportunity and, if memory serves, was first published in a Eugene, Oregon newspaper while an undergraduate at the University of Oregon.

After college, he was a newspaper reporter in Portland for a few months, but he said he was not a good one and did not really want to be. He wanted to write fiction, and the pulp Western market was centered in New York. He went there and survived through several lean years, often walking for hours at a time through Central Park to plot out some high drama of the old frontier. When things began to go well, he returned to Portland where I was born in 1931.

Bugles In The Afternoon first appeared in serial form in *The Saturday Evening Post*. The year was 1943 and its writer was well known as both a skilled and prolific teller of tales about the American West. He had written for the blood-and-thunder pulps in the 1920s and, by the end of that decade, had graduated to the slick magazines. The 30s and early 40s saw a steady stream of Haycox novels and short stories. He was one of the premier writers of fiction of the time.

One short narrative of this period, "Stage to Lordsburg," would become the film, *Stagecoach* in 1939. It was the first, and by all odds the best, of more than half a dozen of his works to become motion pictures. He continued writing in the later 1940s although, by then, his interests had widened and the constraints of serialized, popular fiction had begun to wear thin. He subsequently wrote two transitional novels, both westerns but of a considerably broader dimension. There was much more to come when, at the age of 51, he died of cancer in 1951.

Bugles In The Afternoon comes near the last of the popular book-length works, and it is possibly the best of them. Certainly, it was one of his favorites, for the central historic event of the book, the Custer Massacre, was one he had studied and pondered for many years. It, the massacre, was the grand denouement of a time, and he builds toward this final drama on the Little Bighorn with all the writing skill and dramatic sense that made a Haycox story difficult to set aside and, in fact, frustrating to follow in weekly segments.

I have few detailed recollections about the writing of *Bugles In The Afternoon* or, for that matter, any of his other works. There were through these years occasional dinnertable conversations about this character or that, and how they might develop; but I paid scant attention. Indeed, growing up in a writer's family was, for me, a pleasant, mostly uneventful experience. There were a few exciting months in Hollywood in 1939, when I was eight and he was scripting a motion picture for Sam Goldwyn—one that would not be produced for some years to come. Beyond that excursion, however, there was nothing in my father's activities or moods which suggested to me that his profession much differed from any other.

Aside from an occasional scouting trip to look over country he planned to write about, his regime was steady and methodical. He went to his office in downtown Portland every day, working from 9 to 5. He told me once that learning to sit down at a typewriter and stay there for several hours at a stretch had been the hardest lesson. But it had been well-learned.

On a normal day, he would produce about five, double-spaced pages of rough copy on an aging Underwood upright with a left-hand carriage return. A secretary would reproduce this rough draft, and it would be reviewed and edited the following morning. There were times, he said, when the story struggled and times, too, when things seemed to go particularly well. But a good day with seven or eight pages of copy was always suspect, he said, and almost always required a great deal of next-day repairing.

His ability to write at a steady pace was helped by a remarkable knowledge of the West—a scholarly interest that made him, albeit unclaimed, one of the period's better historians. His own library on the subject, now a special collection at the University of Oregon, ran to several thousand volumes. And there were fat notebooks full of his own research notes gleaned from hours in the archives of historical societies.

However, his sources weren't limited to the writings of others. Much of what he knew about the frontier came from correspondence and conversation with men who had been there. Those recollections were of immense value to him although, he said, some of these pensioners had unreliable memories and others were "polished storytellers if not horrendous liars." I remember one of this number, an ancient hobo who appeared one afternoon at the house with an important message for my father. Our guest was thoroughly mad but harmless, filthy and, in my view, fascinating. He spoke mostly in verse and was, he revealed, the brother of the Lone Ranger.

Historic and descriptive accuracy were expected by the serious Haycox reader; indeed, demanded. He had once "started the sagebrush 100 miles too far east in Nebraska" and said "they formed clubs back there to write and tell me about it."

Such flaws, however, were few. In one of his stories, a character must ride more than 100 miles through the night to save a friend from the hangman's noose. My father did not know if such a feat could be accomplished, and put the question to some of his aging correspondents. One of them would recall, in believable detail, a ride of roughly the dimensions required, the horseman calling ahead as the distant lights of isolated farmhouses along his route appeared: "Saddle a horse. Saddle a horse."

My father's commitment to authenticity was not always to my liking. It was not possible for the family to sit through a western movie without at least occasional grumbling. A cavalry charge with sabers bared was disaster and no amount of pleading would keep him—or the rest of us—in the theater as the bluecoats formed up, unsheathed, and launched pell mell toward the hostiles. "The cavalry never carried sabers on campaign," he would lecture me. "They were useless beyond the parade ground, and were always boxed and left behind." It has taken years of television reruns for me to catch up on some of the action, but he was right. Even in Hollywood, sabers at close quarters are ineffective against all but suspiciously cooperative opponents.

His productivity was slightly affected by the Second World War but not, I suspect, as much as he would have wished. He had been offered a commission in the 41st Infantry Division, his World War I unit, but was at length dissuaded by the family from taking it. He accepted another commission instead as chairman of the local draft board. It must not have been a pleasant assignment and he talked angrily at times about the injustices of the induction system. Young Portland gentlemen who found that deferment might be obtained by some form of temporary agricultural activity were particularly unwelcome supplicants at the hearings of Draft Board No. 1. He would have sent them all to New Guinea, to the embattled 41st, had he been given the power to do so. As it was, I'm told, No. 1 was no place to go with other than a very straight story.

He was, of course, well-known in Oregon and a frequent speaker across the state at all manner of civic events. In time, there would be talk of a political career and, for perhaps a year or two, some serious consideration of a gubernatorial candidacy. But it came to nothing. His writing was the unabandonable first love and, in the late 1940s, he would begin the planning of an ambitious series of works leading from the settlement of Oregon to contemporary times. There weren't enough days left.

I asked him once to tell me what made a writer, and how I could become one. "Hard work," he said. "Talent there may be, but it is 95% hard work." I was instructed to select an object—the branch of a tree, perhaps—and set to work describing it as many ways as I could.

The tree branch, I regret to say, remains undescribed. I did try but found then, as now, that the remaining five percent of the writer's craft is mystery and genius. It is as simple as arranging a few words into a structured sentence and as difficult as separating the atom.

What I have of him in later years is the pleasure of outdoor labor and, in particular, a desire to build with one's hands. In 1939–40, we built a monstrous home in the hills above Portland, a Southern Colonial of some 30 rooms, spacious lawns and gardens. That, however, was only a beginning. He could not be comfortable in something that was simply another man's work. Outbuildings began to spring up—an elaborate, 400-square foot chicken house on concrete footings, followed in line by a building of equal dimension called the "tool house" and, finally, a "pump house" which required for justification the drilling of a deep water-well. All of these were his work, and they were interspersed with the development of a vegetable garden and orchard covering more than an acre of land. He would toil nights and weekends on this neverending task and, on more than one occasion, was assumed by visitors to be the disheveled, well-meaning hired hand. We had those, too, but none could match his energy.

People who met him were surprised to find the writer of deadly drama had not been a cattle rancher or horseman and, had no interest at all in guns or hunting. How could he understand the violent times and rawboned characters he so convincingly portrayed? I don't have the answer but doubt that he was ever totally disassociated from those he created. It seemed reasonable, he told me once, that a fellow who writes about the West ought to be able to live in it.

Ernest Haycox, Jr.
San Francisco, California

An additional note by Jill Haycox:

Bugles In The Afternoon really was my late husband's most popular novel, and it sold the most copies. Erny considered it his favorite novel. He loved that period of time.

I see *Bugles In The Afternoon* at least once a year on television. Naturally, I watch for Haycox novels adapted to motion-pictures.

I renewed the copyright on *Bugles In The Afternoon* on February 10, 1972.

On June 10, 1972 I saw the novel again on television.

It so happened the motion-picture agreement had not included the second copyright period, so of course the present owner of the film was liable.

H. N. Swanson, a Hollywood agent, and long time friend, soon traced the owner.

We decided I would go to New York where the owner had an office.

Naturally, I had to seek legal advice. There is a standard payment for renewal of copyright. After some correspondence I decided to take less than I should have, simply to end this piece of business.

As my lawyer pointed out, I could have kept the owner from showing the picture on television. However, for a court case of this nature to come up, we could have to wait a number of years. The New York courts are so filled with crime cases that my kind of problem would just be shelved.

Scenes from the film version of
Bugles in the Afternoon

A William Cagney Production, released by Warner Brothers, 1952)

Color. 85 minutes.

Director, Roy Rowland; screenplay, Geoffrey Homes and Harry Brown, based on a novel by Ernest Haycox.

Ray Milland (Sgt. Kern Shafter); Helena Carter (Josephine Russell); Hugh Marlowe (Capt. Edward Garnett); Forrest Tucker (Pvt. Donovan); Barton MacLane (Capt. Myles Moylan); George Reeves (Lieut. Smith); James Millican (1st Sgt. Hines); Gertrude Michael (May).

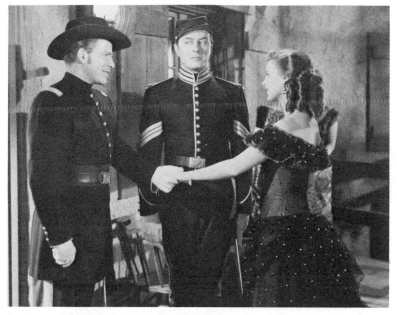

1. Capt. Edward Garnett (Hugh Marlowe) greeting Josephine Russell (Helena Carter) under the watchful eyes of Sgt. Shafter.

2. Capt. Garnett using his powers of persuasion on Josephine.

3. Capt. Garnett prepares the troops for battle.

4. Sgt. Shafter bids farewell to Josephine.

5. Sgt. Shafter tries to talk it over with the Sioux.

6. Charge!

7. Giving fire from behind the covered wagons.

8. A private battle between Sgt. Shafter and Capt. Garnett.

9. The private battle continues . . .

10. As does the larger one.

11. Sgt. Shafter and wounded Pvt. Donovan (Forrest Tucker).

BUGLES IN THE AFTERNOON

Contents

I

That Bright Day — That Far Land

THE TOWN had a name but no shape, no street, no core. It was simply five buildings, flung without thought upon the dusty prairie at the eastern edge of Dakota, and these stood gaunt and hard-angled against the last of day's streaming sunlight. The railroad, which gave the town a single pulse beat once a day, came as a black ribbon out of emptiness, touched this Corapolis with hurried indifference, and moved away into equal emptiness. The five buildings were alone in a gray-yellow space which ran outward in all directions, so empty that the tiring eye never saw where earth ended and sky began. There were no trees in this world, no accents, no relieving interruptions; nothing but the gray soil rolling on and a short brown grass turned crisp and now ready to fade when winter temperatures touched it.

The train — a wood-burning engine and three coaches — had paused and had gone, leaving one woman and one man on the cinders in front of the depot shed; the woman fair and round-bodied and slightly smiling at the land as if it pleased her. Beside her stood a collection of trunks and valises.

Nobody walked abroad, nobody met the train. These two were alone, facing the mute buildings whose western window panes burned yellow in the sunlight. From this cinder platform ran a sinuous pathway through the short grass to a frame building, two stories high, three hundred feet away; in front of the building were a wagon and a team and a pair of saddled ponies. Far out on the prairie a gauzy spiral of dust signaled the passage of riders, inbound or outbound. The man, somewhat farther down the platform, took his view of the town, looked at the woman and her luggage, and moved forward.

"That," he said, pointing toward the two-story building, "is probably the hotel. I presume you are going there. I'll take your light luggage."

She was not more than twenty-five, he thought; she had gray eyes and a pleasantly expressive mouth and her glance, turned upon him, was self-possessed. She smiled and said: "Thank you," and when he took up her valises and turned to the winding pathway she followed him without comment.

There had been a sharp and bright and full sun all day. Now it settled westward and seemed to melt into a shapeless bed of gold flame as it touched the far-away mountains; with its passage the air at once chilled and small streaks of breeze came out of the north with the smell of hard weather. Winter crouched yonder on the rim of the horizon and one day or one night, in the space of an hour, would turn this land black and bitter, shriveling every living thing exposed to it. He knew this land, or land like it; and the feeling of again being in it expanded his tissues and sharpened his zest for living. Yet for all its goodness it was like a smiling and beautiful woman, whose lavish warmth and generosity sprang up from those same strongly primitive sources which could make her cruel.

The wall of the hotel had a door and a set of windows opening upon the dusty earth; and a single railroad tie lay before the door to serve as a step. The man paused to permit the girl to go before him into the place; and then followed. There was a narrow hall and a steep stairway splitting the building into equal halves. To the right of the hall a broad doorway opened into a saloon; another doorway on the left led to a ladies' parlor and office. He followed the girl into the parlor and set down the suitcases, waiting back while she signed the register. The hotelkeeper was a neat and large and taciturn woman. She said, "Together or separate?" When she found out, she said to the girl: "You can take Number Three." As the man stepped up to the register, she watched him a moment, estimating him; and then gave the girl another quick inspection.

He signed his name in a steady-slanting motion, *Kern Shafter,* and his pen momentarily hesitated and then continued, *Cincinnati, O.* It was a slight flaw in his certainty, at once noticed by the hotel woman; her glance held him a longer moment, not so much with interest or suspicion but with a cold steadiness. He laid the pen down, at the same time reading the name of the girl written directly above his own. It was: *Josephine Russell, Bismarck, D.T.*

"You take Seven," said the hotel woman to Shafter. She spoke to both of them with an inclusive glance. "If you're northbound on the stage, it's at half-past four in the mornin'. We serve breakfast at four."

Josephine Russell said: "May I have the key to my room?"

"They were carried away in people's pockets a long time ago. If you shut your door it will stay shut. If you're afraid, prop a chair against the inside knob." She added in a small, grim tone: "You needn't be afraid. I don't stand for anything in this house. You'll have to carry your own luggage. I've got no man handy. Not that men are very handy."

Shafter turned to the valises and carried them up the stairs and waited for the girl to go ahead of him. She led the way down the hall and stepped inside Number Three. She walked across the room to the window and turned to watch him, one last flare of sunlight coming through her window, running over the curve of her shoulders, deepening her breasts. She had removed her hat and he observed that her hair was a dense black; even so she seemed fair of complexion to him. Perhaps it was in the way her lips were shaped against her face or the way her eyes held their smiling.

"I appreciate your help," she said. "Do you think my trunk will be safe on the station platform until morning?"

"I'll bring it to the hotel," he said, and went away.

She remained where she was a moment, her head slightly tilted as she watched the doorway, idly thinking of him. He had worn a cravat which looked as though it might have been the present of some woman. His clothes were excellent clothes for this part of the land, and smiling came easily to him. Yet his hands, she recalled, were very brown; and the palms were square and thick. She swung about and observed that the sun had gone, leaving the land with a strange, thin, glass-colored light. The horsemen out on the prairie were seemingly no nearer now than they had been fifteen minutes before.

But all of it pleased her: the raw running of the earth, the great empty arc of the sky, the smells rendered out by the warm day and the curt bite of approaching winter, this sprawled little town that served as a rendezvous for homesteaders and cow hands and drifters fifty miles roundabout, the sound of men's voices in the saloon below; for Josephine Russell was a western girl returned from a trip east, and this West eased her with its familiar things. She hummed a little song as she took the grime of coach travel from her and prepared herself for supper; she stood awhile, watching the last rose glow of the disappeared sun fade in the high sky. Suddenly, then, the prairie all around her was dark and the shapes of the town's other buildings were sharp-edged shadows in the swift night. She turned down the stairs to the dining room.

There was no door to shut out the barroom and she looked directly into it when she reached the foot of the stairs, noticing that Shafter now sat at a poker table with four other men. He had removed his coat for comfort and sat back in his chair with a long cigar burning between his lips. He seemed cheerful, he seemed content . . .

At four the next morning she came half asleep down the stairs and saw him again, at the same table and in the same chair, finishing up an all-night game. Later, she watched him come into the dining room. He had quickly shaved and, although he showed the lack of sleep, he had the same air of being pleased with everything around him. She smiled at him when he looked toward her, and got his smile back. He had a kind of ease with him, as though he had settled the question of himself and his future, had arrived at a decision and had shrugged off many of the worries or the ambitions that made other men exhaust themselves. His hair was black and bushy and his face was of the long, thick-boned sort, browned by weather and showing the small seams of experience around his eyes. He had quick eyes which looked about him and saw the people and the situations which surrounded him; and it was this kind of watchfulness which inclined her to the belief that he was either western, or had long been in the West. All western men had that same awareness of their surroundings.

The breakfast was bacon and hot cakes and fried potatoes and bitter coffee. Afterwards she walked to the waiting stage in time to see Shafter lift her luggage into the boot. He said to her: "I never saw a stage that wouldn't go off without somebody's luggage. I put a trunk and three valises up there. Is that all?"

"Yes," she said, and stepped into the coach. A pair of young men came aboard and sat on the opposite seat, facing her; a huge man entered, sized up the seating capacity and squeezed himself beside her. Shafter was last, throwing away the unsmoked end of a cigar as he came. He had a long overcoat on his arm and as soon as he took place between the two younger men he opened the coat and laid it over her lap.

"It will be cold for an hour or so," he said.

Daylight flowed over the land in gray, chill waves; the smell of dust lay rank and still upon the earth and all sounds had a brittleness in the air. The brake rod struck sharp against the metal bracket and the driver's hearty cursing put the four horses in motion. They lumbered across the baked earth, leather braces groaning; they turned the hotel's corner with the cry of one townsman coming up from behind: "Don't forget to tell Mike I'll be there tomorrow night!" Suddenly the town disappeared and they were rolling onward, with the coach wheels lifting and dripping an acrid dust.

The coach swayed and shuddered as it struck deeper depressions and the impact went through the five passengers closely crowded on the two seats. The big man sat with his hands on his knees, his bulk spilling against Josephine Russell. He made some small effort to pull himself together but found it impossible; and sat still, a horsy smell flowing from his clothes. He turned his head and grinned at her. "These rigs sure never were made for an ord'nary-size man."

She smiled at him, saying nothing. The smile encouraged him and he said: "I shot buff'lo here five years ago. Ain't none on this side of the Mizzoura any more."

Early morning's dullness was on them. Josephine Russell had, woman fashion, settled herself to endure discomfort as gracefully as possible. The two younger men, each pushed into his corner, looked vacantly out upon the land, while Kern Shafter planted his feet solidly on the coach floor and, using the two men on either side of him as supports, fell promptly asleep.

Josephine Russell passed time's monotony by letting herself be curious about him. He knew how to relax completely in odd circumstances and had dropped asleep almost at once, his chin touching his chest, the long full line of his mouth softening. The wrinkles at the edge of his temples disappeared when his eyes were closed, and the squareness of his upper body went away. She had noticed earlier that when he stood still he carried himself at a balance, which was something civilians didn't often do. He was slightly under six feet; he had big hands and heavy legs. In a country that somehow impelled men to grow sweeping mustaches, burnsides, imperials or Dundrearies, he had remained clean-shaven; and he showed some kind of taste in his clothes and appearance. In the West such a thing was noticeable. He had fine manners with women and he knew how to be easy and smooth with them. That was noticeable, too. Her eyes narrowed slightly on him as she thought that this perhaps explained his reason for being out here; men who came west nearly always had reasons, some of which were gallant and some of which were sordid.

Time dragged on and the day grew warm. Sunlight struck through the coach window, burning on Shafter's face. He was instantly awake at that hot touch, motionless but with his eyes fully open. He looked at the coat still on Josephine's lap, and bent forward and took it and stowed it in a roll beneath his feet; and fell asleep again. The four horses went on at a walk, at a run, at a walk, each change of pace producing its agreeable break and its new discomforts. The wheels lifted the dust in ropy, dripping sheets and this dust traveled as a pall over and around the coach, setting up a landmark that could be seen miles distant; its gauze clouds rolled inside the coach, laying its fine film on everything, and crept into nostril and lung. The morning's coolness was absorbed by the first full rush of sunlight; a dust-stale heat began to collect.

The big man, cramped in the corner of the seat, rolled his eyes around him and, by a series of cautious and self-conscious movements of his arm, burrowed into his pocket and found a cigar. He lighted it and dragged deeply on the smoke, his face growing bland and happier at once. Clouds of smoke spread through the coach and the big man made an ineffectual effort with his hand to sweep them away from Josephine.

The first smell of it woke Shafter at once. He opened his eyes and watched the big man steadily. The big man felt the weight of the glance but avoided it by looking out the window; he sighed heavily, he clenched the cigar between his teeth, he rolled it around his mouth, he took three rapid drags on it, and then irritably stared at Shafter. He held the glance with some defiance, but at last he pitched the cigar out of the window, whereupon Shafter again fell asleep.

At noon the coach, struggling against the endlessness of space, dipped into a coulee and drew before a drab, squat building which sat in a yard littered by tin cans and empty bottles. The passengers moved painfully from their confinement, ate dinner and returned reluctantly to their seats. The big man climbed beside the driver, replacing a slim, wild-haired youth who took his seat inside with a glowering silence. Coach and horses struggled up the coulee's side, faced the rolling sea of grass again, and resumed the steady march. The overhead sun pressed upon the coach, building up a trapped, sulky heat inside; and the dust began to drift up through the cracked floorboards in small, twining eddies. Shafter noticed how the dust touched and clung to the girl's hair; and noticed how the sun played against her face, against the gentle crease of her lips. Humor lived there, even in this discomfort. She had been looking through the window, but felt his glance and met it coolly, now not smiling.

He turned his glance, staring upon the land and the land's gray-brown monotony. Haze came down on the far edges of the world but in that haze indistinct shapes moved — the only motion to be seen anywhere. He watched those shapes for half an hour and noticed them gradually drift in. Presently he knew what they were and his eyelids came closer together and a different expression reached his face. The driver's voice drifted down through the squealing and the coarse grinding noise of wheels and straps and doubletree chains. "Always about here." But the coach's speed neither increased nor decreased.

It was a file of young Indians, slanting forward through the western sunlight on little patch-colored ponies. The Indians rode with a spraddled, keeling motion, their bronze-bare legs shining in the sun. Some of them were breach-clouted only and some wore white man's trousers and white man's shirts dropped outside; a hundred yards from the stage they wheeled and ran abreast of it, the little ponies controlled by single braided rawhide lines attached to their lower jaws. One Indian slowly drew an arrow back in his bow, aimed it, made an imaginary shot, and relaxed the bow; he flung up one finger derisively, whereupon the whole party wheeled and raced away. The driver's voice came down again, windy and relieved. "Agency bucks, but you never know whut they're up to."

Josephine Russell's face was steady and sharp and hardened, but she said nothing. She looked at Shafter.

He said: "Indian kids, just playing at trouble. Nothing to fear."

The sullen young man with the mop of wild hair had remained rigidly drawn together during the affair. Now he relaxed and spoke. "You live in this country?"

"No."

"Then you don't know. There's always trouble. Meet those kids where they thought they had a chance and it would of been different."

"No use worrying about things that don't happen."

The youngster was inclined to be intolerant of this apparent greenhorn, and the presence of a woman made him accent his own frontier wisdom. "If you'd seen what I seen out here — people scalped and whole families with their heads busted in — you wouldn't be so easy about it."

"If it had been spring or summer," said Shafter, "I would have been worried. But winter's coming. These Indians will be on the reservation, eating government beef. They will be good Indians, until spring comes again."

The youngster disliked his point of view being overthrown and he gave Shafter a hard, scowling glance and was evidently tempted to set him in his proper place by a few bolder words. Shafter took the lad's beetling glance and held it, and presently the lad reconsidered his intentions and only said, "If you'd seen what I seen," and reached into his pocket, producing a plug of tobacco from which he chewed an enormous lump and pouched it against one cheek.

Occasionally the stage rolled down the side of a coulee, struck rocky bottom with painful impact and tilted upward, throwing the passengers violently around the seats. The heat clung on with the westering sun and the dust was a screen through which the passengers viewed each other with blurred vision. It dampered normal breathing; it coated the faces of all and presently these faces turned oil-slick and this wetness grew gray and streaky as it formed small rivulets across the dust. The smell of the coach became rank with the odors of bodies rendering out their moisture and the confinement turned from discomfort to actual pain. Shafter noticed that Josephine Russell had taken firm control of herself, pressing back her feelings, and from this he realized she was feeling the ordeal. Now and then, aware of her bedraggled appearance, she pressed her handkerchief against her face.

The road had swung directly into the blast of the low burning sun and therefore it was a surprise when the stage wheeled to a stop before a raw and ungainly house standing alone in all this emptiness. The driver got down, grunting as his feet struck; he called back, "Night stop," and walked away. A man moved from the house toward the horses, and one by one the weary passengers lifted themselves from the vehicle and tried their cramped legs. Shafter stood by, giving the girl a hand down. For a moment he supported her, seeing a faintness come to her face; she touched him with both arms, she held him a little while and then, embarrassed, she stepped away. Shafter climbed to the boot of the coach and sorted amongst the luggage. "Which will you need for overnight?"

"The small gray one," she said.

He found it and brought it down. He stood a moment, surveying the house; he looked to an upper window and saw a woman there, staring out upon the coach. He gave the girl a quick side glance and noticed she had not seen the woman; a short and darker expression crossed his face and he led the way over the packed yard to the door. Three great hounds lifted up and growled at him but a voice — a woman's sharp voice — came out of the house, cowing them.

Josephine Russell murmured: "Are there nothing but women hotelkeepers in eastern Dakota?" She had made a more deliberate appraisal of the place and now she gave Shafter a sober glance. "Is it all right?"

"It will have to be," he said.

A woman met them in the half light of the long front room; a woman once young, and still not old in point of years. She stood back, ample-bosomed and careless of dress; her eyes were ready for Shafter and had warmth for him, but they turned cool and watchful when they swung to the girl. There was a moment — a long and unsure moment — while she studied them. Shafter said in a short voice: "You have a room for this lady?"

"Take the one at the top of the stairs. On the left."

He followed Josephine up the stairs. She stopped before a door and looked back at him a moment, and then opened the door and stepped into the room and stood in the center of it, looking on without expression at the room's furniture, at the rough blankets on the bed. He put down her suitcase and went to the window; he pried it open and looked out, and turned back to her. Her glance came over to him and he saw a slight flicker of embarrassment, calm and self-possessed as she was.

He said: "A hell of a place."

She shrugged her shoulders. "But the only place." Then she said: "Are you going to be around here tonight?"

"Yes," he said. He looked at the door when he left the room and saw that there was no key; he closed the door and walked down the stairs. The woman who ran this doubtful desert shelter stood near by, waiting for him.

He said: "Is that room all right?"

She shrugged her shoulders. "Yes. But I don't ask the genteel to come here."

"This is a stage stop, isn't it?"

"Let it stop some other place," she said. Then she laughed, and her lips were full and heavy and red. "But there's no other place. Do you want a room?"

He said, "No," and color came to him and he turned out to the porch. He walked around the house, sizing it up, its windows blanked out by drawn green roller shades, its paintless angles, its unloveliness. There was an outside stairway running up the east wall, on which he laid a moment's attention; behind the house was another porch, and water and basin. He washed here and beat the dust from his clothes, and resumed his circle of the house. The sun dropped in a silent crash of light and, coming from an apparent nowhere, riders shaped themselves against the sudden twilight. He sat on the porch steps, watching them reach the yard, wheel and step off; all men stamped by their trade, booted and spurred and dusty and scorched by the sun, turned dry by the heat and hollow-hungry, careless and nervous of eye, watching everything and nothing. There was a bar farther back in the house and out of it lights presently rose, and the sound of men talking — and of women talking. He got up and crossed the main room. He paused at the doorway of the bar and had his look at the women; he moved to the bar and took his drink, and stood with his elbows on the bar until he heard the dinner triangle banging. Then he went on to the dining-room door and waited for Josephine.

She came down the stairs and paused to look around; when her eyes found him he saw the relieved lightening of her face. She came up to him, smiling a little, and went into the dining room with him. He saw her glance touch the dozen men at the table and coolly take in the woman at its head — and the two other women also present. She knew them at once, he realized; it was the faintest break on her face, soon covered. After that she took her place and she never looked at them again.

The big plates and platters came circling around, were emptied and carried away by a China boy to be refilled. One man, already drunk, talked steadily; but otherwise the crowd was silent and hungry and ate without conversation. Small talk was a custom of the East; out here men resented making a ceremony out of a meal and wasted no time on it. Ten minutes after they had entered the room, most of the men had finished, and had gone on to the bar; in a little while the rest of the group had deserted the table, leaving Shafter and Josephine to themselves. She sipped at her coffee, tired but relaxed. Through his cigar smoke he watched the lamplight shining against the gray of her eyes, he observed the sweetness and the humor restlessly living in her lip corners. She caught his glance and held it, thoughtfully considering him, making her own silent observations concerning him. Racket began to spread from the saloon and a woman's voice grew strident. The girl shrugged her shoulders and rose from the table.

He followed her back to the big front room and he observed that she stopped at the stairs and looked toward the second floor with an expression of distaste. Suddenly she wheeled toward him and took his arm and they went out of the house and strolled along the vague road. A sickle moon lay far down in the sky, turned butter yellow by the haze in the air, and the stars were great woolly-crystal masses overhead. Sharp-scented dust rose beneath their feet, the fragrance of the earth was strong — the harsh and vigorous emanations of the earth itself. He felt the girl's body sway as she walked; he felt the warmth of her body, the warmth of her thoughts. The desert ran blackly away, formless and mysterious, and far out on the flats a coyote called.

"Do you know this country?" she asked.

"I know the West," he said. "I put in some time in the Southwest."

"Do you like it?"

"It's better than what I've had lately."

They went half a mile onward, slowly pacing; and turned back. The lights of the house gushed from a dozen windows — the only light and the only warmth in all this empty stretch of space; and the sound of laughter, sharply shrill, rode in the little wind.

She said: "What is your name?"

"Kern Shafter. I regret that you have to stay here tonight."

She didn't answer that until they had reached the porch. Then she murmured: "It will do," and passed into the house. At the foot of the stairs she turned to him and asked a question she had asked once before. "You'll be here?"

"Yeo," he oaid. "Good night."

She nodded her head slightly by way of answer, and climbed the stairs.

After she had gone into her room Shafter left the house and went to the coach standing in the yard. He climbed to the boot and found his valise and took out a revolver. He sat on the top of the coach and hefted the gun idly in his palm, feeling its familiar weight, its accustomed and comfortable reality. He thrust it inside his trouser band and lay back to smoke out his cigar while the depth of night increased. The moon's light had no effect on the blind blackness; this yard, touched by house lights, was an island in all the surrounding emptiness. The stars sharply glistened and the scented wind lifted; and mystery closed down and loneliness moved in, with its questions and its far wonder. He sat still, brooding over things behind him, over old injuries still burning and old memories still sweet. When he had thought of them and had felt the heat of them, he closed his mind upon them; and yet, like the leaks in a dam gate, there were apertures in his will and his resolution, through which little seepages of memory still came. He stretched out full length, feeling the goodness of the wind and the ease that came to him. Looking at the sky, he seemed to grow longer and broader, and the space inside him was less crowded. He thought: "I have made one right decision," and felt the peace of knowing it.

With the night also came the quick chill of winter not far away; the starglow had its frigid glitter, the far unseen distance had its threat of storm. Other riders came out of the night, dropped off before the house and moved in, to add to the growing noise. Shafter dropped from the coach and returned to the main room. He found a pair of chairs and drew them together, sitting on one and laying his feet on the other. The big woman who ran the place found him here, so placed that he had a view of the stairs and the doorway of the room directly above.

She stopped before him, smiling down. She lifted his hat and threw it aside and, still with her half smile, ran one finger along the edge of his head. "Your woman will be all right."

"Not mine," he said.

"I guess," she said, "you wouldn't have much trouble with a woman, if you wished. I know your kind."

"No," he said, "you don't."

"Don't tell me what I don't know," she said, half sharp with him. But her brief smile came back as she continued to watch him. "You don't need to curl up like a hound in front of her door. It will get noisy, but nothing will happen."

"Nothing will," he agreed.

"You plan to stay here all night? Right here?"

"Yes."

She ceased to smile. She spoke in a soft, jeering, faintly envious tone. "That's romantic, isn't it? You fool." Suddenly she dropped a hand on his stomach, on the shape of the revolver beneath his coat. "I wouldn't flourish that thing around here. There's a couple men in the bar who could shoot that diamond ring off your finger without scratching your skin."

"Ah," he said, and grinned, "tough ones."

She was puzzled at his reaction. Her lips indecisively loosened while she watched him. He lay back on his chair, a quiet man who didn't seem to care about many things, who didn't give himself away. He dressed well and she knew, without giving it a thought, that he was far above her and perhaps had only a scorn for her. She hated men like that, even more than she hated the rough ones who came here to this house with their appetites; she hated them with a hard desire to use her claws on them — the fashionable, cool ones — and pull them down to her. But she didn't find herself hating this man. It was as she had said before to him: he had a way that women liked and an appeal that women would answer. But he didn't seem to care.

She started to touch him again but checked the gesture. "My God," she murmured, "this is a lonely place. Sometimes . . . If you're crazy enough to sit here all night I'll bring you a blanket later. Maybe some hot coffee."

"I'll be here," he said. She had swung away, but she checked and turned, her eyes scanning him with a small break of hope. Hard living had begun to etch its lines along her face, yet she still was a pretty woman in a loose, heavy, physical way. Carefulness of dress would have done much for her, but she had forgotten to care. She shrugged her shoulders and walked into the saloon, which grew increasingly noisy.

Josephine's room was ceiled with rough lumber whose edges never quite lay together. There was a single window, with a green roller shade discolored by sun and in-beating rain. A lighted lamp stood on a table made up of fragments of boxes which once had contained canned goods; above the table a blemished mirror hung askew. The bed was a four-poster made of solid mahogany, the possible derelict of some wagon train passing through, and on it lay lumpy quilts and a pillow without a slip. The floor had once been covered with a lead-colored paint, but this now had largely broken away so that it was a kind of leprous gray and brown.

Josephine stood in the middle of the room, remembering the people downstairs and hearing the noise which now came up in growing stridency; particularly she heard the voices of the women. She shrugged her shoulders and walked to the bed, pulling back the quilt to explore the two blue army blankets which served as sheets. She bent, looking closely at the blankets; she peeled back the blankets and studied the mattress. She bent still farther down, running a finger along its stitched edge. "At least there are no bedbugs," she thought, and got ready for bed.

She propped the room's lone chair against the doorknob, turned out the light and stood a moment at the window, watching the yard. She saw a man lying on top of the coach, smoking a cigar, and though it was intensely black beyond the range of house lights, she thought she recognized the shape of Shafter's shoulders. The thought of him, vagrant and curious and slightly warm, held her still for a little while; then she crept into bed.

There were men in the adjoining rooms, their lights coming through the warped joining of the wall boards, their voices quite plain as they exchanged stories, each worse than the one before.

She rested, still and wide awake, listening to a fight begin and go through the house in grunting, crashing, falling echoes. Some man yelled out his cursing and a gun exploded and a woman screamed; afterwards a man rushed into the night and presently rode away at a dead run. Near midnight someone came slowly up the stairs, his body making a weight on the flimsy wood. He crawled along the hall, his hands scraping the wall. He touched the knob of the door and stopped, and she heard the knob turn and the door give; after that, she heard another traveler come lightly up the steps. One soft word was said and a sharp blow struck, sending one of the men against the wall. Presently that one fell down the stairs in a tumbling, rocketing fashion. The man who had so lightly come upward now went down with the same soft footfalls. Josephine thought: "He's watching out for me," and thought of Shafter, again with relief. Little by little some kind of order crept into this wild house as its inmates fell asleep, and its guests rode away.

II

West of the River

AT ONE o'clock, Shafter left his seat at the foot of the stairs and went into the barroom. Everybody had gone except one drunk stretched dead to the world across the pool table, and one gloomy houseman cleaning up the debris. Shafter got a glass of whisky and carried it to a table and sat down; the woman who seemed to run this place came up from some other quarter of the house and took a chair across from him. The flame of her vitality obviously burned low, for she sat with her elbows on the table, supporting her head, staring at the table's green felt top. She murmured: —

"Hard way to make a living, isn't it?"

He said nothing and presently his silence made her lift her glance to him. He smiled at her and pushed his drink over the table. She looked at it a long while, all the brightness faded out of her. "No," she murmured, "I hate the sight of it." She looked up at the barman. "Go get us some coffee, Bill." Then she noticed the drunk on the pool table and a raspiness came to her voice. "Roll that dumb beast off there before he digs his spurs into a thousand dollars' worth of woodwork."

The barkeep was a taciturn and a literal man. He moved to the table, put both arms under the sleeping drunk and gave him a short shove. The drunk fell loosely, striking in sections, at the knees and then at the shoulders. His head slammed hard on the floor and his mouth flew open. He rolled slightly, threshed his arms, and ceased to move. Bill went on toward the back of the house.

"Look at him," said the woman in bitter disgust, pointing to the drunk. "That's a man. That's what they all look like. He'll sober up, eat breakfast and go away. But he'll be back in a couple days. That's what I've got to make my living from."

He said: "Feel this way every night?"

"Every night."

"Time to move on then."

"One place is no better than another," she said, and looked at him with a small revival of interest. When she realized he had been steadily watching her, she pulled herself straight and ran her hands lightly over her hair. "Do I look as bad as I feel?"

"What's your name?"

"May," she said. "There's another May here, but she's Straight-Edge May."

"All women are beautiful, May."

"You fool," she murmured, "don't talk like that. You don't mean it. Even if you did mean it, it would get a woman like me to thinking about things she shouldn't any more." But his words had lifted her; they had revived her spirits. "You've knocked around, haven't you?"

"Yes."

"Running from something."

He showed her his smile again, that easy and careless smile which changed him, which took the darkness out of him. He had sympathy for her but he let it show in his eyes rather than spend words on it. He sat with her and took her as she was. "Everybody runs from something, May. Or runs after something."

"In trouble?"

"No. I don't have to watch what's behind me."

"You've never had to come to places like this for your fun, either," she said, judging him with her wealth of man-knowledge. "Your kind uses theater tickets and bonbons, and back rooms at fashionable restaurants."

For the second time this night, she caught him off guard, causing him to flush. "May," he said. "Let's talk about the weather."

She regarded him closely, amused that she could embarrass him but also puzzled by it; embarrassment was a rare thing in a man and somewhat beyond her limits of experience. She shrugged her shoulders. "I guess I don't know much about your kind. I only met one like you. That was a long time ago. If I knew where he was now I'd write him a letter and let him know just how I turned out after he got through with me." A small tinge of bitterness got into her voice. "Maybe it would make him add something extra on the collection plate next time he went to church."

"How do you know he goes to church, May?"

"It's fashionable for his kind to marry somebody respectable and go to church, and buy his way into heaven. No doubt, when he gets sentimental, he sometimes thinks, 'I wonder where she is now.' Not that he's sorry. His kind of man is proud of one good sinful memory. As for the woman, she can just look out for herself." She bent toward him and showed him an old, old anger. "I don't like your kind of men." But as soon as she said it, her mouth softened. "But I like you. I guess that explains how I got here."

Bill came in with two cups of coffee, black and hot and rank, and moved back to his dismal chores. Shafter dumped his whisky into the coffee and drank it slowly. He was loose in the chair, he was thoroughly at rest, enjoying the small tastes and sounds and colors around him. She thought to herself, as she studied him: "I'd figure him a genteel bum, except that he threw George Dixon down the stairs." That made her speak up. "You're too quick for your own good. Dixon didn't mean to go into the lady's room. He was just drunk."

"There is only one way to handle Dixons," he said.

"He may come back," she said. "He's a mean one."

"If you hit Dixons hard," he said, "they don't come back. If you hit them soft, they do."

She said: "You uncover yourself just a little bit at a time. You get different as you go. Is there anything I can do for you?"

He looked at her with a greater attention. "How's that, May?"

"Do you need a stake? I've got plenty of money."

He didn't immediately answer and he didn't smile at her again. He finished his coffee, and rose. Her glance remained on him.

"Didn't hurt your feelings, did I?" she wanted to know.

He shook his head. "No, May, you made me feel fine. But I don't need it."

She followed him from the barroom to the front room. "You don't need to stay down here any more. Take the room across the hall from your lady."

He turned on her, looking down, the quietness of his eyes and the expression in them giving her goodness. She wanted to touch him, to reach up and lay her fingers through his black hair; she wanted to come close upon him and lift her mouth for him. But she stood back, a realist who knew that for him she was a vessel long since drained empty; it was the first time in many years she had felt that way about a man.

"Why did you offer me the grubstake, May?"

"People can always hope," she said. "Maybe you would have taken it. Maybe you would have stayed."

He moved to the stairs and turned back there, one hand lying heavy-spread on the railing. "Remember what I told you," he said. "All women are beautiful."

She shook her head, darkened by what she wanted and couldn't have. "If you wish to be kind, never say that to a woman like me." She watched him all the way up the stairs.

And she was at the foot of the stairs at five in the morning when, following breakfast, he turned out of the house. She had taken pains with her hair; she had pressed away the lines about her eyes with cold towels, and she had put on the dress she used for trips to Fargo. But she didn't speak to him as he went by, for he had Josephine with him, and she knew exactly what her station was. After they had gone out, she moved to the porch, watching the stage swing around in the yard. She saw him bend and look through the window at her; and she stood still and watched the stage roll away through its dust and become at last a point in the distance.

The man who had been capsized from the table the night before now moved out of the house in painful slowness. He stopped beside her, puzzled as to the soreness of his bones. "By God," he said, "it must of been a big night. Somebody ride a horse through the barroom, May? I been stepped on, all over."

"No," she said. "You just fell down."

"Must of been from the roof," he murmured and went on to his horse. He groaned when he went into the saddle; he turned and waved a hand. "See you soon, May."

She still watched the stage, but she said, with a piece of a smile: "All right, Tom. Be good and come again."

The coach ran along the twin ruts of the road, outward upon the prairie, under the rising flood of clear and brilliant sunshine. For the space of half an hour, the world stood bathed in morning's freshness, in its coolness, in its bright cleansing light; and for that half hour the horizons were sharp lines in the distance. Then the coolness went away and the faint fog began to rise and the enveloping dust settled within the coach and the monotony of the ride gripped them again. Three of the passengers had dropped off at the night station, leaving only the heavy man, Josephine and Shafter inside. Shafter propped his shoulders in the corner of the coach, braced his feet on the floor and fell asleep.

When he awoke, there was a series of small, ragged up-and-down black strokes against the emptiness and the horses had smelled their destination and were now running freely without the urging of the driver; somewhat later the stage moved into the mouth of Fargo's main street, passed a row of raw-boarded houses to either side, turned a corner and stopped at a depot shed standing beside a single track.

The driver got down, shouting, "Fargo, and yore train's in sight," and went up to the boot, throwing down the luggage without regard for the contents. Shafter stepped out and gave Josephine a hand; he found her luggage and piled it near the track, standing back to light a cigar. The train had come out of the east, its progress singing forward on the rails and its whistle hoarsely warning the town. Townsmen strolled up to break the day's tedium and to touch again for an instant that East out of which they had come; to catch, in the train's steamy bustle, the feeling of motion and excitement and freedom which had impelled most of them to come west but which they had lost as soon as they had taken root here.

Josephine turned to Shafter and regarded him with soberness. "You have been kind. If I should not see you again, let me wish you all good luck."

"I'll be on the train."

"Bismarck?" asked Josephine, and showed him a remote pleasure with her eyes.

He nodded instead of speaking; for the engine coasted by with its bell steadily clanging and its exhausts ejaculating gusts of steam. Two baggage cars and five coaches growled to a jerky stop, and passengers looked curiously through the grimed car windows; and an army captain stepped to the runway and began a vigorous constitutional, his cap slanted rakishly on a head of long, bright red hair. The conductor stood on the runway and shouted, "Fargo — Fargo, twenty minutes for lunch!"

Passengers now descended and ran for the lunchroom sitting at the edge of the platform. Josephine meanwhile turned to the train, whereupon Shafter gave her an arm up the nearest coach platform, collected her luggage and carried it into the car. He stowed his own valise on an empty seat and left the train, crossing to the lunchroom. Some of the passengers had seated themselves along a table, before a row of dishes prepared for hasty service; and other passengers, unable to find seats, reached over the heads of the fortunate ones and improvised sandwiches for themselves. Shafter noticed a pile of lunch boxes made up, took two of them, paid the bill and returned to Josephine.

"You never know when these trains get where they're going," he said, leaving a lunch box with her.

He returned to his own seat and began on his meal. The engine bell had begun to sound again and the conductor stood on the runway, crying "Bo-o-o-ard," to summon passengers from the lunchroom. The engine released its brakes and gave a first hard *chuff,* sending a preliminary quiver through the coaches. The train slid forward, gathering speed, while a woman on the train began to scream as a last man rushed from the lunchroom, sprinted along the runway and caught the grab rails of the last coach. The gathered townsmen cheered this extra touch of melodrama, and the engine whistled its throaty farewell as it gathered speed, and the vacuum of its passage lifted eddies of dust and paper on the tracks. It left behind the smell of steam and coal smoke and warm lubricating oil; it left behind the memory of liveliness and motion and it left behind,

in the heart of more than one townsman, the half-formed decision
to pull up his roots again, as he had before, and move into that
bright West whose unknown distances held perpetual promise of
fortune and adventure.

The coaches, castoffs of other lines in the East, swayed with the
not yet thoroughly settled grade of this new railroad, stretched taut
on their couplings, and slammed together when the engine slightly
abated speed. Cinders pelted the windows and smoke streamed back
the length of the train; and the engine whistle laid out its hoarse
notice upon the land. Here and there a siding ran briefly beside the
main line and here and there a yellow section shanty stood lonely
in the sun. Out in the distance an occasional antelope band, startled
from grazing, fled away in beautiful smoothness. Once in a great
while Shafter saw a ranch house or a rider, or cattle. Propping his
feet on the opposite seat, he fell asleep, and later woke to find the
train stopping at a town that was four little shanties facing the
tracks; and slept again until he heard the conductor cry, "Bismarck!"

The town's gray out-sheds and slovenly shanties and corrals slid
forward and its main street appeared — one long row of saloons,
stores, livery barns and freighter sheds crowded side by side, un-
evenly joined and roughly thrown together. The train stopped, heads
bobbed beside the car windows and presently people came in to
search for friends. Shafter picked up his valise and left the coach.

The sun was down and coolness already began to move over the
earth. There had been rain in Bismarck, turning the yellow dust
gray and slick, and coating the boots of the gathered crowd. An
army ambulance stood near the track, held by a cavalry corporal,
and a pair of ladies crossed to it and were whirled away. Josephine
Russell meanwhile descended, walked to a gray-haired man and
kissed him. The gray-haired man took her luggage and turned
off, but for a moment Josephine Russell paused to look back at
Shafter. Impulse moved her to him.

"I wish you luck," she said.

"I'll remember your wish," he answered and lifted his hat to her
and watched her walk on. She was an alert, happy woman; she
had presented him with that fair and serene face which he most

admired, and as he looked at her retreating shape he had his slight regret — the regret of a man who sees beauty and grace disappear.

The cars were now empty, the engine had been uncoupled and moved on; for this was the farthest west of the railroad, in this year of 1875. Beyond Bismarck was the yellow Missouri, and beyond the Missouri lay the unknown lands of the Sioux where, intermittently for ten years, little columns and detachments of the army had marched and fought, had won and had been defeated. Shafter lifted his valise and moved toward a wagon wherein sat a driver. He spoke to the driver: —

"Where's Fort Abraham Lincoln?"

The driver pointed a finger southwesterly. "Along that road, four miles to the Point. Ferry there." Then he said: "Get in."

Shafter dumped his valise into the wagon's bed and took place beside the driver who now set his team down the street at a trot. At the end of the street the road moved in dog-leg fashion up and down and around little folds of earth, past an occasional house, past Indians riding head down and indifferent, their toes pointed outward, their shoulders stooped. The team kept up an easy mincing trot, making a little melody of harness chains, and so covered four miles, coming then to a highland upon which sat a collection of houses sitting apart and facing all directions. Beyond this highland the terrain rolled into bottom lands and reached the Missouri. Beyond the river stood the fort on its bluff, its line of houses square and trim and formidable. The driver slammed on his brakes as the wagon descended the grade to the ferry dock; and pointed at the houses to either hand.

"If you got money to spend, don't come here. This is the Point. It's off the military reservation. It is a bad place, my friend." He let go the brakes and the wagon rolled to the deck of a river steamer, once glamorous but now converted to something little better than a scow with steam; on the pilot house a gilded sign gave its name, THE UNION. The name was its only substantial part, for when the lines were cast off the ancient engines shook the boat in all its frames. They surged forward through the near shore's back eddy, came upon the middle channel and were seized by a current that lay deceptively beneath this murky river's surface. The *Union* shuddered throughout, paused and lost steerage way. It skewed across the current, fell five hundred yards downriver, and reached slack water on the far side, with its engines racking its ancient frame, It worked slowly upstream and nosed into the slip. The wagoner released his brakes, whipped his team into a run and went up the grade to the top of the bluff. When he reached it he sat back and blew out a breath.

"Damn boat someday is goin' to keep going right on down to Yankton. Or blow up."

The walls of this fort were formed by the back edges of barracks, storehouses, officers' quarters and stables, all these facing a great parade ground running a thousand feet or better in each direction. The teamster drew before the guardhouse post, said "Commissary," and was waved in.

"You know where the adjutant's office might be?" asked Shafter.

"Down there by the end of the quartermaster building."

"Thanks for the ride," offered Shafter and dropped off with his valise. He went along the east side of the parade ground, traveling on a board walk which skirted troop quarters; and as he passed these long barracks he heard the clatter of dishes coming up from the mess hall in the rear of each barrack. This was supper time, the sun just dropping below the ridge to the west of the fort; and the ceremony of retreat was not far away, for orderlies were now cutting out of the stable area, leading horses across the parade to Officers' Row. He had just reached the doorway of the adjutant's office when the trumpeter at the guard gate blew first call.

He stepped inside in time to see a huge, tall first lieutenant clap on a dress helmet with its plume, thrust the chin strap into place and hook up his sword. Dundreary whiskers grew in silken luxury along his jowls, out of which showed a big-fleshed mouth, a solid nose and a pair of darkly sharp eyes. He looked at Shafter. He said, "Yes?" and started for the door. "Yes?"

"I'll wait until the lieutenant returns from retreat," said Shafter.

The lieutenant said, "Very well," and flung himself through the door, followed by a sergeant major empurpled with years of weather and hard living. A corporal remained behind in the office, his arm hanging from a sling.

Shafter watched five cavalry companies file out from the stables to the parade ground. The hark of officers came sharp through the still air. "Column right! Left into line! Com-m-pany, halt!" Horsemen trotted briskly here and there, lifting quick puffs of dust from the hard parade. One by one, the five companies came into regimental front, each company mounted on horses of matched color, each company's guidon colorfully waving from the pole affixed in the stirrup socket of the guidon corporal's stirrup. For a moment the regiment remained still, each trooper sitting with a grooved ease in his McClellan, legs well down and back arched, saber hanging on loosened sling to left side, carbine suspended from belt swivel to right, dress helmet cowled down to the level of his eyes. Thus the Seventh sat in disciplined, impassive form — a long double rank of dark, largely mustached faces — homely, burned faces, Irish faces, seasoned and youthful faces, faces of solid value and faces of wildness — all pointed frontward to the company commander and to the adjutant now taking his report. Presently, the adjutant wheeled his horse, trotted it fifty feet forward and came to a halt before a slim shape poised lithe and watchful on his mount.

Even at this distance Shafter recognized the commanding officer — that long, bushy fall of almost golden hair which even the cowling of the dress helmet could not conceal, that sweeping tawny dragoon's mustache which sharpened the bony, hawkish nose and accented the depth of eye sockets, that sinuous and muscularly restless body now held in momentary restraint against its own incessant rebellion. There sat the man who was a living legend, the least-disciplined and poorest scholar of his West Point class of 1861; whose wild charges and consuming love of naked action had turned him into a major general by brevet at the age of twenty-five and who was, in the shrunken peacetime army, Lieutenant Colonel of the Seventh Cavalry and its commander by virtue of the absence of Colonel Sturgis. Everybody in America knew the face of the man; it was a household familiarity, the thin lips half concealed by the waterfall mustache, the hungry boniness of the jaw, the blue inset eyes seeking attention, seeking any audacity to prove the right to attention.

Custer's arm answered the adjutant's salute with a swift nervous jerk. A word was spoken. The band burst into a quick march, still stationary on the right of the line. The officers of the regiment rode slowly front and center, formed a rank and moved upon the commanding officer. Shafter heard the brittle crack of an officer's voice halt them. He watched them salute Custer, and receive his return salute, after which they took place behind him. Suddenly now the band swung around and marched down the front of the regiment, in full tune, and wheeled and marched back. Silence came completely; all the shapes upon this parade turned still as the massed buglers tossed up their trumpets and sounded retreat. Hard upon the heels of the last trumpet note the little brass cannon at the foot of the flagpole boomed out, its echo rocketing into the western ridge and out across the Missouri. The flag began to descend and the band struck up a national air. Shafter pulled his heels together and removed his hat; he stood balanced, facing the flag as it slid down the pole toward the trooper waiting to receive it. In the ensuing quiet, Custer's strident voice carried the length and breadth of the parade.

"Pass in review!"

The first sergeants, now commanding the companies, wheeled about, harking their stiff calls. The band broke into a march tune, the regimental front broke like a fan and came into platoon column; it turned the corners of the parade and passed before the commanding officer with hard dust smoking up around it. Down at the far end of the parade ground, each company pulled away toward its own stable. The ceremony was done.

Out by the flagstaff the officers surrendered their horses and moved idly along the walk toward their quarters. The adjutant took his last orders and departed. An orderly galloped forward to take Custer's horse, but the general swung his mount and flung it headlong across the parade, wheeled and raced it back. Arriving before his quarters he sprang to the ground, tossed over the reins and stamped up the porch of his house; it had been one sudden outburst of energy which could no longer be dammed up.

Shafter meanwhile stepped back into the adjutant's office. Presently the adjutant came in, slightly sweating; he removed his dress hat and laid it on a desk, he unbuckled his saber and hung it to a peg on the wall and, having done this, he looked at Shafter.

"Well, sir."

"I should like to enlist in this regiment," said Shafter.

"Where are you from?"

"Ohio."

"How was it you did not enlist at the nearest recruiting service?"

"I prefer to pick my regiment."

"That involved considerable train fare," observed the adjutant, and took time to consider Shafter with a very cool eye. "Normally we are recruited from Jefferson Barracks. Still, we can enlist you." He turned to the corporal with the bad arm. "Get an enlistment form, Jackson. Get a doctor's blank, too."

Jackson searched another desk for the required forms and the adjutant lowered his rather massive frame into a chair and considered the work on his desk. The corporal sat down at another desk and beckoned Shafter before him. "Name?" he said, and began to take Shafter's history. "Recent address? Next of kin?"

"No next of kin."

"Closest friend, then."

"None," said Shafter.

The corporal leaned back and chewed his pen a moment, looking at Shafter. The adjutant raised his head to consider this new recruit. "Are you that alone in this world?" he asked, with some skepticism. But he nodded at the corporal and murmured, "Let it go." Both the corporal and the lieutenant, Shafter realized, were thinking the same thing: that he was another drifter running from a past. These regiments on the border had many such men; it was an old story.

"Birthplace, parents' names? Age, weight, color of hair and eyes? Height? Distinguishing marks?" The clerk rattled off the inquiries and scrawled them down. It grew late and he was impatient to be free — to join the poker game at troop barrack, to meet a woman

across the river at the Point, to sleep — or perhaps simply to sit idle
and dream of the comfort and the freedom of civilian life. Shafter
quietly supplied the answers required of him, thinking of that same
civilian life with no regrets and no particular warmth. Insofar as
he had a home, this army post would satisfy him completely; the uniform would be the answer to his wants. He heard men come into
the adjutant's office behind him. He heard the adjutant say: —

"It is slightly late, Doctor. But could you examine this man for
enlistment?"

"Yes."

Shafter turned and saw the doctor, standing by the adjutant's desk.
But his eyes lingered on the man only a moment; for there was another officer now in the room, a captain looking out from beneath
the rim of his dress helmet at Shafter, with a keen attention. He
was a heavy, stocky man with a broad practical face, with a heavy
sand-colored mustache guarding his upper mouth. It was a service-
able, unemotional Irish countenance, a face disciplined by duty and
routine and largely beyond the whims of excitement. Shafter looked
back at him gravely. The doctor said, "Step in the room," pointing
to a doorway back of the adjutant, "and strip."

He followed Shafter, he waited, his mind obviously on other
things. He took a mechanical survey of Shafter's naked frame and
pointed to the thick whitened welt of a scar that made a foot-long
crescent on Shafter's left flank, above the hip. "What was that?"

"Saber cut."

"Ah," said the doctor, and made his tapping inspection of Shafter's chest. "How old?"

"Thirty-two."

The doctor completed the rest of his routine in silence and motioned for Shafter to resume his clothes, meanwhile himself leaving
the room. He sat down at the edge of the adjutant's desk, complet-
ing the physical form. "He'll do physically," he said to the adjutant.

The captain still remained in the room. Now he said: "I'll take
that man."

The adjutant grinned. "You want everything for A Company,
Moylan."

"I'm down to fifty-three men," said Captain Moylan.

"You're no worse off than the other companies."

"I'd like to have him, Cooke," said Captain Moylan, pressing the point.

The adjutant looked at the enlistment blank placed on his desk by the corporal. The corporal had gone. Cooke read through it. "He came all the way out here to enlist. You're buying a pig in the poke. Probably he's using the uniform to hide."

"He's had service before," said the doctor. "Saber scar."

Cooke said: "Jackson forgot to ask that question. It doesn't show here."

"Do I get him?" asked Moylan.

"You can have him, but the other company commanders will charge me with partiality."

"One more thing," said Moylan. "Let me swear him in."

Both Cooke and the doctor showed some degree of surprise. Cooke was on the point of asking a question, but at that moment Shafter, having dressed, returned to the office and took stand in front of the adjutant's desk. Cooke now gave Shafter a more thorough glance, noting his posture, his drawn-together carriage, his composed silence. Cooke said: —

"Do you leave any felonies behind you?"

"No," said Shafter.

"Have you had prior service?"

Shafter's answer came after a small pause, noticeable to all of them. "Yes," he said.

"What organization?"

The small delay was again noticeable. "Fourteenth Ohio."

"That would be the Civil War," said Cooke.

"Yes."

"What was the quality of your discharge?"

"Honorably mustered out, end of war."

Cooke nodded. He took a little brown volume of army regulations from a pile on the desk, searched through it and found a page. He handed the open book to Captain Moylan. Shafter turned to face the captain and, without being requested, raised his right hand.

Moylan looked at the page and began the oath: "Do you solemnly swear . . . "

When it was done with, Moylan gravely listened to Shafter's "I do," watched his face a considerable moment, and tossed the book of regulations on the table. "Very well," he softly said. "You are now a private in the Seventh Cavalry, attached to A Company. Follow me over to barracks."

"Yes sir," said Shafter, and moved out of the office behind Moylan. Cooke sat with his chin propped in one massive, meaty hand, watching the two go. "That was odd, Porter. Something there, I fancy."

"He's no raw Irishman off the boat," commented Porter. "He smells like a broken-down gentleman to me."

"I didn't seem to catch the broken-down part. If he is a gentleman, may God help him. We've got a few of them. They're very forlorn souls. Well." He rose and made a halfhearted gesture of creating some sort of neatness on his desk. "A little game tonight?"

"I've been invited to dance the opening set at D Company's ball," said Porter. "I'll meet you later."

Out on the baked parade ground, Shafter fell in step with Moylan, to the left and slightly behind the captain. First twilight had come to the land, the low hills to the west of the fort turning dark and edged against the sky, the great endless prairie to the east slowly foreshortening, as night crept over it. A guard relief detachment went scuffing by, the sergeant saluting Moylan as he passed. Moylan returned it absent-mindedly. He spoke to Shafter without turning his head.

"This was considerable of a surprise, Kern."

"I hadn't realized you were with the Seventh."

"I'm damned glad to see you. Often thought of you. It has been a long time since Winchester and Cumberland Gap. I don't suppose you expected to see old Myles Moylan as a captain of cavalry. It has been a hard route. I was sergeant major in this outfit before I got my commission. Coming up through the ranks is not the easy way to do it."

"God bless you," said Shafter. "I can think of nothing better."

"I asked Cooke to attach you to my company," said Moylan.

"I didn't say why. You didn't wish me to say why, did you?"

"No."

"It was a hard, hard thing," murmured Moylan. "I have never ceased to feel anger over it. Have you done anything about it?"

"Nothing to be done."

Moylan walked a full twenty feet before speaking again; and his words were troubled. "The strangeness of it does not stop with my being here and you being here. It is more than that. I wish I could have had the chance of speaking to you quietly before you took the oath. I think you wouldn't have stayed. Garnett is here. Or did you know that, and come to hunt him especially out?"

"I didn't know it," said Shafter, and said nothing more. He walked steadily beside Moylan, his chin dropped, expression drained from his face.

Moylan said: "He is first lieutenant of L. That is why I had Cooke assign you to my company. It would have been highly unpleasant for you to have served under him."

"It is strange how a thing never ends," said Shafter.

Moylan stepped to the porch of a barrack at the south end of the parade; a first sergeant sat there with a pipe in his mouth; he came to his feet and snatched the pipe from his mouth. "Hines," said Moylan, "this recruit is assigned to A. Take care of him."

"Yes sir," said the sergeant. Moylan swung off, going at a steady, fast pace down the walk, into the gathering twilight. The first sergeant gave Shafter a considerable stare. "What's your name?"

"Shafter."

"Well, then, Shafter, come with me," said Hines.

The barracks was a building thirty feet wide and better than a hundred long, with peeled logs standing upright as supports and a floor of rammed earth. A continuous row of double-decked bunks ran down the walls. At the foot of each bunk was a small locker for each man's effects and a rack for sabers and gear and carbines and other equipment. At the far end of the building was a little office over the door of which was a painted sign, ORDERLY ROOM. A door led back into what seemed a mess hall. Meanwhile the sergeant strode along the bunk row, past men already asleep, past men lying

awake on their blankets, past a table where men sat at a poker game
and looked up at Shafter with an indifferent interest. The first sergeant stopped at a bunk. "This," he said, "is yours. Do I have to
teach you to ride and handle a gun and mind your orders or   "
and he studied Shafter with a closer eye — "is it that you've had service before?"

"Yes," said Shafter.

"Cavalry?"

"Yes."

"Alcott," called Hines, and drew another sergeant across the room
with a waggle of his hand. "Take this man — Shafter's his name —
and give him an outfit."

"Come along," said Alcott and towed him into a dark little cub-
byhole of a quartermaster's supply room. The sergeant did a moment's measuring on Shafter with his eyes, then turned to his
shelves and began to toss pieces of uniform over his shoulder.

Twenty minutes later Shafter emerged with an outfit stacked from
his outspread arms to his chin — underwear, socks, field boots and
garrison shoes, blue pants and blue blouse and two blue wool shirts,
campaign hat, forage cap and dress helmet with plume, saber and
saber sling, carbine with its sling, Colt revolver, Springfield carbine, ammunition, cartridge belt, canteen, mess outfit, intrenching
tools, saddle bags, housewife kit, bridle, lariat and hobbles and picket
pin, a razor, a silvered mirror, a cake of soap, a comb, two blankets,
a straw tick, a box of shoe polish and a dauber, an overcoat, a rubber poncho with a hole through its center, a pair of wool gloves, a
bacon can, currycomb and brush, and a pair of collar ornaments with
cross-saber, the regimental number 7 above and the troop letter A
below.

He laid these things on his bunk, took up his tick and left the
room, headed for the stables. A hard-packed area lay between them
and the rear of the barrack hall, used for troop assembly; beyond
the stables stood the edge of the bluff which dropped to the Missouri now blackly running on into the night with a soft rustle of
its silted waters. Beyond the river winked the lights of the Point
and over the water at this moment slid the *Union* with a panting

chow—chow of its engines. Shafter found the straw stack and knelt to fill his tick; he heard the casual stamping of the horses and smelled the rankness of horses — and the night came blackly down upon him and from afar drifted the rolling tune of the band, made beautiful by the distance, by the night, by the shining of the stars. When he had finished his chore he returned to the barrack hall, laid the tick on the bunk and made his bed. He took off his civilian suit and pulled on the army pants and shirt; he rolled up his civilian clothes and stood a moment looking at them, and had his long, backward thoughts. He turned around, speaking down the barrack hall.

"Anybody getting a discharge soon?"

"Yes," said a trooper, and sat up from his bunk. "I'm leavin' next week."

"How big are you?"

"Five-ten, one hundred and sixty."

Shafter rolled the suit into a ball and threw it at the man on the bunk. "The tailor can pull in the trouser legs and cinch up the coat. It's yours. When you get to New York, walk into the Netherlands House, and tell the headwaiter who wore those clothes last. You'll get a free meal out of it."

The guardhouse trumpet drew the slow notes of tattoo across the silence of the night, softly and beautifully. Shafter got a cigar from his luggage on the cot. He lighted it and strolled in his stocking feet to the barrack porch. Across the thousand-foot parade ground the lights of Officers' Row were pleasantly shining and somewhere about the fort the regimental band still was playing dance music. Out from Number One Post at the guardhouse came the sentry's call: "Nine o'clock — all's well," and the call was picked up, post by post, until it ran all around the fort. He thrust his hands into the pockets of the pants, feeling the roughness of them; they had the smell of the storehouse on them and they were stiff. But they covered him and they brought back to him recollections of the years gone, and all those recollections were satisfying. It was like coming home; nothing was strange. The voices of the men within the barrack, the sight of the carbines racked together, the sabers hanging at the foot of the bunks

— all this was familiar. It was a way of living which, once surrendered, he now embraced again.

The darkness was a complete, moonless dark. Beyond Officers' Row lay the low, curved silhouette of the western ridge, over which a soft wind came with its scent of winter, with its scent of farther wildness. Out there, far out, lay a country as mysterious as the heart of Africa. Across it, during the past ten years, occasional military expeditions had traveled, had fought, had won and lost — but never had penetrated the core of it. That was Sioux land, the last refuge of a race which had given ground before the promises, the threats and the treacheries of the white man's frontier; and now had vowed to retreat no farther. Out there Sioux tepees made their rows and clusters along the Powder, the Yellowstone, the Tongue and the Rosebud; and along a stream which the Indians called the Greasy Grass but which was known to white men as the Little Bighorn.

III

The Ritual of Acceptance

"ABBOTT!"

"Yo!"

"Allen!"

"Yo!"

"Benzen!"

"Here!"

This was at five-thirty in the morning, the company assembled
unarmed and dismounted behind its barrack to answer roll call.
A mist lay hard upon the Missouri, hiding the water, but holding
in suspension all the river's rich, dank and racy smells, and day's
first light pressed down upon the mist from above. The troop stood
glumly double-ranked in the chill air. The sergeant's nose was a
reddening thermometer of both his temperature and his disposition.
Upon completion of roll call, he made an about-face and rendered
his slowly precise salute to the sharp-visaged young second lieutenant waiting by.

"Present or accounted for, sir."

The lieutenant acknowledged the salute and thus, having ful-
filled regulations, walked away. Hines turned back upon the troop,
morning-sour and professionally cranky. "I never saw a filthier yard,
nor a dirtier barrack. After breakfast you'll all turn out for police
on it. Mind me, you have been doin' too much soldierin' on your
bunks. Corp'ril King and squad, wood detail. Costain, duty at the
orderly room. Melish, Duker and Straub, kitchen. Sergeant McDermott, Corp'ril Roy, Privates Bean, Ryneerson, Hoch and Muldoon,
guard duty tonight." He thought a moment and thereafter opened
his roster book again. "By order of this date, Private Shafter appointed sergeant. Dismiss."

The heavy smell of coffee came reeking out of the mess-hall

wing as they broke up and ran back to barrack. All down the parade sounded the brisk mess call. Day broke through the mist, sparkling against the dew-beaded grass. Shafter got his mess outfit from his bunk, crossed to the hall, and joined the forming line. A private with a vein-netted face and a pair of flushed eyes overhung with a solid lacework of stiff black brows came up behind him, growling. "A sergeant," he said, "does nawt éat with us common ones. You belong at the head o' the line."

"I'll wait until I sew the stripes on," said Shafter and gave this new one a thoughtful appraisal. The man had muscular shoulders; he was full of bone and meat, but his belly was round and liquor had softened him. On his sleeve was a faded spot where, not long before, sergeant stripes had been.

"The rank came easy, did it not?" said the man, accenting his insolence.

"As easy as yours went away," said Shafter.

"I worked for mine," said the man. "Four years. I licked nobody's boots for 'em. I gave 'em up because it was me own wish."

"So that you could breathe freer into a whisky bottle," said Shafter.

"You've got a tongue, I do observe," said the man. He lifted his voice a little and half the line of men heard this. "To be a sergeant is not a matter of tongue in this outfit, bucky. It is a matter of knuckles. Do you know what I think? I think you'll not last long."

The line moved up, passing before the cook's table where a pair of troopers served out breakfast from kitchen kettles. Shafter got his oatmeal, his bacon and biscuits and held out his cup for coffee. The trooper handling the pot let his hand waver a little so that the coffee spilled over, scalding Shafter's hand; and then the trooper gave him a blank stare. Shafter looked back at him, a little light dancing gray-bright in his eyes, and passed on to a long table. That was the way it would be in this troop; he was untested, and suddenly a sergeant — made so by Captain Moylan out of memory of incidents long ago. Moylan must have known that he put his new sergeant in a hard position.

Hines passed by and dropped a brusque word. "Come to the orderly room."

In a little while Shafter followed him into the small room at the end of the barracks. Hines was at his desk. He said, "Shut the damned door," and waited until it was done. "I'm too old a man to remark upon my company commander's choices. You've been in the army before?"

"Yes."

"Moylan knew you somewhere?"

"Let's let that slide," said Shafter.

Hines was displeased, and his stare was like the slap of his heavy hand. "It is his choice to make, but it is me that has to keep the company runnin' like a company should run. There is somethin' here which the company will not like, and I cannot put my hand upon any man to stop him from givin' you the roll of his eye. I will not have this outfit go sour because of the advancement of a rooky to sergeant. So, then, you must lick somebody to show what you've got. It will be the one that was sergeant and got broke for tryin' to lap up all the whisky in Bismarck. That's Donovan."

Shafter remembered the meaty one with the round belly. "He's opened the door already."

"See that you walk right through that door," said Hines. "You must give him a hell of a beating, or you'll never draw any water in this outfit as a noncom. If he should give you the beatin'— and it is my bet that he'll do just that— there is but one thing for you to do. You will turn in your stripes."

Shafter stood easy in front of the first sergeant, smiling a little. "You have got a fine collection of savages for a company, Sergeant. I shall tame one of them for you."

"So," said Hines and was not impressed. Four hashmarks on his sleeve testified his service; in the rounds of his eyes lay an iron, taciturn wisdom. The army had made and shaped him until he was all that the army stood for, a solid, short-tempered and thoroughly valuable man. "You talk like a damned gentleman. Get your stripes sewed on. At stable call you will be assigned a horse. Afternoon you will hitch up the light wagon and go to Bismarck to do errands for the captain and his lady. You will stay until the train comes in, pick up the first lieutenant of this company, who arrives from St. Paul — the Lieutenant Smith."

"Who is the officer that took roll call this morning?"

"That one is Varnum. He has some knowledge of Indians, which God knows we'll need when they break out again next spring."

Stable call came sharp upon the parade ground, pulling Shafter from the orderly room. The fog had lifted and bright sunshine slanted out of the east; he was assigned his horse, and his stall, and spent time grooming the horse. Sick call came, and first call for drill; at nine o'clock the sharp-faced Lieutenant Varnum took the company out upon the parade. Heat lay like a thinned film in the windless air, only suggesting what it had been a few short months before, but the fine dust rose beneath the hoofs of the turning horses as the five companies, each on a section of the parade, went through their close-order maneuvers, wheeling in column, fours left, fours right, left into line, walk, trot, gallop; the horses, old in the business, automatically responding, crowding upon each other, grunting, precisely coming about. At eleven-thirty recall sounded; and mess call came at noon. Afterwards, Shafter hitched up the light wagon to a pair of horses and, with a shopping list from Mrs. Moylan in his pocket, drove through Lincoln's guard gate — past the post gardens and hospital and band quarters, past the barracks of the regimental noncommissioned staff, past bakery and officers' club and civilian quarters and post trader's store — and so came to the ferry.

Over the river, he drove through the Point which lay exhausted after its night's excesses, and followed the straggling road into Bismarck. As soon as he arrived there he did the shopping for Mrs. Moylan; after that he hunted up a tailor and sat in his underclothes for an hour, reading an old copy of the *New York Tribune* while the tailor cut his uniform to better size, sewed on the sergeant's chevrons and the yellow noncom strip down each trouser leg.

He still had an hour to spend before train time; and walked the length of Bismarck's street, the sun's warmth going through his heavy blue blouse and bringing out its woolly smell; he turned and strolled back and, in front of the town's big grocery store, he came upon Josephine Russell. She halted at once, showing surprise; she tipped her head as she studied him.

"So that is why you came west?"

"Yes."

She said: "I think you've worn the uniform before. I thought that when I saw you standing in front of the depot at Corapolis."

She carried a basket of groceries, and she had a roll of checked red-and-white oilcloth under her arm. Shafter relieved her of these bundles. "Where can I carry these for you?"

"You're on duty, aren't you?"

"Waiting for the train to come in."

They moved down the street, side by side. She wore a light dress, and she had no hat, and she seemed fairer to him than before; her gray eyes were calm and pleased in the way they looked at him. Her lips held their steady hint of a smile.

"It's good to see you," he said.

She gave him a quick side glance, slightly speculative, her eyes gently narrowing. Her lips made a softly pursed line and afterwards she walked on in silence, looking before her. This day the town was crowded. Half a dozen punchers came up the walk, shoulder to shoulder, thrown slightly forward by the high heels of their riding boots — all sharp-eyed, roughly dressed men, and all keenly alive. They broke aside to let Josephine pass, and eyed her with surreptitious admiration. Indians sat against a stable wall, dourly indifferent. Up from a warehouse at the lower end of town moved a caravan of ox-drawn wagons crowded to the canvas tops with freight, headed outward from the railroad into that southward distance which ran three hundred miles to Yankton without the break of a town or settlement, except for the dreary little army posts or steamboat landings along the Missouri.

A man sat on the steps of a barbershop with a carbine and calmly shot between the traffic at a target over near the railroad tracks; and drew up his gun to let Josephine and Shafter pass by. At the foot of the street Josephine turned the corner of a feed store and moved back upon the prairie to a house standing somewhat removed from the town. A picket fence surrounded it, but otherwise it was without ornament, shade or grass.

Josephine opened the gate and led Shafter to the porch, there relieving him of the packages. She dropped them inside the house door and turned back. "If you must wait somewhere, it might be just as comfortable waiting here. Sit down."

There were a chair and a rocker on the porch, both made of merchandise packing boxes. Josephine took the chair and Shafter settled himself in the rocker and let his long legs sprawl before him. The gesture brought an instant smile and comment from the girl. "You have a wonderful gift of just going loose all over whenever you can."

"I got that from the army. A man learns, when he's on long marches, to make the short stops count."

"The uniform changes you entirely. My first judgment of you was a great deal different." Her glance turned thoughtful. "In civilian clothes you seemed a somewhat skeptical man, perhaps accustomed to the good things of life."

He showed some embarrassment at the remark. He said: "I guess that's true."

She realized she had struck something in him which was vulnerable; he had a sensitive spot, and she was sorry she had touched it and changed the subject. "You were lucky to get a uniform that fitted you."

"I had the tailor work on it," he said. "Well, whatever I was, I still am. You can't change a man by clothes. But I have wanted to get back into the uniform for ten years. I remembered that when I was a soldier last time I had about as much complete peace of mind, as much personal contentment, as I ever had. That's why I came back. I do not require much comfort and I do not need many possessions. What I need, I guess, is to be with plain and honest men."

"Men can be plain and honest outside the army."

"Then," he said, "it must be something else the uniform has that I have needed. At any rate, I feel at home, which is something I have not felt for a long time."

"Adventure?" she murmured. "The sound of bugles?"

He shook his head. "I went through four years of the Civil War. I heard a lot of bugles blowing for the charge. I saw a lot of men fall, a lot of good friends die. That's the other side of adventure. I am no longer a young man dreaming of gallantry in action."

She bent a little in the chair, smiling and curious. "You make yourself a greater puzzle to me, Sergeant." Then she rose and went into the house. He reached into his blouse for a cigar, and lighted it and relaxed wholly in the rocker. The afternoon was warm, all of summer's scorch gone out of it. The deep haze of summer, this far west, had lightened, so that the prairie was a tawny floor, running immeasurably away into the distance. The railroad line marched eastward, marked by the single row of telegraph poles; and in that direction was the smudge of the afternoon train coming on. Josephine Russell came back with a tall glass of milk and handed it to him.

"How long have you lived out here?" he asked.

"Two years. We have always been moving up on the edge of the frontier. I suppose in two or three years more we'll be out there in Montana somewhere. My father has that store — where you saw me. But he is restless, and more so since my mother died."

"You like it here?"

"I like whatever place I am." A more sober expression came to her face. "It was nice to visit the East, though. I don't know when I shall see it again."

The train flung its long warning whistle forward from the distance, reminding Shafter of his duty. He rose with reluctance and stood easy-balanced on his feet, looking down at her with his expression of personal interest, and he repeated what he had said earlier: "It is good to see you again."

"The post can be a very lonely place. Are you sure it won't bore you?"

"I don't need much in the way of distraction."

She said: "This house is open, if you feel like visiting."

He nodded, he said: "I shall do that," and walked back toward town. She watched him go, his shoulders cut against the sunlight, his long frame swinging. She had known, as soon as she saw him in uniform, that the sergeant's stripes did not represent what he once had been. Somewhere in the past he had been a man with a career, had met disaster, and had stepped away from the wreckage with a shrug of his shoulder. She had guessed that much about him two days before, and was more certain of it now. There was, she thought, a woman somewhere involved. Reluctantly she lifted her guard against him. "I should not," she murmured, "be very much interested in him," and continued to watch him until he swung around the corner of a building and disappeared.

Shafter drove the small wagon to the station and arrived just as the train did. He watched the passengers come out, saw only one army officer, and walked toward him. Lieutenant Algernon Smith was a dark, chunky-shouldered man with a bushy black cavalry mustache, heavy black brows, a solid chin and sharp eyes. He took Shafter's salute.

"Sergeant Shafter, sir. I am to drive you to the post."

The lieutenant said: "You're new?"

"I enlisted yesterday, sir."

"Rapid promotion," said the lieutenant enigmatically and nothing more. He had a small portmanteau which he flung into the wagon when he reached it, and stepped up to the seat, folding his arms across his chest like an artilleryman riding a caisson. Shafter ran the team out of town and down the rutty road. Past the Point he saw the ferry ready to cast off, whereupon he whipped the team into a dead run down the incline and put it aboard with a sudden shock of brakes. Lieutenant Smith grabbed the edge of the seat to prevent falling out, and gave Shafter the benefit of his dry voice: "I guess you have dash enough for cavalry service."

Once inside the guard gate, Shafter drove over the parade to Officers' Row, let off the lieutenant and went on to Captain Moylan's quarters. He carried the packages to the back door, delivered them to the captain's striker, and returned the wagon and team to stables. It was past five o'clock then, afternoon stable call having occurred while he was gone; therefore he curried his horse and walked into the barrack. As soon as he reached his bunk he saw that it had been ripped apart. His box of cigars, which he had placed beneath the tick, now lay in sight, its lid open and the cigars gone.

The men of the troop sat around the barrack, waiting mess call, cleaning up equipment for retreat, or lying back on their bunks. Donovan, he noticed, was at one of the tables, playing a game of solitaire. Donovan was smoking a cigar and, to make the point clearer, Donovan had a row of cigars lying on the table before him. A scar-mouthed trooper stood by, thinly grinning and watching Shafter from the evil corners of his eyes. It was a published thing in the barrack room; everybody knew what was happening, and waited for the rest of it to happen.

Shafter turned to the table and stood beside it, looking down on the red surface of Donovan's neck. The ex-sergeant kept on with his solitaire, aware of Shafter's presence but ignoring it. He had his feet planted squarely on the floor, beneath the table; he had his forearms lightly braced on the table's top so that one warning would bring him roaring up to his feet.

"Donovan," said Shafter, easy and plain, "where do we have this fight?"

"Behind the stables," said Donovan with equal calmness. "Tinney, have a cigar. They're good ones, picked by a gentleman lately come among us to dodge a warrant. I guess we have smoked the gentleman out." He slapped a hand down on the table so hard that the cards jumped and he leaned back and shouted out a heavy laughter at his own joke.

The scar-mouthed trooper grinned and reached for a cigar. He was not entirely sure of his act, however, and cast a sly glance at Shafter. He held his hand on the cigar, dividing his attention between the two men, and for a moment he seemed to debate on which side of this coming fight the power lay — and safety for him. Presently he decided the question in Donovan's favor, picked up the cigar and turned away. In the background Shafter saw the other troopers watching, interested and speculative. It was a break in the dull day, a flash of violence feeding their hungry appetites.

"I'll be behind the stables after tattoo," said Shafter. "Better smoke those things up now, Donovan. You'll be sick of cigars later."

Donovan continued imperturbably with his playing. He said to the room at large, "Listen to the gentleman's words carefully, boys. The gentleman is a sergeant. He is an educated sergeant, sent among us heathens to bring us knowledge."

Supper was over and retreat gone by; twilight came, layer on layer, with its sharpening chill. Along the quadrangle, lights splashed their yellow lanes out of doorways, poured their fan-shaped patterns through dusty windows. A patrol, half a company in strength, came in from the western distance and moved with jaded temper across the parade, equipment clinking in the dark. Shafter strolled along the barracks walk with his cigar, hearing the talk of men come out in drawling eddies, in sudden bursts of laughter, in sharpness, in murmuring. A guard detail tramped briskly by, an officer crossed the parade at a full-out gallop; and somewhere a deep voice yelled: "Flynn—hey, Flynn!"

The stars were up, turned brilliant by the cold air, and for a moment Shafter stopped to watch them. Other troopers moved by him, some with idleness and some hurrying to reach the ferry and the gaudy dens beyond the river at the Point. Across the parade, General Custer's house was filled with light and officers and their ladies strolled toward it, the quick and gay voices of these people coming over the long stretch of ground in softened cadence. He listened a moment to those tones of warmth and he stood still with his eyes half closed, and then swung on with the idle current of troopers, moving past the guard gate toward the post trader's store.

He turned about before he reached it, remembering that he had a date with Donovan after tattoo, and he paced back through the outthrown lights of the guardhouse, indifferently noticing an officer appear from the guardhouse, and swung toward Officers' Row at a quick and nervous pace. Twenty feet onward, he heard the officer's stride cease and he heard the officer call at him:—

"Hold up there."

He had not seen the officer's face, but a ruffling chill ran along his back and a strange tight spasm went through his belly as he swung. The officer stood waiting twenty feet away, his face obscured by the shadows; and then the officer murmured in a long, odd voice: "Come here, Sergeant."

Shafter moved up, watching the other man's face take on shape and form — and identity. When he was ten feet removed, he discovered whom he faced and a feeling greater than any feeling he had known for years broke through him and shook him from top to bottom. He came to a stand and remembered he was in uniform, and made his salute.

The lieutenant did not return the salute. He looked upon Shafter with a face exceedingly sharpened by astonishment, by the shock of past memories, by the rousing of old rages and evils. He had no motion in him at that moment, he had only one thought, and this escaped him with a slicing-sharp expelling of wind.

"How in God's name did you get here?"

Shafter could think of but one answer, and made it: "It is a small world, Mr. Garnett. A very small world to a man trying to escape his conscience."

"Your conscience?" said Lieutenant Edward Christian Garnett.

"Yours," said Shafter.

The lieutenant stood still and began to curse Shafter with a softly terrible voice. He pulled up his high shoulders, he straightened his long body and he used his words as he would have used a whip, to cut, to disfigure, to destroy. The guard patrol swung around the corner of the quadrangle and passed close at hand, stopping the lieutenant's voice for a little while, and in this silence Shafter saw the man's pale wedge of a face — so handsome and tempting a face to women — show its hard evil, its unforgiving and brutal blackness. This was Garnett, formed like an aristocrat out of a French novel, with dark round eyes well recessed in their sockets, with a head of dark hair that broke along his forehead in a dashing wave, and a gallant mustache trimmed above a full, thick-centered mouth. He had the whitest of teeth; he had a smile, Shafter remembered, which could charm a woman and capture her without effort. He was a man with the obsession of conquest — the conquest of a woman; he had the predatory instincts of a tiger and no morals, no scruples, no decencies. He had touched nothing that he had not destroyed, so that all along his career was the wreckage of his passing. He was, Shafter bitterly knew, an inner rottenness covered by a uniform, and cloaked by a kind of gallantry which passed for courage.

The patrol passed on. Garnett said, sharply: "See to it that you are not in this fort tomorrow."

"What are you afraid of, Mr. Garnett?"

"Damn you," said Garnett, "speak to me properly."

"Then let us start right. Return the salute I offered you. You were always a slovenly soldier."

Garnett stared at him. "I could prefer charges against you, Shafter."

"Do you want to open the record of the past, Mr. Garnett?" murmured Shafter.

"And how could you open it?" answered Garnett, thinly malicious. "Your word against mine? Who would take it?"

"Captain Moylan is also here," said Shafter. "As a gentleman, I suppose he has kept his knowledge of you to himself. How would you like the ladies of the post to know of the events of your past? It would interfere with your prowling. I think you will never prefer charges against me."

Garnett stepped nearer him. "Listen to me. I have got a hundred ways of getting at you. Believe me, I'll use them all. I'll break your damned back and I'll break your heart. Before I'm through with you, you'll crawl over the hill one dark night and never come back."

"You are a dog, Mr. Garnett," said Shafter.

Garnett lifted a hand and hit him one cracking blow across the face with his open palm. The effect of it roared through Shafter's head; he stepped away and then he stepped forward, to find Garnett backed four paces from him and holding a drawn revolver on him. "Go ahead," Garnett softly murmured. "You are in a hard regiment, Shafter, with damned little mercy shown on insubordination. The colonel would have you shot, as he has had others shot before you."

Over by the guardhouse, the bugler softly breathed into his instrument, readying his lips for tattoo. Shafter waited out the dismal silence, pulling his impulses back into safe place, and spoke to this man he both despised and hated more than any other person upon earth. "I did not know you were here," he said. "Probably I would not have come if I had known it. Still, I'm here. Here I shall stay. And now that you have used your hands on me, I'll tell you something: One way or another, I'll destroy you."

Lieutenant Garnett held the gun on him, watching him with strict attention. He said, "You may go now, Sergeant."

They were alone in the darkness, thus facing. Shafter thought of this, knowing that he had the advantage. By daylight he could not pass the strict line which divided him from Garnett; by daylight Garnett could make him dance. But there would always be times when he might catch this man on even terms; for Garnett would take no chances on his own blemished reputation being published at this post. So Shafter stood his ground and gave Garnett a taste of what would come.

"Put up the revolver and turn about and march away. I think Moylan would relish the opportunity of exposing you."

Garnett cursed him again, in his whispering wicked way. Tattoo broke over the parade, drowning out the sound of Garnett's voice; but he watched the lieutenant's lips form their blasphemies and then close thinly together. The lieutenant holstered his gun, swung and went toward Custer's quarters at a long-reaching pace.

He left behind him a man who, once turned bitter against the world, had mastered his bitterness; and suddenly now was bitter again. He left behind him an enemy of dangerous shape, a man tempered and toughened by a war, knowing its trickeries, its subterfuges, its brutal modes of combat. All that knowledge Shafter had subdued and put aside during the ten following years, but it returned to him as he turned back toward A Company's barrack with tattoo's last notes falling away in softened, melancholy loveliness across the parade and across the dark yonder earth. Nine-o'clock call began to run from post to post as he rounded the barrack and moved through the dark space between barrack and stable. He cut about the stable and found A Company's men waiting in the blackness, all ranked along the river bluff. He saw a shape lift from the earth and heard the shape say: —

"What kept you? Now where's that lantern?"

It was Donovan speaking. He stood heavy-shouldered in the dark, stripped to his shirt, with his paunch spilling over the belt of his trousers. A man moved up and pulled a blanket away from a lantern, so that its light danced in yellow crystals upon the night. Donovan clapped his meaty hands together and held them dropped before him, grinning at Shafter. He was a confident old hand, facing another routine battle; and the battle was life to him, so that he gave no thought to hurt or to injury or to scars. There was no real anger in the man, Shafter understood; Donovan had only used his sarcasm and his ridicule as a weapon to produce the fight he needed as much as he needed food. "Take off your blouse — take off your shirt. I'll have no advantage. I need none."

It was a full ten degrees colder than on the previous night, and a wind played out of the north as an idle warning. Stripping off blouse and shirt, Shafter studied Donovan's bullet-round head, the blunt bevel of his shoulders, the softening pads of fat which lay along his upper arm. The man's coolness, the man's complete calm warned him; this Donovan had been a professional somewhere and thought of his opponent as only another green, awkward one to be pounded down and added to his list. He saw Donovan winking at the dark shape of the crowd.

"If the gentleman is ready," said Donovan with his ridiculing tone, "let's be off to the fair."

He waited no longer. He took a striding, squatty plunge forward, his left fist feinting, his right thundering out. Shafter came in, caught that right-armed blow on his elbow and threw it aside. He hit Donovan hard in the belly; he felt his fist sink into the doughlike fat. He heard Donovan's blast of expelled wind; he shifted his hips as Donovan tried to ram a knee into his crotch; he trapped both of Donovan's arms under his elbows and he rode around a circle as Donovan used his strength to pull free. He let go, hooked a punch against Donovan's kidney and moved away.

Donovan shook his head. Donovan's mouth was open, sucking wind. Donovan's face was rouge red. He gave an impatient cry, his narrowed eyes showing a crimson, sly fury as they studied Shafter. He stood still. He stamped the ground with one foot, shuffled forward and feinted with his body, luring Shafter in. He dropped his arms, opening himself wide, and rushed forward again with his head down, growling strange things under his breath; he was suddenly hard to hit. Shafter tried for the man's belly, missed, and then, before he could swing clear, he was thrown back on his heel and knocked to the ground by a savage punch he had never seen. He rolled and saw Donovan's legs striding forward; he seized Donovan's foot and turned with it and brought the man down. The ex-sergeant struck hard, and the fall drew its grunt, and after that Donovan was a fat ball of fury, reaching and striking and kicking.

Shafter flung himself away, stood up and watched Donovan rise. He hit the Irishman, left and right hand, in the belly and brought Donovan's guard down. He saw his opening, stepped in and sledged Donovan at the side of the neck. He got two hard blows in before Donovan reached for him and tied him up. He went loose, letting Donovan pay out his strength in the struggle.

Donovan cried, "You damned leech, stand out and fight it!" He used all his muscles and heaved Shafter clear, and raised a hand to brush his sweaty face. Shafter slid in, driving for the man's belly, and saw the sick look that came to Donovan's mouth. Donovan reached for him but Shafter whirled aside, found his chance, and hit him in the kidney again. The man's softness was crawling up on him; he had his mouth sprung wide and his eyes were not clear. Helplessness seemed to come to him, for he shook his head and let his arms drop. Shafter started in, but feinted back as Donovan, playing possum, came to life and struck out in long-reaching left and right blows. He missed and now, off balance, stumbled forward. Shafter caught him with a short, up-cutting blow beneath the chin. Donovan sighed; the power went out of him and he fell slowly and cumbersomely to the dust, his face striking.

The light bobbed up and down in Tinney's hands. Tinney said, "For God's sakes Donovan, quit foolin'!" He ran forward and tickled Donovan with the toe of his boot; he bent nearer and straightened back, to say in a dull astonishment: "He's out."

"Water bucket," said Shafter.

Somebody went running back to the stable while Tinney helplessly circled Donovan with the lantern. "Donovan — hey, Donovan," he pleaded. Troopers formed a fascinated, silent circle. Shafter said, "Tinney, how did you like that cigar?" and watched Tinney's head spring up. Tinney opened his scar-shaped mouth to speak, found nothing to say and slowly backed off. The messenger ran in from the stable and flung a full bucket of water on Donovan's naked torso. The Irishman, half-wakened by it, made a wild swing and got to his hands and knees. He shook his head and looked up. He saw Shafter. He ran a hand over his face to slash the water away. "I got licked?" he said.

"You should quit smoking, Donovan," said Shafter. "Cigars are bad on the wind."

Donovan pulled himself to his feet. He said, "What fool dumped the bucket on me? Because a man is on his knees is nothin'." Then he said curiously, "Was I out?"

"Dead out," said Shafter.

"Then I got licked," said Donovan in a practical voice. He studied Shafter at some length, without resentment. He put out his hand. "That's the end of it," he said. "I never bear a grudge."

Shafter took Donovan's hand, whereupon Donovan thought of something and swung around, pointing a finger at the men of A Company. "When I'm licked, I'm licked. But don't none of you lads think you can do better than me. Don't none of you get fresh with me. I'm still man enough to lick the lot of you. Another thing — if you back-talk the professor here, I'll beat your ears down. You hear?"

He started for the barracks, his head dropped in weariness. Shafter came up to him and laid an arm on his shoulder, so that the two went on through the dark. Donovan murmured: "I'll buy the cigars, bucko. You're all right. If you can lick me, you can wear the stripes. I'd like to see the man that can take 'em off you."

"Donovan," said Shafter. "One night soon we'll take a few of the lads and drop over the river. A little drinking will do no harm."

"Ah," said Donovan, "you're my kind. But if I'd lay off the whisky you'd never of had me. Professor, this is a damned good outfit."

Shafter moved through the barrack room, putting on his shirt as he walked; he continued on to the porch which confronted the parade and he stood there and felt the ache of his bruises, the loosening aftereffect of the fight. But he knew he had ceased to be an outsider. He had joined the company; he could tell that by the way the men looked at him. This was why he had joined — to be one of a company of men. To be with them and a part of them; remembering away back, he knew that it was in this closeness he had been happiest. Maybe it was discipline or maybe it was service, or maybe it was the feeling of a man as he rode with other men, joined in the roughness, in the brawling and in the fighting, in the lust and evil and in the honesty and the faithfulness that bound them all together. He stood still, coming close to the reason, but never quite grasping the tangible form of it. As he searched himself, going down into the strange places where lived those prime hungers which made him a man, he remembered what things had been important to him in the past, and what things he had missed in civilian life. They were little things, but all of them strong — the sweat that started out of his pores and stung his eyes, the heavy dust rising up from a marching column, the wind against his face when he rode through some early March morning with the fog lifting out of the lowlands of the Wilderness; the rain beating hard upon him until the smell of his uniform was woolly and rank; the pure pleasure that had come to him when, dried and exhausted, he dropped to his belly beside a sluggish branch in Virginia and drank the brackish water until he could hold no more; the evening shadows with the campfires glittering through them and the sound of tired voices coming from afar; the stretch of his leg muscles as he lifted in the saddle for a run; the wicked satisfaction that came of taking a blow and giving one; and the comfort of the earth as he lay against it — and the calm dark mystery of the heavens as he looked up to them. Each was a little thing, but each one fashioned and formed him and fed him and made life full.

A trooper came out of the barrack and stood silently by; he was a young lad, tall but still not wholly filled out with man's muscles. He had light hair and a fair face and he smiled in an engaging way when Shafter looked at him. He was not more than eighteen. He said wistfully: "I wish I knew how to fight. I mean, well enough to take care of myself."

"It will come," said Shafter.

"Funny thing," said the boy, "I never had a fight."

"It may be you can get through the next forty years without one," said Shafter. "I hope you do."

"A man's got to fight sometime," said the boy.

"Don't look for one — don't give it a thought," said Shafter. "Wait until it comes — and perhaps it will never come." He fell silent, noting the boy's puzzled face. What he had said seemed a contradiction to the lad; and so he quietly added: "Men are not dogs to be growling at each other."

"Well, I suppose so," said the youngster and, still puzzled, moved down the parade toward the south; in that direction, beyond the quartermaster quarters, lay Suds Row, which was a line of houses occupied by married sergeants whose wives were troop laundresses. He heard the boy whistle a little as he moved into the darkness.

Shafter returned to his bunk and pulled off his uniform. Donovan walked out of the washroom, stripped naked. He tapped his paunch, turned red by the punches Shafter had put there. He was grinning. "A good fight, bucko." The first sergeant came out of the orderly room and paused to look at these two.

"What happened to your belly, Donovan?"

"I fell on a picket pin," said Donovan, and grinned again.

Hines said: "I'll have to send a detail out to pull up all these picket pins which the men of this troop keep stumblin' over." He showed Shafter a sardonic humor and passed on, grumbling at a group of poker players. "Break up that. Taps is comin'." He left the barrack and went at an old soldier's steady, established pace through the dark, along the side of the quartermaster department and the commissary building; he turned down Officers' Row and stopped and tapped on the door of Captain Moylan's house. When the captain came out, he rendered his slow, grooved salute and said: "He licked Donovan, sir."

"So," said Moylan, and was pleased. "It will be all right."

"It will be better than I thought," agreed Hines. "Now, can he soldier?"

"As good as you or I, Hines."

"Let us not be givin' him too much credit," said Hines. "If the man is half as good as either of us, Captain, he is an angel."

"You'll see," said Moylan.

IV

On Officers' Row

LIEUTENANT GARNETT moved rapidly over the parade toward Officers' Row, preoccupied and scowling, with the shock of the meeting still affecting him, with fear still a sharp sensation in him. As he came before General Custer's house, he paused to pull himself straight, to compose the expression on his face and to make a few quick jerks at the tail of his coat. Once more in trim, he crossed the porch with his cap removed and tucked in the crook of his left arm.

Mrs. Custer met him, touched his elbow and led him forward to the crowd arranged in groups around the room. She was a demure woman, quietly charming and with a light and softhearted manner of meeting people. She said: "I believe you know everybody, except perhaps our very young and very pretty guest from Bismarck."

She paused before Josephine Russell, who was seated on the piano stool. Lieutenant Garnett's back sprung into a tenser arch, like a race horse waiting the drop of the barrier; his deep-set and slightly mournful eyes saw the girl's prettiness and the hunting instinct in him rose and fashioned a flashing smile, and all the proper gestures of gallantry; he made a show in his uniform — the long straight sweep of his trousers with their broad yellow stripes, the tight brass-buttoned coat above which lay the white wing collar and black cravat. He had a long wedge of a face with an olive pallor which no amount of sun changed and this, against the intense blackness of his wavy hair, made him an extremely striking man.

"Josephine," said Mrs. Custer, "let me present Mr. Garnett. This is Josephine Russell." And then, because Mrs. Custer had a motherly instinct for the men of the command, and loved to make matches, she added with her air of bright and gentle interest, "Mr. Garnett is so wedded to his profession that I fear he has never had time for ladies."

Lieutenant Garnett gave Mrs. Custer a quick glance, suspecting irony; but he saw only a very human pleasure on the face of the commanding officer's wife and so turned and made his distinguished bow. "I must warn you, Miss Russell. There are many bachelors and you will be rushed."

"Ah," said Mrs. Custer, "all the eligible bachelors of the post have rushed her."

"I propose to join their ranks immediately," said Garnett.

Josephine acknowledged the compliment with a smile; she sat with her hands on her lap, pleasantly reposed. Her hair lay darkly back on top of her head, exposing the small and dainty ears with their pearl pendants. She had a soft roundness to her bosom, and she had a reserve in her eyes; and the shadow of strength and intensity behind her smiling greatly intrigued the lieutenant. She said: "The gallantry of the Seventh is well known, Mr. Garnett."

Mrs. Custer went away and for a little while the lieutenant tried his best wares on Josephine, idly but deceptively probing and drawing her out, testing the metal in her, searching for some entry through her vanity, her weaknesses, her romantic notions or her pride. He was a clever man and presently when the general's brother, Captain Tom Custer, came up — a slim, restless man with a boyish and daredevil face topped by lank light hair — the lieutenant passed on to pay his respects to the other officers and their ladies. The general was in a corner, having some sort of tactical discussion with Major Reno and Captain Weir of D Company and the tawny Yates who was commander of F. Garnett left that weighty circle to itself, said a few words to Algernon Smith and Mrs. Smith, joined in with Calhoun and Edgerly for a moment — the latter as handsome a man as himself — and so, punctiliously leaving his word and his smile from person to person, he came finally to Major Barrows and his lady, the major being here on tour of duty from the inspector general's department.

The major was on the small and lean side, leaf brown and quiet of face, very soft of voice and with a taciturn cast to his eyes. A small mustache and imperial gave a tempered sharpness to an otherwise gentle set of features, and his manner in addressing Garnett had a kind of formal courtesy. "Good evening, Mr. Garnett. A pleasant evening."

"Pleasant, but there's a chill in it. Winter's coming."

"Always does," said Major Barrows, inflecting a most common-place remark with his dryness.

Garnett, usually extraordinarily attentive to the ladies, talked on with the major for a full minute or more before turning his head and looking down at Mrs. Barrows; and then gave her a smile and a word, nothing more. She looked up at him, a woman somewhat younger than her husband, still of feature and with only her eyes showing much expression. She sat back in the chair, her head rested against it so that her throat revealed its ivory lines. Her lids dropped and for a moment her lashes touched as she watched this man — darkly, indifferently, strangely.

The major divided an inexpressive glance between them and then thought to say: "You have met, have you not?"

The major's wife smiled slightly. "Of course. Two or three times."

"My memory for things social has grown rusty," apologized the major. He sought his coat for a cigar, cast a glance at the general and his party and made a little bow to be excused, going over to join that discussion. Garnett thrust his arms across his chest, matching the depthless inspection of the woman with one of his own. In the little pocket of her throat he saw her heart beating and he knew he had stirred her. He had met her at a party like this only a month before, had smiled at her; he had sat beside her at Major Tilford's dinner slightly later, studying her silence and her indifference until he knew what it was. This was his third meeting and he understood what his method was to be with her; it was to be dark and somber, with soft words carrying more in tone than in meaning. The major's wife, he guessed, was a lonely woman with unspent emotions.

"Do you enjoy it here?" he asked.

"Yes," she said, and continued to watch him out of her half-closed eyes. It was a challenge to be met and he murmured: "Of what are you thinking?"

"Many things."

"Have you walked through these shadows, late at night, by yourself?"

"Yes. Often."

"I know what you have felt. I know what you have thought," he said.

"Do you?" she asked. Her eyes grew wider and a slight warmth escaped her control and showed on her lips. He watched her suppress it, he heard practicalness return to her voice: "You are gallant, Mr. Garnett."

He had interested her but, like a wise campaigner, he did not overdo his pressing; he nodded and turned back to join Calhoun and Edgerly who stood before Josephine. Presently the talk of the older officers interested him and he drifted that way. Weir was speaking: —

"It is absurd to suppose that the Sioux, having had their best country in the Black Hills opened up to the white miner, will not brood upon it. We have respected no treaty we ever made with them. They know we never will. What good is a treaty, solemnly made in Washington, when a month later five hundred white men cross the deadline? The prospector, the emigrant and the squatter have a hunger for gold and land that we cannot stop by treaty. We have spent two years trying to run the whites out of country which we have promised shall be the Indian's. It is an impossible job. The Indian knows we will continue to back him westward until we have pushed him into the ocean. All the Sioux leaders see it. They will make a stand. Of course there will be a campaign next year."

"If so," said Custer, "we shall decisively defeat them."

"I wish," said Weir, "I were as optimistic. All this summer the traders have been freighting repeating rifles up the Missouri, trading for fur. Winchesters and Henrys. They are better arms in many ways than ours. Did I tell you that last week when I took out my company for target practice one third of all our carbines jammed after the fifth shot?"

"Tell your recruits to keep the breech mechanism clean."

"That is not the trouble. These cartridges have got a lot of soft base metal in them. The cartridge expands quickly and sticks in the breech. The extractor tears through the rim of the shell — and there's a gun you've got to hack at with a pocket knife."

"Major," said Custer to Barrows, "I wish you'd stress things like that in your report to the department. I have written so many critical letters that I'm regarded as a dangerous and undisciplined officer. I am heartsick at the things I see which I cannot improve. Things which lead a very slimy trail right back to Washington."

Mrs. Custer overheard him and gave him a wifely side glance. But the general, impetuous in any kind of attack, used his words as he would have used a saber. "The post-trader situation is rotten. It is corrupt, it is venal. The prices charged by the post trader here are outrageous. Do you know what his excuse is? It is that his expenses in getting the job were so enormous that he must recoup himself. Why were they enormous? Because there are gentlemen in Washington who sell these post-traderships to the highest bidder. How can such a situation exist? Because there exists a corrupt ring in Washington, so protected by extremely high-placed officials that they cannot be touched."

The group of officers appeared mildly embarrassed. Major Barrows cast his reserved, taciturn glance at the general. "That is a risky thing for an army officer to say, Custer."

"I don't give a continental," said the general. "I personally know of a brother of one official — one of the highest in our land — " he checked himself, looked about the group with his bony, flushed face, and plunged on — "in fact the brother of the very highest public official of our land, who is receiving financial reward for using his indirect influence in assisting civilians to receive these post-traderships from the Department of Interior."

"Custer," said Major Barrows, "no army officer who wishes for a successful career can afford to question civil authority in Washington."

"I shall be in Washington soon," said Custer. "I shall mention the evil as I see it."

Mrs. Custer moved forward and lightly laid her hand on her husband's arm. "You must not ignore the rest of your guests," she said, smiling the dangerous subject away.

Custer immediately grew gentle at her touch. His sharp blue eyes sent a dancing glance around the room and saw his brother, Captain Tom Custer, seated alone in a rear corner of the room, hands over his stomach as he caught a bit of sleep.

"All right, Libby," he told his wife, "I'll be mealy-mouthed." But his eyes returned to the figure of Tom Custer and an edged grin formed beneath the tawny fall of his mustache; he made a signal at Lieutenant Edgerly, who came immediately near. He whispered something in Edgerly's ear. The lieutenant left the room at once.

Major Barrows said: "How certain are you of a spring campaign?"

"Wholly certain," said Captain Weir. "Nothing will stop the Sioux from defending their ground, if we push at them."

"How do you know you'll get orders to push at them?" asked Barrows.

Garnett had meanwhile drifted away and now was again in the corner with Mrs. Barrows. The major slightly changed his stand so that he saw them without turning his head greatly; he watched them as they talked, he watched his wife's face.

Weir said: "People on the frontier want to move west. They see the Indians barring their way. So they shoot a few Indians and then the Indians shoot them. That creates an incident. People here then cry to Congress and Congress puts pressure upon the War Department. We shall be sent out."

Major Reno had not spoken thus far. He was a stocky, rumpled figure, round and sallow of face with black hair pressed down upon his head and a pair of round recessed eyes, darkly circled. He seemed not wholly a part of the group; he seemed outside of it. But he said now: "It will not be a summer's jaunt. We shall face formidable resistance."

"Oh, pshaw," said Custer. "I know Indians. They will see us, and break. The question will not be one of fighting them. The question will be, can we reach them soon enough to surround them before they break into little bands and disappear. I can take this regiment and handle the situation entirely."

"Your regiment," said Barrows, "has an average muster of sixty-four men per company. Full strength, you might take eight hundred men into the field. A third of those are apt to be recruits. It is not an extraordinary show of strength."

The general said, with his dogmatic certainty: "The Seventh can whip any collection of Indians on the plains," and turned to meet Edgerly, who had returned with a hank of clothesline. The general looked at his brother Tom, still snoozing in the chair, and chuckled as he took the line. He walked along the edge of the wall; he got down on his hands and knees and crept forward until he was behind Tom Custer's chair. Crouched there, he looped the clothesline around Tom Custer's boot at the instep, made a slip knot and softly drew it tight; then he crawled to a rear window, standing open to the night, and made the other end of the clothesline fast to the window's latch.

Edgerly had meanwhile brought in the guard trumpeter. The general tiptoed to the front of the room and whispered to the trumpeter; he went around to the other officers and softly spoke to them — with Majors Reno and Barrows alone standing indifferent and puzzled in the group. Edgerly closed the front door and the trumpeter retreated into the general's study. The rest of the officers had risen and were waiting Custer's signal.

Suddenly he cut his hand sharply down through the air, the trumpeter blasted boots and saddles into the room and the officers began to rush pell-mell for the door, shouting: "Sioux! Edgerly, get to your troop! They're attacking the back side! My God, they're coming down the hill by the hundreds!"

Custer yelled, "Where's my hat? Reno, take the first troops assembled — Weir — " Somebody yanked open the front door and rushed out, shouting back: "Hurry up!" and hard after that a gun cracked through the night.

Tom Custer came up from his chair in one bound, roused out of his peaceful catnap. Reacting with an old soldier's pure impulse, he made a headlong rush for the door. Three steps took him to the end of the clothesline, which snapped tight and cut his legs from beneath him. He fell in one flat, long-bodied crash, face flat on the floor.

Everybody yelled in terrific delight and even Reno permitted himself a smile. General Custer staggered to the nearest wall and laid himself against it, laughing so uncontrollably that tears rolled along his face. Mrs. Custer, in all this pandemonium, stood still and

smiled her gentle smile while Tom Custer, the holder of two Congressional medals of honor, sat up in the middle of the floor and
unhooked the clothesline from his boot. He shook his head, staring
at all the convulsed shapes around him; he pointed a finger at the
general and shook his head, and began to grin. "That was a frivolous
kind of amusement. I damned near shook out my teeth."

The general drew a handkerchief from his pocket and wiped
away his ribald tears. Major Barrows looked at his wife, who rose;
and the two made their expressions of pleasure and departed. Edgerly
brought around a rig for Josephine. Gradually the rest of the visitors
said good night and went away until the general and his wife were
alone.

Mrs. Custer moved upstairs, leaving the general to a restless back-
and-forth pacing. He had his hands clasped behind him and now and
then stopped to rearrange some object on the table, to change the
location of a chair, to lift or lower one of the frayed window shades;
and then resumed his nervous traveling. Presently he passed through
the doorless arch into a room whose walls were crowded with animal
heads, guns and Indian relics. Two large pictures looked down upon
his desk; one was of McClellan — to whom he gave a loyalty he seldom gave any other man — and one was of himself in his flamboyant
uniform. He sat down and picked up a pen, and sighed his dislike
for the chore before him. But physical energy nagged at him and
so in a moment he resumed the article he was writing on frontier
life for an eastern magazine, sending the pen across the page in
a rapid, plunging scrawl.

He worked for an hour, tense and aggressive in this thing as he
was in all things, and abruptly stopped and sat back, listening to the
faint scratches of sound coming through the lonely house. Taps
blew and the guard call went around. He fidgeted in the chair and
lifted his voice: "Libby!"

She descended the stairs, wrapped in an old blue robe, her hair
done back for the night and her eyes sleepy. "Libby," he said, "how
can I write if you're not around?"

She smiled at him and settled in a chair, all curled in it, and
watched him as he read what he had written; she watched his face,

her eyes soft and affectionate, and when he had finished she said: "That's very good, Autie."

"Is it?" he asked, like a small boy, anxious for praise. "Is it any good?"

"Nothing you put your hand to is not good."

"Then," he said, "I shall send it, though the Lord knows why they should want to pay me two hundred dollars for it. It will help out on our next trip east, old lady."

"Yes," she said, absent-mindedly. Her thoughts were elsewhere; they revealed a half fear on her face. "Autie—all this talk of a campaign next summer—do you think it will come?"

"I expect so."

"Then I hope winter never passes," she said, suddenly intense.

"Libby," he said, "you were a little cool toward Reno tonight."

"It is not in my heart to be nice to anybody who is not your friend."

"Still, he's an officer of this regiment. We must show no favorites. We must be the same to all."

"I'll try," she murmured.

He smiled at her and rose and went around to her. He lifted her out of the chair and carried her around the rooms, her small protests coming against his chest: "Autie—let me down. Autie—"

"Blow out the lamps," he said, and lowered her by the tables while she blew; and in the darkness he carried her up the stairs. "Autie," she murmured, "I'm too old a woman for such romantic foolishness."

"You are a child," said he.

Major Barrows moved slowly down the walk with his wife, silent as he usually was, preoccupied by his own reflections. Margaret Barrows did not disturb them for she was engaged in thoughts of her own, and so the two reached the house assigned to them. The major lighted the lamp and stood a moment by it, his taciturn eyes observing the willow shape of his wife as she moved about the room, the luminous gravity of her face, the shining in her eyes.

"Pleasant evening," he said.

"Yes."

"Custer was indiscreet. He always is. Nothing saves him but a reputation for dash. That will not save him forever, unless he grows humbler than he is now."

She moved toward him and watched him with that strange expression which always deeply disturbed him; for he was not a stupid man and he knew the depths of his wife's nature, and struggled in his own way to satisfy the rich, racy current of vitality within her. But the stiffness of his nature was a hard thing to change, so that he knew he could not satisfy the romantic side of her character. It troubled him that she stood here now and wanted only some little display of ordinary affection, some word that would please her; and the best he could contrive was a stolid, "I think I'll finish my smoke on the porch. You're a beautiful woman, Margaret. I was conscious of that tonight." He bent forward and kissed her and straightened. She stood a moment longer, permitting him to see the iron control come to her again, and he knew he had failed. She said: "Good night," and went into the bedroom.

The major walked to the porch and sat down, hooking his feet to the rail; there to brood over the fragrance of his cigar. Lieutenant Smith and his wife strolled past, on the way to their own quarters. Mrs. Smith's musical voice came to him. "Good night, Major."

He said, "Good night," and watched the two move through the shadows. They were a well-matched couple, a very gay and companionable woman and a very handsome man; after several years of married life they were still close to each other. Some marriages were like that, he thought, in which the dispositions, the tastes and hungers of two people were so perfectly matched that the union was indestructible. It was an uncommon thing, and a beautiful thing to see, and it made him keenly feel his own failure. Life was mostly humdrum, drudgery and tedious hours stretched end on end; for him that was well enough but for his wife it was a kind of suffocation against which she fought. She needed brightness and drama and moments when her cry for beauty would be answered. He thought: "If I could play the gallant part, if I could go to her as a swashbuckling man and sweep her up and arouse her and stir her all through — " But he shook his head, knowing he was not that kind of man; even if he tried to play the part it would not come off. Some men were born for one thing, some for another. As he sat there, thinking of this and knowing his wife's terrible need for some kind of release, he felt a tragic unhappiness for her.

Lieutenant Smith and his wife moved into their quarters and made ready for bed. Smith said: "That was strong meat Custer was serving up — that talk about graft and scandal. All true, every word of it, but he's on dangerous ground talking about it."

"He loves dangerous ground," said his wife. She sat on a chair scarred by repeated ownerships and changes of station, before a bureau made of scrap lumber by some trooper of the command. There was a mirror one foot square on the wall and into this she looked as she took down her hair. It was another threadbare room to match all the threadbare rooms along Officers' Row, with a dull neutral wallpaper pasted against the uneven walls. The floor was bare boards painted brown and at the windows hung those same green sun-cracked shades which were to be seen in all the quarters. One austere army rule covered these habitations: No house should be better than another house and no family was to have more comforts than another family. Therefore all quarters were shabby and mean and without grace, except as the small pocketbook of the officer could improve them. In the East these houses would have been tenements belonging near the railroad track.

"So he does," said Smith. He pulled off his shoes, removed his shirt, and sat back to enjoy a last fragment of his cigar.

"I never cease to think of that," said Mrs. Smith.

"What?"

"All of you — forty officers and eight hundred men — are in the hands of one impulsive commander. When he courts danger for himself, he courts it for you."

"That's the way of soldiering. You're old enough a campaigner by now to know it couldn't be otherwise."

"I'm old enough a campaigner to know that no commander has

the right to take risks for the fun of it, or for personal glory, or for newspaper stories back east, or to show his enemies what a great soldier he is."

He looked at his wife with some surprise. "How long have you been thinking these things?"

"A long while."

"You shouldn't harbor them in your head. It's been a long stretch for you out here in this dreary nowhere. I should have sent you east last fall."

She looked at him, disturbed yet affectionate. "You know we couldn't afford it. If we could have, I wouldn't have gone without you. What fun would that be?"

"Well," he said, "it would have been nearer possible last year than now."

"Are we broke?"

He grinned, taking it in an easy way. "Just more broke than usual. That last change of station set us back a lot in railroad fare." He thought about it a long interval, then sighed and said, "Maybe some-day the government will be generous enough to pay for the trans-portation of an officer's wife when she follows her husband from post to post." Then he added, "Not that I'm complaining. We have had good times. We're healthy. We sleep well. We have few wor-ries."

"And when you die," said Mrs. Smith with a touch of irony, "the government will even be generous enough to bury you without expense."

"Ah, now," he said, and grinned, "you get that out of your head, old girl."

She was not a woman to complain and not a woman to fret with him or to add to his worries; yet tonight a good many small things seemed to collect in her mind and make her restless.

"I heard the general speak of a campaign next spring. Is it that certain?"

"Looks so. Government has been sending expeditions out there year after year without results. The Sioux grow more discontented. The settlers become more insistent on opening the country. We've been hearing that government intends to order all Sioux back to their reservations permanently. The Sioux will not comply. I think we shall see a big campaign, intended to end the question once and for all."

She sat still, thinking of his words; and her face darkened and he saw worry he had not seen before. It made him say again, very regretfully: "I wish I'd sent you back east for a vacation."

"No," she said, "it isn't that. I can't help thinking of the general's temper. He would throw this regiment away, all in a moment of recklessness."

"He would be at the head of it when he threw it," Smith gently reminded her.

"I believe," she said, "you'd appreciate a campaign full of fighting."

He gave that a moment's consideration and arrived at his basic belief in the matter. "After a winter of garrison confinement, I'm always glad to be riding out. But after a summer of eating dust I'm always glad to come back. No, I think I prefer easy ways to hard ones. But that's scarcely the point, is it? The government has trained me to take the hard ways. We're not in the hands of Custer, old girl. We're all in the hands of our country."

She shrugged her shoulders and went to bed. Smith finished his cigar and walked through the house in his nightgown, blowing out the lights; and came beside his wife. He put his arm around her. "You're a little blue tonight."

"I wish," she whispered, "I knew what was troubling me. It is there, but I can't name it. Sometimes it is a lump in my stomach."

"Maybe we'd better have Porter give you a looking-over."

"You idiot," she said, "you know I'm healthy as a horse," and moved against him.

After leaving Shafter, the young trooper — Frank Lovelace — walked into the night, his desires setting a compass course toward Suds Row. He thought of Shafter in youth's instinctively admiring way. He was greatly impressed by the sergeant's coolness and quietness under strain and he wistfully wished that he might have the same kind of qualities. His age made him dream of great things;

and his vivid imagination placed him in the sergeant's shoes, so that he saw himself equally cool and brave and triumphant. This was the world he made for himself, but he was young and therefore he was unsure, not knowing his capacities and secretly doubting himself.

He turned into Suds Row and passed along the row of small houses occupied by the married sergeants. He had been walking rapidly; now he dropped to a slow saunter and began to whistle. When he passed the house of Mary Mulrane, he gave the lighted window a swift sidewise glance and saw Mary's father, old Mulrane who was a sergeant major, bowed over a paper on the table. Young Lovelace continued his stroll to the end of the row and stood a moment listening to the Missouri lap at the base of the bluff. He turned back. Mulrane's door had opened, letting out a bright gush of light; it closed again and he felt dispirited. But when he came abreast the house he found Mary waiting.

He turned in and saw her face pale in the shadows; he touched her with his hand and he drew her smile. He stood still, a wonder and a wanting rushing through him and setting off the purest and most violent kind of flame, and he drew a long sigh and thought of nothing to say. He saw the way she held up her head and he thought he might kiss her; but he never had kissed her and he didn't want her to think the wrong thing about him. She waited, watching him, the smile steady on her face. Presently she came from the wall and slipped her hand into his hand and walked back down the row beside him.

He said: "It's cold tonight. Aren't you cold?"

"No. I'm not cold at all."

"I should think you would be."

"It's pretty tonight."

"Yes," he said. "The darkness just kind of stretches away. Like it was moving." They came to the edge of the bluff and he reached down and got a chunk of earth; he threw it and waited, and long afterwards heard it strike the river. He said: "The river's always going somewhere. I wish I could get in a rowboat and just drift. Next week, Yankton. Then St. Louis. Then New Orleans."

She didn't answer him and he felt her somehow draw away from him. She didn't stir, but she wasn't as near him as she had been. He could feel it distinctly. Then she said: "Do you want to go that bad?"

"Oh," he said, "it isn't that. I'd just like to be doing something. I'd like to see the country."

"The girls in the South," she said, "are supposed to be very pretty."

"I wasn't thinking of that," he answered at once. "I'd like — " But he didn't know what it was. It was something formless; it pushed at him and it pulled at him, it filled him up.

"You're funny," she murmured.

He looked at her and saw her smiling again. She was near him, she was watching him closely. He said: "It's tough to just stand around when everything is happening everywhere. I've got three more years to serve. When I get out, what'll I be? Nothing at all."

She murmured: "I think you're something."

He looked at her, his pulse beating faster. He waited a long while, on the edge of what he wanted; he felt himself shoved toward it but he knew he never would take the chance of making her think he was another easy trooper. She made a little motion with her head and she looked away from him a moment and took his hand again, standing still. "I get lonely too, sometimes," she said, and turned her face toward him. Suddenly a kind of terror went through him for what he knew he was about to do, but he couldn't help it. He put one arm around her and saw that she didn't draw back. Her face was still near him and just below him. He put both arms around her and kissed her. He was trembling, he was hot, he was cold. He squeezed her until a sigh came out of her; he felt the heat and the urgent sweetness of her mouth and it astonished him to realize she held him as tightly as he held her. He felt her fingers at the back of his neck.

She stepped away, looked at him a moment; she dropped her head against his chest and continued to hold him. He heard her murmur: "Did you mean that, Frank? It wasn't just something you'd do to any girl if you got the chance?"

"Oh, no," he said, shocked.

"I'm glad. I wouldn't let anybody else do it."

They heard Mulrane calling in his thick Irish voice: "Mary," and turned to see the sergeant blocked against the light of his open door. Mary Mulrane softly laughed and seized young Lovelace's hand and walked up the street with him. Young Lovelace felt the sergeant's hard eyes on him, and was embarrassed. But Mary held his hand so that her father could see it.

"Going out like that," said Mulrane, "in a cold night without a coat. Where is your mind awanderin'?"

"It isn't cold," said Mary.

"Ah," said the sergeant, "it isn't cold, is it?" And he grunted something under his breath. "You come in. And you, Lovelace, you had better get back before you're picked up by the rounds. Taps will be blowin'."

"Yes," said Lovelace and started up the street. He had gone a few feet when he heard Mary murmur something. In another few feet the sergeant's voice came after him. "Come to Sunday supper, Lovelace."

"Thanks," said Lovelace, and went on. The earth came up and struck his boots; but it was soft — the earth was — and it seemed to roll and sink with his weight. The air was fine and cold and full of fine smells and the night's sky sparkled with its diamond stars. He could not breathe enough; he could not feel enough. Taps broke as he entered the barrack. Tinney saw him and Tinney gave him an evil grin. "Pickin' up your washin' again? I saw Purple down that way tonight. Maybe he was pickin' up his laundry too."

Lovelace said, "Ah," and turned to his bunk. But after the lights were out he lay on the bunk and was racked by doubt, by a deep hate of Tinney and Purple. He thought: "I've got to learn to fight." He lay still and suffered.

V

Rehearsal for a Tragedy

AT SIX o'clock in the morning Lieutenant Algernon Smith led twenty men of A Company out upon the parade, joined a platoon of L Company waiting there under Garnett, and made a motion of his hand which put the combined column across the parade. The troopers moved two by two through the guardhouse gate, rode up the slope of the ridge east of the post and came to its crest, facing the desert's long western reach, now a-smolder with the tan and ashy colors of fresh sunlight.

Shafter rode as right guide at the head of the column, Smith beside him. Adjoining the lieutenant was the civilian guide, a tall and very thin man wearing a sloppy blue serge coat and a hat scorched by many campfires and discolored by many a dip into wayside creeks. His name was Bannack Bill and he had a gaunt neck up and down which an Adam's apple slid like a loose chestnut; his calico eyes, half hidden behind dropped lids, never ceased to search the landscape.

Early morning glumness held the troopers silent; they rode half awake, slumped on their McClellans, gradually taking on life as the sun warmed them and the steady riding loosened their muscles. All this was familiar country, and the ride just one more scout detail flung out daily to keep an eye on the Sioux, who moved in mercurial restlessness over the land. East of the river the Indians lived in sulky peace and paid their visits to Bismarck, sitting in motionless rows along the sidewalk. East of the river they were a subjugated race. But west of the river they were a free and intractable people, at peace if it pleased them and at war if it pleased them, made haughty and insolent by the memory of the many evils done them by white people, made proud by the recollection of their vanishing freedom, made warlike by nature. They came into the post to hold council with the general and the pipe was smoked and presents passed and gestures of friendship made; but at night these same warriors waited in the darkness outside the guard line to cut down whatever foolish trooper strayed beyond the limit of safety. East of the river a man might sleep at night in safety but west of the river was only an uneasy peace maintained by the threat of guns — Indians and soldiers facing each other with the knowledge that the penned-up flood of hatred and vengeance grew stronger and stronger behind its barrier.

Bannack Bill made a little gesture and rode wide of the column, staring toward the ground as he traveled. He came back. "Small party headin' south. Half a dozen bucks. Dozen kids and women. Four travwaws."

Algernon Smith turned to Shafter. "You're new. Maybe you don't know what we're doing."

"No sir."

"Keeping watch on these people. Never know what they might do. Maybe they'd strike against the fort some night to drive off stock. Maybe they might try to raid the guard lines. The only way we can guess their state of mind is to watch the trails they make — to see if they're collecting any place in a big bunch, which is always indication of something in the wind. Unusual activity is a good sign that they're disturbed. Right now it is customary for them to collect from summer villages and go down to the Agency for the winter. If they go down in big numbers we can guess they're going to cause us no trouble until spring. If they stay away from the Agency we can expect something." A little later the lieutenant added: "Of course there are many villages, farther west, who never come in. They're beyond our reach."

The middle of the morning, some thirteen miles from the fort, the column came upon little hills and bluffs bordering the meandering course of Heart River. At this time of the year the river had receded to a small creek, over which the command passed easily, wound through willow and cottonwood and filed through a series of gullies. A ridge ran to either side of the column, shutting off the farther view of the land. Lieutenant Smith scanned it with a moment's professional interest, turned and made a motion of his hand which was sufficient to send a pair of troopers forward to act as points for the column, to send another pair galloping up the side of the left ridge — and a third pair toward the summit of the right ridge.

Bannack Bill meanwhile had found himself another interesting set of tracks and pursued them forward at a trot, his light body jiggling up and down on the saddle. Lieutenant Garnett, hitherto riding halfway down the column, now came forward to travel beside Smith.

"Usual course this time, Smith?"

"Unless we run into something that draws us aside."

Shafter sat easy in the saddle, pleased as he had not been pleased for ten years. Behind him were the usual sounds of troopers in motion, the squeezing sibilance of leather, the off-key clinking of metal gear and the slap of canteens, the murmuring play of talk among the men, the sudden chuffering of a horse. He turned and saw the column stretch two and two behind him in blue-figure line, the men so dark of face that their eyes seemed to glitter; it was a tough, rawboned line — like a sinuous whip being dragged across the country. Carbines lay athwart each man's pommel; the yellow seam of each noncom's pants leg made a splash of color. He saw Donovan's round raw face slowly grin and Donovan's eyelid slowly wink; he settled himself frontward again and he thought: "A damned fine life I have been missing." Around him eddied the odor of dust and the odor of his horse — and the smell of his own body rendering up its warmth. All of it was good.

Smith said: "Tell flankers and point men to get farther ahead," and sent off the trumpeter with the message. The trumpeter's name was Kane and he was a round and ruddy-faced boy who had creased the front brim of his cavalry hat upward so that it gave him a dash; he left the column like a gunshot, flinging his horse into an instant run, body swinging on the saddle. Directly in rear of Shafter, Corporal Bierss and a private by the name of Jordan were rolling out the tempting juices of one obscene story and another, each man matching story for story. Donovan, overhearing this, called forward to Bierss. "Lad, you talk too big. You don't know that many women."

"I meet 'em quick — I get rid of 'em quick."

"Like Kimono Lizzie in the Big Bend House," said Donovan.

The column liked that and laughed at it, though the laughter didn't trouble Bierss. He said amiably: "She wasn't no lady, so I left."

"By the second-story window," said Donovan.

"It was too much trouble walkin' back down the stairs," said Bierss.

"Just so," jeered Donovan. "There was a sergeant from D Company comin' up the stairs, him havin' a better track on Lizzie."

That did disturb Bierss, who said: "The hell with any sergeant from D. I wouldn't walk a foot from none of that crowd. And he didn't have no better track than I had."

"Whut'd you jump out the window for then?"

Bierss thought rapidly and came out with a virtuous answer. "I wouldn't compromise a lady."

A shout of laughter exploded and rolled down the column and came echoing back. The effect of it pleased Bierss, who grinned beneath his ragged dragoon mustaches and shook his shoulders into squarer shape. The two officers rode on in self-enforced isolation, hearing it all but ignoring it. The column came up from a long ravine and faced a desert studded with glacial rocks. Ahead of them stretched a bumpier country, and still farther ahead the misshapen outline of badlands showed through the thin fall haze.

The point scouts had gone forward, the flankers were working off to a greater distance, and the civilian guide was two miles in advance, just now entering a scattered fringe of trees which marked a creek flowing from the northwest. Smith shook his head. "Bill's too old a hand to be doing that. He might get jumped before we could reach him."

"Old ones get careless," said Garnett.

"Damned seldom," said Smith. "That's why they live to be old."

He had not sent out advance scouts to survey the previous crossing. But they were now thirty miles from the fort, and in deeper Indian land, wherefore he watched the two point men as they moved cautiously upon the timber before them and presently turned his head to Shafter. "Take six men and go up there."

Shafter half swung in his saddle. He made a motion that pulled the three nearest sets of twos away from the column, and set his horse to the gallop across the ground. He had Corporal Bierss with him and Bierss still held on with his stories: —

"So I saw she was lookin' at me with somethin' in her eyes and I knew all I had to do was . . ."

Shafter watched the two point men fade into the timber; when he got within a hundred feet of it he waggled a hand to left and right, bringing his six men into skirmish line. All these troopers knew their business and spread farther and farther apart as they approached the timber, and so went into it, threshing carefully through. They crossed a creek, breasted a loose thicket and reached the top of a small bluff. Shafter stopped here, waiting for the main command to come up. They dismounted and crouched down to break the riding monotony, and Bierss took time to catch a smoke.

"You been at this kind of business before, Sarge?"

"Yes."

"I thought so. Ever in the South?"

"Yes."

"The girls down there," said Bierss dreamily, "have got skin the color of cream."

"Beautiful faces," agreed Shafter.

"Wasn't talking about their faces," said Bierss.

The main column splashed over the creek, came grunting up the side of the bluff. The advance group went to the saddle and fell in at the head of the column. Smith swung it left, climbing again to the crest of a ridge wherefrom he might see the roundabout pockets and ravines; the flankers in the distance were rising and falling across this rough ground like small boats in a heavy sea-swell. Smith grunted and shaded his eyes against the western sun, looking at the small figure of the guide who, two miles forward, now turned his horse and rode a steady circle in signal. Smith said "Gallop," and put the troop to a run.

The troop whirled down the ridge, the horses grunting as they pitched across the uneven ground, accouterments banging and slapping down. The civilian guide waited sedately, and pointed to the south, whereupon Smith brought the column to a halt with a down-thrust of his hand. He looked back at the strung-out column. He called testily: "Stop that sleeping on your elbows. Close up — close up! Sergeant McDermott, what are you back there for?" Then he looked ahead once more in the direction which had drawn the guide's interest.

Off there, now showing on a ridge, now lost in a depression, Shafter saw a column moving beneath the shape of its own dust — a long string of ponies and riders and travois; and over the distance he heard Indian dogs barking.

"Biggest one yet," said the guide. "Fifty lodges in that outfit."

Garnett said, with a show of eagerness: "Let's go have a look."

Smith was a cooler and more reflective man, with considerable experience in frontier campaigning. He considered Garnett's wish, and rejected it. "As long as they're heading for the Agency there's no point in our stopping them. They might misjudge our intentions as we rode up, and prepare for a fight. One shot by a careless buck would start trouble which nobody wants or intends."

"I hate like hell to let them think we're avoiding them," grumbled Garnett.

"That's scarcely the point," Smith said dryly, and put the column forward at its former pace and in its day-long direction. This march carried them along the ridge, so that they were in plain sight, and gradually as they moved west they had a better view of the long Indian column as it wound through and around and over the depressions and hummocks of the land. The head of the column passed out of sight on the yonder side of a ridge, but a group of warriors came streaming back on their ponies, stopped at the end of their column and stood watchfully there, faced against the cavalry. Presently, as the tail of the column dropped over the ridge, this rearguard wheeled and went scudding away — a thin yell of defiance floating back.

"That's all right — that's all right," grumbled Garnett. "We'll take care of that someday."

"Possible," said Smith, still dry-toned, and gestured the command forward.

The sun's violent flame rolled back like sea waves across butte and ridge and far-scattered clumps of timber; into that yellow flare the column rode with growing weariness and longer silences. At six o'clock Smith rose in his stirrups to have a look before him; at six-thirty the command had camped in a grove beside another small creek, the horses standing on picket, the guards posted, the camp-fires burning and the smell of coffee and bacon drifting in a chilling air. Men went beating along the earth with sticks, routing out rattle-snakes, and the sun sank and twilight fell full-handed upon the earth — and then the stars were all a-shine across infinity's pure space and the campfires became round, dull spots in the black. Shafter rolled in his blanket, settled his head on the saddle and for a few drowsy moments listened to the murmuring around him. The creek left a smooth, undulating tone behind as it ran north and the smell of the half-dead fires drifted against Shafter's face to remind him of a thousand bivouacs, and so to revive one by one the tangled memories of his past. Weariness played through his bones — the wonderful luxury of physical looseness rolling all along his body; and his cares and strange involved wanderings went away, taking him back to the pure simplicity of being one tired man sleep-ing near other tired men.

There were no trumpet calls on scout patrol. Men stirred out of sleep and saw daylight crack through the eastern blackness; and sat up to put on their hats, their blouses and their boots, thus rising full-dressed. One trooper gave a springing shout and jumped aside and began to swear; he got a stick and beat the life out of a rattle-snake which, drawn by warmth, had spent part of the night curled against his blanket. A water detail took the horses down to the creek, vanishing in the damp fog. Fires sprang up, rich yellow in the half light, and the smell of coffee and bacon pungently spread. An hour before sunrise the company moved out, silent and cold and morose.

The way now was southwest as the column began to make its curve upon the land and strike homeward; but the guide said, "I'll look yander a bit," and rode straight into the west. Somewhere near the tail end of the column a trooper began to sing and was stopped by half a dozen grumbling voices. A bleak chill lay in the still air, its thin edge cutting against face and hand; the breath of the horses laid little puffs of visible moisture against the light. Sunrise broke tawny in the east, bright but heatless, and the sleazy fog lying over the earth vanished. The horses' hoofs struck and rattled along scattered rock brought down by glaciers tens of thousands of years before, and little patches of alkali showed on the ground, and clouds of small black birds wheeled up and went away in wheeling billows.

Far ahead of them the guide came into view on a ridge and circled his horse as he had done the preceding night. Smith watched the guide a long while but forbore to push the troop into a gallop because of the rocky underfooting. He swung the column to higher ground and then, clearing the gravel, simply waved his hand overhead; the column burst into a steady run, with the lieutenant's glance now and then going back to see how the formation was. His voice laid down a growling insistence.

"Keep up — keep up. Dooly, handle your horse." Garnett had come abreast of Smith again, but the senior lieutenant gave him a tough look and said: "Ride back." Garnett dropped to the rear. The lieutenant, Shafter decided, was that kind of officer who kept his amiability and charm for the social hours; on duty he was a brusque man attending strictly to business and determined that others under him should attend to theirs.

The column followed Bannack Bill downgrade toward a thin fringe of willows scattered along a creek. There was something scattered on the ground which, upon a steady inspection, had to Shafter a familiar attitude; he had seen many men thus, arms crooked carelessly, bodies lying in the disheveled posture of death. The guide waited near by and said nothing when Smith halted the column. There were three men stripped naked, two of them apparently beyond middle age and a young one. This was not entirely a matter of certainty, for they had all been scalped, their heads cracked in and their bodies mutilated. Each man had half a dozen arrows thrust into him.

"Look like prospectors coming back from the Black Hills," commented Smith. "Ever see them before, Bill?"

"Can't recognize 'em."

"Not dead long. They've not swollen much."

"Sometime yesterday afternoon," said the guide. He got down from his piebald horse and had a look around the ground. "They hadn't started a fire and so I guess they were just makin' camp."

There wasn't much to show the story for there was nothing left except the bodies. Horses, equipment and supplies had been carried off. One white trail showed where a warrior had dumped the prospector's flour and, a few yards from the scene, a muslin bag of beans lay spilled on the ground.

"It was that party we passed yesterday late," said Bannack Bill.

"How sure are you of it?" asked Smith.

"A party of bucks would of sculped these fellers and let it go like that. That knife work was done by squaws and the arrers prob'ly by kids practisin' up on their shootin'. You'll find them scalps with that party."

"We'll go see," said Smith.

He led the column to the creek and let it water, and then swung back into the southwest, moving at a walk through the rough gravel-strewn valley. They traveled steadily, passing over small ridges and into other small lands of level grass, and through broken formations and areas of upheaval. Near eleven o'clock they cut the trail of the large party bound south for the reservation and came upon an old Indian lying alone in the half-warm sun. He rose to his elbows and looked at them with a bitter-black glance out of his shrunken, disease-ravaged face, half expecting death at the hands of the troopers; and fell back on his side, not caring. The troop passed on.

Smith spoke to Shafter. "You've had campaign service?"

"Yes sir."

"How much?"

"Four years and a half."

"Any against Indians?"

"Half a year against the Comanches down in the Nations."

"I like to know how far I can depend on my sergeants," said Smith briefly, and fell silent. He had followed the Indian trail directly for an hour when he left it and moved over a hill to the west and set his troop into a gallop along a sandy valley. They went this way, walking and running, until the sun tipped over the line and started down; and then the lieutenant stopped the command for half an hour's nooning. When he moved the column on again it was straight to the south in a line that roughly paralleled the course of the Indian band. Around two o'clock he called Garnett forward.

"Take Shafter and the first ten troopers and scout to the left. Don't expose yourself. My desire is to come in ahead of the Sioux and catch them before they can set themselves for trouble. If you sight them, send back a messenger and wait for me to come up."

Garnett nodded his head and started away with his detachment. Smith's voice came after him, sharply inquisitive. "Do you thoroughly understand you are not to precipitate any action of your own if you sight them?"

"Yes," said Garnett, and rode on.

Shafter moved beside the lieutenant, jarred out of his calm, suddenly heated by his anger and his contempt and his savage distrust of Garnett. He ignored the lieutenant as they slanted up the side of the valley's east ridge, zigzagging around rock shoulders, following old deer and antelope trails. Looking back, he saw the rest of the command streaming directly south, kicking up a heavy pall of dust. A hundred feet short of the ridge's crest, Garnett stopped his detachment and nodded at Shafter.

"Climb up there on foot and see what's beyond."

There was still some distance that might have been covered on horse, relieving that much foot labor, but Shafter got out of the saddle, handed over his reins to Corporal Bierss and climbed upward over the spongy soil, his boots sliding back on the slick, summer-cured grass. The climb made him reach for wind and he knew this was Garnett's idea of hazing him. Near the crest of the ridge he flattened down, removed his hat and looked over. There was a succession of low, choppy ridges before him, and no sight of Indians. He turned and gestured the command forward, and got into his saddle when it came.

Garnett led his detachment down the far side of the ridge at a quartering run, crossed through a series of little pockets and started up the side of another ridge. Halfway to the top he spoke to Shafter again. "Scout ahead on foot. Make it faster. We're losing time."

Shafter dropped to the ground, catching a puzzled stare from Bierss; he moved up the slope, digging his heels against the turf, and flattened and looked over the high ground into a small cross ravine which led from the valley in which the main column moved to the one where the Sioux were presumably traveling. He saw nothing and once more signaled up the detachment. Garnett, when he arrived, said: —

"You ride ahead. Half a mile. When you come near the summit of these rolls of ground, go up afoot and have a look. You'll have to move fast to keep ahead of us."

Shafter got on his saddle and started away. Garnett's sudden-loud voice turned him. "Did you hear what I told you?"

"Yes sir," said Shafter.

"Then speak up when I give you an order," said Garnett.

"Yes sir," said Shafter and swung off. He dropped down into the canyon and slanted up another slope until he got within ten feet of its summit, and went the rest of the way afoot. A plateau lay before him, badly broken into gullies, dappled with small knobs and minor pinnacles, and beyond that there seemed to be a drop-off into a definite valley. He stopped long enough to signal the detachment forward and proceeded into the rough terrain.

There was no clear view of any of this for more than three hundred yards in any direction and therefore he kept a sharp watch around him, realizing that it was likely the Indian party might have its own scouts out. Garnett, he guessed, had thought of the same thing in sending him forward alone. The lieutenant had a fixed hatred of him.

He passed around a knob and looked back in time to see the detachment rise to the crest behind him. He waved at it and dipped into a gully, followed it to a butte and circled the butte; and thus he veered and tacked his way forward until he reached what seemed to be the final ridge on the plateau. He crawled the last few yards and looked over the crest into a plain running eastward toward the Missouri. Out there, close by the base of the plateau, the Indian band moved sedately southward, enveloped in its own dust.

He made his way leisurely down the hill and lay back on the ground until the detachment came up. Garnett rode his horse almost on top of him. Shafter rose slowly, and enjoying the black flash of temper he saw leap into Garnett's eyes. "Over the ridge, just below us," he said and swung to the saddle.

Garnett said: "Maybe we should have brought a bed for you," and wheeled the column away. Shafter turned to look back at Bierss; he saw Bierss grinning, and he winked at Bierss, knowing that the lieutenant also saw this from the corner of his eyes. They ran along the foot of the ridge, turned a corner of an intervening butte, and discovered Smith riding upgrade from the west with the rest of the command. Garnett lifted in his saddle and made a wheeling gesture with his arm, pointing east. Smith acknowledged it but made no effort to hurry his command on the slope of the hill; therefore Garnett halted his group and waited. There was a quarter-hour delay, but Garnett held his men tight in their saddles, giving them no chance to dismount. He sat still, completely ignoring the command.

Smith came up and said: "Whereabouts?"

"Over the ridge."

"Garnett," said Smith, "you should know enough to rest your men when you have the chance." He led the column forward, staying beneath the shelter of the ridge and following it across the plateau until it pinched out. When they broke over the summit of the plateau they were within five hundred feet of the Sioux, face-on with them. Smith trotted his column forward. He turned in the saddle to speak back to the troopers. "No false motions now," he said. "Wait for my commands." He spoke in a lower tone to Garnett. "We shall ferret out the warriors who did the killing. I propose to take them back to Lincoln."

"Like hunting for a piece of coal in the cellar on a black night without a match."

"There are ways of doing it," said Smith. "Hold yourself ready to do what I say. When I swing side to side in the saddle, drift the column into a skirmish line very slowly."

"Very well," murmured Garnett, a touch of irritation in his voice. Smith heard that and gave his junior officer a sharp glance. "I don't want any damned notions of gallantry or dash to upset this job." The column of Sioux was immediately before him and he flung up his hand to halt the troopers. He said to Shafter and to Bannack Bill, "Come with me," and rode forward.

A line of warriors milled out from the rear of the long Indian column, racing forward, low-bent and weaving on their ponies. The older men in the forefront of the procession ranked themselves and sat still. Smith stopped in front of them and murmured to Bannack Bill: —

"Tell them I'm glad to see them and hope they have had a good summer. Tell them I presume they're going to the Agency for winter. Tell them we're pleased to have them come in, that the meat is fat at the Agency. Tell them any compliment you happen to think of for about two minutes. I want to watch these young bucks while you're talking."

Bannack Bill began to speak, using his hands to cut sign across the air. The leading Sioux, all old men with faces bronzed and chiseled by weather and years, listened. They were wholly still except for their eyes, which lay on Bill as he spoke, and darted covert glances at the lieutenant, and struck shrewdly farther out to the waiting troopers. The younger men of the band had drifted forward, forming a scattered semicircle.

Shafter murmured: "There's a fresh scalp hanging to the arrow pouch of that pug-nosed lad out on the left."

"Very good, Sergeant," said Smith coolly. "That's what we're looking for."

"You'll probably find the blankets and the clothes among the squaws."

"Ever try to handle a squaw?" said Smith, dryly. "We'll leave those dusky beauties alone."

Bannack Bill finished his interpreting and sat idle in the saddle. All the old men remained silent, thereby lending dignity to the parley. A good deal later one of them straightened on his horse and spoke in the guttural, abrupt Sioux tongue.

Bill said: "He says he's very happy to see the government soldiers. They are his friends. He is their friend. All Sioux are friends of all whites. All whites should be friends of the Sioux, though sometimes they are not. He says he is on his way to the Agency and is glad to hear the beef is fat. Most years, he says, it is very poor and the Indians starve. Why is that, he asks."

"Don't tell him I said so, Bill," said Smith, "but there isn't any answer to that question. There are as many white thieves as red ones and probably he's dead right. Tell him I'm happy to see him in such good health, tell him things like that for a couple more minutes."

"By God," said Bill, "I can only invent about so many lies. Anyhow, these old codgers know what you're up to." ·

"How do they know?"

"You got here too fast from where they saw you last."

"Tell him we're all happy," said Smith.

Shafter said: "The lad next to the lad with the scalp has got a gold watch and chain wrapped around his neck."

"Two out of three will do nicely," said Smith. "You've got a good eye, Sergeant." He eased himself in the saddle, rolling from side to side, which was his signal to Garnett a hundred feet behind him. The old Sioux men watched him in beady interest, their glances flicking back to the troopers now idly deploying into skirmish line. The young bucks saw it as well and stirred uneasily, drifting their ponies back and forth.

"Bill," said Smith, "tell him we're happy over everything but the murder of the three white men. Ask him if he knows of that evil thing."

Bannack Bill murmured: "You sure you're ready to start the fireworks?"

"Let it start," said Smith. He waited until Bannack Bill began speaking; then he turned his head and gave Shafter the kind of glance which not only delved for toughness in another man, but mirrored his own essentially hard spirit. "We need a display of decision here, Sergeant. It has to be done quietly, but without any show of hesitation. When I give the word, ride over and bring out those two bucks. I shall back you up."

Shafter said, "Yes sir," and felt the continuing force of Smith's glance. The lieutenant was aware of the risk involved in so brisk a show of power, for the warriors in this band were all well-armed and they could muster as much strength as the detachment Meanwhile Bannack Bill said his say and waited for reply. It was not long in coming. The old spokesman of the Sioux straightened himself, pointed to the earth, to the sky and to the four cardinal points, no doubt invoking all the gods he knew about to attest his sincerity, and launched into speech.

"Winding himself up," murmured Smith and impassively listened. When the old one had finished, Bannack Bill paused a moment to summarize what he had heard, and proceeded to translate it free-hand.

"The old codger decorates his damned lie as follows: His heart is pure, his mouth is wide open to truth, his soul is hurt to think the lieutenant would think that Red Owl's band would hurt a white man. Not one of his people touched a hair on those three prospectors. He has seen many bad things done by the whites but he's ready to forgive and forget and would share his blanket with any white man to show he means it. He says likewise it is gettin' late and he's got forty miles more to go before reachin' the Agency. The nights are growin' chilly and some of his old ones are hungry. Which is a way of sayin' to us that it is time to quit the foolin' around."

Smith nodded, meeting the old warrior's eyes. They were eyes of black liquid, full of pride and complete confidence — and touched with shrewd scheming as they stared back at the lieutenant. Smith said: "Tell him I'm glad to hear of his peaceful intentions. Ask him this: If he knew that some of his young men had killed the prospectors, would he bring them to the fort as a sign of his good will?"

Bannack Bill asked it. Out on the wings of the crowd the young bucks grew increasingly restive and there was a murmuring among them. The old one placed a hand on his heart and briefly answered the question. Bannack Bill said: "He says he would bring in his own son if his son had done it."

"Go get them, Sergeant," murmured Smith, not turning his head. He stared at the old one. "Tell him I believe his word to be true. Tell him he has no doubt been deceived by his own young men, for we see the scalp and we see the watch. Tell him we take him at his word and will carry the two young men back to the fort with us."

Bannack Bill hesitated, casting a bland stare at Smith. "I hope you got the best cards in this game, Lieutenant."

"Tell him," said Smith.

Shafter had meanwhile turned and now rode directly and unhurriedly to the left, passing along the ranks of the younger warriors. They sat still, staring back at him with their haughty faces, with the snake-twining of insolence in their eyes. He came to the warrior who had the fresh scalp hanging from his quiver and to the warrior with the watch wrapped by its chain around his neck. He stopped, looking at the scalp and at the watch. Suddenly other bucks crowded close to these two and grasped their carbines and lifted them suggestively and a steady, thick stream of Sioux words went back and forth along the line, growing sharper, growing more excited.

Shafter heard Bannack Bill say: "He says there must be a mistake. That is an old scalp, from many years ago. The watch was a present."

"Tell him we shall take the two warriors to Lincoln. If he speaks the truth we shall release them."

Shafter pulled his .44 and laid it on the buck with the scalp. He pointed his finger at that one, and at the other one. He made a gesture of command. These two sat dead still and stared back, animosity burning brightly in them; but the younger men began to push around them to make a screen that Shafter could not get through and, seeing this, he shoved his horse forward and swung it and laid the muzzle of his gun against the ribs of the warrior with the scalp. He pushed on the muzzle. He said: "Move out." A sudden crying freshened about him. He heard the clicking of carbine hammers and he watched the young bucks drift in to trap him. One buck swung his arm toward his revolver. Shafter laid the gun on him at once and stopped him, and pulled the weapon back to his original target. He heard Smith coolly say: "Ask him if a chief swallows his words as soon as they are spoken."

Bannack Bill repeated it to Red Owl and Red Owl sat still thoughtfully. Back in the column the women were beginning to lift their shrill voices, the savage intent of their words scraping Shafter's nerves and inciting the young warriors to greater violence. One brave flung his carbine around and took a steady aim on Shafter. Then Red Owl's voice came out quickly and spoke three words that settled the question, for the two wanted warriors moved out of the group, Shafter behind them. They rode straight toward the waiting cavalry, never turning their heads.

Smith said crisply: "Tell Red Owl I'm pleased he keeps his word," and wheeled back to the detachment. He called to it, "Hold your places," and swung to watch the Indian band take up its forward motion. The old ones rode by in stony silence but the bucks, fermenting with rage, dashed back and forth along the cavalry line, shrilly crying, flinging up their guns in provocation. They wheeled and charged at the troopers, sliding down from their ponies in beautiful displays of horsemanship, coming full tilt against the troopers' outspread line, and wheeling away with a derisive shouting.

"Hold steady," said Smith.

Garnett watched the Sioux with the clearest kind of desire on his wedge-shaped face. He spoke in strong enough tone for his words to carry through the troopers. "It would be better to kill them now than wait until next year when they may kill us."

"Garnett," said Lieutenant Smith, "there's women and children in that group."

"They're worse than the men."

"Never mind," said Smith.

The procession went slowly by, the squaws all shouting at the troopers and some of them crying wildly. The travois dragged up dust and the young warriors suddenly drove the Sioux horse-herd through the deployed troopers. This was a moment of danger and Smith saw it and called sharply again: "Hold tight," and watched the scene with the sharpest attention until horses and Sioux had passed on. Then he said: "Column of twos — forward — walk." The troopers came in, resuming formation. Smith settled himself taciturnly at the head of the group.

"It was a question in my mind how we'd come out," murmured Bannack Bill.

"They had their women and kids along," said Smith. "That kept them from fighting." He turned to Shafter, who rode with the two captive Sioux. "Very good, Sergeant," he said, and pointed the column due east. He was disposed to let the silence continue, being naturally a blunt man who seldom saw the necessity of extended conversation. But Bannack Bill, who knew a good deal about Indians, had the recent scene still in his mind. "Something else to make them hate us. You know how an Indian hates, Smith? It is like one of these fires that burns in a coal bed out there on the Bad Lands. Goes down underneath and smokes and gets hotter. It just never goes out. One day it breaks into the open — the damnedest blaze you ever saw."

"That may come," admitted Smith.

"Sure it's comin'. These Sioux have been pushed back as fur as they'll push. They're right now on the last of their huntin' land. Last buff'lo is there. Last freedom is there. They have made up their minds to go no further. I know."

"If I were a Sioux," said Smith, "I'd feel the same way. We can only hope that the authority in Washington will see the point and let the Sioux alone."

"The authority in Washington," stated Bannack Bill, "will order the Seventh out for a campaign when spring comes. I been here a long time on the frontier. It is the same old story."

Smith rode a long distance in silence; he was a soldierly shape, he was that kind of officer whose presence reassured the command, practical and assured and humane, with the habit of decision and the knowledge of men well-blended in him. A dozen years of soldiering had seasoned him, taught him rough-and-tumble, swiftness of action; it had taught him the distinction between caution and daring. West Point and the campaign field had made of him an excellent sample of that type of officer and gentleman which the army regarded as its ideal.

Now and then his thoughts laid a temporary shadow across his face; now and then he shook his head as his thinking took him to impassable ground. Presently he shrugged his shoulders. "You're right," he said. "There will be a campaign. Well, it is one of those things over which a soldier has no control, and never will. We do what we are told to do, and presently we shall be told to subjugate the Indians. The fault is higher up." Then he corrected that. "Still, the men higher up are not free agents either. Something pushes them on, whether they like it or not. It goes back to one race against another race. The white man's idea against the red man's idea. If the situation were reversed, the Indians would be doing to us what we are now trying to do to them. White men have fought each other since the beginning of time. Red men have fought each other. Now the races fight. Well, we're in the hands of history, and history is a cruel thing."

"Lieutenant," said Bannack Bill, "just remember one thing when you're campaignin'. Every man in Red Owl's band has got the memory of you and me and the sergeant here burned deep in his head. He would know us next week, next month, next year. And he has got his notions of what he'll do when he meets us. Finger by finger and joint by joint and one chunk of flesh after another. Remember that next summer and take damned good care you don't fall in their hands."

"Things sometimes drift on for years," said Smith. "Nothing happens. Just reveille and retreat, summer and winter. Sort of a holiday in a man's life. Then a cloud gathers and you smell bad weather. You feel it in your bones, as I have been feeling it for months. Never tell me there isn't such a thing as a sixth sense. Well then, the storm breaks. When it is over, you look around and you see a lot of faces missing. That's the hard thing — to recall all those men who once were beside you on the firing line, and now are gone."

"It is coming," said Bannack Bill.

Smith lifted his shoulders and reclaimed his practical manner. "Never pays to speculate upon the future."

It was then three o'clock. At ten, the command reached the guard gate at Fort Lincoln, answered the challenge and passed in. Taps ran the cold air as Shafter stepped wearily from his saddle.

VI

The Ride to Rice

COLDER weather squeezed the land; a thin crust formed on water buckets and barrels and the ground showed crazed frost patterns. Troopers turned out for morning roll call in overcoats and Berlin mittens. Sergeant Hines's voice had a more brittle snap to it and his nose, which was an adequate weather vane, made a scarlet point in the gray dawn. After he had announced the details for the day he said: "Shafter, harness up the light wagon and report to commanding officer's house. Take along a couple blankets, your carbine and fifty rounds of ammunition. Dismiss."

Shafter had his breakfast, hitched the team and rolled over the parade through a woolly fog, through a stillness that was unlike any other stillness. The sun lay somewhere above this fog, without heat enough to dispel it or to break the steady cold. He rolled before Custer's house and stepped to the porch as Custer came out with Mrs. Custer and Josephine Russell.

Shafter saluted and noticed the general's sharp eyes go around the horizon. Custer said: "Not quite time for a blizzard, but it will be cold. Are you dressed warm enough?"

"I'm stuffed and padded," said Josephine.

"Sergeant," said Custer, "drive Miss Russell to Fort Rice, remain overnight, and bring her back. Be sure you leave Rice soon enough to make the fort before sundown." Custer gave the girl a hand to the seat of the light wagon, saw to it that a blanket was folded over her legs, and meanwhile cast a professional eye on the carbine lying under the seat. Mrs. Custer called from the porch: "Give my love to Mrs. Benteen and the other ladies and say I hope to see them soon." Shafter sent the team over the parade at a willing trot, passed commissary and quartermaster buildings, rolled down Laundress Row, and set out upon the road which ran south beside the swinging loops of the river toward Fort Rice twenty miles away. The morning-fresh team went spanking along.

He had not seen Josephine for a week, and experienced a good deal of pleasure at her presence. "I have been wondering how you were."

"So have I," she said. "I grew rather curious to see how the experiment was turning out."

"What experiment?"

"Your coming back to an old trade. Other men have tried it and seldom found it satisfactory."

"Do you think I'll regret it?"

"You seemed a different sort of person. I mean — accustomed to better circumstances than you are in now." She paused, opening the subject for him. When he refused the opening she calmly qualified her observation. "It didn't seem to me that you would deliberately accept so rough a life."

"Not as rough as it looks," he commented. "It is a very good life in fact."

"I know something of soldiers," she said. "I have heard them talk and I have seen them drunk."

"Both the genteel and the common get drunk."

She sat straight, looking before her for a few thoughtful moments. "I suppose I was rude."

"No," he said. "Not rude. You don't know my kind of people."

"Those are not your kind of people," she said, now on firm ground again. "That is why you are such a puzzle to me."

"When did you bother to think of me at all?"

"Why," she said, as though surprised that he should doubt her interest, "don't you know any woman is intrigued by contradictions? You are a contradiction. I wanted to go visit Mrs. Benteen — and I suggested to Mrs. Custer that you were undoubtedly a good driver."

He turned, smiling, to her and watched her smile answer him. The cold day rouged her cheeks and sparkled in her eyes. She had a beautifully fashioned face, all its features generous and capable of robust emotion, all of them graceful. She was a girl with a great degree of vitality and imagination, these things held under careful restraint. He saw the hint of her will, or of her pride, in the corners of her eyes and lips.

"I am flattered," he said.

"Under pressure," she said, with quick humor, "you do rise to gallantry. Do you know — I think your thoughts of women are sometimes less than generous."

He said, very seriously: "I hope I've never shown it to you."

"It is only a guess," she said and at once changed the subject. "A beautiful day."

The fog had closed in, bringing the horizons close upon them. It was colder than it had been, with grayer shadows lying upon the dull earth. To the left of them the Missouri ran between its crumbling banks, to the right lay a strip of moderately level country, this running up to a low ridge; and this ridge marched southward a matter of miles and dwindled away into a general plain. They came, late in the morning, to a narrow wooden bridge over the Little Heart, which trembled to their passage; they followed the road's rutty course steadily southward, steam beginning to rise from the winter-thick wool of the horses. At intervals during the morning a courier ran full speed by them and later they overtook a slow-laboring freight outfit bound southward from Bismarck. Near eleven o'clock the Bismarck-Black Hills stage came out of the lonely land to the southwest, pitching on its fore and aft straps.

"I have never liked the sharp line between officers and men," Josephine suddenly said.

She had been following some line of thought; and this was its conclusion. He tried to guess what the thought had been but failed. He said: "A regiment is a machine built for violent action. Men make up the parts of the machine — and each part has to perform its particular chore. There's no time to argue about it when a fight starts; so it has to be settled a long time beforehand. Every man must understand his place."

She said, in a lightly speculative voice: "I should not think you'd be happy in your place."

"Why not?"

"You've had a higher place."

He smiled a little. "You're an indiscreet woman."

"Perhaps," she said calmly. "After all, a woman has two privileges. To be inconsistent and to be indiscreet."

He said, now grown sober, "I have had both qualities used on me. It has made me wonder what a man's privileges are."

"To walk away when he grows weary of it," she said promptly. "That's what you did, didn't you?"

She hit hard when she chose to. He looked at her and saw her half-smile temper the cool realism of her thinking.

"Many men have walked away," he admitted. "But few men ever walked away whole. They left some of themselves behind. The ability to trust, maybe. Faith. The first idealism they had. The wonderful dream of youth. Love is supposed to be the core of a woman, it is supposed to be the entire meaning of her life. The philosophers, at least, say so. A man is supposed to have many interests, of which love is only one. So the wreck of a love is supposed to leave a woman bankrupt, whereas it is presumed that a man easily mends his heart and hunts for another love. That is entirely a fiction of the philosophers."

"Are you quite sure?" she asked, gentle with her voice.

"It is the woman who mends her heart and finds another love," he said. "She knows she's got to do it, if she's to get along with the business of living. So she does it. She's far more realistic than the man. She gets her balance back and moves forward. Very frequently he doesn't."

"It was as I thought," she murmured. "You are skeptical regarding women."

"Yes," he said. "I am."

Her answer to that was extremely soft. "I am so sorry."

"Why should you be?"

"It leaves you so little."

"There is still the world of men for a man to be comfortable in."

Fort Rice came through the fog, a blur and then a square shape huddled against the earth. He slapped the team into a trot and looked at her and saw that she was quietly studying him; and he caught an expression on her face that was wholly mature and far-thinking. She said: "This has been a nice trip, Sergeant. At least I have relieved you from drill, haven't I?"

"Yes," he said, and drove into Rice as mess call sounded. Mrs. Benteen, a tall and tired-appearing woman, came to the porch of one of the half-dozen homely houses to greet Josephine. Shafter took the girl's portmanteau into the house, came back and drove the rig around to the stables and put up the horses. He had no particular mess assignment and therefore hunted up a sergeant and got permission to attach himself to H Company. After noon meal he took a stroll around the post.

It was only a shabby collection of buildings, made of warped cottonwood lumber, closely surrounded by a stockade of logs set upright in the ground and capped at each corner by a small bastion from which sentries might view the roundabout country at night. All the ground was worn smooth of vegetation and all the quarters were paintless, their walls warped apart by the reaction of sun and rain. Thus shabby and forlorn, Fort Rice commanded the Missouri's bluff, exposed to the full rigors of winter wind and to summer's brutal heat. For the people of this post there were no diversions, no entertainment, no break in a dull and confined life. East and west of them stretched an empty land. Forty miles to the south lay the Agency, twenty miles northward were Lincoln and Bismarck — too far away for a casual ride.

He sat on the barracks porch, watching the two skeleton companies drill briefly in the afternoon; and later he made a circle outside the post. There was a cemetery lying slightly beyond the post on a small knoll with little mounds slowly losing identity as weather faded them back to the blank anonymity of the gray earth. In a short while the very mark of these people would be gone — they who had been round-formed and fair, their bodies taut with hunger, their lips red and warm and all their dreams making them great. For a short while they had lived, had voice and motion and were set apart from other living things; they left footprints upon the earth and their hands formed objects which were dear to them, but now the shifting sands filled in the crevices which marked the oblong spot where they lay and the same wind which once had blown its fragrance against them now blew where they were not. They had occupied space beneath the sky and above the earth; that space was now empty. Somewhere, somebody still remembered the touch of these people, but in time that remembrance would grow fainter until at last there would be no living thing that knew them — and the great void of time would have absorbed them into its nothingness.

He thought of this and it was a gesture of rebellion which made him draw his boot along the edge of one fading grave, to sharpen its outline and thus postpone that inevitable oblivion; and he turned and made his circuit of the post, coming upon the crumbling bluff of the river. A wooden incline led down the side of the bluff, upon which stood a wooden platform with wheels, and a keg. To the machine was attached a pair of ropes by which the keg was run to the river for its cargo of water and drawn up. He stood awhile, smoking a cigar and watching the later afternoon grow gray. The strange fog held on, thickening and rolling forward until the river became a silver blur beneath the woolly overcast. A wind came up with its keen cold.

After supper and after retreat, he sat awhile in H Company's barrack-room, watching men sit taciturnly at poker tables, watching them lie back on their bunks. A big-bellied cast-iron stove slowly grew red and tobacco smoke rolled in sleazy layers through the room, through which the barrels of the carbines played a dull blue gleaming. One trooper squatted on his bunk, plucking a sad tune from a guitar, while two other troopers stood close by and tried to make a harmony from the tune. Out of the washroom stalked a lean-flanked cavalryman, naked entirely, with a pure white skin which ran up to a sun-blackened collar line. The wind had risen and sang a soft song at the barrack eaves and men lifted their heads, shrewdly listening to that warning. Gun oil and dressed leather and men's bodies and the horse-impregnated uniforms made a heavy male odor in the room.

"Who's goin' to be mail sergeant this winter?" asked somebody.

A corporal sitting by had an answer. "John Tunis took his discharge this week. They're breakin' in a new man at Lincoln."

"What's that?" asked Shafter.

"Always a sergeant detached to carry mail in the winter when the railroad stops runnin'. Lincoln to Fargo and back, twice a month. A team and a sleigh. Tunis was the only one who could make his way through a blizzard."

Shafter moved from the barracks, into the windy blackness. Lights glistened along the cramped parade and the bastions at each corner of the stockade stood lonesome against the shadows. There was a party in Benteen's quarters, all lights gleaming cheerfully upon the cold world. Through the shadeless windows he saw the officers and ladies of the post gathered, with Josephine surrounded by young lieutenants. He pulled on his cigar, and was surprised that he stood here. "I am well past sentimental longings," he thought. But he stood fast, and observed her carefully. One of the lieutenants drew laughter from her — from this self-contained girl who was so careful of her inner riches; she lifted her head and he had a full view of her face, changed by the laughter, and he said to himself: "She's damned attractive," and for a moment he felt a small thread of loneliness, of outsideness and was reminded of many things in his past. Turning away, he returned to the barracks, coming suddenly upon a scene.

Men sat motionless on the bunks looking toward the end of the big room; and those at the tables had suddenly quit their games. The first sergeant of H, a leather-lean man with four hashmarks across his sleeve, stood in the middle of the room and faced a man at the far end. He was speaking in a cool, persuasive voice to that one. "Put it down, Stampfer. When you're drunk you've got no business handling a gun — and you're damned drunk now."

The trooper at the end of the room had placed his back against the wall. He was short and chunky, with a wildness burning in his eyes and a mass of hair half fallen down over his forehead. His mouth opened and closed and opened again; and then he said with a drunk-mad distinctness: "I am going to kill you!" He brought up the carbine in his hand. He patted it with one hand. "The only friend I've got in the whole damned world. It don't sneak around behind me. It don't steal things out of my bunk. It don't take my rights away."

"Now," said the first sergeant in a most practical voice, "what's the good of shootin' me, Stampfer? You want to be hung?"

"I'm smarter than that," said Stampfer. "I'll leave one bullet for myself."

"You're makin' a damn fool out of yourself in front of the lads," said the first sergeant. "Put the gun down."

"Sure," said Stampfer. "All of you think I'm a damned fool. Don't think I don't know that. I seen you laugh behind me. I hear what you say about me. I'm nothin' but a dog around here!" His voice went up-pitch, uncontrolled and half screaming. "I hate the lot of you. I could kill you all and beat your brains out! That's for you, Beckett — and I'm goin' to kill you first! Then I'm goin' out to hunt the officers of this troop — the dirty slave drivers. I'm goin' to kill Benteen and I'm goin' to put a slug right through Gibson's guts." He shouted it out. "I've had enough of it — from all of you — from this stinking hell hole — from these bastard officers that look at us like we was scum and give us the butt end of their tongues whenever they please! You can cringe! You can stick it out when they drive you like cattle through the heat! You can stand guard duty this winter when it's so cold your fingers rot off! That's fine — that's fine! I won't — not me!"

He stopped in quivering exhaustion. He lifted the gun half to his shoulder and fired at Sergeant Beckett, who never moved a muscle. The sound slammed through quarters and one man, crouched on a bunk near Stampfer, now flung himself forward. Stampfer swung the muzzle of the gun and caught the trooper on the side of the head, dropping him senseless to the floor. Suddenly the whole half end of the barrack rose and rushed at him. Stampfer swept the gun before him like a scythe; a second trooper went down, but a third one ducked in and caught the gun. After that H Company went to work.

Stampfer was against the wall and the liquor's madness had added strength to his heavy frame. He took these men as they came to him, breaking his knuckles against them, plunging his feet into their bellies. He caught them at the arms and butted his head sharp under the chins; he slashed his fingers across their faces and drew blood.

He was struck, and struck again until sight left him, but he stood on his feet and fought as a blind and senseless brute would fight. One man got a strangle hold on him, was carried around and around and flung off, another trooper tackled him at the waist and had his face smashed by Stampfer's up-driving knee. All this carried the fight away from the wall toward the center of the room. Suddenly Sergeant Beckett drew his revolver, made a quick pace forward and cracked the barrel across Stampfer's skull. Stampfer went down, no more motion in him.

He left wreckage behind him, two men knocked completely out, one man kneeling dazed on the floor with a broken nose, and half a dozen others nursing lesser injuries. The sergeant stood still, staring at Stampfer and cursing him. "Two months since the last spell. I have warned you boys to offer him no booze."

"He had a bottle. It was full half an hour ago. It's empty now."

"Dump him on his bunk and tie him to it," said Beckett. He saw somebody coming in the door, turned about and yelled, "Attention." He stood stiff before the entering officer, who was Captain Benteen.

Benteen said in a querulous, rasping voice: "What's this?"

"Stampfer again."

Benteen was an officer of long service. He had a thatch of snow-white hair, a round stubborn face and a mouth made for acid comment. Benteen was a cranky realist and a disciplinarian; he wasted no sympathy on Stampfer. "Did you lay him out?"

"Cold enough."

Benteen looked at the carbine on the floor. "Was that his shot I heard?"

"It was so."

The captain saw the two men lying unconscious. "Badly hurt?"

"Just knocked out," said the sergeant. "They'll come around."

"Sergeant," said Benteen, "next time he draws a gun on any man of this company, shoot him. You have that as an order from me. Now tomorrow when he comes to you with his regrets, make up a pack for him with seventy pounds of bricks in it. He'll march around this post with that until he falls down."

"Yes sir," said the sergeant.

Benteen gave the troop a harsh stare and turned from the room. Outside at the moment taps ran the post and the sentries were calling. The trooper with the smashed face rose with his lips redly smeared. He clapped a hand to his mouth, swearing. "He broke one of me front teeth with his damned knee, Sarge!"

The sergeant went to the man. He said gruffly, "Hold up your head," and used his fingers to pull back the man's bruised lips as he would have opened the mouth of a horse. He looked at the tooth sharply snapped off and he murmured: "You'll have a hell of a toothache if that thing stays in. It has got to come out. I'll get my pliers."

He went to the man who had made the first jump at Stampfer; he bent down, and rose up. "Neely," he said softly, "go fetch the surgeon."

VII

Of Many Incidents

AT ONE o'clock Shafter brought the light wagon before Captain Benteen's door, gave Josephine a lift to the seat and stood by while Benteen arranged the robe around her with an old man's motions of gallantry. The captain looked at the sky a moment, suspecting the weather. "Sergeant," he said, "waste no time in returning to Lincoln. Do you know what an oncoming blizzard smells like? Do you know the signs?"

"Yes sir."

"If bad weather blows up before you reach the Little Heart River bridge, turn back to this post. If you should be unable to return, take cover in the bridge. It has served such purpose before."

"You mustn't worry," said Josephine. "I have been out in many a storm."

There was a wind, and the wind ruffled the captain's white mane when he removed his garrison cap. He gave the girl a hard smile. "A blizzard is not a storm. A blizzard is the world upside down. It is the wind gone mad and the world drowned out. It will drive the breath from your lungs and the heat from your body. When the blizzard blows it brings on a fury that will pound the reason from your head. Nothing stands against it — nothing at all. You know that. However, I am merely cautioning you against a remote possibility. If I thought a storm likely I should not permit you to return to Lincoln. I think it is too early in the winter. But don't waste time, Sergeant."

"It has been most pleasant," said Josephine. "I shall tell the Custers how kind you were."

Benteen gave the girl an oblique glance. "Convey our regards to the general and his lady," he said and turned away. It had not been an effusive message.

Shafter rolled through the guard gate at a trot, facing a gray plain upon which the winter fog pressed and thickened and was churned by the stiff wind moving out of the north. It was colder than the day before and the sun was a thin refraction of light above the overcast. Summer and fall had departed from the plains in the space of thirty-six hours and the smell of the air was raw, almost dangerous. Shafter was smiling. "What is amusing?" asked Josephine.

"Benteen's reluctant courtesy to Custer."

"It was rather wryly given. I noticed it."

"Have you heard the story?"

"Not all of it."

"About seven years ago the Seventh had a battle down on the Washita in the dead of winter and wiped out Black Kettle's band of Cheyennes. It was somewhat of a fight and a small detachment under Major Elliot wandered off and didn't come back. Custer considered himself in a tight fix — other bands being in the neighborhood — and spent a couple days getting his regiment and supply train together before looking for Elliot. He found Elliot and nineteen men dead. Benteen considered Custer had exhibited complete callousness in the matter and wrote a letter about it to the newspapers. It was quite an affair. Benteen despises Custer. If you consider the man's face you can see he would be capable of a good robust hate."

"The regiment seems a very close and agreeable family."

"You can't put a group of men — and their wives — together over a period of years without having animosities. This regiment has its factions. The general is an extremely dashing man, very proud of his abilities. You will remember he was a boy general in the Civil War. He hasn't forgotten it and neither have some other officers who are serving under him, twenty years older than he is. Some of them feel he has too much dash and too little judgment. Others would follow him into point-blank artillery fire if he ordered it."

"I admire him," said Josephine. "Very much."

"He is either loved or hated. He commands no lesser feelings in men."

"How do you feel about him?"

He gave her an easy, half-smiling glance. "I shall reserve my judgment until I serve my first campaign under him."

She said, very soberly, "Are you that sure there will be fighting?"

"Yes," he said, "I'm very sure there will be."

He rode along in silence, not thinking seriously of very much but simply sitting by while the day touched him with its fingers. The damp fog moved over his face like soft fine bristles and a smell, slightly rank and rotten, came from the near-by river. High up beyond the overcast was the subdued murmuring of geese, scudding delayed before the onset of winter.

"Sergeant," she said, "I'm glad to be riding back with you."

When he turned he saw that she was smiling at him and then he remembered how blunt she had been with him the day before; and was struck by the change. She had drawn the curtain of reserve away and seemed to like him and seemed to wish to be liked by him. She had a teasing expression of gaiety in her eyes; she had a provocative challenge in them — and all this made her a more complex and unfathomable woman, and a more striking woman.

"I appreciate the honor," he said. "It was different yesterday."

"Ah," she said, and didn't bother to explain the change. "Isn't it a wonderful day?"

"When you feel good," he said, "any day is good."

"It is the country," she said. "It makes you spread out inside. It makes you giddy. It even makes you reckless. It is easy to cry or laugh here. Or to love, or kill."

"Killing and loving are close together sometimes."

They rolled on over the prairie, jarred steadily by the dry-baked ruts. There was a sound ahead of them, of riders moving fast through the thickening mists, and presently a lithe little officer sitting forward on his horse like a jockey darted out of the haze with a file of six troopers behind him; they fled by, one shout dropping from them, and faded into the haze again.

He remembered, suddenly, that she had fallen long silent and turned to see darkness on her face. She said: "That was a strange remark. It came out of experience."

"Yes."

She looked at him as she had the previous afternoon — judging him. "You should not permit your experiences to sour you."

"Yes," he said, "it is a nice day."

She was wholly mature at the moment, alert enough to understand the undercurrent between them, to fathom his desire to push her away from his secrets. She said: "That was a rebuff wasn't it, Sergeant?"

"There is no real gallantry in me."

She thought of it, and watched him with a half-lidded attention. She was very cool, and very frank with her eyes. "It was unnecessary to warn me. You see, Sergeant, I was brought up to believe that each person must stand the consequences of his own actions. I never could expect sympathy from my people when I hurt myself doing some foolish thing. So, if I do a foolish thing now, I shall not cry. You needn't worry."

"What is the foolish thing?"

"I have decided I like you."

He gave her a half-embarrassed and half-astonished glance, whereupon her soberness unexpectedly left her and she put a hand lightly on his arm and laughed. She had a way of laughing that was extremely attractive, her chin tilting up and her lips curving in pretty lines. A small dimple appeared at the left of her mouth and light danced in her eyes.

He said brusquely, "You're a damned strange woman."

"The simplest kind of a woman. There is no complexity to a woman until a man puts it there."

He shook his head and let the talk drop, but he thought about it through the long stretch of following silence. The Little Heart bridge shaped up through the fog murk. They passed it and dropped their booming echoes behind; the horses, sensing home, stepped briskly through the chilling wind.

"Have a nice visit?" he asked.

"Yes. All officers of this regiment are gallant. There was one young lad newly from West Point — the colonel's son. Sturgis. It is confusing. Do you suppose Colonel Sturgis will ever return to take the command from Custer?"

"I doubt it. The War Department seems to regard it as Custer's command. He's been in charge of it for ten years or so — except for a season when he was courtmartialed and deprived of authority."

"What was his transgression?"

"Rode a hundred miles to see his wife — and wore out his escort troopers getting there. All this without permission to leave his post."

"It was a romantic gesture," she murmured.

"It was something he would have arrested one of his own officers for doing. He is a man with violent swings of temper. Inconsistent and unpredictable. You can never know for a certainty what he'll do next. That's been his history. Steadfastness is not one of his virtues."

She said unexpectedly: "Did I see you strolling through the dark last night, past Captain Benteen's quarters?"

"Yes."

"Smoking your cigar. I understand a cigar and a woman go together in a man's mind. Was there a woman in your mind?"

"I wondered," he said, "if you were enjoying yourself."

"I was also thinking of you," she murmured.

He looked at her and noticed the sweetness of her expression and was greatly troubled. He had started out with this girl pretty much as a stranger; and found himself now somehow engaged in her emotions. It threw him back on his honor, and he searched himself carefully, wondering if he had given her encouragement. He thought: "She's old enough to know her mind, she knows what she's doing." But he was uneasy with the responsibility which lay with him. It bore hard against him, the more he thought of it, the farther he silently traveled, until he came to his abrupt conclusion. "It will have to be settled," he thought.

He stopped the team and wrapped the reins around the brake bar, turning to her. Her eyes lifted to him, narrowed and watchful, but she made no motion when he bent and put his arms around her; for a small moment he hesitated, looking carefully at her lips and the expression in her glance, and saw nothing but the layered darkness in her eyes. He bent down and kissed her, and held the kiss longer than he intended, and drew away. She had made no gesture and no sound; she had put no resistance against him. But now she said, in a curt, precise voice: "I think I heard the general say we should be home by supper-time."

He sent the team on at a faster clip, much more uncertain than he had been. He thought with some self-disgust: "There is no such thing as a study of women. Nothing is to be learned from them. A man gains no permanent wisdom." It was then past the middle of the afternoon, and the sky turning gray; at five o'clock he passed through Lincoln's south gate, and drew before Custer's house. He got down to give her a hand, and felt the weight of her body momentarily spring against his arm. She had a light perfume that drifted to him — a sudden, disturbing fragrance. He started back around the horses and was halted by her clear, sharp voice: —

"One moment, Sergeant."

He turned and watched her come forward. She was on guard, she was cool and quite self-assured, and smiling. It was not a soft smile, not tender or indulgent; it came out to him as the reflection of tumult and stirred emotions.

"You meant to frighten me away, didn't you?"

"To show you that your knowledge of me was incomplete. You must not take men at face value."

He saw the fire and the intensity within her, the swift feelings under hard control. "I think you'll find it was a dangerous subterfuge, Sergeant," she said evenly.

He lifted his cap as she turned away; he climbed to the seat and drove the rig through the sweeping wind, back to stable quarters. He unharnessed and stalled the horses and backed the wagon into its proper place. Having missed stable call, he groomed his own horse in the gathering dusk. But all this while he remembered the taste of her lips and her fragrance and the stillness of her body, neither accepting nor rejecting him. That got into him and suddenly he realized she had broken through his barrier. Afterwards, walking back to quarters, he recalled her voice as she had said: "You'll find it a dangerous subterfuge," and wondered at her meaning.

He reached the barracks with all this churning through his head, and heard first call for drill rocketing down the parade. "It comes early tonight," he said to Hines.

"For the rest of the winter it will be before supper."

He stood retreat and for a while the ceremony took the girl out of his head. There was this power in the trumpets and in the music of the band, in the old grooved ritual of arms, in the voice of the adjutant calling all across the parade's distance, in the somber, stilled ranks of the men and in the pageantry of troopers wheeling by the commanding officer and the bright flash of gold epaulet and the swords tossed gallantly up. It was a thing that was in his blood and bones, not so much because of its color but because of all that it meant in the way of men faithfully standing together — of hard and proud men, of evil ones, of young ones and old ones — all for the moment surrendering what they individually were to become something greater than they could ever individually be. That was it, he thought; that was the thing that brought peace to him, and comfort — this faith in a symbol, in an idea. He rode back to stables in a better frame of mind, but at supper table the recollection of the afternoon scenes recurred and turned him irritable. Afterwards he lighted up a cigar and moved around the big room, as undecided as he had been for many weeks. Sergeant McDermott and Corporal Bierss had started a poker game. McDermott said, "Sit down, Shafter."

Shafter took a chair and waited for his cards. He saw Donovan at the far end of the room with half a dozen other troopers, all of them talking over something. Donovan saw him and came over. Donovan murmured: "This is a good night to get wet, Professor. How you feelin'?"

"Any night's a good night," said Shafter. "Where you goin'?"

"There's a place across the river called the Stud Horse," said Donovan. "Bierss here knows it's a lively spot. A little fun, Professor?"

"Let the man alone," said Sergeant McDermott. "He's just about to catch up on his arithmetic."

"A lad from L dropped word there'd be a group of his boys over there," said Donovan. "It was a kind of an invitation. He said if we had the guts to drop in — "

McDermott and Bierss showed immediate interest. McDermott said: "Why didn't you say that to begin with? You comin', Shafter?"

Shafter got up, still undecided. Maybe, he thought, this was the way to knock his troubles out of his head, maybe it wasn't. But this was his troop and the lads had let him into it; he was one of the crowd. "I had a notion to go into Bismarck," he said. "How long can you keep that fight on ice?"

"It won't get started until the police patrol clears out, after tattoo."

"I'll be there," said Shafter.

McDermott and Bierss and Donovan went into a close study. McDermott said: "Last time we got licked. We didn't take the best scrappers along. Get Rusk and O'Mallon and Carter. Get . . ."

Troopers drifted forward. Lovelace came up and heard what was in the making. He said: "I'll go, too."

McDermott looked at him, critical but not unkind. "You ain't had much experience in this business, son. Barroom fightin' is a science. You'd get your head knocked off before you turned around. L Company will bring along its best scrappers."

Lovelace revealed embarrassment. He held his place and he repeated his wish. "How am I going to learn if I don't start sometime? Let me go along, Sarge."

Shafter studied the boy a moment, knowing exactly what lay in Lovelace's mind. Presently Shafter said to McDermott: "Take Lovelace, Mac."

McDermott shrugged his shoulders. "All right. You get a couple boats and take 'em over to the other shore, son."

"What are the boats for?" asked Shafter. "There's a ferry."

"It will be after taps," said McDermott, "so we can't come back on the ferry. Who's guard on Number Six Post at ten o'clock?"

"Don't know," said Donovan.

"I'll go see the sergeant of the guard," said McDermott. "Last time there was a green lad who didn't know much about soldierin'. He might have caused us trouble."

Shafter turned away, but he heard McDermott's voice call after him: "We ain't ever had enough foxy scrappers to cope with that outfit. By God, it will be a different tune tonight. You be there sure, Professor."

"Sure," said Shafter. He put on his overcoat and stepped into the raw, steady wind. Beyond the guard gate he caught a late-traveling ambulance, crossed the wind-chopped river and so rode into Bismarck.

Earlier that afternoon Major Barrows' wife rode out of the post on a dark bay horse and swung toward the ferry at the same time Lieutenant Garnett came trotting off the old Fort McKean road with half a platoon behind him. He saw her and lifted his hat and smiled. Afterwards, inside the post, he nodded at one of the troopers. "Purple, report to me at my quarters." He surrendered his horse and strode over the parade to bachelors' quarters at his usual pacing gate, every inch of his frame taut and soldierly. He was thinking of Mrs. Barrows in his aggressive way when he moved into the frame house at the end of Officers' Row and entered his own particular room. He was still appraising her as he washed up and groomed himself before his mirror. He thought: "Lonesome as hell, and ready for a little flirting." He corrected himself on that. "Not the precise flirting type, I think. Probably trying to be honest with a husband who is somewhat of a fool in his handling of her."

Purple presently tapped on the door and came in and stood by with a half-respectful, half-knowing interest. Jack Purple was the lieutenant's striker, doing the necessary valet chores, running the usual errands and, on occasion, executing chores which were scarcely routine. He had followed the lieutenant through two enlistments, being transferred at his instance from one outfit to another so that he might serve Garnett. He was in many respects a cheaper edition of the lieutenant, as base and as fundamentally predatory, but lacking Garnett's covering veneer. He was a lean man with a sharp face in whose crevices a kind of handsomeness dwelled in company with a poorly reined boldness. He imitated the lieutenant's long hair-cut, the lieutenant's fastidiousness of dress and in his way he tried to copy the lieutenant's dash. An apt and willing pupil, he had learned many of Garnett's methods with women and after eight years of association he knew more of the lieutenant's secrets than any other man, so that the relation between them was a thing compounded of servility, trust, and contempt. Bound together as they were, they had no illusions, and each man secretly harbored his opinion of the other.

"Purple," said Garnett, "keep my boots in a better state. Your private affairs have made you forgetful."

"The lieutenant knows," said Purple with a veiled grin, "that I have nothing new to trouble me."

"You're lying," said Garnett. "I know about that girl on Laundress Row."

Purple showed concern. "My God, Lieutenant, you ain't got your eyes on her have you?"

"No, but she's going with a boy in A Company."

"Oh, him," said Purple with indifference. "Lovelace is his name. A dummy."

"Never take a woman away from a man who's liable to cripple you, Purple. You never see me doing that, do you?"

"I'll take care of him."

"That's your affair. Now listen to me. I want a man in this outfit soundly whipped. I want him busted up."

"Lieutenant," said Purple, "some things I can do, some I can't do."

"Not you," said Garnett. "Get Conboy to do it. Just drop the word to Conboy that you can get him a hundred dollars if he does a first-rate job."

"It will be first-rate if Conboy does it," said Purple. "Who you wastin' that money on?"

"The new sergeant in A Company. Shafter."

"The one that licked Donovan?"

"Did he?" said Garnett and looked displeased.

"He did," said Purple and stood still, trying to remember where Shafter had cut Garnett's past trail. "But it shouldn't be much for Conboy. Conboy licked Donovan twice. This Shafter won't reach him at all."

"Go see Conboy," said Garnett. "Keep my name out of it of course."

"The man's a sergeant. How could he be after any woman you wanted? Was it a long time ago, Lieutenant?"

"Get out of here," said Garnett. "Bring my horse around."

He pulled on his overcoat, buttoned it and snugged his shoulders into it until the cloth lay smooth; he gave his hair a last brushing at the edges and took care to adjust his garrison cap; and he stood a moment before the mirror, watching his face. "She will play the deep game," he thought. "She will want me to play it." He went out to his horse and swung up with a last word for Purple. "See Conboy right away," he said, and broke into a gallop across the parade, through the guard gate and along the ferry road. Mrs. Barrows waited at the slip for the ferry now nosing in; she turned her head when she heard Garnett approaching.

He lifted his cap to her, not smiling; he had the exact expression on his face he wished her to see — a repressed look which came from stirred feelings, a gentleman of honor hard-drawn to a woman but holding himself in. He noticed the violet coloring of her eyes and he closely watched the small change around her lips. These little fugitive shifts on a woman's face, the varying sounds of a woman's voice, the small gestures or phrases half spoken — these were things on which he always laid much emphasis. He was not certain, but he thought he made an effect on her.

"To Bismarck?"

She nodded and put her horse across the staging to the boat. She rode through to the boat's far end, Garnett following. "My destination also. Do you wish to dismount?"

"No."

He made nothing of her brevity. It was a thing to be read either way. She was, in his own expert judgment, a fully formed and beautiful woman, an instrument of many strings, awaiting somebody's touch.

"Winter's here."

"Yes," she said. Then, as though conscious that her sparing conversation might be rude, she gave him a full glance, murmuring: "Now the light goes out until spring. I dread it."

"There's still a train back," he pointed out.

"An officer's wife has no business living apart from her husband."

"I understand that," he said.

"Do you?" she softly said.

For all his assurance he was halted by the remark; he made nothing of it and saw no lead for him. He thought with impatience: "Have I misjudged this woman?" He tried a few idle phrases, and was answered with equally idle phrases as the boat labored with the current, reached the eastern shore and dropped its plank. The two moved upgrade to the forking of the road — one branch going through the Point, the other swinging wide of the place and running along the bluff. He said: —

"Shall we take the roundabout road?"

She gave him an odd glance. She said, "I don't believe in avoiding the realities, Mr. Garnett. The Point can't be ignored by circling it." But she looked behind her at the east side of the river, which at this distance was covered by the day's thin fog; then her eyes touched him, the excitement in them quite distinct. "But if you wish," she said in a quicker, shallower voice, and turned to the side road.

He felt a quick elation. She had made a decision and had indirectly told him why she had made it. They moved up the road to the top of the bluff and came in another quarter hour to the scar of the railroad right-of-way being built west of Bismarck and now abandoned for winter. They rode along the right-of-way until, by her gesture, they swung into the flat prairie. Presently they were two figures riding along in the mist. "I like it better this way."

"Strange," he said. "I should think you'd like to stick to lights and comfort. I should not think you'd enjoy lonely places."

"Lonely people for lonely places," she said.

"I recognized the loneliness in you."

"I suspect you are rather clever at reading people, Mr. Garnett. Have you been wasting your time reading me?"

"Yes. Is it a waste of time?"

"Better if it were."

"It is a damned hard thing," he said, his voice rough and edged.

"What is?"

"To see a woman — to know that woman is your kind of a woman.

Dreaming the same kind of dreams. Ready to laugh at the same things, to feel the same loves, the same passions. To lie awake at night — "

"Mr. Garnett," she murmured in the softest of voices. He looked down and saw her hands tightly gripping the pommel; he saw hurt and hard restraint on her face. He had struck her emotions forcibly and he knew this was the moment he had waited for. "Wait," he said, and stopped his horse and got down. He came beside her, looking up; the things he felt were hot enough and real enough at this moment to show upon him and the woman saw them as she stared at him and struggled with herself. "No," she murmured, "get back on your horse."

"Come down," he said, and touched her. He felt her body trembling as she hung to the pommel, he noticed a weakening in her, he recognized something almost like terror on her face; and then that broke and she crossed the deadline she had set herself, and suddenly put out her arms and came down to him. He had her in his arms and his mouth upon her and he held her like that over the lengthening moments, feeling surrender soften her. When she pulled her lips away she was silently crying, even as she clung to him; she dropped her head and laid it against his chest.

"I knew this was coming," she whispered. "I knew it at the Custers'. I sat there and could look ahead and see all of it. You're not a good man, Mr. Garnett. I know that."

He said: "I am very much in love with you."

She lifted her head and showed him her bitter glance. "You needn't lie. It isn't necessary."

Her realism had not left her and this threw him off balance and made his next words ridiculous even in his own ears. "Do you think I'd touch you if I didn't have the deepest kind of feelings — "

"Yes," she said, "you would. I know you — and now I think you know me. You have studied me rather carefully haven't you? Help me up, please."

He gave her a hand to the side saddle, flushing at the position in which he had been placed. She made him seem awkward and amateurish and that was to him an unforgivable thing. He got to his own saddle and quickly attempted to get the scene back within his control. "Mrs. Barrows," he said, "if you believe that about me I shall certainly not come near you again."

She stared into the thickening, graying mist of the afternoon and then she turned and gave him a glance which revealed the fatalism in her. "Yes, you will. And you know also that when you come, I'll be where you want me. That is the way it will be, Edward. We both know what we are and we both know there is no help for us. I'm going back to the fort. Don't come with me."

She turned her horse and started away, then checked around and rode back to him. Her voice softened and her face showed a more tender side of her character. Her eyes searched him and seemed to have hope in him. "Edward," she murmured, "we can be better people. Let's try to be."

He gave her a dark, rash look. He said, "I want you. I've got to have you."

Her voice lifted to a sudden passionate appeal. "Let me alone!"

"No," he said, "I can't. I want you and I know you want me. That's enough isn't it? What else matters at all? I can't play a hypocritical part. Neither can you. There's too much in both of us."

She watched him a long moment, her shoulders dropping and the softness going from her face — the odd glow of beauty dying. A long sigh escaped from her. "All right, Edward," she whispered. "All right," and turned from him.

He watched her grow smaller and dimmer in the rapid-falling twilight, and at last vanish. He had a twinge of conscience, not at his conquest of her, but in permitting her to return home alone. He had done better than he expected; he had caught her sooner than he believed possible, and now said to himself: "A ripe peach ready to drop from the tree." As soon as he said it, he thought differently of her, he valued his triumph less highly, and he had another cynical thought: "From what she said I don't suppose I'm the first man to come along." Even so, he was thinking of when he should next see her, and of what he would say. With this in his mind to excite him, he pointed his horse southeastward, hearing the fort's sunset gun send its echo up along the river's canyon in rocketing waves. At late dusk he arrived in Bismarck, stabled his horse and went into the restaurant frequently patronized by the post's unattached officers. He discovered Edgerly in the back of the place.

"Got tired of the food at Bachelor Hall?" asked Garnett.

"Been tired of it for years," said Edgerly.

"You should do as I do — get yourself invited more often to married quarters for your meals."

"I've been a star boarder at every table in the garrison," said Edgerly. "A man can push his luck just so far. Then he becomes a damned bore."

"Maybe our salvation," said Garnett, "lies in marriage."

"That," said Edgerly, "is a damned bizarre suggestion, coming from you."

Garnett accepted the remark with a grin, but he felt the pointed edge of it. He envied Edgerly's magnificent stature and was jealous of Edgerly's thoroughly masculine appearance. The man was as handsome as hell and was the cynosure of many a woman's eyes. While he ordered and ate, he turned Edgerly's remark over in his head, possessing a Beau Brummel's sensitiveness to the opinions of other men; and he wondered if he had acquired a reputation among his brother officers of which he was not aware. The thought inevitably brought along its companion worry: Had any part of his past caught up with him? There were only two men in the post — Captain Moylan and Shafter — who knew his reputation and both these men, being gentlemen of their own standards, would keep silent; a gentleman, he thought with a return of cynicism, was a man who suppressed his natural desires for fear of what people would say.

"You came in here looking rather pleased," observed Edgerly. "Had luck?"

"Luck?" said Garnett and felt himself betray a certain embarrassment. Edgerly had a sharp pair of eyes and it seemed to him that Edgerly now watched him with something more than casual curiosity. "Just the winter air vitalizing me, I suppose." He lighted a cigar with his coffee, taking such ease as could be found in the restaurant's drab atmosphere. The place had become crowded with the odd assortment of rough frontier types — cowhands, railroad men, gamblers and freighters. A buxom and floridly handsome woman swept into the place, wearing a vivid mauve dress fitted snug at bosom and hips; she took a table and she called out in her hearty voice: "Hurry it up, Charley," and cast a speculative glance at the two officers.

"Shall we take in the opera?" suggested Garnett sardonically.

"The girls at the Wave put on a pretty good show," said Edgerly. "Rough but diverting. However, I think I'll go back to the post and spend the evening with Upton's *Tactics*."

"Scarcely answers the problems of a Sioux campaign," said Garnett. "Upton conceives of cavalry as a solid force meeting a solid enemy. The Sioux simply do not subscribe to the doctrine of staying in one place or in sufficient force to be met and defeated. It is like charging a cloud of dust."

"The answer is," suggested Edgerly, "for the cavalry to in turn do the same thing. Make rapid night marches, hide by day, split and come together."

"That would be practical if we had no wagon train, no luggage, no such impediments as saddles, intrenching tools and so on. The Anglo-Saxon horse soldier is a cumbersome object moving along at five miles an hour. The element of surprise is not in him unless he is fighting equally cumbersome opposition. If you attempt to split forces in front of the Sioux the result is that the Sioux see it and destroy each force separately."

Edgerly said: "It depends a great deal on the commander."

"Our commanders are still fighting the Civil War — mass against mass. They come out here with a total lack of information regarding Indians."

"Scarcely true of Custer."

"Edgerly," said Garnett, "doesn't it strike you a little odd to hear him say that one white soldier can match ten Indians? Do you believe that? I don't. I believe it to be the kind of reasoning which may lead us into difficulty."

"You sound like Benteen," said Edgerly. "I had not known you were a Benteen adherent."

"No," said Garnett, "I have not aligned myself."

"For my part," said Edgerly, "I believe the regiment will acquit itself with credit when the campaign comes. Did you hear Custer is presently leaving for the East on vacation?"

The two rose, paid their bill and went out — a pair of tall and extremely distinguished-appearing men drawing the covertly admiring glance of the buxom woman at the table. They stepped into a street turned robust and lively by Saturday night's traffic. The gush of Bismarck's lamps played upon the street's moisture-clodded dust and cappers stood before the gaming houses, each with his patter and his urgent invitation. A line of soldiers were spread along a shooting gallery's arcade, the twenty-two–caliber rifle bullets clanging on the metal targets. Edgerly paused a moment to look on, and to make his observation. "That's something we could stand more of in the regiment. We've got too many recruits who are indifferent shots." Half a dozen cowhands whirled through the night's darkness, primed for excitement, and sending their high sudden shouting into the clamor; the town marshal paced taciturnly by on his steady rounds and a tall, white-mustached man came down the street side by side with Josephine Russell.

Edgerly paused before them and lifted his hat, smiling. He shook hands with the elderly man and he made a gallant bow before Josephine, who said: "Night-hawking, gentlemen?"

"A couple of soldiers on the prowl," agreed Edgerly and then, remembering that Garnett had not previously met Josephine's father, made the introduction.

Garnett made his bow and accepted Russell's hand. The girl's presence straightened him like a cold shock and placed him on his best and most charming manner. He observed the girl's casual glance, and met it, and his fast mind began to hunt for the usual signs that would give him a proper lead. He held her attention until she swung her glance to Edgerly.

Russell said: "You've had a cold ride over from the fort, and mighty little entertainment to. be had here to pay for it. Happy to have you both join us at our house for a cup of coffee."

Edgerly said, "I should be back at the post, but I shall accept, in

order to give Garnett here a view into one of the few civilized homes
in this territory."

"You must be thinking of our new plush chair," said Josephine.
Edgerly made a move to drop beside her and was forestalled by
Garnett who smoothly turned and took her arm. She gave Garnett an
amused glance and then again diverted her attention to Edgerly.

"How was the last scout?"

"No excitement. None at all. The Sioux are all coming in will-
ingly for a winter of free beef at the Agency."

"Don't you folks be deceived," said Russell. "There's more things
brewing than you're familiar with. I talk to the traders and teamsters. They catch what's going on."

"What's going on?" asked Edgerly.

"The Sioux have got plenty of guns and plenty of shells and plenty
of horses. They been visiting, band to band, all this fall. Sitting Bull's
been around talking to Gall and Two Moons and Crazy Horse and
the other chiefs. It is unusual for Indians to make plans that way.
Each band most always goes it alone."

"What are they talking about?"

"You'd never get a Sioux, not even a renegade Sioux, to tell you
that."

Edgerly spoke soberly: "Let it be, if they want to fight it out next
spring. We shall settle the Indian question once and for all."

Mr. Russell gave the lieutenant an old man's glance of reserved
knowledge. "The army's said that for ten years, and it has tried.
It has nothing yet to show for its campaigning." But then his courtesy made him smooth over the reflection. "Let's not discuss politics.
Coffee will be good after this cold wind. Early winter coming."

VIII

At the Stud Horse

SHAFTER came into Bismarck half an hour later and entered the nearest saloon; he strolled along the filled tables, he watched the faro rig and he tried a dollar on the roulette wheel. One of A's troopers, a Dutchman by the name of Kanser, sat at the blackjack table, having luck. Kanser looked up at him, pointed to his pile and said: "Sit in, Sarge. I'll bank you. I'm lucky." Shafter shook his head and passed on out of the saloon into the gathering wind. He had reached the far end of the street before he quite realized where he was bound, and then he shrugged his shoulders and continued on across the empty area toward Josephine Russell's. Suddenly he knew that she had been in his mind ever since he had dropped her at the Custer house. He had the clearest picture of her smile, the strongest recollection of her voice. He was going back to her, he told himself, to straighten out a misunderstanding. He had meant nothing by the kiss; he wanted her to know that.

He wasn't aware of visitors until he had knocked; and then it was too late to turn back, for Josephine opened the door at once and seemed pleased to see him. She took his arm, saying, "Come in out of the cold," and drew him through the door. As soon as he got inside he saw Edgerly and Garnett.

He stood still and his thorough knowledge of the gulf that separated officer and enlisted man made him realize the embarrassment of his position, even though he was on the neutral ground of a civilian house. Edgerly was faintly smiling the smile of a man who looked upon an awkward situation with some puzzlement; and he was quick to say, "Good evening, Sergeant."

"Good evening, sir," said Shafter. He was at the moment watching Garnett's eyes display a malice and a thin pleasure, and the sight of that heated him physically and hatred of Garnett was a force that kicked him in his stomach. He thought rapidly of one means or another by which he might gracefully retire from a situation which was as painful to his hosts and to Edgerly as to himself.

The girl understood this as well as he did. She saw the whole scene quite clearly, Shafter's stony attitude of attention in front of his superior officers, Edgerly's gentlemanly effort to break the restraint with his friendly smile, and the satisfaction visible on Garnett's face. She said to Shafter in a soft and hurried voice: "Wouldn't you like to have a cup of coffee?"

He said: "I've had supper."

Edgerly meanwhile had done his quick thinking. Now he said: "Did you find the horse I sent you after?"

"Yes sir," said Shafter.

"That's fine, Sergeant. Where was he?"

"Beyond the Point."

"Take him back to the fort for me, Sergeant," suggested Edgerly, and gave Shafter his repressed grin.

Shafter turned out of the house at once. The girl followed him, closing the door. He had stepped from the porch when her voice stopped and turned him. He stood still, watching her move forward. "I'm very sorry," she murmured. "I suppose it was my fault. If I hadn't invited you inside you wouldn't have been placed in an uncomfortable situation. But it would have seemed very rude if I hadn't asked you in, wouldn't it? You wouldn't have known the reason and you would have thought me without any manners at all."

"It doesn't matter," he said.

But she shook her head as she watched him. "I'm afraid it does. You're quite angry."

"No," he said. "I have no privilege to be angry. Good night."

He was down the steps when she stopped him again. "Just a moment," she said and turned into the house. Presently she came out with a heavy coat wrapped around her. She took his arm, not saying anything, and she walked with him back through the windy darkness toward Bismarck's street. When they reached the foot of the street he stopped and faced her. "That was nice of you."

She said: "I hate that military distinction between officers and men. I really hate it."

"It can't be otherwise," he said.

"Edgerly was very thoughtful."

"The man is a gentleman by instinct."

"There's something very bitter between you and the other one — Garnett. I think that's what made you most angry."

He looked at her and was ashamed of the trouble he had caused her. He said: "I apologize for bringing any of my feelings into your house. You shouldn't give it another thought. I had no right to come to you."

She chose her words with a good deal of care. "I have my own rules of right and wrong. You must let me feel the way I wish to feel about it."

He smiled down at her somewhat in his old and easy way, but she knew he was still inwardly rankling and then she was completely convinced that her prior judgment of him was correct. Had he never been of a higher grade than sergeant he would have accepted the scene in her house without a second thought and automatically would have made his departure. But he had felt embarrassment, even though he knew the rules of the game; he had made his exit as gracefully as possible, to save her feelings as well as his own. He had once been something better, and perhaps the memory of that was the thing that had most hurt him.

"You have a gentle heart," he said. "Do you wish me to see you back to the house?"

"No. Come to supper Wednesday night."

She thought he meant to refuse, for he stood silent as he considered it. Then she saw his smile come again. "That will be something to look forward to," he said and lifted his hat to her and went up the street.

She stood a moment, watching him stride away, sharing his embarrassment and made angry at the scene which had produced it. Presently she shrugged her shoulders and moved back toward the house. "Some of it I don't understand," she thought. "Some of it came from the other officer — from Garnett."

At the south end of the street Shafter hailed a freighter moving out of town and climbed aboard, to sit in heavy silence beside a taciturn driver whose sole remark was "Hyah Lily, hyah, Don!" The blackness of the night closed in and the fog broke like a fine rain against them, very cold. "Damn him," Shafter thought, "he's moved into another home, to stalk another woman." There was no feeling as bad as the one which that knowledge brought; it whetted his temper dangerously, it brought up from the past small pieces of memory one by one and revived a story he had never been able wholly to forget. "He'll spoil her if he can, knowing I know her. God damn him!" He slammed the palm of a hand hard down on the seat from thinking of it, drawing the teamster's slanted glance. "No mosquitoes this time of year," said the driver.

Three quarters of an hour later the lights of the Point began to make crystal blooms through the fog and by degrees the sound of music moved forward. They passed a building strongly lighted and skirted others one by one. "Which is the Stud Horse?" asked Shafter.

The driver pointed with his arm. Then he said: "Been there before?"

"No."

"Then you're a fool for goin' near it."

Shafter said, "That may be," and dropped into a road slowly turning to mud beneath the wheels of the steady-passing wagons. When he reached the door of the Stud Horse he noticed a few troopers hanging back in the darkness, grouped together. Passing through he came upon a room the approximate size of A Company's quarters, with its bar running the full length of one wall, with the customary grouping of poker tables and other gambling layouts. There was a small floor for dancing and a raised platform at one end on which sat a piano, and a pianist in a velveteen jacket, an accordion player and a fiddler. There was additionally on the platform a raw-boned girl singing a song about a soldier lad who would hear no more bugles to the muted accompaniment of the violin. Fragments of the song came through a considerable racket, for the place was well occupied by soldiers from the post, and this was the latter part of the evening so that the fun had gotten moderately rough. He saw Lovelace standing at the bar and walked toward him. The youngster gave him a look and murmured: "The crowd's been waitin' for you. They're in the back room."

Lovelace's hair was as yellow as a girl's and he had a nice pair of eyes. A glass of whisky stood before him on the bar, so far untouched; he moved it between his hands with short restless gestures and he seemed nervous.

"I'd let that stuff alone until later," said Shafter.

"I wish this was over with," said the lad. "But we got to wait until the patrol comes through. L Company's outside. I saw 'em awhile ago."

"You been in this kind of fighting before?"

"No," said Lovelace. "I'm not afraid of it, but maybe this drink would help."

"Wait awhile," said Shafter and pushed the whisky away. The front door opened and a file of troopers came briskly in, headed by a sergeant. The sergeant bawled: "All out for the ferry. Make it sharp now, boys. Get away from that bar — cash in. I won't be tellin' you twice." The detail tramped out.

"We'll go out and circle the place to the back room," said Lovelace. The music stopped and Shafter and Lovelace moved with the crowd into the sparkling, damp air. Voices called through the blind fog and somewhere a woman started to laugh and kept on until she ran out of breath. He heard the patrol sergeant shouting in and out of the Point's various dens. Lights died here and there as Lovelace led him around the corner of the Stud Horse, past a group of waiting troopers. He heard one of them say: —

"That's that new sergeant of A Company."

"Can he fight?"

"He licked Donovan."

"He's my oyster, boys. Where'd that damned patrol go to?"

Lovelace led him to the rear of the building and opened a door into a little room crowded with A troopers. A lamp burned on the table and smoke filled the place. Donovan said: —

"You're a man to keep a date on the dot, Professor. Nine it is. The patrol's gone by."

"Hold it a minute," said Sergeant McDermott. "Hackett is patrol sergeant tonight and he knows about this. So he said, don't start a fight until he gets out of hearin'."

"You think of everything," said Donovan.

"There's a right way to fix things — and a wrong way," said McDermott. "Lovelace, how many L men did you see?"

"Eight or nine."

"The agreement was not more than ten to a side," said McDermott, "but you got to watch that outfit. It is not to be trusted."

Shafter counted noses. He said: "We've got twelve here, Mac."

"That's entirely different," said McDermott. "Just in case they got more."

Shafter grinned at the men around him, at Donovan's scarred professional fighting face, at the wholly unconcerned Bierss, at Lovelace who was worried and tried to hide it, at Tinney whom he felt to be treacherous, at the other troopers standing shoulder to shoulder around the room; it was the troop spirit that drew them here — the pride of it in their bones and the rank lust of living in their blood. They would be bruised and they would be hurt and some of them would carry scars afterwards, but still it was the faith of one man to another that brought them here.

There was a scratching and a murmuring out in the big room. McDermott said: "That's them," and opened the little room's inner door and stepped through with A's troopers behind him. McDermott looked across the room at the L troopers drawn into a kind of line; he said, politely formal, "Well, gentlemen, here we are. How many have you got?"

There was a sergeant to speak for L — a rawboned heavy man with pure-black mustaches roping down from either side of his mouth. "You can count, Mac."

"So I can, and I count thirteen. That's more than ten."

"Ain't it, though," retorted L's sergeant. "And I can count, too, and I count twelve. You tryin' to fool us again?"

"I said to the boys," said McDermott, "that you could never trust L. I was right, wasn't I?"

"Twelve and twelve then," said L's sergeant, and turned to point a finger at one of his men. "You, Gatch, stand aside and stay out of it."

McDermott took a look at the discarded L trooper and was derisive. "Him? Hell, leave him in the fun. He ain't goin' to be of any use to you anyhow."

The two troops had spread out and had gradually drifted nearer. A man came from the bar, speaking to them: "What you pick my place for? I get the worst of it all the time. Take your scrap over to the City of Paris for a change. You bust up any more poker tables for me and I'm goin' to turn you in to Custer."

"Yeah," said McDermott, "you do that. He'll pay the bill." But then he stopped his forward drifting and stabbed an arm at one of the troopers in front of him. "Conboy, what're you doin' here? This is strictly between A and L."

But L's sergeant said in a cool and crafty voice: "Nothin' was said about that."

Conboy was built short and broad and muscular. He had a bull's neck and a jet-black head of hair cropped close to his skull and when he looked out upon A Company's ranks he dropped his head and scanned them from beneath his heavy brows. He was a knuckle-scarred man, flat of lip and flat of nose, and he rubbed his shoes gently back and forth on the floor, his knees springing into a slight crouch. Donovan protested at once. "Nothin' was said about bringin' in outside bruisers, either. Is this an honest fight, or ain't it?"

"Now will you listen to who's speakin' those words?" jeered L's sergeant.

"All right," said Donovan. "Pair off as you want, but I'll take Conboy."

"I've licked you before, Donovan," said Conboy, now speaking for himself. "I want fresh meat this time."

"So you've got down to pickin' your meat easy," said Donovan with heavy sarcasm. "You should be proud of that, Conboy."

"I'll take one man," said Conboy with a kind of insolent weariness. "When I have done him up I'll back off. That leaves things even enough."

"Who's the man?" demanded McDermott.

"Him," said Conboy and pointed at Shafter. "I hear he thinks he's a fighter."

McDermott was outraged at the affair and said so. "Martin," he said to L's sergeant, "if that damned misfit outfit of yours is so afraid of itself that it has got to ring in professional talent to win a scrap, you can go to hell before you get any further consideration from us."

Donovan had drifted beside Shafter and now whispered. "The man is a bruiser. He fought all the big ones in England. I have fought him twice. He's better than me, Professor. He's better than you."

Conboy stood watching Shafter with an idle, lowering light in his pale-blue eyes, with his scarred head dropped after the fashion of a dangerous bull half ready to charge. He was barrel-chested and he had massive legs but his girth bulged out from his hips like pillow stuffing; he was past his prime and no longer kept himself hard, but the crafty skill of his long years was more than enough among amateurs. He was, Shafter guessed, beyond thirty-five.

Conboy said: "You ready?"

Shafter moved to the bar and peeled off his overcoat and blouse and shirt. He heard Conboy say in a vast, confident voice: "The rest of you lads hold off your fight till we have ours. I like a proper audience."

"A knockdown is a round?" asked Donovan. "You back off when he's on the floor?"

"So it is," said Conboy shortly.

"Then it is understood," said Donovan. "Everything proper. If you forget that, Conboy, I'll come up behind you with a chair."

Conboy had stripped to the waist, and now he squatted slightly, one foot forward and both enormous fists cocked stiffly before him. Shafter squared off before him, standing balanced with his arms down. Conboy stared at him from under his shaggy brows. "Get your guard up, you fool. I'll not play around with a green man. Come on, guinea, give me a fight — give me a fight."

The troopers had fashioned a circle to watch this; other troopers were returning to the Stud Horse, drawn by the rumor of trouble. Shafter looked at Conboy's feet, so solidly planted on the floor, anchored there by the man's vast bulk, and experimentally he slowly circled Conboy at a distance, watching Conboy's shoes make little shuffling turns; suddenly Shafter whipped back in the opposite direction and saw Conboy's feet stop and reverse. Conboy's footwork had been slow and Conboy knew it as well as Shafter, for his pale eyes heated up and he let out a huge roar and came rushing forward with his head down and his big hands reaching out in feinting punches. Shafter slid by him, hooked a hard jab into the man's belly, swung and caught Conboy on the side of the neck. Conboy, never off balance, whirled catlike and launched his rush; he missed with his right hand and reached full out with his left fist and caught Shafter on the shoulder, shaking Shafter backward. He followed up his chance, pursuing Shafter. Shafter wheeled aside, swinging behind Conboy and waiting there.

Conboy came around with an irritated scowl. "Come on — quit the fancy stuff and give me a fight!" He stood still, his flanks heaving softly to his breathing. He jiggled his fists up and down, feinting as he remained in his tracks and watching Shafter with his alert and crafty eyes. L Company's men were beginning to ride Shafter with their comment: —

"That's monseer, the dancer."

"Take a crack at him, Shafter. It won't hurt any worse to get killed now than later."

Shafter moved sidewise again, slowly turning a circle while Conboy irritably wound about. Shafter heard Donovan murmur: "Take your time Professor. Make him come to you. The big tub of guts is too heavy to move."

Conboy heard it and flung his head aside to shout at Donovan: "I moved fast enough for you, lad — "

Shafter slipped in, cracked him on the side of the face and laced a jab into his flank; he had learned something about the man at the first exchange of punches, and learned something now, for Conboy's ruffled temper gave him speed and he came around in a flash, smashed through Shafter's fending arm and hit him with a left-hand blow on the chest. It had a crushing effect, turning Shafter cold. All he saw for that moment was Conboy's red face and pale-blue eyes moving against him; he ducked and barely avoided a killing punch that went windy past his cheek; in self-defense he fell against Conboy, locked Conboy's arms and laid his weight against Conboy. Donovan yelled: "That's it — that's it!"

Conboy roared, "Is it now?" and threw his bullet round head forward, cracking Shafter hard on lip and nose. Shafter locked his fingers together behind Conboy's back and squeezed, but it was like squeezing into sponge rubber; he could not spring the man's ribs. He bore Conboy backward by his dead weight, he shifted his legs to protect his crotch against the up-driving of Conboy's knees and he brought his heel hard down on Conboy's instep. The heavy man had grown angry and his wind began to trouble him as he tried to fling Shafter away. They had wheeled around the circle, with the circle giving away, and now they came to the bar. Conboy used a sudden concentration of energy to swing and hurl Shafter against the bar. Shafter, who realized what the man wanted to do, let himself be carried around, and then flung his own strength into the wrestling.

Conboy, overbalanced, struck the bar and was pinned to it. Shafter surged against him, driving the man's shoulders backward. He heard Conboy grunt and wheeze and he pushed Conboy far enough to draw one of the man's legs from the ground. He let go, smashed him under the neck with two hard side-swinging punches, saw Conboy's arms lift and then drove in with his knee full into Conboy's belly.

For a little while he had Conboy cornered and he grew reckless of his own defense. He battered Conboy's kidneys, he flung himself against the man again with all his weight and threw his forearm across Conboy's windpipe, springing the man's back on the edge of the bar. He matched Conboy's strength with his own and he balanced his weight against Conboy's. He heard L Company shouting at him, outraged at the turn of the affair and disliking this kind of fighting. He heard something crash and then the truce snapped and the troopers rushed yelling at one another.

He saw Conboy's face grow crimson from strain and he felt the man's oxlike heart slug through his shirt. He let go the pressure and stepped back and drove a right-hand blow with all the power he had into Conboy's belly. He saw Conboy sag; but that was all he saw. Fired up and aggressive, he momentarily forgot that this man had

spent a lifetime learning rough-and-tumble; suddenly out of nowhere Conboy's fist caught him on the head and the explosion of it
lighted his brain brilliantly and he felt himself spin away and go
backward. He never knew when he hit the floor.

When he awoke he had a thundering headache and a sick hollow-
ness in his belly. There was a stillness in the saloon and out of the
stillness a man said: "That patrol will be back here in a minute.
Maybe we better carry him."

He couldn't see who did the talking, but he said: "Damned if you
will," and rolled and put the palms of his hands on the floor, pushing
himself up. Then he heard Donovan's husky, gravelly voice close by.
"Now that's the lad, Professor. A drink will fix it, and we've just
got time for one."

He stood up with the help of Donovan's arm. Donovan's face
was a shimmering object behind a fog; it moved gradually out of
the fog and became clear. Looking around him he saw A Company's
men, worse for the wear and tear of a hard brawl; but he saw L's
troopers here too. The affair seemed to be over and no bad feelings
left. He spotted Conboy at the bar, both elbows hooked to its edge.
Conboy's face was still red and he looked tired. Shafter walked over
to his blouse and overcoat and put them on, feeling the pull of his
sore places; the ache of his head pounded steadily on.

McDermott slapped the bar with his palm. "Let's get that drink,
boys. We can't hold off that patrol all night."

"Conboy," said Shafter, "what'd you hit me with?"

"Me hand, damn you," said Conboy, morosely. He swung himself
around to the bar and leaned on it, a tired man and a disgruntled
one. Donovan stood by Shafter, feeling good.

"Next time, Conboy, he'll lick you."

"Will he," said Conboy, sourly. "Will he indeed?"

"A month's pay he will," said Donovan.

Conboy gave Donovan a pale and dismal stare and downed his
whisky at a toss and looked dourly at the empty glass. "A man's a
fool to be doin' this thing forever."

This crowd was tired, the ferment spilled out of it in one sudden
climax of brawling; but it was cheerful. Troopers stood along the

bar shoulder to shoulder and drank the cheap Stud Horse whisky in content while the houseman bitterly complained.

"Who's payin' for those tables? Who's in charge here? By God, I'll go over to the fort tomorrow."

Conboy turned his sour glance to Shafter. "What's the 'Professor' for?"

"Just a jackleg title," said Shafter.

"You'll do," said Conboy grudgingly. "I had to work for that hundred dollars."

Donovan gave him a look. "What hundred dollars?"

There was a man beside Conboy, a trooper with a dandy's haircut and a weakly handsome face; and this one said softly to Conboy, "Shut up, Conboy."

McDermott had gone out of the saloon, and now came hurriedly back. "Back door — back door. Patrol's comin'."

The troopers made a run for the saloon's rear doorways and went scrambling into the darkness; out front the sergeant of the patrol made an unnecessary racket with his command. "Patrol, halt! Patrol at ease! Jackson, you go over to the City of Paris while I see if everything's clear in the Stud Horse!" His voice carried clearly through the misty, cold night; it was a fire-alarm warning to everybody before him, as he knew it would be. Donovan caught Shafter's arm. "Come on, Professor. No use causin' Hackett any trouble."

"Donovan," said Shafter. "Who was the slick one with Conboy?"

"Him? That's Lieutenant Garnett's striker. Purple's his name."

McDermott herded his band together, softly grumbling: "Follow me," and led the way down the bluff and across the sandy lowlands to the river. Lovelace trotted into the darkness and presently called: "Down here." Following his voice, the A Company detachment came upon two boats drawn upon the beach. "Six to a boat," said McDermott. "Pile in."

They shoved the boats into the water, troopers wading out and climbing aboard. These boats were average size and the weight of six troopers pulled them down until the oarlocks were a bare six inches above the water. Donovan had the oars in Shafter's boat and he swore placidly at the troopers crouched on the bottom. "How the hell can I brace my legs?" There was a steady wind out of the north

— the cold all-day wind with its bite of winter; as soon as they cleared the beach small waves began to lick against them. McDermott said: "Don't get this damned thing broadside, Donovan, or we'll swamp."

"Say," said Corporal Bierss, "can anybody swim?"

Nobody answered him. The laden boat rose sluggishly with the swells but never quite made the summit; water broke at the bow and sprayed inboard. Somebody let out a yell. "Fine," said Bierss, "I'm glad one man can walk home if we sink."

"Listen," said somebody else in an uneasy voice, "let's go back."

"Shut up," said Bierss. "Other people want to enjoy the music."

"What music?"

"Ah," said Bierss, "the fiddles of heaven are playing."

Donovan had the nose slightly swung toward the west bank and therefore the waves, coming close upon each other in this narrow stretch of water, took the boat on the quarter and gave it a twisting, heaving motion. The fog had closed densely in, shutting off the lights from the fort, the Point, and the stars. The second boat had disappeared and the sound of the troopers in it faded somewhere downstream. They were in a black gut that had no direction, with the wind beating down the river's shallow canyon and the boat wallowing. The Missouri came aboard in flat sheets and somebody stirred, and drew protest from McDermott.

"Lie still."

Bierss said in his idle, unexcitable voice: "If anybody gets sick on this packet, just remember which way the wind blows."

"We ought to be near shore. How wide is this damned creek?"

"It runs from bank to bank," drawled Bierss. "But my mother always liked to say that no river was as wide as it looked and no chore as hard as it seemed."

"Was she ever on the Missouri in the middle of the night with a bunch of drunks?"

Lovelace spoke up, distinguishable to Shafter by his more careful use of words. "Next time I think I could lick that fellow."

Four men spoke up practically in unison. "You licked him this time."

There was a silence, and then Lovelace said in a surprised, greatly elated voice: "Did I? Did I really lick him? You know, he wasn't a bad fellow."

"Why," said Bierss, "none of 'em are bad after you've had a fight with them."

Donovan had said nothing all this while, being full of labor at the oars and extremely careful in his management of the boat. Now suddenly either his vigilance wavered or the wind swung a curler from a broader angle, for the boat rose on its side, took the shock of a wave's wallop nearly broadside and went teetering into a trough. It dipped into the river like a bucket, whereupon one trooper lifted himself off the floor and further unbalanced the boat. There was a moment of real danger. Shafter felt the craft sink and felt it grow unmanageable. Water rolled back and forth along the bottom.

"Bierss and Mack," he said, "overboard and hang on." He was at the bow and swung and straddled it and let himself into the river, hanging to the bow's point. He heard Bierss say cheerfully: "Nature's own way of taking a bath." Shafter felt the boat lighten as it lost something like five hundred pounds of load. "Donovan," he called, "you can't row upstream with the three of us dragging. Just keep the nose angling toward the bank and let the current set you over." He went under as a wave broke across the bow — and he came up spitting. Wind made a sibilant rough sound on the river. Bierss was saying: —

". . . and so Reginald said to Mary, 'Will you walk hand and hand down life's pathway with me?' And so she did and her oldest son grew up to join the cavalry. Donovan, stop long enough for me to shake the water out of my boots."

"It ain't so damned funny," grumbled somebody.

There was a dull crystal glow above them, which would be the fort lights coming through the fog, and the waves had lost force. Donovan rowed steadily and a last curler broke over Shafter's head, the muddiness of it making a taste in his mouth. Now with calmer water, Donovan swung the nose of the craft and headed directly for shore, and presently Shafter felt bottom beneath his feet. He walked into shallower water, pulling the boat with him.

The troopers got out and hauled the boat to dry land while

McDermott murmured, "Wait," and disappeared in the downstream darkness. Donovan also moved away and in a little while returned. "We're half a mile below Post Ten." Somewhat later McDermott came back with the troopers who had been in the other boat.

"This river," said Donovan thoughtfully, "ain't anything to fool with. I never did like water."

The party walked upstream into the cutting wind. Shafter felt coldness slice through him; water drained down his body and collected in his boots and his boots squealed as he stepped forward. After ten minutes of this forward groping McDermott whispered back: "Follow me," and tackled the bluff.

They moved Indian file to the bluff's edge and lay flat, waiting the sentry's passage. It was now past taps with the lights of barracks darkened, but a glow came on from Officers' Row and from the buildings scattered outside the post proper. A shape emerged from the misty blackness, paused and faced the river. McDermott waited a decent interval and then called softly forward: —

"For God's sakes, Killen, move on to the end of your post. We're cold."

The sentry growled: "Keep your mouth shut. You want me to violate the articles of war?" He walked into the darkness.

The file of troopers rose up, passed the stables and crept to the rear of the barrack. McDermott opened the door and led the way into the room's warm darkness; one by one the troopers groped to their bunks, the sound of waterlogged boots betraying them. Shafter stripped naked, laid his clothes at the foot of the bunk and slid into his blankets.

The night was over, leaving him with his bruises and his headache; the left side of his face was numb from the last blow landed by Conboy. Otherwise he felt content, relieved of his cares and made sweet again by the swift burning-out of excess energy; all through the barrack he heard men whispering and the soft laughter of troopers as they remembered back — and this sound was a good sound and gave him peace.

Then he recalled Conboy's hundred-dollar chore and realized it was Garnett who had offered the money to have Conboy cut him into ribbons; he had been tired but now he lay long awake, his fresh hatred rising. He was still awake when Hines stepped from the orderly room with a lantern and played its light upon the row of bunks; he had stayed discreetly away until he was certain of the party's return and now, like an indulgent father, came to see if all were accounted for.

IX

Word from the Past

ONE DAY, the restless Custer took his wife and brother Tom east for winter; he took with him also the driving energy which whipped the regiment's temper, so that without his presence the Seventh settled into a slower routine. Early winter rains slashed out of slate-colored skies lifting the Missouri a full five feet and driftwood wheeled down the river's mud-greasy surface while the quickening current began to undercut the crumbling bluffs. Standing near A Company's stable, Shafter watched huge sections of earth crash into the water and send small tidal waves onward. Two soldiers were caught in a squall while crossing from the Point and were never seen again. Three babies were born within the post and a sergeant's wife on Laundress Row committed suicide.

Continued reports of disaffection came from the various Indian agencies. Runners arrived with news that the Sioux, half starved for want of enough government-issued beef, were beginning to leave the reservations and return to their own lands westward. The Seventh, now under Reno, scouted steadily in that direction to turn stragglers back, but it was like spreading a net against the wind. The spirit of revolt and resistance was a growing thing throughout the Indian bands as Sitting Bull's couriers traveled from village to village. Near the end of November Calhoun and thirty men had a brush with a fleeing party of Sioux on the Heart River in which one trooper was injured; the Sioux disappeared in the darkness.

A hundred recruits arrived from Jefferson Barracks to fill the Seventh's thin ranks. Lieutenant Benny Hodgson, about to surrender his commission and return to civil life, decided to stay through the summer campaign which he felt to be coming, and was made battalion adjutant under Reno. Young Jim Sturgis, the colonel's son, newly minted from West Point, joined his father's regiment and was attached to M Company quartered at Rice. There was the rumor of a War Department scandal coming out of the East as well as half-verified news of army plans being laid by Grant and Sherman and Sheridan for a winter campaign to crush the Sioux. Custer, the post learned, was in New York, being feted and dined and enjoying the company of that great Shakespearean actor Lawrence Barrett. General Terry, the department commander at St. Paul, sent on urgent orders for the Seventh to overhaul its equipment and to whip its recruits into shape as rapidly as possible; whereby on the windy bitter mornings the troops went through their monotonous evolutions on the parade, marched outside the fort for rifle-range practice, and daily scouted westward. Freighters broke the first light snowfall with supplies for the quartermaster and commissary depots on the reservation. Miners began to stream back from the Black Hills, forced out by weather and by the fear of Sioux revenge in the spring. The Far West, Captain Grant Marsh commanding, came downriver and stopped briefly to report he had been fired on four times in four days along the upper stretches of the Missouri. On December 6 the telegraph flashed news from the East that couriers would be sent out to instruct the recalcitrant Sioux to come into the reservations by January 31, or be treated thereafter as hostiles. That same day the first hard blizzard swept out of the north and pounded Lincoln for thirty-six hours, marking the end of train service from the East until spring.

First Sergeant Hines opened the orderly room directly after morning sick call and waggled a finger at Shafter. When he reached the room, Shafter found Captain Moylan at the little desk with a letter in his hand. The captain said: "Hines, step out a moment," and waited until the old sergeant had gone.

"Kern," said Moylan, and nodded at the letter, "this came to headquarters three or four days ago. Cooke gave it to me to handle as I saw fit." He handed it to Shafter and he sat back to watch Shafter's face as the latter looked down on the single page with its scent so familiar, with its light quick handwriting: —

The Commanding Officer,
Seventh Cavalry,
Fort Lincoln, D.T.

As a particular favor to one who is vitally interested in knowing
the whereabouts of Kern Shafter, is he a member of your regiment?

Very truly,

ALICE MACDOUGALL

The scent raced across the years and the sight of that handwriting
made him vividly remember the smiling and the laughter and the
love that once had been without bottom or boundary. Her person-
ality was a fire glowing against the blackness of time; her voice
was a light bell stroking its melody through long emptiness, rousing
his memories so fully that the hurt of all that had been was a
physical pain. He folded the page into smaller and smaller squares,
tore it across, and dropped the pieces into the iron stove in the
middle of the orderly room.

"No answer?" asked Moylan.

Shafter turned his head slowly from side to side. "None at all."

"I remember her very distinctly," said Moylan. "Last time was
behind the lines at Fredericksburg." He sat idle, a heavy, sandy-
haired, bluff-featured man with memories in turn sweet and acid.
"You were the officer then, and I was the sergeant. Very odd to
recall. You've never seen her since?"

"Once," said Shafter. "Once in Baltimore."

The captain said in a careful way: "I always wondered one thing.
Did Garnett marry her?"

"No."

"God damn him," growled the captain, "he's got a lot to answer
for on Judgment Day." He looked up. "She still remembers you.
Is this the first time you've heard of her — since Baltimore?"

"No," said Shafter. "I have heard indirectly of her many times.
She has spent a fortune tracing me."

"She has a fortune to spend," said Moylan.

"She always had everything she wanted," said Shafter.

"Until she met Garnett," amended Moylan. "Then she had nothing." He sat heavily in thought, and at last shook his head. "It didn't take her long to find out she guessed wrong, did it? She has apparently been sorry for ten years — and wishes to see you. That's a long time for a woman to regret a thing. Doesn't it have any effect on you?"

"No," said Shafter.

Moylan looked at Shafter with steady attention. "It is logical that you should hate Garnett. He'll not be easy with you around here. He'll use his weight on you where he can. He's already tried, has he not?"

"Yes," said Shafter. "But that can work both ways, Myles."

"Do nothing you'll regret."

"Regret?" said Shafter and gave the captain a metal-sharp glance. "If it were in my power to put a bullet through his heart, I'd have no regrets."

"That is not what I meant," said Moylan. "He ruined you professionally once. Do not open yourself to that again by any act."

Shafter said nothing and the captain knew the man well enough to realize his words made no effect on one who, ten years before, had been a wild and headlong kind of warrior. The intervening years had settled Shafter, had given him some wisdom and some tolerance; it had not changed his essential character at all. He was now what he had always been, the proof of it being his return to soldiering after long absence. That caused Moylan a question.

"What brought you back to the uniform, Kern?"

"I was never very happy out of it."

"The old songs, the old bugle calls, the old duties —"

"Not sentiment, Myles. I'm a little old for that, and a little too jaded to be romantic. Maybe I got tired of being my own man doing whatever I pleased, and therefore doing nothing."

"I know you better," said Moylan. "The answer is that soldiering was your lot, as it is to some men more than others. The dust and misery of it, and the content of it as well. The romance of soldiering, of course, is all nonsense in the hands of civilians who know no better. The real part of soldiering is a thing they never know — to come off a scout dirty and frozen to the bone — and to sit at night in comfort and to know you've done a day's good work, and that other men around you have done it, too." He stopped his talking, looked down at his broad hands, and said in a different voice: "We've got need of a sergeant to ride the mail. I told Cooke I had the man for it. You are the man."

"Yes, sir," said Shafter and smiled a little. "You want me out of the post this winter."

"I want no collision between you and Garnett," said Moylan. "Report to Cooke for further instructions. You're listed on A's roster as detached beginning today."

He sat back after Shafter had gone. Hines returned and set about the ritual of paper work. Moylan said: "I gave him the job."

"Does he know about bad weather?"

"Yes," said Moylan and drew a piece of paper before him. He dipped the pen and stroked the corners of his mustaches for a moment and then began: —

My dear General:

It would require the colonel's approval to carry this matter to the adjutant general's attention. Therefore, I write directly to you as an old friend, to bring to your attention the case of Kern Shafter, once an officer of the Fourteenth Ohio . . .

"Captain," said Hines, "is there a feelin' between Shafter and the Lieutenant Garnett?"

"Why?" asked the captain.

"It is information among the boys that Garnett paid Conboy a hundred dollars to bruise up the lad."

Moylan grumbled in his throat and sat heavy at the table, his silence giving Hines assent. Hines said discreetly: "There are other things, regardin' the lieutenant's habits —"

Moylan swung about. He stared at Hines. "A woman?"

"A woman."

"I know about that," said Moylan. "But keep your mouth shut, Hines."

Shafter pulled on his heavy coat and Berlin mittens and moved into the white outer world. The wind, driving from the north, had banked all exposed walls of the post eave-high with snow, had laid a two-foot covering across the parade. The roofs of the buildings were puffed up like thatched cottages, the glittering white surface broken only by the dark smudge of chimney. The wind which at the height of the storm had blown at a sixty-mile rate had ceased entirely so that the post had a dampered stillness across which the voices of men carried with a lively sharpness. Shafter moved along the narrow shoulder-high lane carved out by the shovel details, and reported to the adjutant's office. Cooke gave him his instructions.

"You'll have a sleigh and two mules and a week's rations. You'll eat and be quartered along the route, but the rations will be for emergency if you get snowed in anywhere. The round trip to Fargo is approximately two weeks, depending on weather. You'll be wise to follow the railroad closely. You can't see the track but the telegraph poles will always guide you. Here is a list of ranches and shelters along the way. Better spend the morning picking your team and putting your storm pack together. Draw on the quartermaster for extra robes and blankets. Leave at reveille tomorrow. Get the pouches at the fort's post office and drop back here for special despatches. You'll also take the outgoing mail from Bismarck. That is a courtesy to the town. I have no more to add, except that you should watch your weather most closely. Sometimes you'll never have more than an hour's warning of a blizzard."

Shafter saluted and left the adjutant's office, going out to the big mule barn behind the post to pick a team. He spent an hour doing this, and the rest of the morning stowing the sleigh. Then, with nothing more on his mind and being his own master while on detached duty, he hitched his mules to the sleigh and left the fort for a trial run. In the middle of the afternoon he drew up before Josephine Russell's house and saw her come to the door.

"If you're staying awhile," she called, "drive your outfit into the barn."

He circled the house, left the team and sleigh tied in the barn's runway, and struggled back to the house. The snow was fresh and

needed both settling and hardening in order to make decent footing
for the mules; a cold night, he thought, ought to put it in shape.
He slid out of his heavy coat in the room's warmth and stood with
his back to the heater's isinglass windows, watching Josephine's
clever hands work at her knitting needles. She sat near a window
for the sake of the light, her face now lifting to him, now dropping
to her work. She had on a dress the color of dark roses, with a
large cameo brooch pinned at the neck; and she seemed pleased
with his presence. There were certain things which always gave a
woman a cozy, demure air; knitting, he decided, was one of those
things.

"What's your errand today, Kern?"

"Just trying out a pair of mules, for the Fargo mail run."

She stopped her work to give him a serious appraisal. "Did you
put in for that?"

"It was assigned to me, but I have no objections."

Her smile came quickly up through the soberness of her face,
giving it warmth and charm. He watched her lips softly change.
"No," she said, "you wouldn't object. When I first met you, Kern,
I thought you were a very sophisticated character. In fact I thought
perhaps you were of the faded gentleman type. When I heard you
had joined the Seventh I thought, 'There goes a man with delusions
of romantic adventure.'" She smiled again to remove whatever sting
there might have been in her words. "But you have done very well
for yourself. Is that little purple spot on your temple the place
Conboy hit you?"

"Who tells you of these things, Josephine?"

"An army post is the biggest whispering gallery on earth."

"I got knocked out," he said and stretched his feet before him,
loose in the chair and very comfortable. The girl went about her
knitting, her head bent. She had turned sober again and he thought
she held some displeasure of him behind her silence. After a little
while she murmured: —

"What do the women look like in that place?"

He came to his own defense immediately. "Do you think my
tastes are on that level?"

"Then what were you there for?" she asked, and looked at him with sharp criticism.

"It was a little family affair between A and L Companies," he said. "The boys asked me to join the party." He thought it over and added: "You could call it my initiation into the troop."

She held herself still, once more debating him in her mind. "The opinion of other men means a great deal to you, Kern."

"The opinion of my kind of men," he amended.

"Are they your kind?" she asked. "The ones you bunk with and march with? Are they really?"

"That's why I joined," he said. "To get back where I belong."

She shook her head, murmuring, "You're strange," and resumed her knitting. "You've had education and many pleasant things, but you go back to a raw and very rough kind of life. Doesn't it cause you any remorse to give up those nice things?"

He sat silent, turning it over in his own mind. Nothing had bothered him since joining, no regrets and no moments of indecision. He remembered now that he had felt at home when he stepped onto Fort Lincoln's parade; weight and care had fallen from him, and the feeling of emptiness within him had somehow been filled. Not one day since that time had he lacked peace of mind.

"You are thinking that I'm ducking out of civil life because it was too hard — letting the government do my thinking in return for eighteen dollars a month."

"It has occurred to me," she said.

"I had no obligations in civil life," he told her. "I had nothing — and I knew it. A man must feel he belongs to something. As long as he floats around space doing little chores that start and end with his hands and never reach his heart, he's no good to himself. Some things are real and some are only tinsel paper that people wrap themselves in, having nothing more important to do with their time. Dust is an honest thing, and so is sweat and the bruises you get from fighting."

"Do you suppose these other troopers think of that?" she said.

"Some do and some don't. Some are good and some are pretty

bad. But the point is that when the trumpet blows boots and saddles, they'll all swing up together, and when action begins they'll run forward together. That is what men were made for, Josephine."

She held her eyes down to her work while he talked, she kept them there. Shafter sank low in the chair, the back of his hair ruffled against it and his body sprawled in lank and bony lines. He watched her fingers move with the knitting needles, making little half circles of gracefulness. Small shades of expression softly darkened and softly lightened her face and her lips made their elusive changes as her thinking varied. He got up to fill the stove and noticed that the woodbox was empty; he left the house and got an armload of wood and brought it back. The silence of the house was a pleasant silence; he tipped his head, watching the ceiling, listening to the ticking of a clock. Now and then an echo from Bismarck's main street reached out.

"How old are you, Kern?"

"Thirty-two."

Her knitting needles wove in and out beneath her absorbed eyes, her profile against the strong light of the window was full-lipped and serene.

"Have you ever been married?"

"No," he said.

"Engaged?"

"Yes."

"Are you now?"

"No," he said.

She laid down her knitting and let her hands lie idle in her lap while she gave him an exacting appraisal. She was thoroughly serious, wholly wrapped up by her momentary interest in him. "It was something painful, wasn't it?"

He nodded and let that serve for an answer. Her glance searched all the way through him, and presently she shook her head and took up her knitting again, speaking as much to herself as to him. "It has left its effect. It isn't that you are cynical about women. I've never caught that in your talk, but you distrust women. You look at them as though they had qualities which men should be on guard against."

"Women," he said in his idle, speculative way, "are the only real beauty in the world. What good is a lovely sunset if a man can't embrace it? There is a need in him that neither sky nor earth nor music can fill. Only a woman can fill it."

She murmured: "You say that as if you believed it but didn't want to believe it."

"A woman is a wind, wild and sweet. A woman is a song. I have never thought differently."

"Kern," she said, "your trouble was that you wanted too much. No woman can be all that."

"There are rare meetings like that — of a man carrying to a woman all that he feels and needs, and receiving from her all that he hoped for."

"You have been deeply disappointed," she said.

"A man's not entitled to disappointment," he said. "The fault is more apt to be in him than in the woman. Therefore, he draws back and forgets about it."

"You have not forgotten."

"I have not forgotten that I was a fool," he said, quite careful with his words. "I will not be a fool twice."

She kept her attention on her knitting, her mouth drawn together in almost severe lines. She made no attempt to break the silence; she seemed done with him. Presently, in a little gesture of impatience, she put the needlework aside and rose and went into the kitchen. He heard her call back: —

"When does A Company have its ball for the enlisted men?"

"Two weeks away, I believe."

"It will remind you of other days."

"I had no intention of attending," he said.

She came out in a little while with a cup of coffee for him, and one for herself. She took her chair again. "One stretch of road between here and Fargo you'll want to watch. There's no shelter of any kind for thirty miles if a blizzard should catch you. It is between Romain's ranch and a little section house called Fossil Siding. When do you leave — when will you be back?"

"Leave in the morning. Should return in ten or twelve days unless the weather stops me."

She put her coffee cup aside and rose and stood at the window with her back to him. Her shoulders were square but rounded softly at the points and her black hair lay rolled and heavy on her head. She touched the pane idly and turned to him, looking across the room with a restless light in her eyes. He sat still, meeting her glance and seeing the shadow and shape of odd things come and vanish. She wasn't smiling but the thought of a smile was a hint at the corners of her mouth, in the tilt of her head. She took his coffee cup and went into the kitchen. He heard her move and then stand still; and suddenly his mind was fully on her and the thought of her went through him and kicked up its reaction. He got up and reached for his coat.

"This is a lazy man's life."

She came into the living room. "Have supper here."

"There's the team on my hands. Otherwise I'd accept."

She watched him button up the big overcoat and grow bulky. His shoulders made a sweep and the uniform took much of the first-noticed softness from him, toughening him. She noticed the scars on his knuckles.

"So you had your fight and crossed the river on a dark, rough night — and almost swamped. Is that what you like?"

He grinned. "That's what I like," he said. "It was a good party."

"I haven't been to a dance since early fall," she murmured.

He looked at her a moment. "It's strictly an enlisted man's ball. No officers and officers' ladies."

"So then?"

"You're for gentlemen and officers, Josephine."

"Am I?" she asked him, coolly meeting his attention. "How do you know that?"

He saw in her at that moment a reckless spirit. She had wanted something and she had asked for it; her eyes held his glance, with the hint of a temper as aggressive as his own. He said: "I can't be put in the position of refusing a lady's wish. Will you go to the ball with me?"

"Of course," she said.

She was smiling slightly, knowing what she had done to him, knowing also the boldness of her asking. He moved to the door and turned there; she was alert, she was carefully exploring his face with her eyes for things she seemed to want to know. "You gave yourself away," she told him. "If you weren't a gentleman it wouldn't have been difficult to refuse me."

"Maybe," he said, "I really wanted to take you." But he shook his head at her. "It is not a good thing for you. It will cut you out from being invited to officers' dances. When you let yourself be seen with an enlisted man, you are crossing one of the toughest boundaries in the world."

She started to tell him something, thought better of it, and moved around him to open the door. Then she said: "You are a rough-and-tumble man, Sergeant. But I think I can hold my own with you."

He grinned as he lifted his cap, and then went into the snow, openly laughing, and presently curled around the house with the sleigh. She was on the front porch and waved at him as he went by. She stood a considerable while in the biting, still air, now wishing she had told Shafter that Garnett had invited her to officers' ball and that she had accepted. It was the reason she had deliberately forced an invitation to the enlisted men's ball from Shafter. She knew, as a matter of intuition, that he disliked the officer. This, then, was her way of balancing the situation, of taking the edge from any resentment he might feel toward her for going with Garnett.

She turned into the house and closed the door, and stood with her back to it. "Why should I bother to go to the trouble of saving his feelings? What do his feelings matter to me? I am simply another woman he means to keep at a proper distance."

She remembered all that he had said, and she knew much that he had not said — the streaks of hopelessness and resentment, the imagination that he could not entirely subdue, the hunger that no amount of self-discipline could kill. He had partly given himself away, she realized. "The woman," she thought, "left her marks all over him. She must have been brutal about it, to produce his present state of mind. Yet even now he is not sure he doesn't love her. That's behind it all."

She moved across the room, despising the woman, whoever she was; ashamed of the woman, and outraged at a story she could only guess at.

X

Mr. Garnett Tries His Luck

AT REVEILLE he was up; by eight o'clock he had put the fort and the river behind him. There was a hundred pounds of mail in the sleigh, a week's emergency rations and a roll of bedding, and extra grain for the mules. Bismarck dropped behind a steel-gray winter haze — its housetops and its little winding columns of smoke; ahead of him stretched a white smoothness broken only by the line of telegraph poles and, at great intervals, the low-lying smudge of a ranch house. That first day out he saw several of these ranches; and put up at one of them that night. The second day brought a duller sky and a greater emptiness. The mules went steadily on, hauling the sleigh at a brisk clip where the snow lay thoroughly hardened by alternate freezing and thawing. When they reached soft patches the team fell to a slow, exhausting struggle. He passed two houses on the second day; on the third, he ran almost his whole trip with nothing in sight but the telegraph poles. He crossed little creeks frozen to the bottom, he flushed small bands of antelopes and saw where they had scratched away the snow for forage. The fourth day he came upon a party of warriors cutting out of the north on a hunting trip; they saw him and advanced until they identified his uniform and then turned away, sending back their insolent cries. The fifth evening brought him to a stalled freight train waiting for a snowplow; he stayed that night in the train's caboose, stabling the mules in an abandoned sod hut. The following afternoon, passing close-grouped farms, he came into Fargo — which was only another version of Bismarck. By daybreak the following morning he was on his way back, bearing not only mail but several packages for Bismarck merchants and a little pouch of despatches from department headquarters at St. Paul.

He brought with him also a week's collection of newspapers and read them at night, in one ranch house or another. President Grant

had taken the Indian matter into his hands and had ordered a
winter campaign to follow the failure of the Indians to return
peacefully to their reservations on the deadline of January 31. One
headline said: CUSTER WILL LEAD WINTER EXPEDITION. CAN BOY
GENERAL REPEAT BRILLIANT WASHITA STRATEGY? The *New York
Tribune* had a long and tempered essay on the ills and evils of
Indian affairs, deplored the instances of corruption and misdealing
which had characterized so much of white relations with the savage,
but sadly concluded that the march of white man's progress could
not be stopped, therefore making rigorous treatment of the Indian
the most humane in the long run. The *Boston Post* bitterly assailed
the greed of the white man and the white man's consistent disregard of his obligations.

The history of relations between white man and red has been an
unbroken story of rapacity, cruelty and of complete lack of feeling
on the part of the white. Nothing has been constant with him except
his sacred right to seize whatever land he wished from whatever
Indian tribe he wished. We have no reason to be proud of our
dealings with the weaker savage race. We have no right to call
ourselves a civilized or cultured people with that record against us.

But the *St. Louis Globe* reflected the view of the western settler
and trader and land-hungry emigrant.

There is no use entering into a discussion of the morals of the
white man versus the red man. All the debate in Christendom cannot blink the fact that the white man is a surging tide of conquest,
of settlement and progress, whereas the Indian is content to rove
nomadically across the land as he has done for the tens of thousands of years, ignoring an earth which could provide him riches
were he industrious enough to cultivate it. Primitive indolence and
barbaric narrowness is his character, nor does he wish for anything we call civilization. Let us not shed tears over the ills done
poor Lo. Poor Lo has been at the business of killing and raiding
and stealing for many centuries before the white man came. It is
his one great object in life, it is his profession and his pastime.
Whereas a white boy is taught to believe that the purpose of a man

is scientific and literary and social advancement, the one and only training an Indian boy ever receives is to go out and kill his enemy, thereby becoming great in his own tribe. Were the race of the Indian to die off tomorrow there would be no permanent handiwork behind him, no inventions, no scholarship except a few primitive daubs on this or that rock, no system of ethics at all, not one worthy thing to justify his tenantry upon the fairest of all continents. By contrast look upon the white man's record in a brief 250 years here. That should be answer enough to all the silly sentimentality current in the East. It is time now to end the endless marching and countermarching of skeleton cavalry columns commanded by officers who know nothing of savage warfare. It is time now to send in one large and determined expedition to crush savage resistance permanently and to confine the red man to the reservation, so that at last the white race may get on with its appointed destiny, which is to harness the continent and to build civilization's network across it.

The system of post traderships was under fire and Congressman Clymer had asked the House for authority to investigate the Indian Bureau and the War Department, suggesting scandal. Secretary of War Belknap was quoted as saying that yellow journalism made a mockery of an honest man's attempt at efficient administration. There was definitely, in all the papers, a growing preoccupation with the Indian question — and a growing scent of trouble brewing. There were also many items regarding Custer. He had given a talk at the Lotus Club. His spectacular presence was noted and admired at the theater.

Custer [said the *New York Herald*] has as much right as any man living to speak of Indians. His statement that one regiment of cavalry — with pardonable pride he mentions his own Seventh — could handle the Sioux in one campaign as effectively as ten years of treaty making and treaty breaking, must be seriously regarded. In any such campaign, who else has the skill, the matchless daring to equal his leadership? The Boy General of 1864 is now the mature Indian fighter, the darling of his troops, and in the full prime of his great powers.

There was the smell of bad weather in the air as Shafter moved westward over the empty, dull-glittering plain toward Lincoln.

They had been to see "Julius Caesar" played by their closest friend, Lawrence Barrett; and afterwards they had gone up to a mansion facing Central Park where, surrounded by money and power and considerable beauty, Custer had dominated the conversation both by his exuberance and by his reputation. Now, at two o'clock in the morning, the general and his wife returned to their hotel rooms.

The general was keyed up by the fullness of the evening, and at the mercy of his inexhaustible energy; he flung his hat and cape and dress coat the full length of the room and missed the chair at which he aimed. He let them lie and walked a circle of the sitting room while his wife went into the adjoining bedroom.

"Vacation's about gone, old girl," he called out. "We're coming to the end of our period in heaven."

"I'll regret going back," she said. "I've had such a nice time. And you've enjoyed yourself so much."

"No more shows, no more parties for another year. Maybe for two or three years. The army is a strange thing. A little glitter at retreat when the band plays and everybody's in full dress. A little of that followed by hours of drudgery and tedium. It is the tedium that eats out an officer's heart. Year after year of it."

She came out to him in her robe. "Autie, you shouldn't be restless. We've had such a good time. It's nice to have a famous husband. We're welcome in the homes of the rich, the powerful, the artistic, the intelligent. George Armstrong Custer rings the bell and the door opens. I thought of that tonight, watching you talk. I was very proud of you."

He looked at her, he smiled at her; he stood in a moment's rare repose, gentled by her softness, by her love. But it was only for a moment. He had supped at the table of the mighty, and the mighty had been deferent to him because he was General Custer; now he saw that ended as he turned back to his frontier post. He saw more than that. He saw the undramatic years stretch out ahead of him —a continuation of the long eleven years which had followed the

Civil War. And as he thought of those years of patience and plodding and unspectacular duties performed, he had his fear. He was a child of adventure; his fame had come of moments of crisis and headlong action. Routine was death to him, but he saw nothing forward but routine. He had reached the pinnacle at twenty-five and all the subsequent years had been anticlimax, a wasting away of those precious hours which a man so meagerly possessed — those hours in which he had his chance at everlasting glory. At thirty-six he was less than he had been at twenty-five. In another ten years he would be forty-six, one more middle-aged Civil War officer whose greatness was only a fading memory with the people, whose place in the sun was taken by younger men seizing their moments of luck.

"Oh, Libby," he said, almost groaning, "I'm in a blind alley. There's no chance open, nothing to reach for. I see the stupid and the dull all around me, rising above me, fawning or tricking their way to power. My enemies are in command of the War Department, cheating me out of chances, giving other men places I ought to have, entrusting incompetent officers to places of responsibility to which I'm entitled. I'm handcuffed. If there was a break I might make, if there was an alley, an opening anywhere, I'd seize it."

"Autie," said Mrs. Custer, whose softness was strength, whose quietness was the only discipline he knew, "what more could you want?"

He sighed greatly and smiled at her. He went forward and kissed her, turned obedient and teasing. "You have a hell of a time with me, don't you, Libby?"

She said: "Civilization is not too good for you. I think we will be happier when we return to the command." But a cloud passed across her expressive face as she remembered that spring was not far away. Spring was her dread, spring was a black cloud that shut out her life's sun — for spring meant campaigning, it meant Autie marching away. Suddenly she turned back into the bedroom.

Custer seized the day's paper and lay out full length on the floor of the room to read it. He became engrossed in a front-page story concerning Congressman Clymer's proposed investigation of the War Department; and presently he sprang up, went to the writing table and sat down at it. Mrs. Custer heard his pen scratching violently through the quietness.

"To whom are you writing, Autie?"

"I'm offering my services as witness to Clymer. I think we shall get to the bottom of some scandal, and I know enough of it to lend a hand."

She was silent a moment, then spoke again. "Do you think it wise?"

"Wise or not," he said, "I shall do it."

He finished his letter, addressed the envelope and sealed it; he leaned back in the chair, feeling a thrust of hope. It might lead somewhere; it might lead to an opportunity. It might give him an opportunity to smash at his enemies, to bring him before the people on an issue. It was, at least, an opening — and openings were rare things for a frontier officer. He studied this and grew slightly excited at the thought. He saw himself once more in the current, as he had been before; he saw himself out of the slack water at last. He had to have action to survive, since action was his only gift; and survival and triumph and public acclaim were to him the same sources of life they were to the other public men who fought tooth and claw for them. Fame was a jungle in which predatory beasts roamed; there were no rules in that jungle, only a bitterest kind of fighting. And at fighting he had considerable skill.

Garnett called for Josephine at eight, stood a moment in the Russell living room to give her his full admiring glance and murmured: "You must forgive me for using a very old phrase. I had no idea you were so — " he paused and seemed to search himself for the word, and went on in an impulsive way —"so damned beautiful."

She was round and mature within a black dress whose solid coloring was broken by little streaks of gold thread along her breasts and sleeves. Her hair, extremely black, lay high and shining on her head, exposing white neck and ears, and a pair of earrings moved slightly as her head turned. She watched him, smiling but not entirely taken in. "I hear you're a gallant man, Lieutenant."

He gave her a keen answering smile and stood sharp-eyed before

her. The smile gradually faded. "I suppose so," he agreed. "I suppose
the presence of women inclines me toward the kind of speech they
want to hear. My feeling is that a woman living out here, with little
enough in the way of comfort or luxury, has got something extremely
fine in her soul. Even the washerwoman who follows her sergeant
from one dismal hovel to another."

"Particularly that woman," corrected Josephine.

"Gallantry or not," he said and was wholly serious, "I mean what
I say about you."

"It is at least pleasant to hear."

"And now to the ball," he said, suddenly returned to his high
humor; and escorted her to the cutter. They made a rapid passage
to the fort and came upon the commissary building, which served as
the ballroom, its stores pushed aside and its bare walls and rafters
decorated with colored paper shields, crossed arms and bunting. The
regimental band sat on a platform at one end of the room. Major
Reno, commanding in the absence of Custer, led the grand march
with his wife; afterwards the crowd broke into sets for the quadrille.

The officers of the five companies stationed at Lincoln were present in full dress uniforms, gold epaulets, sash and regimental cord
draped over the shoulder; and this color flashed and glittered against
the dresses of the ladies, and there was a sharp exuberance in all
of them, a health and a happiness and a childlike response to one
night's freedom. The Benteens and DeRudios and Gibsons came up
from Rice where H and M Companies were stationed — and remem-
brances were spoken for the five troops on far-away station — for
Captain Keogh's I Company and Captain Ilsley's E Company at
Fort Totten, and for B, G and K in distant Louisiana. The regiment was a clannish thing even though it had not been together as
a complete unit for many years; in spite of its jealousies and cliques
and animosities, the Seventh was tied together by its traditions, its
decade of service.

There were other townspeople, besides Josephine, at the ball; and
now and then she saw Charley Reynolds, reputed to be the best
scout in the West, come shyly inside and watch the proceedings. He
was a small man, very quiet and very soft of speech, dressed in a

neat blue suit and black tie; somewhere he had a past which he never mentioned but his eyes were sad blue eyes above a round, smooth face and a semicircle mustache carefully kept. Other officers from the infantry companies stationed at the post were likewise in attendance.

They danced the sets, they danced the polka, the schottische and the waltz. Josephine went swinging away in the arms of this officer or that one; she stood in one little group or another, all of them gay and all charged with little bursts of gossip and laughter and bantering. They stood at the punch bowl — lemonade made with citric acid — they lightly ridiculed one another, out of familiar association, repeating the old, old jokes and the ancient recollections.

"I admire that dress," said Mrs. Smith to Josephine.

"I bought it this fall in the East. I suppose it's the last new one I'll have for three or four years."

"Why," said Mrs. Smith, "I'm wearing one six years old."

Mrs. Calhoun smiled regretfully. "I bought this in 1869. I've never been close enough to the East to get another. It has been altered and let out so often that it is nothing but a mass of thread and stitches. Miss Russell makes old women out of all of us."

Annie Yates and her husband joined the group. Captain Yates ran the back of his fingers across his yellow mustaches. "Myles, I hear your saddler got drunk and snowbound last night."

Moylan nodded. "We are thawing him out one section at a time."

"It shows," said Yates slyly, "what drunkenness will do for a company."

Moylan grinned. "Just have your first sergeant mention it to my first sergeant, if you want to know which outfit is the best at indoor fighting. For recommendations, ask L Company."

"What about that fracas?" asked Yates, turning to Garnett.

Garnett gave Moylan a quick glance and met the captain's cool attention. He flushed a little when he answered Yates. "I know nothing of it."

"Quite a brawl, I heard," said Yates indifferently and moved to his partner as the music began. Major Barrows bowed at Josephine and led her away, leaving his wife for Garnett's attention. Garnett put his arm about her slim waist, adjusted himself at the proper waltz distance and swung her out upon the floor.

Neither of them spoke for a considerable time, he staring over the top of her dark hair and she watching the couples about her with an expressionless disinterest. Now and then she caught sight of Josephine and followed the girl with a narrowed glance, her lips moving together by a pure reaction over which she had no control. Finally she said in her coolest voice: "Your taste is excellent, Edward."

Garnett said, equally cool, "Do you object?"

"Why should I?"

But he knew she was furious, and the knowledge pleased him. "I wish," he murmured, "I might hold you closer."

"Be careful," she murmured, "my husband is watching."

"Does he suspect?"

"It is never possible to know what he thinks or what he knows, Edward. But we must be very discreet."

"I shall have the cutter at the same place tomorrow afternoon."

"No," she murmured, "not so soon. I can't always be finding reasonable excuses to go to town."

He said nothing but when she looked up she noticed the shadow of sulkiness on his face; the tips of her fingers dug into his shoulder. "Don't," she whispered. "Don't, Edward."

"I can't help it," he said.

She grew coldly, politely angry with him. "You can help it well enough to bring a very pretty girl to the ball. Don't act out a part."

They danced the rest of it in complete silence, once around the huge hall. The music found them at the far end. He took her arm and walked her slowly back toward her husband. He looked straight ahead of him when he spoke. "Tomorrow afternoon, Margaret?"

They had almost rejoined the group when he heard her soft, smothered answer: "All right." Then she turned from him to her husband who stood by with his usual taciturnity. She smiled at him. "Are you having a good time, Joseph?"

He looked down at her in the manner with which she was so familiar — some part of his mind and heart loving her, some part

of him grimly hanging to his iron reserve. "I always enjoy myself
when I see you having a good time."

She kept her eyes on him until he turned to speak to Calhoun;
and then she ventured a surreptitious side glance at Josephine Rus
sell, who stood beside Garnett. She hated the girl in the proud way
of a beautiful woman recognizing loveliness in another woman;
and, knowing Garnett, she wondered what secrets might lie behind
Josephine's calm. Benteen came up to claim her, his cheeks scarlet
against the silver-white magnificence of his hair. Crusty and con-
tentious as he was, he unbent to her. "My pleasure, Mrs. Barrows."

At two in the morning the ball ended and the various couples
met in one house or another for coffee and bacon, and carefully
treasured eggs long packed down in water glass. At three, Garnett
returned Josephine to her house and at her invitation stepped inside.
The elder Russell sat asleep in a rocker with a stout fire going; and
woke and moved off to bed. Garnett stood in the middle of the
room, holding his dress hat tucked under an arm, letting his glance
openly admire the girl. She removed her coat and stood by the stove,
as fresh and as awake now as she had been seven hours before;
there was a tremendous amount of vitality in her, and a great deal
of practical wisdom which now and then came out with its faint
irony, and a capacity for emotion lying well down within her. He
wondered if any man had stirred it.

"Thank you, Mr. Garnett, for the most delightful kind of an
evening."

He made a little bow with his head, still watching her with his
appreciative eyes. She turned to warm her hands at the stove and
her attitude at the moment — the straightness of her body with its
round and full outlines — kicked a hard emotion through him. He
was so interested in her that when she suddenly turned her head
she caught him with this unguarded appreciation in his eyes; and
her glance came back to him knowing what he thought. He was a
handsome creature whose judgment was critical and therefore his
interest was a flattering thing; she admitted that to herself. He was
dangerous as well — his smile, his gallantry, and his words.

"Am I welcome in this house?" he asked.

"Yes," she said.

"I should like to pick you up for a ride in the cutter some morning."

She didn't answer it; she simply nodded. He drew a breath and walked toward her until she was within reach of him and he looked down at her and waited for a break in her eyes.

"Don't spoil a good impression, Mr. Garnett."

"You're still thinking I am particularly solicitous of ladies, aren't you?"

"I think," she said, "they are a challenge to your talents."

Sometimes she threw him off stride by her frankness; in moments like this, when he wished for tenderness and emotion, her words were cold water flung in his face. He flushed somewhat. "I find myself in a bad situation with you. I don't want you to suspect me. Women have played their light games of flirt with me. I have responded in kind. You seem to be aware of that."

"Let's not be too serious at three o'clock in the morning."

"I don't want to be misunderstood. I want you to know I'm dead serious toward you. This is no game with me, Josephine. When I leave here tonight I'll be troubled with myself all the way home."

"Now why, for mercy's sakes?" she demanded, really surprised.

He shrugged his shoulders. "As you stood there at the stove just now I grew completely disgusted with myself. I never thought any woman could humble me in that manner. Do you see what I mean?"

"Perhaps," she said, studying him with considerable penetration. She had a great deal of self-control, and much pride. She was, he thought, as strong a woman emotionally as he had seen; but in her lips, in her voice tones, in the slanted glances she sometimes gave him there was the hint of powerful convictions and will. He had the feeling that she could, if necessary, draw a revolver and shoot a man down and not go to pieces afterwards; it was that thing he chiefly discovered as he analyzed her, that courage and simplicity of action which was near to being primitive. The truth was, he knew less of her from observation than he knew of most women; her character had a way of eluding his inspection.

"Why should we be too involved in all this, Edward?"

He made a little bow to her and said "Good night," and turned to the door. As he opened it he swung back, and said with a complete confidence: "You must know me for what I am. I mean to have you, I mean to make you want me."

Trooper Lovelace ate his supper in a hurry, a fact noticed and commented on by Bierss. "What's the matter with your appetite, Lovelace?"

The young lad flushed under the attention of the roundabout troopers and got up from the table. "Nothing," he said. "Nothing at all."

"Love's bad for the appetite," said Bierss. But he went easy on Lovelace. Crude and obscene as his comment could be, he forbore using it now. All he added was, "You got Purple to beat, Lovelace. He's stickin' close to Suds Row."

"Who said anything about Suds Row?" retorted Lovelace and left the mess hall. He was relieved to get away from the crowd, for he lived in deadly fear that one of the troopers might say something concerning Mary which would compel him to fight. It wasn't the fighting which troubled him so much; it was her name being mentioned at all in the barrack. He wrapped his heavy coat around him and passed into the frigid night; and eagerness to see her again caused him to buck his way rapidly through the snow.

When he came before Mulrane's house he stopped, the shyness in him making it difficult for him to knock on the door and face the family. He stepped away and moved on toward the bluff, but he hadn't gone far when he saw a pair coming up the street, and heard Mary's voice carry forward in the brittle-cold air. The other figure was tall against her, whereby he knew it was Purple.

He went dead cold and his stomach turned over. He hated Purple violently, and he was shocked at Mary; but most of all he felt the humiliation of standing here as they came forward and saw him. They moved on until he saw Purple's grinning face — and heard Purple speak to him like a grown man making talk to a little boy: "You're out late, son."

"Is that so?" said Lovelace, and felt self-disdain for so feeble an answer. Mary's face was round and troubled in the darkness. Her voice was softly hurried.

"Frank," she said, "we're going in the house now. Come on."

"No," he said, "I was just walking by," and cut around them and went on. He heard Purple say something, and laugh; and the sound of it burned like an iron through him. He stopped at the edge of the bluff and swung around. They were before her house and a little later he heard Purple's boots go gritting through the snow. The house door opened, and closed. She had gone inside. Lovelace moved up the street, thinking of a dozen sharp and challenging things he might have said to Purple, in answer to the man's arrogant manner. He thought of them now; but now they were too late. He passed the Mulrane house with his head down, and heard Mary speak to him.

"Frank," she said, "wait a minute."

She had opened and closed the door, but she hadn't gone in. She stood in the shadows, waiting for him, and as he came up she lifted her head and smiled for him. "Come in now, Frank."

"No," he said.

"You're angry."

"No," he said. "I didn't mean to butt in."

"I didn't know you were coming," she said. "How was I to know?" Then she grew a little irritated. "Am I supposed to just sit around and wait for you and turn everybody away?"

"No," he said. "Not at all."

"Well, then," she said, "don't be foolish."

"A little cold for taking a walk, wasn't it?"

She tossed her head at him. "I've walked in colder weather, with you."

"And kissed him, too, I suppose."

She delayed her answer, watching him, troubled and uncertain with this scene. "I let him kiss me," she admitted slowly.

"Well," he said, stricken dull, "good night."

"Wait. A girl has to know things, doesn't she? She has to know whether she thinks more of one man than another. A girl isn't a bolt of cloth to be wrapped up and set on the shelf by the first man that comes along. She's got to know who's right. A man looks around to find the right one, doesn't he?"

"Well," said Lovelace, "maybe he's the right one, and maybe I'm not. When I kiss a girl I'm not fooling around."

"You shouldn't say that to me, Frank. I'll do what I please until I make up my mind."

He descended lower and lower into a sweltering gloom. He sank like a rock through layers of disillusion and renouncement and broken dreams. He said, "All right, Mary," and moved up the street with personal tragedy weighting his shoulders down.

Her voice came after him: "Aren't you going to invite me to your troop ball?"

"No," he said. "Good-by, Mary."

He moved through the guard gate and tramped along the row of barracks; he went all the distance to the north guard gate and turned back to company quarters. He stretched out on his bunk, face up; he was wholly crushed and there was no hope in him. He thought of deserting and going to Mexico. Then he said to himself: "No, I'll stay here until summer campaign. She'll see."

XI

Memory of a Woman

SHAFTER reached Fort Lincoln thirteen days after his departure from it and dropped off his mail and despatches. He had brought back from Fargo a barrel of apples, something rarely had on the frontier. Half of the barrel he left in the barrack room; the other half he divided into three sacks, taking one to Mrs. Moylan and one to Lieutenant Smith's wife. Both ladies were genuinely appreciative. Mrs. Smith looked at them and took up one and laid it against her cheek. "When I was a child in New York, Sergeant, I used to do this to take the winter chill out of them. We had a big root cellar with bins on each side for apples and potatoes. Sometimes the snow got so deep between the house and the root cellar that we tunneled a passageway between." She looked beyond the sergeant, the vision of it very clear to her, drawing her back to her younger years. "Apples and nuts and home-cured raisins at night around the big fireplace. There were eight of us — eight children, and now they're scattered all over the earth." She gave him a bright short smile. "Your present took me back, Sergeant. Thank you."

He carried the mail on through for Fort Rice that same afternoon and returned to Lincoln next noon. This was Saturday, and the men of the troop had spent most of the day dressing up the quartermaster building for their ball that night. Receiving Moylan's permission to use the mail sleigh, Shafter presented himself at Josephine's house promptly at seven-thirty.

When she came to the door, he was astonished at the rough shock that went through him. Her presence did that to him, the smile breaking over her lips, the touch of her hand on his arm, the sudden view of loveliness she presented to him. He closed the door and stood against it, watching her move away and turn and face him. She said: "It is a little early. Take off your overcoat for a moment."

He was a tall sharp shape inside the coat's length and heaviness. It fitted snug against shoulders and chest and added to his height.

He stood wholly attentive as he watched her, a black-haired man with long and broad bones and a face whipped by the wind; and the wind and darkness — and the sight of her — sharpened his eyes. She noticed it and made a slight turn and a slight gesture with her arms and stood before him for his inspection, the smile steady. "Will I do for your ball, Kern?"

He said: "I've not seen anyone like you."

"Come now," she said, "you've seen no woman at all for a week. That's no comparison."

"I can go farther back than that," he said, soberly deliberate.

She tipped her head, immensely curious as to his past, caring about it with a genuine emotion. Her smile changed and grew smaller. "How far back must you go to find a woman you'd want to stand beside me?"

"Once," he said, "a long time ago, there was one."

"She meant a great deal?" asked Josephine, very softly.

He nodded. "At the time it was one of those affairs which seemed — " and a self-amused and slightly harder tone came into his voice — "eternal. The kind you make everlasting vows on. When the earth is wonderful and everything is fair to behold and you could fight all the dragons on earth."

She had ceased to smile; the glow left her face and she stood still, listening. "Where is she now?"

"Somewhere, alive."

"Alive in you. I hear her walking around your heart."

"All you hear is echoes."

"How long since you've seen her?"

"Eight years."

"Echoes don't last that long. Only hope does."

"Or disillusion. I have no desire to hope."

She turned slowly away, moving toward the corner table in the room. She put her hands lightly on a book, and moved the book, and spoke over her shoulder. "It must have been an intense affair to leave so lasting an impression."

"A man and woman in love," he said, "is scarcely a mild thing, is it?"

"That depends on the woman and on the man."

"I'm speaking for myself."

"Yes, you have a great deal of depth. I have only recently discovered that in you."

"A man learns to cover himself and protect himself from further commitments which will break him apart. He goes sour and skeptical."

"You're not."

"You've not heard me express it."

She turned about. "Kern, I don't think I like to be the instrument which brings back those memories to you."

Humor moved into his eyes. He had an edge to his spirits, and appreciation of her was a clear print on his face. He had changed a great deal in the short time he had been in the army, she thought; he was a more aggressive man, a simpler and less involved man enjoying the physical sensations, the hearty pleasures, the old, sentimental loyalties. Still, she remembered his one grim remark concerning disillusion, and was troubled by it, though she failed to understand why she should let it disturb her. For a moment the fine, glowing feeling of his presence had left her; suddenly she shrugged her shoulders and smiled again.

"What a strange way to start an evening. Time to go, isn't it?"

He moved over the room to lift her coat from a chair. He held it for her and was for the moment close to her, so that when she turned to him and looked up she saw the image of her face in his eyes. His lids crept together as he watched her, as her presence hit him again with its sound jolt. She saw what was happening to him but she stood still, her lips slightly apart. She thought: "This is foolish," and felt the heavy undertow of feeling sweep against her, unsettle her resolution, and turn her reckless. She made one sharp move to break that moment, and wheeled away. He stood still and presently she swung back, her face almost severe in its darkness, but her eyes glowing against him. For a moment they watched each other, completely still; and then she lifted her chin, breaking the turbulence of feeling between them, and took his arm.

"Time to go," she repeated.

He brought her back at one in the morning and escorted her to the door. He lifted his hat and he said: "Thank you. Now you've tried the high and the low. Good night."

She said. "Come in for coffee."

"No," he said.

She had a way of lifting her head in a sudden motion when she was angry and when she was determined. She said: "Tie the mules and put the blankets over them. Then come in, Sergeant."

When he had taken care of the mules he came into the house and found Russell standing sleepily by the stove. Russell said: "My girl is staying out late. Three last week and one o'clock tonight."

"My record is better than the lieutenant's by two hours," said Shafter.

"That's right," said Russell and left the room. Josephine had dropped her coat on a chair and for a moment had watched Shafter's face; now she went into the kitchen. Shafter stood with his back to the stove, hearing her move about the other room. He got a cigar from his pocket and lighted it and he drew in the heavy smoke and relished it, at the same time thinking of the waltz tune swinging them around and around the hall. It was Sergeant Hines who had privately said to him, during a break in the dancing: "You're flyin' high, Shafter. She was at officers' ball last week with Garnett."

He listened to her footfalls and admitted that she drew his attention, and he recalled that he had thought of her during the thirteen days between Fargo and Bismarck. He pulled the cigar from his mouth and stood with his face tipped toward the floor, gravely aware of what was happening to him and stubbornly convinced that he had to prevent it from happening.

She came from the kitchen with coffee for both of them and a little tray with bread and honey and cheese. She put these things on a table and motioned to him. He brought up a chair and sat down opposite her. She sat back with her coffee, her eyes scanning him over the rim of the cup, quite thoughtful. "Who told you about my going with Garnett?"

"One of the boys."

"I should have told you two weeks ago that I planned to go with him."

"If I'd known it I wouldn't have taken you."

"Why?"

"A woman can't play both sides of the line. I'm on one side of it and Garnett's on the other. You're an officers' woman. In going with me you have shut yourself out of being invited to the officers' side again."

"Isn't that my affair more than yours?"

"No," he said.

She sipped at her coffee, never for a moment taking her eyes from him. He was seemingly at ease, but she knew he was violently angry and she hated to have him that way.

"It really isn't that," she told him. "It's Garnett, isn't it?"

"Let's forget it."

"Nothing would please me better," she coolly answered. "But you have no intention of forgetting it. So it had better be talked out before it gets worse."

He used his calm, stubborn voice on her. "How would it help?"

"I don't know," she said. "That's what I'm trying to discover. You were embarrassed by him in this house once. Is that the cause of your disliking him so greatly?"

"Josephine," he said, "I hope you had a pleasant evening," and rose. He smiled at her, but he had drawn away from her. She sat still, watching him pull into his coat, and she wanted to ask him if common jealousy lay at the roots of his change toward her but she could not bring herself to the direct question.

"It started out very well, Kern," she told him, "and ended badly. But I really forced myself on you, so I shall not complain." Abruptly she began to feel a slow outrage at the whole situation. "I have liked most of the changes I have seen in you. I do not like this one at all."

It broke through the reserve behind which he seemed to want to take shelter. "It is Garnett," he admitted. "But it goes a long way back. There's no use adding to that."

"If it is so far in the past, why bring it forward to influence your judgment of me? I have nothing to do with your past, or your quarrels."

"That's right," he said, very dry. "You're also trying to tell me I have no business in making an issue of your going with Garnett."

"Yes," she said. "I was trying to tell you that."

"You're right. And that leaves the matter pretty straight. As I said before, you're an officers' woman and I have no business here at all." He took up his dress hat and bowed slightly at her and turned to the door.

"Is that your way of saying good-by, Kern?"

He swung. She had shaken him out of his hardness and she had made him sad. She saw the sadness lie darkly around his eyes and his mouth. He nodded. "I don't believe in tangling up somebody's life — and I've spent a good many years trying to untangle my own."

She rose and spoke in an almost antagonistic tone. "Where is the tangling? Aren't you taking in too much territory to make anything out of a dinner, a few visits and a dance?"

"You misjudge yourself, Josephine," he said.

She had not convinced him, she had not changed him, and she was not holding him. Knowing it she hit him with deliberate unfairness. "Did you run from Garnett once before — as you're doing now?"

He let an enormous sigh out of his chest as he came back to her. She hated what she had done and she was ashamed of herself and stood still when he looked down with his gray, dismal expression. "You don't know me very well," he said and took her arms and pulled her forward. "It would have been better if you'd left me alone." He dropped his head and kissed her, holding her so strongly with his hands that she felt pain in her ribs. Then he stepped back. "That was foolish," he said.

"Was it?" she asked.

"You knew it was coming," he said, thoughtfully watching her.

"I usually know when a man wants to kiss me."

"That's not hard to read on a man. The difficult thing is to know what he means by the kiss."

"Last time you kissed me it was for the purpose of offending me and getting rid of me. What was your meaning this time?"

"We're fighting now," he said. "It isn't worth that."

"What would you fight for?"

"A crooked deal at cards," he said, "a spilled drink, a dirty name — a shove in the ribs."

His words deliberately crowded her out, deliberately kept him inside a man's world. She was hurt by the way he spoke, and she thought she knew why he had spoken. "You've had one fight over a woman and now you think there's no woman worth that trouble. You have taken most of the nonsense out of your life, haven't you, Kern? You are very safe with your little comforts."

She was greatly embittered and she wanted to punish him. Even so she listened carefully to him when he spoke, seeking to pull aside the screening of his words to fathom what terrible experience had left him so dull and without faith.

"A woman is beauty, Josephine, and all men worship beauty. Some men always see it from a safe distance and die happy with their illusion. Some men come upon a woman and touch her and possess her and never regret it. But there are men who have no such luck. When they come upon their shrine and touch the beauty they have worshiped from afar for so long — all that beauty fades and dies out." He paused a moment and then added the one and terrible comment: "It is hard for a man to come upon this shrine and see the finger marks of other worshipers before him."

"From you," she said, pitying him even as she hated him. "From you who have rolled in the dust and been beaten down in barroom brawls."

"Different," he said with his gray smile remaining. "A man's sins are honest. He wants his beauty to be the same way." He looked at her with the smile disappearing. "How did I come to speak of all this?"

"I drew you out. I don't like you, Kern."

"The first honest thing said tonight." Then he shook his head. "No, the kiss was also honest. But it is better to end a thing properly than to nourish miserable illusions."

She said: "You will never cease to nourish your illusions."

"Then," he said, "I'm a fool."

She threw his words back to him. "Yes, you're a fool. But for the opposite reason. For thinking you can live without illusions. You'll never have anything else half as real. Good night."

She listened to him cross the porch and drop into the snow. Later she heard him run the sleigh and team around the house, heading away for the post. He was still before her in the room, his shape, his height, his face with its swings of feeling. Until this night he had guarded himself well, and then had let the screen slip aside to expose the wreckage within — the old love that had run through him like a fire and had burned out to leave nothing but the charred skeleton of hope behind. "I was right," she thought, "I should never have permitted myself to be interested in him."

It surprised her that he had so profoundly shaken her, had aroused a momentary fury against him, and then a pity. He was a man emptied out by catastrophe and now living in a state of guarded suspense, fearing that some other catastrophe might shake him again. He had pulled away from all the fine prodigal emotions of living because of that. Yet she corrected herself, knowing she had wrongly estimated him. He had too much in him deliberately to starve out all his feelings and therefore he had retreated to the world of men.

It was a tragedy and she felt it. She stood still, wondering why it should go so hard with her, and presently she understood. She had allowed herself to put her first hopes in him, his smile, his strength, his imagination and tenderness — all those things which made a man sound and good; and now stood by and watched him throw those things contemptuously aside. It hurt her badly.

XII

The Gods Cease to Smile

SHAFTER was in Fargo on Christmas Day. He had dinner at the rail-road restaurant and moved to the saloon to play poker until the mood went out of him and he bucked his way through a hard-driving snowstorm to the hotel and lay long awake, listening to the wind whining thin and sharp along the wall of the building. Darkness pressed down upon Fargo so heavily that the town's lights, passing through window pane and doorway, were at once absorbed. On the blackened, weather-riddled street a gunfight erupted and briefly lasted. Somewhere in the hotel a music machine pricked out sentimental tunes steadily; he listened to those little tinny melodies and was carried back and carried down until he turned savage from the memories of his life.

The storm pounded the earth for three days. It screamed through the town and drove drifts against the windward side of buildings until men were able to walk out of second-story windows. It snapped telegraph lines eastward and stopped trains from St. Paul. It moved out of the northern emptiness like great wild sea waves, higher and higher, more and more violent, until the impact of this fury thundered against Fargo's walls and carried away all insecure things, and shook each building on its foundation. Fargo's citizens counted ranks and named those who had been caught away from home and knew that death rode abroad.

There was a rope stretched from the hotel to the restaurant and from the restaurant to the saloon; along this confined pathway the citizens blindly moved. Men who had come in from the outskirts of town at the beginning of the blizzard dared not attempt the half-mile journey to their homes. They slept in the hotel, ate in the restaurant and spent the rest of their hours in the saloon. A poker game, started on the first day, went intermittently on to the end; and when

Shafter rose from the table on the morning of the fourth day and heard the strange, hollow stillness abroad, he had five hundred dollars in his pockets.

It was beyond New Year, however, before the mail from St. Paul came in; and the homeward journey across the drift-drowned land took him ten days. When he came into A Company's barracks, Hines said: "Where were you when it started?"

"Fargo."

"The boys were bettin' even money you were caught out."

That night Garnett dropped into Josephine's house for dinner and mentioned the arrival of the mail. Josephine said: "Did he have trouble getting through?"

"Shafter? I don't know." He observed the girl's lightened spirits and after the elder Russell had taken himself off to bed, Garnett commented on it. "You have a fancy for him don't you?"

"I'd worry about any man traveling in this weather," she said.

It was not a direct answer, Garnett realized, and he pushed his point. "That wasn't what I asked."

"Yes," she told him, "I like the sergeant."

He smiled his best smile. "I envy any living thing which has part of your heart or your interest."

"Edward, did you know him before he came here?"

He had been smiling at her, and he still smiled; but she noticed him change within, grow reticent, grow cautious. He struggled with his answer, not wishing to answer her, but she kept the pressure of her glance on him, making him say with great reluctance: "Yes, I knew him."

"Were you once friends?"

He said, "Good friends, once."

"Why did you quarrel?"

"Do you have to know that, Josephine?"

"I suppose I'm too curious," she said, and turned away from him to the far corner of the room. She sat down and picked up her knitting, at once absorbed in it. She changed the conversation by saying: "This is your first winter out here, isn't it? You must watch the weather from now until April. It can be very treacherous."

"I've heard that," he said. But he was troubled at the way the scene had gone, and dissatisfied at the showing he made with her. A woman's mind was a fertile thing. She would perhaps ask him no more about his past, but she would invent one answer after another to fill in the unsolved story — and by this process he might be injured in her eyes. He sat in the chair with a posed ease, the warmth of the room making his ivory cheeks ruddy; his hair tumbled forward on his head and gave him a negligent handsomeness. He tapped the chair with the index finger of his right hand — a broad, long hand with a heavy diamond ring showing out its glitter; he dropped into a somber study.

She looked up and saw him thus off guard and tried to fathom the realness of the man. There were times when he deliberately put himself on his best behavior toward her; she always knew these times and always discounted them. There were other moments when she felt he wanted her to see him for whatever he was, when he tried to be only human and natural, as though he had discovered in her a realism which cut through any pose he might adopt. He knew his own striking appearance and he took pains to be seen at his best, and yet, in his own way, he had much of the rough masculinity she had observed in Shafter. Always, in studying Garnett, she had Shafter in her mind; he was a constant reminder in her head so that now he was somewhere in the room, looking at her with his gray eyes and with his smile which covered his real feelings.

"Edward," she murmured, "don't chase your thoughts around."

"Well," he said, "I've never been noted for heavy thinking. I'm surprised at myself. The things I keep going back to, the things I keep stumbling over. Regrets — and all that."

"What regrets?"

"Things that would have been better undone."

"Women, I suppose."

"Looking at you, they're just shadows."

"That's a strange thing to say."

"It is strange for me to be here wishing I could say what I want to say."

"I never knew you to lack self-expression."

THE GODS CEASE TO SMILE

"I never have," he admitted. "That's it. I have told other women how beautiful I thought they were. I have even told a woman I was in love with her. I have said those things, not entirely meaning them. Now I want to say them because I mean them. I wish I had never used those words before."

"You're frank at least."

"It is my only chance, with you." He got up, walking toward her. He looked down. "Do you expect him tonight? He came back today. I suppose he'll come to see you."

"I don't think so," she said.

"You've been kind to me lately. Do you have any particular feeling toward him, Josephine?"

She answered him with an almost irritable impatience. "No."

"Do you trust me?"

She ceased her knitting and looked up, carefully choosing her answer. "Yes," she said, "I trust you."

It made a tremendous impression on him. He grew buoyant, he made a swift motion with his arms. "I'd like to wrap you in fur and drive you down the Avenue in the most elegant cab in New York. I'd like to dine you at Terry's and take you to the theater. I'd like to sit by and watch your lips grow red when you smile. You are the most beautiful woman in the world in evening clothes. There is body and strength to you. There's — "

"Edward," she said, "don't."

His intemperate feelings controlled him. "You see," he murmured, "that's how I feel. If you trust me, believe me also." He swung around and got his coat and shrugged himself into it. She laid aside her knitting to watch him and noticed how, unconsciously, he straightened himself before her to show himself to best advantage; it was a thing he couldn't help. "There's a place in New Orleans, in the Quarter. When I think of it I think of you. A restaurant down an alley, with a back courtyard and an old man who plays the violin while you eat — "

"Did you take a woman last time you were there?"

"Yes."

"Shame on you for wishing to take me there then."

"I know," he said. "I know. You see how it is? Well, let's go for a sleigh ride out to the Benson farm tomorrow."

"Don't you ever have duty at the post?"

"Winter's a dreary time for soldiering. Nothing to do. Old stories, old faces. We all get sick of one another, and therefore try to keep away from each other. Two o'clock?"

She murmured: "We had a drive two days ago. Let's wait another week, Edward."

"Then invite me to supper."

"I shall," she said. "But not this week."

He said quietly, "I understand."

She found herself irritated. "What do you understand, Edward?"

"You do expect Shafter. Good night, Josephine."

He was not a humble man and therefore it was remarkable to her that he left with so much quietness. She took up her knitting but held it still; she listened to the wall clock strike nine and restlessness destroyed her sense of comfort. She put the knitting aside and got her coat and hat and an old wool muffler and stepped into the night. Coldness held both wind and blackness in its frozen grip and the sliding of her feet on the snow brought up crackling echoes which went abnormally large before her. She turned into Bismarck's street and strolled along it, almost alone. The night marshal passed her and stopped to leave his warning. "Twenty-seven below, Josephine. Don't stay out in this too long." She went on until she reached the post office. It was closed, as she knew it would be, but she looked both ways on the street with hope in her heart, and then turned into her father's store.

The night clerk was serving a last customer before closing time. She moved idly around the counter and got herself a cracker and cut a piece of cheese and dipped a pickle from the big barrel; she sat on the counter's edge and swung one leg while she ate. Two squaws came in and made signs for tobacco. She made the transaction, speaking a few Sioux words to them, and watched them leave.

"Why don't you go home, Jo?" asked the clerk. "That pickle will spoil your sleep."

She wrapped the muffler around her neck and stepped back into the night's iron-hard cold and saw Shafter standing at the edge of the walk, facing her. He had come along in the sleigh and had gotten out of it.

She realized then that this was the hope that had brought her here; but now she was uncertain, and uncertainty made her turn half away, and stop and turn back. His glance had followed her and was intently on her. He lifted his hat.

"You're going home alone?"

"Yes," she said.

He made a motion toward the sleigh. He came forward and took her arm and gave her a hand into it. "Better wrap that muffler tighter. Part of your ear is exposed."

She said: "Did the storm catch you?"

"I was in Fargo," he said and sent the mules walking down the street. "Didn't get away until after New Year."

"I wondered if you were safe," she said.

"Two weeks in Fargo," he said, "is a dull experience."

"There must have been a poker game."

"That runs out, too."

They turned the corner and moved over the gap toward her house. He brought the sleigh before the door and held the mules in check. "Nice Christmas?"

"The Calhouns had a party at the fort. Somebody had sent in a plum pudding; and we had Tom-and-Jerries without the eggs. There were three eggs, but they all turned out bad. The band played Christmas carols and we went around singing until Major Reno ordered us back to shelter before we froze. Yes, it was a pleasant Christmas. Only one shooting in Bismarck."

"Christmas . . . " he started to say, and shook his head and let it go like that. He looked at her in the way she best knew him, smiling and easy — all this covering up the heat in him. She sat still a long moment, gripping her hands together beneath the robe. She thought: "I should ask him inside. I should break this wall between us." But her pride was harder than her wishes and presently she slipped from the sleigh. "Good night."

"Good night," he said and lifted the reins. He was ten feet on when she called to him. She said, "Happy New Year, Kern."

He swung in the seat, the glow from the snowbound earth shining faintly on him. "And many of them," he said and disappeared.

She waited until she no longer saw the outline of the sleigh and no longer heard the sibilant slicing of team and runners on the snow; then she turned inside, profoundly sad.

He was in Fargo in February when news came over the wire that the Indian Commissioner had surrendered control of all Sioux not on their reservations to the War Department. He was at Fort Lincoln a week later when Terry's order to be ready for a winter campaign came to the Seventh. Making his back-and-forth circuit during the following weeks, Shafter watched the story unfold. The Sioux and Cheyenne, frightened by the intentions of the War Department, fled from their reservations, going back through bitterest weather to their old grounds on the Powder, on the Rosebud, on the Tongue. The General of the Army, Sherman, had given Terry full freedom of action. Meanwhile Sherman had despatched a column under Crook north from Fetterman, the intent being that Crook and Terry, coming from different directions, should catch the Sioux in a nut cracker. Crook's column beat its way through terrible weather, launched a surprise attack on the village of Crazy Horse, on the upper sources of the Powder, and for a moment had victory within its grasp. But Crazy Horse, fighting in desperate recklessness, gathered his warriors and threw Crook's column into disorder and drove it back to Fetterman. Terry, meanwhile, found his plans wrecked by the steady succession of blizzards blowing over the land and delayed his campaign.

Early in March, the long simmering scandal which had sent its forewarning taint out of Washington for a year or more boiled over. A broker in New York came forward with evidence that Belknap, or Belknap's wife, had taken money as reward for aiding certain men to secure profitable post-traderships. Belknap resigned as Secretary of War on the eve of a Congressional investigation. At the same time Custer, whose leave had expired, took the train west to St. Paul with his wife and there reported to General Terry.

Terry gave him his orders. Custer was to go on to Lincoln at once, to put his regiment in readiness and to march at the first break of weather, to meet the Sioux and to gather them in or to crush them. "I had hoped to be started long before this," said Terry, "in order to work in conjunction with Crook. As soon as practicable, Sherman will get Crook in motion again, headed north."

Custer took a special train from St. Paul. Halfway between Fargo and Lincoln the blizzard snowed him in and he cooled his impatient heels in a frigid coach until a detachment from Lincoln came out to his rescue. Once at the fort, his nervous, driving, impetuous will galvanized the seven troops of the regiment into feverish action; and at the same time, departmental orders went out from Washington, sending the three companies in Louisiana and the two at Fort Totten back to Lincoln. For the first time in many years the regiment was again to be whole. Custer flung himself into his job with all the terrific energy of a man who could not bear quietness.

He had scarcely returned to duty, however, when a telegram arrived from the Congressional investigating committee ordering his return to Washington in order to testify against Belknap. On the eve of a campaign, with all the glory that might accrue to the regiment and to him, his own indiscreet offer to Clymer had at last caught up with him. In this dilemma he wired his appeal to the committee: —

I AM ENGAGED UPON AN IMPORTANT EXPEDITION. . . . I EXPECT TO TAKE THE FIELD EARLY IN APRIL. . . . MY PRESENCE HERE IS DEEMED VERY NECESSARY. . . . WOULD IT NOT BE POSSIBLE TO ALLOW ME TO RETURN MY REPLIES BY MAIL?

The committee thought not, and so near the end of March Custer returned to Washington. Sergeant Hines spoke his mind confidentially to Shafter about this.

"If the general would keep his mouth shut maybe he wouldn't get in so much trouble."

Terry had based his plans on Custer since the latter was to his mind the best Indian campaigner under his command. Therefore the campaign lagged, waiting Custer's return from Washington. The days and the weeks dragged on while the committee slowly worked its way through the mass of testimony, prejudice, politics and recrimination. One by one the lost companies of the Seventh returned from their out-of-way assignments and the quarters at Lincoln, never meant for a full regiment, spilled over. The ice in the river went out one day with a grinding and a crashing like unto the cannonade of an artillery battle but the weather still was dangerous, now clear, now swinging down with its northern fury. Day after day the regiment drilled and made its preparations, and by means of the newspapers followed the testimony of their commander in Washington who, prodded by question upon question, at last produced this one startling thing: —

> "Fraud among the sutlers could not have been carried on without the connivance of the Secretary of War. . . . You ask me of the morale and character of the army. The service has not been demoralized even though the head of it, the Secretary of War, has shown himself to be so unworthy."

Captain Benteen, consistent in his hatred of Custer, smiled a wintry smile when he read that. "The God-damned fool," he said to his lieutenant, Francis Gibson. "Belknap was President Grant's friend. In saying Belknap was a scoundrel, Custer is telling the people publicly that he thinks the President is a scoundrel. Do you think Grant will stand that in silence? It is a matter of discipline. No little jackass lieutenant colonel in the United States Army can speak of the commander-in-chief that way. Right or wrong, an officer keeps his mouth shut. But Custer never had sense enough to know that. He has courtmartialed many a man within his regiment for insubordination, and now exhibits the worst insubordination possible. Wait and see what Grant does to him."

Out in St. Paul, General Terry waited for Custer's release from Washington. All arrangements had been made, now that spring was close by. Crook was to start up from Fetterman again. General Gibbon, with all the troops he could scrape together from the isolated and remote posts of Montana Territory, was to march east, reach the Yellowstone, and follow it until he joined with the Seventh Cavalry which meanwhile would be marching west. Thus the three columns, flushing Sioux before them, would drive the red men into a pocket, there to trap them and induce them to return to the reservation, or to subdue them by pitched battle. The plan was made and Terry waited for the commander of the Fort Lincoln column to return from Washington.

The Congressional committee finished its initial hearings but held Custer in the capital for future use. Now, with the campaign hourly growing nearer, Custer saw himself in danger of being left behind — his regiment marching without him. He appealed to Sherman, who was the General of the Army. Sherman said: "You had better see the President. It is in his hands entirely."

"I have been there twice. He refuses to see me," said Custer.

"Better try again," said Sherman.

Custer went wearily back to the White House and handed in his card. He sat in the anteroom, a lank, flamboyant man slowly being humbled and made conscious of his own helplessness as the hours passed. Men went by him, in and out of the President's office. Old officer friends from the Civil War paused to say hello, but he thought there was constraint in their manner. The sun had ceased to shine upon him. At five o'clock in the evening, as gray day came to its end, the President's secretary came out with his message.

"The President," said the secretary, "will not see you."

Custer stood up, paling a little. He remained still, the dash and the rankling vigor for the moment crushed from him. Then he murmured, "Very well, sir," and left the room. That night, with his wife, he caught the train west. As he stepped from the train at Chicago to transfer for St. Paul an aide of General Sheridan's came to him, offered a polite salute and handed to him a copy of a telegram despatched from Sherman to Terry: —

GENERAL: I AM AT THIS MOMENT ADVISED THAT GENERAL CUSTER STARTED LAST NIGHT FOR ST. PAUL AND FORT ABRAHAM LINCOLN. HE WAS NOT JUSTIFIED IN LEAVING WITHOUT SEEING THE PRESIDENT OR MYSELF. PLEASE INTERCEPT HIM AT CHICAGO OR ST. PAUL AND ORDER HIM TO HALT AND WAIT FOR FURTHER ORDERS. MEANWHILE, LET THE EXPEDITION FROM FORT LINCOLN PROCEED WITHOUT HIM.

Custer gave his wife an odd, desperate glance — the wildness of feeling rushing to his bony face, into his piercing eyes. "Libby," he said, "they have stripped me of my command."

Discipline had reached out and struck him with its brutal hand; and the hand was Grant's, whose reputation Custer had so rashly impugned before the Congressional committee. Custer at once boarded the train for St. Paul with Libby. He was afraid — he who never had known fear before. He was humiliated and humbled and felt the sting of it so keenly that all the appreciation of life went from him. His vaulting ambition to challenge the President, with the public as an audience to the combat, fell completely out of him; his audacity wavered and his intense physical energy, with its accompanying self-assurance, faltered. He who had been the darling of America stood bereft of his power, brought short up, stripped and held still by the brooding presence in the White House. His entire career lay in the hollow of Grant's stubby palm.

Reason and persuasion were methods for which Custer held a secret contempt, because of his impetuous nature; but force was a thing he understood, and this blunt blow reduced him to the stature of a man begging for his life. As soon as he reached St. Paul he went directly to his immediate superior, Terry. Terry, he knew, had always liked him, and had faith in him as a fighter. Terry was now his last resort.

"I am entirely in your hands, General," said Custer. "Neither Sherman nor Sheridan will intercede for me. The President would not see me, although I repeatedly attempted to see him. When I found it was useless, I took the train west. Now I am condemned for not having visited the President before I left. What was I to do? They have me trapped in a cage and it pleases them to poke sticks at me. If it is the President's wish to humiliate me before the country, he is succeeding. I do not believe I deserve it."

Terry was a mild man, a man deeply humane, tolerant and sympathetic. There was a Christian mellowness in him, and a great capacity of forbearance. Even so, he delivered a gentle reprimand.

"You should have known better. You've been in the service long enough to know the impropriety of making public comment on your superiors."

At any other time Custer would have reiterated his fiery impatience with hypocrisy. Now he played a meek hand. "I have never been anything but a soldier, General. I do not understand politicians. They have used me."

"No man can be used unless he permits himself to be used. Or unless he is very stupid. Certainly you're not stupid."

Custer flushed, but held his peace. Terry thoughtfully considered the problem and was at loss for an answer. He had counted on Custer for the campaign. "I have definite instructions not to take you. Even if it were possible to take you, I now propose to go as commander of the eastern column."

"Put yourself in my place," said Custer. "If my regiment marches without me I shall be intolerably disgraced."

Terry thought about that, slowly and with great doubt. "I have learned not to question the orders of my superiors. That is a lesson I doubt if you've learned. But you must learn it. Impetuousness has been your lifelong creed. It is an admirable thing until it runs into something else, which is insubordination. An officer of your rank, commanding the lives of eight hundred men, must have respect for order and for caution. The lives of all these men are entirely at your disposition. I have complete faith in you as a fighter and I should feel much better with you in personal command of the Seventh, but I cannot deny that the President has cause enough to suspend you from duty."

"Is there no way you can put in a word for me?" said Custer.

Terry turned to his desk and took up his pen, very carefully composing a message; upon finishing, he passed it to Custer. It read: —

I have no desire to question the orders of the President. Whether Lieutenant Colonel Custer shall be permitted to accompany the column or not, I shall go in command of it. I do not know the reasons upon which the orders given rest; but if these reasons do not forbid it, Lieutenant Colonel Custer's services would be very valuable with his regiment.

Custer's relief came up strong and ruddy to his face; his spirits rushed from extreme depth to extreme height. He said: "I am forever under debt to you, General," and left the room.

There was now nothing to do but wait while the slow wheels ground; and days passed, intolerably long to Custer, and to his wife who had to bear his moods which were penitent and hopeful and downcast and bitter by turn. The message went to the division commander at St. Louis, General Sheridan, who added his endorsement.

> On a previous occasion, in 1868, I asked executive clemency for Colonel Custer to enable him to accompany his regiment against the Indians and I sincerely hope that if granted this time it may have sufficient effect to prevent him from again attempting to throw discredit upon his profession and his brother officers.

It was then forwarded to General Sherman who despatched it to the White House, and there it rested in the hands of Grant — a man whose convictions were as immovable as polar ice, whose enemies were seldom forgiven, whose injuries were always remembered. Yet the President was a military man and the western campaign waited, and Terry had expressed an inclination for Custer's services. Somewhere during the same day upon which he received Terry's application, he weighed his personal feelings in relation to the wishes of Terry, an old soldier whose faithfulness was unquestioned; and so he despatched his answer to Sherman, who wired it to Terry: —

> THE PRESIDENT SENDS ME WORD THAT IF YOU WANT GENERAL CUSTER
> ALONG, HE WITHDRAWS HIS OBJECTIONS. ADVISE CUSTER TO BE PRUDENT,
> NOT TO TAKE ANY NEWSPAPERMEN, WHO ALWAYS MAKE MISCHIEF, AND
> TO ABSTAIN FROM PERSONALITIES IN THE FUTURE.

Nothing but a sense of propriety restrained a wild whoop of triumph from Custer when Terry gave him the news. All his restlessness and vitality and abundant confidence came back at a single bound. He stood by to hear Terry's final instructions: "Return to Lincoln by the first train and pull your regiment together. I shall join you at the first opportunity. I wish to march as soon as I arrive."

Custer left Terry's office and repaired immediately to his hotel. In the lobby he met Captain Ludlow, who once had campaigned with him and now was passing through the city. His troubles were common knowledge among the army, and Ludlow expressed a friendly sorrow. "But," he said, "you look uncommonly cheerful for a disgraced man."

"I've been restored to duty," said Custer. "I am taking the next train west."

"Capital," said Ludlow. "When will Terry join you?"

"Directly."

"You'll be under an excellent officer. A little on the cautious side for a man of your temper, but an able one. I hope it won't cramp your freedom of action too much."

Custer gave him a smile and a rash, penetrating glance. "Oh, once we're in the field, I shall pull away from Terry."

Ludlow lifted his eyebrows and stifled a comment. Custer gave him a hearty slap on the back, departing. When he entrained for Lincoln, he was a man with a fixed idea. Behind him lay intolerable injustice and deep personal humiliation; but ahead of him lay redemption in the form of one more glorious opportunity. The Seventh was his regiment, as all the country knew; his name and the Seventh were inseparable. It would be the Seventh which seized the chance and pressed it — and restored his prestige. Who then could stand before him? In this game of power — played before the audience of the nation — he meant to produce a trump against Grant. He meant to seize his chance, by whatever means it had to be obtained. He looked ahead, and saw no great difficulty in gaining complete freedom of movement from Terry, once he was in the field.

XIII

The Past Comes Forward

SPRING came slowly, fitfully to the plains; now with the pale sun dissolving the snow, now with half-warmed rains pelting down, now with nights of searing coldness. The Missouri boiled yellow and heavy between its crumbling banks and rose until it lapped at the foundation timbers of the Point. All across the flatlands the river eddied and cut its way, and great chunks of earth dropped into an already mud-engorged stream. The *Far West,* Captain Marsh commanding, nosed up from Yankton and tied at the fort to take on supplies which it would carry upstream for the troops, as far as the Powder and the Tongue, or even beyond if Terry so ordered. In memory of past ambuscades, Captain Marsh had the sides of the engine room double-planked and the pilot house shielded with thin iron plates against Sioux rifle fire.

Toward the middle of April, Shafter left Lincoln for what he believed would be the last mail trip. Snow still blanketed the ground and lay bank-full in the coulees; but here and there on the railroad's right-of-way it had begun to shrink back, permitting section crews to repair the unsettled grade and the warped track. Trains would be soon in operation.

Four miles from Fargo, he passed the Benson farm and stopped long enough to pick up their private mail. The earliest spring birds were returning, sweeping in graceful clouds upon the small knolls swept clear of snow; and high overhead at night he heard the honking of geese — the earliest vanguard of itinerant millions to follow. The weather was raw and windy, but in the wind was the rank smell of winter's breakup, of rotted earth about to come alive. By early morning he crossed swales coated with ice; by late afternoon similar swales farther east had turned into brimming lakes under the wan warmth of the day. Here and there, the receding snow line disgorged its tragedies, a buffalo fallen, a cow long dead but still intact from its winter's refrigeration. Far away on the horizon he saw the smoke of a work train.

He arrived at Yankton to find the despatches not yet arrived from St. Paul, and was delayed a week, waiting their arrival. The mail, the newspapers and the telegraph wires were teeming with news of freshened activity. Great things were stirring, great plans were making, and hopes ran high for a permanent settlement of the Indian problem; the campaign was drawing near. Crook had already started north from Fetterman to carry out his part of the plan, which was to box the Sioux on the south, to drive them north toward the Missouri or to prevent them from drifting away from the Missouri. Meanwhile, in Montana, General Gibbon had formed a column from troops stationed at Forts Shaw and Ellis and had gotten under way the middle of March, pushing through the bitterest of winter weather in order that he might fulfill the orders Terry had given him. Coming out of the west, Gibbon was to push east to the Yellowstone and follow it, scouting, making contact with the Sioux, and pressing them toward the Dakota column which would be advancing from Lincoln. Somewhere in the almost unknown region west of the Missouri and south of the Yellowstone, Terry's plan called for a junction of these three columns — his own, Crook's and Gibbon's. Somewhere in that same area the Sioux moved like shadows upon the earth, keyed up by their great leaders and their medicine men.

The despatches from St. Paul arrived at last on a Saturday train. Shafter went to the post office, got the pouches for Fort Lincoln and Bismarck and returned to his hotel with them late in the afternoon. Afterwards he dropped by the stable to have a look at the mules, and went to the hotel for supper. Darkness came down again and a rough wind whirled through the town. He sat awhile in the saloon, half interested in a poker game, and finally gave it up and climbed to his room.

A week of inaction was a hard thing. He made a slow circle around the cold room, half of a mind to go back to the saloon; there was this restlessness in him which had lately grown greater, destroying his satisfaction. He thought, "Same thing as cabin fever. It's been a hell of a long winter. A little sunshine, a little sweat and a smell of dust will cure it." He stopped and stood by the window, listening to the wind with an experienced ear. It made a racket and it shook the hotel with its force; but the venom had gone out of it. Spring was on the way. In another sixty days the regiment would be in motion across the plains; the thought of it cheered him enormously. "Probably this is my last mail trip," he reflected. "Snowplows and work trains are halfway to Bismarck now. Should be a train in there next week."

Somebody knocked on his door and he said, "Come in," but for a moment he remained at the window, interested in a little scene on the street below. A dray, drawn by four horses, came around the corner, the horses breast high in the snow. They stalled there and the driver, seeing trouble ahead of him, now tried to back out and got his two teams snarled. Presently Shafter remembered the knock at his door and turned. A woman stood in the doorway and made a little gesture with her hand. She tried to smile, and failed; and suddenly she closed the door and placed her back to it.

"Kern," she said. "Kern. Come to me."

It was like springing out of a sound sleep. The same physical shock went through him, the same quick and heavy pounding of his heart oppressed him. A queer thought came to him. "Why," he said, "she's ten years older." He saw that at once. Her shape was the same straight and lovely shape he had known so long ago; her face was the same expressive face, the lips warm and ready, the eyes watching him and willing to respond. She had always worn excellent clothes, and wore them now; the jade pendants at her ears reminded him somehow of the night he had found her with Garnett; perhaps they were the same ones. She wore the ring he had given her, the sight of which had a far-away effect on him, as though he turned back the pages of a book and saw himself as a man half familiar, half strange.

"Hello, Alice," he said.

"Come to me Kern."

He kept thinking that she was ten years older. There was nothing he could see on her to prove it; but the effect of those years was somewhere in her. They had made a change, the nature of which he could not tell. He lowered his eyes and remembered how many hundreds of times he had called her back to his mind and had created the image of her. The image was clear and distinct, engraved in his memory by the years of recollection. He lifted his glance quickly, to match the image with her presence before him; and there was an instant in which the image lay upon the reality and made a small blur. The two did not perfectly blend. Then the image died and the realness of her presence was with him. But he remembered that one moment and he thought: "Ten years have made a difference."

She had waited for him and he had not moved. She said: "I've spent a long time looking for you, Kern. Years of looking for you. I found you were at Lincoln. I was on my way to Lincoln. Then I saw you tonight on the street. After all that, can't you come the last ten feet?"

But she saw he had no intention of coming and, with a gesture of her shoulders, she walked toward him, her eyes holding his attention completely. There was a blackness and a care in her eyes; there was a terrible concentration of feeling in them, as though her life depended upon him. She touched him and looked up, and then she slid her arms around him and brought her body to him and gave him a full and long kiss.

He made a gesture of placing his arms around her and a great embarrassment went through him at his lack of response. She felt it as well and presently stepped back, hopelessness and half-terror in her eyes. She murmured: "Would it do any good to go all the way back, Kern? To explain the kind of a girl I was, the foolishness in me, the strange things I seemed to want and then found out I didn't want? Would it help if I said I made a mistake, and knew it as soon as you were gone, and have lived ever since trying to find you and repair the mistake?"

"No," he said, "it wouldn't do any good."

"I can't believe the deepness of all we felt could die out entirely. I can't believe it would die at all. It was everything to us. How could it be nothing now?"

"Was it everything to you?"

"When it was too late, I knew it was. But you were always the steadfast one. I never expected to come to you and find there wasn't a trace of me left in your heart. I knew I had hurt you as badly as if I'd shot you. That's been on my mind ten years — to make it up. But I thought you'd remember me, and remember the best of what we had. That maybe you would carry a hope, as bitter as you were toward me, that someday it might be different. That we could go back."

He heard, in her words, all that he himself had secretly believed. He had nourished the wish, even as he had closed himself up, made himself over, and sought simplicity for his life. His disillusion, he realized, was a screen behind which he covered his hope. Now she was here — and he could revive the hope. Yet, with Alice Macdougall before him, he had no desire to revive it. Something had happened to him. Maybe it was the weariness of ten years. Maybe it was something else. He wanted to express all this to her, and found it impossible; and only shook his head.

She looked closely at him. She begged him in silence to change, to come to her; she begged him to lie to her and say the things, out of pity, that he didn't believe. The wish and the appeal was on her face; the willingness to come to him on any terms was there. He knew it and felt the shame of her position and was embarrassed again. "No," he said, "nothing can come back, for us."

She made a sharp turn from him and walked across the room to the door. She swung back. The capacity for crying was burned out of her, he guessed; her expression was dull and indifferent.

"Kern," she said, "it would help me if I knew one thing. Do you hate me so much?"

"No. I don't hate you at all."

"Then," she said, "I know you never loved me as deeply as you thought you did. I haven't really wrecked your life. I only wrecked my own."

He wished he could answer that. He wanted to tell her how the long years had been with him, how empty they had been, how far he had traveled to escape the memory of her, how long he had

dreamed of her. But he saw that she was comforted by her belief
that he had failed in depth of emotion. It restored her self-respect.
She stood still, giving him a long and smileless glance; she was a
woman taking away some final memento to mark the end of a
part of her life. She murmured: "You've changed very little. You
look well." She drew a breath, she said in a low and uneven voice:
"Remember, Kern, I tried to come back." Then she opened the
door and went away.

He walked over and closed the door. He stood with his face to it,
trying to explain to himself why the memory of her had been so
powerful in him and now meant nothing. He was free in a way he
had not been free before; there was nothing left of her now but a
sentimental recollection. He thought: "Something's happened and
I have not been aware of it."

He left Fargo on a dull and lowering morning. Winter this year
had been one of the most severe on record; it released its grip for
a few hours, and renewed it again with its bleak, slicing winds. At
Hatton's Ranch he woke to a bright morning. A bland warm wind
blew from the south, and all that day the snow beneath him turned
to slush and the mules carried a thin vapor of steam around their
flanks from sudden sweating. That night, at Bell T Ranch, old
George MacGoffin warned him.

"Too damned sudden and too damned fair. It's like a woman
hatin' you all year and then beginnin' to smile. There's a knife in
that smile."

"Never had the experience of a woman throwing a knife at
me," said Shafter.

"My experience has been with Injun women," said MacGoffin.
"I ain't had no chance at the other kind."

That morning he started with one day's run into Lincoln remaining, and therefore was on the road earlier than usual. The
previous day's thaw had hardened by night into a tough crust which
made bad footing for the mules. At noon Shafter stopped to boil
his coffee and fry his bacon. Before resuming his journey he buckled
on to each mule a set of smaller leather snowshoes designed to

give better traction. Far ahead of him, barely visible in the steel-colored haze, lay Romain's ranch and, beyond that, the Benson ranch which was four miles short of Bismarck.

As he rode forward the haze thinned and gave him a better view of the horizons; at three o'clock he passed the Romain ranch and pointed toward Benson's house. Somewhere in the course of the next hour a feeling rolled through him and ruffled his flesh, a queer sensation that had no apparent origin. He sat still, alert to the feeling and now aware of a forming darkness distant in the north. The air was wholly motionless and the sound of mules and sleigh made more than the usual racket in an increasingly thin air. His feet and the exposed flesh of his face registered the increased bite of weather, by which he knew the temperature had swung sharply down in one of the prairie's freak twists. It was the weather change, then, that had made its reaction in him.

The Romain ranch was by then an hour behind him, the Benson house two hours ahead. He thought of the possibilities of shelter between those two points — the culverts into which a man might dig his way and find scant comfort, and one small section house. These were his secondary defenses against the storm now display-ing itself northward in the shape of a ragged wall of cloud columns kicked high by wind.

He had played his game with these blizzards all during the winter; had seen them form and come on, sometimes slowly, some-times with the speed of an express train. On occasion he had been given far-away warning; on other occasions he had been struck within a period of ten minutes. So now he studied the clouds with a searching attention over a quarter hour, sending the sleigh along at a fast clip. It would be a storm of some severity, he decided, but probably not as dangerous as those of midwinter had been and not possessing that dense drive of snow which completely blotted out the earth. By this time he had reached the halfway point between Romain's and Benson's. In one sudden flip of decision he made up his mind to continue to Benson's.

He had enough experience to possess great respect for those northern clouds bearing down upon him; therefore he checked his position in relation to the nearest culvert on the railroad and made a quick guess of the length of time it would take him to reach Benson's. He oriented himself carefully, knowing that when darkness closed in he would have to depend entirely on the feeling of the earth as it lifted and dropped beneath the sleigh. The telegraph poles ran die-straight westward, the yellow station house at Tie Siding marched up and fell behind. He got out his watch and marked the time he passed it. If the storm closed in he would then have one kind of a bearing when he turned about.

Nothing yet disturbed the cold still air around him; up north the height and breadth of the jagged clouds told of a tremendous wind rushing forward — and behind the clouds marched a spreading blackness in which fury lived. The sight of it made him revise his judgment, made him take out his compass and get a course on the Benson house. It lay directly along the telegraph poles, one point south of due west. As long as light lasted the telegraph poles would be sufficient, but when the storm's strange night fell, with its wild crying and its pressure against the team and its smother of snow, the poles would be indistinguishable ten feet distant.

At four o'clock, the Benson house was forty-five minutes before him and in clear view. At ten minutes after four there was no Benson house to be seen. Day drained out of the sky and through the stillness he heard the distant reverberation of wind, like the trembling echo of a waterfall, like the shuddering of volcanic action. He looked into the sleigh's bed to see if his mail and light cargo were secure; he snugged his collar around his neck and lifted his scarf to the bridge of his nose and suddenly put the team to a run. He had sensed a possibility of outracing the storm by a scant margin.

In another ten minutes he hauled the team down to a steady walk. He had lost his race even then and realized he had to conserve the mules for the emergency which would come when the blizzard struck. Blackness moved over the sky like an unrolling carpet and one first streak of wind puffed softly across the stillness. The mules had been plugging steadily along but now the touch of the wind disturbed them and they broke into a trot. Shafter let them keep the pace, meanwhile watching the gray wall, boiling from earth to heaven, move on with its stately terrible power; great lances of grayness puffed forward from its crests, like the spray blown from mile-wide, mile-high waves. Wind grew brisker about Shafter and as the churning blackness rushed upon him he heard the voice of the storm slowly lift at him with its mixture of tortured sounds. He looked at his watch, putting his head close to the dial. The time was then twenty-five minutes past four and the Benson house was another thirty minutes ahead. Looking up from the watch he thought he saw a flash of light reach forward from the house, but at once realized it was a single wafer of snow whipping by. He had scarcely stuffed the watch into his pocket when the full pressure of the blizzard, moving across the earth at fifty miles an hour, came upon him and round about him and seized him and shook him in the sleigh's seat and became a great yelling in his ears. A wall of hardened snow hit him and closed steadily down until he had only a vague sight of the mules.

He felt them give to the wind's pressure and pulled them back, northward, and felt them give again. He changed course slightly, passing a telegraph pole within arm's distance and calculating the location of the next pole; in this way, fighting the team's drift, he made his departure from one pole and his landfall on another, observing that he missed the poles by wider and wider margins as he went on. The pressure of the storm thus grew greater and his forward progress became a game of guessing how far northward it was necessary to swing. Meanwhile he took to counting the poles, realizing he could not read the watch in the pit-black darkness now surrounding him. He made his rapid estimate of distance. It was a rough four miles to Benson's and there were thirty poles to the mile; that would make 120 poles between this point and Benson's, the poles standing 176 feet apart.

He drew hard to the north. He counted the approximate distance before the next pole should show its thin blur near by, and saw nothing; he hauled hard to the north again, tension pulling at the muscles of his belly. He counted the seconds slowly in his head. He thought: "Maybe I'm swinging too much," and strain piled up in him. But the force of the wind had gotten always greater and he

knew his own senses were tricking him and therefore kept drawing to the right until it appeared to him he was traveling due
north.

He had by then gone a distance sufficient to include three poles
and had seen nothing. There was only one way left him of checking
his whereabouts. Pulling around through what seemed a forty-five-
degree turn, he headed full into the teeth of the wind. The team
fought him and fell off against the wind; he brought it back and
used the ends of his reins to push it on. The sleigh rose with a roll
of snow and tipped down and he felt the runners grit and bump
along spotty covering over the railroad ties. He had struck the right-
of-way.

He turned with it and followed it. A snowplow had recently cut
a partial way through here, leaving shoulders to either side of the
track; thus more or less guided, the mules could not swing off as
freely, and now settled to a steady pulling. Meanwhile he counted
the poles he could not see, judging the distance between. When he
passed the thirtieth pole he started from the beginning again and
in this manner covered the second mile.

The wind and the sheer weight of the coldness got through him.
He felt it first in his legs as a stiffness and then as a pain; and then
he felt it in his bones. He began to kick his feet against the sleigh's
floor. "Twenty-three," he said, and kicked the floor, "twenty-four,"
and kicked again. He had the muffler drawn twice around his head,
but the wind flung its rioting racket against his ears until the steady
pulse of sound bothered him.

This was the first break in a man's armor, the first aperture
through which the blizzard flung itself eventually to break down
sense of direction, to destroy hope, to bring on the panic that made
men disbelieve themselves and at last turn with the wind and let it
carry them to destruction. It was the incessant sound which first
drummed the balance out of a man's mind, and afterwards it was a
knowledge of legs slowly freezing. He was in the center of blackness, feeling the blackness whirl around him so swiftly and so powerfully that he grew dizzy. For a moment he closed his eyes. When he
opened them the team had stopped.

He brought the reins sharply down on the mules' rumps. He said, "Thirty. Two more miles."

The mules started, went a few halfhearted feet, and again stopped. He lifted the ends of the reins, but suddenly remembered that there was a short low trestle over a coulee two miles east of Benson's house; the mules had come upon the trestle and were afraid of it. Pulling them around, he drove over a hump of snow and sighted a pole as it slid by, and now once more he aimed his course from pole to pole.

He was in the middle of the third mile when he realized the mules were playing out. The poles came up from the blackness more slowly and the team swung farther from the wind and was harder to rein back. At the twenty-sixth pole on the third mile the team faltered and came to a stop.

He lashed out with the ends of his reins and got the sleigh going. He said "Twenty-seven," and waited what seemed a long while for the twenty-eighth pole. He picked it up and then sat back for the next one. Suddenly he thought: "I was pretty slow in reaching out to slap those mules." He had thought he had swung his arm instantly, but now that he got to studying it, he realized he had sat motionless for a good ten seconds. The bitter cold had begun to paralyze his mind and the knowledge of it flashed the sense of danger through him. He stamped his feet on the sleigh's floor and he yelled into the wind, "Now I'll stretch my right arm," and felt his muscles gradually respond. It was like sending a ball rolling down a bowling alley and waiting for it to strike — his will moving that reluctantly toward his muscles.

He reached the first pole of the fourth mile. The wind keeled him on the seat; the force of it shoved the sleigh sidewise and the screaming sound of the storm grew more and more shrill until his ears vibrated from the steadiness of the impact. He pulled the mules around with greater difficulty and knew that he could afford to waste little more energy in this kind of wrestling and turned the team north again, rising onto a shoulder of snow and dropping into the railroad cut. It took a great load off his mind thus to be traveling in a certain direction; at the same time he began again to count slowly, thereby estimating the passage of the telegraph poles, which he could not see. The thirtieth pole should, if his calculations had been right, bring him opposite Benson's house. If he missed Benson's, the road would carry him directly into Bismarck, but he knew he could not nurse the team the additional five miles.

He kept stamping his feet until he discovered he had lost all feeling in them; his right side, so steadily pounded by the wind, had grown stiff. He stopped the team as soon as he thus realized he was slowly freezing, and stepped from the sleigh. He held the reins and walked forward, no sensation of weight on his feet, and got to the head of the team and led it forward.

The physical exertion warmed him, but it tired him. He thought: "I'm not that soft," and knew at once how much the blizzard had sapped him. He put the reins over his shoulder, guiding the mules as well as pulling them on against their inclination to stop. He had passed the fifteenth pole when he began to watch the left forward distance for Benson's house lights. He thought he saw those lights and stared steadily until the mealy agitation of snow made a heaving up-and-down confusion in his brain. He closed his eyes and walked half a dozen paces, and opened them again. There were no lights.

When he had counted the twentieth pole he began to visualize the ten poles remaining. He made a picture of them in his mind and saw how far they stretched out and he thought: "I may have to let the team go and walk on." But he argued himself out of the impulse. He had a terrible feeling of futility and a growing conviction that he lacked the energy to cover the distance. Then he pushed the doubt out of his mind by arguing with himself about the mules again. "It's too good a team to abandon. The off mule is a little the smartest, and a little the meanest. Same as people are. The smarter they are the crueler they can be. Something there for me to think about when I reach Lincoln. Can't give up the mules. Or the mail . . . "

He walked straight into a signal post stuck up beside the right-of-way and struck it with his face. It should have hurt him badly, but the pain was something that traveled very slowly to his consciousness. The team had stopped behind him. He put his hand on the post and felt upward until he reached the square board on top of the post — and he stood still, the wind pushing him against the post and the scream of the wind pulling his thoughts apart. He put them patiently together again, trying to make a picture of the railroad as it moved toward Bismarck, trying to spot the signal board's location.

"Why, hell," he said, "this is the Benson whistle-stop sign. The house is two hundred feet straight south."

The discovery shot a jet of warmth through him. He crawled back along the side of the near mule and got into the sleigh and he squared the team into the south, with the wind full at his back. Then he said: "There's one more sign, a mile away from the Benson sign, but I can't have misjudged my distance that much." The whole thing now was a toss-up, for he was no longer certain, and he sat still, knowing that if he failed to strike the Benson house at the first try, the team would not face the weather and return to the track. Suddenly he brought the rein ends down on the mules. "Hya — hya," he yelled. "Get on Babe. Butcher!"

They had stood still too long and now were slow in starting. He slashed their rumps with the reins and got them into motion. He felt them strain upward on the ridge of snow and falter. He hit them again and yelled at the top of his voice. The sleigh tilted, came to the snow's summit and dropped down. The mules, driven by the wind, slogged slowly through the snow.

He was again counting time slowly, and guessing distance. He stared ahead of him for Benson's lights and he grumbled, "Come on — put that lamp in the window. Forty-two seconds, forty-three seconds . . . "

There was a flurry of snow in front of him, a flickering screen of it across his eyes; and then he realized it was a ray of house light which had made the snow visible. The mules had stopped again and when he watched the snow a moment he saw the light shining ahead. He was directly against the house's porch.

It never occurred to him to step down and go to the house. Instead, he guided the team to the left and made a patient circle, driving the sleigh close by the walls. Darkness came solidly down again as soon as the house light faded, but he had the picture of Benson's

yard wholly clear in his mind and went on with confidence. When
the team stopped, Shafter got down and went ahead, touching the
wall of Benson's barn. He scraped his hand along the wall until he
found a door latch and rolled the door open and pulled team and
sleigh into the barn's runway. He hauled the door almost shut and
turned and put his back to it. He spoke to himself aloud, with a
drunken man's labored distinctness:—

"Better stay here until I thaw out. Better not go into a warm
house."

Exhaustion hit him on the head like a maul. He let his feet slide
forward a little so that he was braced against the wall. His belly
was empty and his throat dry; and his body was a patchwork of
feeling and stinging aches and numbness. He slapped his hands together and he said: "They're all right." He took off his Berlin gloves
and slid his hands underneath the muffler which lay ice-cemented
around his throat and ears. He pinched his ears. He pulled away the
muffler and began a steady rubbing. Streaks of colored light swam
across his pupils and he was distinctly unbalanced from the pounding of the storm, and for a little while the quietness in the barn
bothered him. He felt the wind lean against the wall and strain it
and he heard the shrilling of the eaves and the rattle of sleet against
the roof. Sensation came to his ears.

He walked through the darkness toward the mules. He said:
"Babe — Butch," and walked around and around the sleigh, stamping his feet as he traveled. He was greatly tired and wanted to
sit down, but he kept himself moving. He said, "Babe," again and
unhitched the team and groped in the dark for a quarter hour to
remove the harness. He was as weak as a man recovering from a
long fever, every motion of his hand requiring a deliberate push of
his will. He let the harness fall on the ground and he let the mules
go and turned to the door. When he stepped outside, the storm
nailed him to the wall so that he had to wheel sideways and go
shoulder first into the wind; he guided himself by the faint light
he saw and reached the house's back door. He hit it once with his
hand, opened the door and passed into a dark room. There was a
farther door open, through which a light burned with extraordinary

brilliance. He went through that doorway and saw two blurred forms ahead of him. A woman's voice came sharply at him.

"Kern — where've you been?"

She came to him, reaching toward the scarf around his neck and when she pulled it away, the crusted ice rattling on the floor, she laid her hands on his ears. "Kern," she said, "you can't stay in a warm room."

"That's all right. I thawed out in the barn." He closed his eyes and pushed his fingers against the lids, and opened them to find Josephine watching him.

"I'll get you some coffee. Are you sure your feet are all right?"

"Coffee's fine," he said. He looked at the man standing near the stove in the corner of the room, but the pounding of the weather still affected his eyes and the heat of the room put a film on them. Josephine had gone back toward the kitchen. He looked around the room and saw an army cot made up like a divan and he went to it and sat down. He bent over and supported his head with his hands braced against his knees. This was uncomfortable and presently he lay back on the cot.

When Josephine returned he was sound asleep. She stood over him a moment, worrying about him. "He was coming from Fargo and got caught in it. He must have lost his team. Edward, help me take his boots and socks off. If his feet are frozen we'll have to wake him up."

Garnett said irritably: "It is a strange thing he should come to this house, with two hundred miles of space between Fargo and Bismarck."

She looked back at the lieutenant. "Under the circumstances, I'm very glad he's here. Help me with his boots."

Garnett said: "I'd do anything for you, Josephine, but I will not touch him."

"This is no time to be hating him. He may lose his feet."

"Let him crawl around on his hands and knees."

"Edward," she said, shocked, "no human being should carry that kind of thought in his head."

"You don't know," he murmured. "You can't possibly know how

I feel about him, or how he feels about me. There is no use of hiding it. I'd be lying to you if I said I was sorry for him. I regret he survived the storm. For his part, he would stand over me and let me die and never lift a hand."

He stood back and watched her haul at Shafter's boots. She got them off and stripped away his heavy wool socks. She put her hands on Shafter's feet; she pinched the white skin around his ankles and watched a faint spot of color come to the flesh. Garnett's expression turned distasteful as he viewed this. A protest came out of him. "Don't dirty your beautiful hands on him."

"I wish I knew what was between you two. You've done something to him, haven't you, Edward?"

"I have done my best to ruin him," said Garnett coolly. "As he has done his best to ruin me."

"I think he has more generosity in him than you have, Edward."

Garnett's mouth formed a small, acid smile. "Wait and see." Then he remained still a long while, his hands laced behind him, darkly speculating. "Josephine," he said finally, "no matter what happens next, please remember I have never said an insincere thing to you."

"Why? What can happen?"

"Wait and see," said Garnett.

XIV

A Sinner Turned Holy

SHAFTER woke with one thought uppermost in his mind: "I've got to get up and find a place to sleep tonight." The room was dark, and the windows showed the blackness of the outer world. The storm had blown itself away, its abrupt end a surprise to him. He turned his head to see a light in the kitchen and a woman moving about. He lifted himself on the cot; his clothes were on but his shoes had been removed, and he had blankets over him. The weariness was gone. This little half hour's nap had freshened him and taken even the memory of the storm's beating from his head; he felt fine, and said to himself: "I'm almost as good now at thirty-two as I was at twenty." Almost as good, but not quite, for no man could expect to keep forever the bubble of energy of that younger age; and when a man got older he got wiser — and wisdom always had a little bit of fear in it. "When you're young," he thought, "you're too dumb to know all the things that could kill you."

He got up and moved into the kitchen to find Josephine at the stove. The little kitchen table was set and the smell of coffee and bacon was a stimulant to him. Josephine said: "How do you feel?" She smiled at him.

"Fine," he said, "fine. Half an hour's rest does a lot."

"Nearer ten hours," she said. "It is six o'clock in the morning."

He looked out of the window; he looked at his watch. "That's a strange one," he said, and went to the back porch. He cracked the ice from a water bucket and washed his face. Josephine opened the door briefly to hand him a towel, and he stood in the brittle stillness of the morning, savoring the softer, warmer smell that this day brought. Light made a dull crack in the east, but there was a silver haze hanging over the land — the kind of fog that would last indefinitely and shut out the sun. Snowdrifts lay in molded shapes against the walls of the house, banked halfway up the windows. The blizzard had punished him, and left his skin as tender as though it had been seared by fire, but even so he had already forgotten the misery of that four-mile ride. He was in good spirits, and hungry, and pleased with his survival as he turned back into the kitchen.

He sat down to breakfast. Josephine poured coffee for him and for herself and took a place opposite. She sat quietly by, her face turned rose-colored and pretty by the stove's heat; she sipped her coffee, now and then watching him but offering no comment.

"How do you come to be here?" he asked.

"We were out for a ride and saw the blizzard coming. We got here about two hours before you did. Where were you when it started?"

"Halfway between here and Romain's. What time did I get here?"

"It was half-past seven."

"Four miles in two hours and a half," he said. He shook his head. "I didn't think it took that long. No wonder I got cold."

"You were dead-beat," she said.

He ate his meal and sat back with his cigar. Josephine rose to pour him another cup of coffee, a serene and thoughtful expression composing her face. He noticed it now as he had so often before. "Where are the Bensons?" he asked.

"They were on the way to Bismarck when we passed them. So I suppose the storm held them in town."

Daylight slowly seeped through the windows, muddy and sullen. He got up from his place, now thinking about his mules. "Time to get on. It was a first-class blizzard. The last shot in the carbine, I guess, before spring comes. I doubt if we'll have another. My last trip, more than likely. The train will be running next week."

He heard somebody stepping along the front room, behind him, and he noticed the girl's face tighten. He thought nothing about it as he stood there; he felt like a man who had gone through a big drunk — bruised and sore but all sweet and cleaned out inside. Everything was fine and he had no bad memories or cares.

"Where did you get that cut on your head?"

He raised his hand to it and ran a finger along a welt which stretched from the bridge of his nose back to the line of his hair.

He had to stop to think about it before he remembered. "I walked into the signal post out in front of the house. That's what saved my bacon. I knew I was on top of Benson's then. It steered me right in."

"You took chances, Kern."

"I thought I could beat out the storm. I guess I got a little careless." He turned around and faced the living-room doorway, and at that same moment he saw Garnett come across the front room and stop. Garnett looked at him, his eyes narrowed, his mouth pulled long and firm; there was a thin and bright attentiveness in his glance and he held himself on guard, as though he knew trouble had to come between them.

Shafter removed his cigar. Red color showed freshly along his neck and a rough expression tumbled over his face. He looked, the girl thought, like a man who suddenly had stumbled upon something dangerous and unpleasant, something for whom he had maintained a lifelong animosity. He held the cigar in his hand, reading Garnett, and being read by Garnett. Presently Shafter turned his head to the girl and she saw what he thought.

"This is the man you came riding with?"

"Yes," she said. "It is as I explained to you. The storm caught us."

"I know," said Shafter, very quietly. Then he asked her an odd question. "Has he had breakfast?"

"No. But why?"

He almost smiled as he pointed to the revolver and belt on Garnett's waist. "He eats breakfast with his gun."

"You know why it's there," said Garnett.

"Why is it?" Josephine asked.

"He's away from the fort," said Shafter, murmuring the words.

"There's nothing on this side of the river to be afraid of," she pointed out. "These Indians on the east bank are all right."

"That's right," said Shafter. "But I'm here."

"You see?" said Garnett to her. "He knows why I've got it."

She studied the two, worried and gradually growing impatient. "I think you are both fools."

"That's probably true," said Shafter.

"You've had your meal," said Garnett. "Go on, get out of here."

Shafter's face held its creased half-smile. He had his head slightly
bent as he watched the lieutenant. He murmured: "Up to the same
old tricks, Garnett?"

The girl caught the meaning of it and spoke quietly, ignoring the
chance to grow furious at him. "I told you how it was. You were
caught in the same blizzard, weren't you?"

"Don't explain anything to him," said Garnett sharply.

"That's right," agreed Shafter. "The lieutenant never explains.
There isn't time enough — even if he lived to be an old man — for
him to explain all he's got behind him."

"Sergeant," said Garnett coolly, "mind what I tell you or I'll have
you courtmartialed for disobeying me."

"Stand aside from the door," said Shafter. "I'm going in there to
get my cap and I don't want to get the smell of a scoundrel on me."

"According to the record," said Garnett in a jeering tone, "who's
the scoundrel? You're making a scene for the lady. If I had you in
my company I'd break you."

"If I were in your company," said Shafter, "somebody would be
broken in due time, no doubt. Stand aside, Beau."

The name, the girl noticed, pricked Garnett's coldness. His eyes
heated and for a moment he balanced in the doorway, thinking of
the answer he wanted to make. Then he stepped into the kitchen and
cleared the doorway. Shafter went past him and crossed the room to
the cot. He got his cap off the floor and he took his muffler from a
wall hook where it had been hung by Josephine to dry during the
night. He stood with his back to the kitchen while he wrapped the
muffler around his neck. He started to put on his overcoat, but then
he got a thought in his head which turned his face tough, and he
folded the coat over his arm and went back to the kitchen.

Garnett had taken a seat at the end of the table. He sat on the
edge of the chair, his body turned so that he might watch Shafter,
who now came through the doorway and paused. Shafter looked at
the girl. He said softly: "My advice to you is to get out of this
house."

She was under strain, fearing what might happen. "Kern," she
said, "don't say any more. You've said enough."

"That's right," he agreed. "I've talked enough." He dropped the coat and came against the back of Garnett's chair. Garnett started to rise, but Shafter's arms closed about him and pinned him to the chair; then he let go with one arm and used the butt of his palm to crack Garnett on the temple, and after that he reached down and knocked away Garnett's hand as it struggled to reach the gun. He caught the gun out of Garnett's holster and stepped back and threw it to the far corner of the kitchen. He was laughing quietly.

"Now, Beau."

Garnett sat still a long dragged-out moment, his head sagged down. The girl mistook his silence and sharply spoke: "Kern, you've injured him! Don't you know what he can have done to you — "

Garnett made a springing rush from the chair, avoiding Shafter's outreaching arm. He raced through the doorway, momentarily out of sight. Shafter wheeled and started after him, hearing Josephine's voice suddenly grow shrill: —

"Benson's rifle — on the wall!"

He rushed through the door in time to see Garnett rip the rifle from the wall and bring it up to him. The round, dark muzzle centered on Shafter and wavered a moment. He whirled and ducked as the roar of the gun filled the room with its dry crash and he felt the wind of the bullet against him and heard it tick through the far wall. He charged straight against Garnett as the latter took two backward steps. He knocked the gun aside and hit Garnett with the point of his shoulder and smashed him against the wall; he brought up one arm and rammed it across Garnett's windpipe, and seized the gun and got it free and flung it into a corner. He stepped back again, his head still slightly bent as he watched the man.

"Now's the time, Beau."

"Do you know what I'll have done to you?" cried Garnett.

"You're hiding behind somebody else again," said Shafter. "You're always trying to find somebody else to settle your scores. Like Conboy. Like other times I could bring back to you. But right now, it is just the two of us. Do you know what I'm going to do, Beau? I am going to destroy an illusion of manliness. I am going to cripple you past the point where any other woman will want you. When I think of the women — "

Josephine, now at the kitchen doorway, cried at Shafter: "Don't, Kern!"

Garnett stepped sidewise along the wall, toward a corner, as Shafter watched him. Suddenly Garnett reached a chair and seized it and flung it up over his head and came forward, his face slashed by the intensity of his thinking as he swung the chair and flung it down and forward. Shafter raised one arm and took the blow, and shunted the chair aside. He stepped on and drove a punch deep into Garnett's flank, into the soft flesh just above the hip. Garnett cried out a hurt breath and let the chair drop and wheeled and sprang at Shafter, both hands swinging. One of his fists struck Shafter on the cheek, sending Shafter back.

But he was still hunting for a weapon, and momentarily turned his head, thus exposing himself. Shafter jumped in and staggered the lieutenant with a blow against his belly. Garnett struck the wall and his mouth sprang open and in this defenseless moment he was at Shafter's mercy. Shafter hit him slantingly on the mouth, drawing blood. He watched Garnett's head drop and roll aside. He waited for his chance and when he saw it he hooked another side blow across Garnett's nose. He knew he had done the man damage, for he heard Garnett's yell rise.

Garnett came against him and took his punishment; he seized Shafter around the waist and held on and pushed Shafter toward the stove with a great burst of strength. He shoved Shafter against its hot sides and he stiffened his legs behind him and spent all his remaining energy in that one effort to hold Shafter there.

The smell of Shafter's scorched clothing began to stink in the room. Shafter felt the flare of pain on the backs of his legs. He got an arm around Garnett's head and gave it a twist that threw the man off balance. He slid suddenly aside and saw Garnett throw both hands against the hot top of the stove to keep himself upright. Garnett cried out and drew back with his hands half open before him. The pain of it made him forget Shafter who, now behind him, came up and sledged him on the side of the neck and drove him across the room. Garnett turned and shoved his arms defensively before him. Shafter hit him on the mouth and drove a punch into his belly and watched the man drop.

He stood over Garnett, breath drawing deep, and bitterly regretted he had not more permanently damaged those handsome features which had caused so much ruin. This was not like his fight with Conboy, in which the end of the struggle brought also an end to bad feeling; this was like no other fight in his life. He was dissatisfied, his thirst unquenched; he looked down and hated the man more violently than before, and knew he would never cease to hate him. He waited there with the hope that Garnett would rise up and try again. He said: "Now's the time, Beau. Get up. Just one more try. Maybe you can reach another chair. Maybe you can get one of the guns. You can try, Beau. If you shot me, you wouldn't be held for it. You know that. Get up and try it."

He stepped back another pace, giving Garnett a chance to make his turn, his jump, his lunge. He thought the man's silence was faked; he thought Garnett heard him, and waited. Blood rolled down Garnett's lips and he breathed in the shallow, fast and sucking way of an exhausted man; suddenly he gave a hard groan and rolled to his back and laid a hand over his broken nose. Shafter got a glance at the man's eyes and knew then the fight was over.

He stood still with the memory of a ten-year injustice burning through him, unquenched. He murmured: "God damn you, Garnett, you've always got a way of sliding out. You'll crawl out of this, like you crawled out before, and you'll carry your rotten business on. I ought to break your back."

Garnett swayed gently from side to side, on the floor. His legs rose and dropped as steady reflexes of pain pulsed through him. He groaned: "You've broken my nose."

"I hope it heals crooked," said Shafter. He had grown cooler and now he shrugged his shoulders and turned into the kitchen. Halfway to the rear door he wheeled rapidly, entered the living room again and picked up Benson's rifle. He ejected the shells and put them in his pocket and laid the gun on its rack; in the kitchen

he retrieved Garnett's revolver and removed its loads and left the
gun empty on the table.

Josephine had come into the kitchen. When he moved toward the
back door she halted him with her voice.

"He'll have you courtmartialed. You have put yourself in his
hands."

He had forgotten her for a little while. He stared at her, aware
of her beauty as he always was. She was a fair woman, with hungry
dreams seeking answer; and Garnett, whose profession was women,
had at once known the vividness of her dreaming, her eagerness to
believe and to respond to those things which seemed to come as
answers to all longings. It was a cheap and easy and dirty profession, preying upon the near things of a woman's soul, betraying
them and leaving the woman stripped of illusion.

"No," he said. "He won't. He can't bring charges against me
without explaining the circumstances and involving you. He won't
do that. Not that he'd have any scruples about giving you away, but
he'd be exposing himself."

"Exposing himself to what?" she asked.

"To other women who now think they share his interest exclusively," said Shafter.

She stood stone-quiet, her face fixed in a cold distasteful expression. She murmured: "You make this a very unpleasant affair,
don't you?"

"I know the man," said Shafter.

"Do you know me?" she said.

"You went out for an afternoon's ride," he said. "That was all."

Her answer tumbled swiftly back at him. "Where is the wrong,
Kern? Dig down as deep as you want and find me an answer —
the worst answer you can find."

"There's your answer," he said and pointed through the door
toward the living room. Garnett had risen from the floor and now
walked slowly forward and supported himself in the doorway. He
looked upon these two with his battered face, his crushed lips and
his bold nose now broken at the bridge; he looked at them with a

dull indifference, and listened as though their words came through fog to him.

"What has he to do with me?" she demanded.

"Everything he touches — "

She cut in and finished the phrase for him. "Turns bad. That's what you think. You were hurt once, and you stopped growing. You have spent the last years of your life shrinking smaller, drawing away for fear of getting hurt again. You've done a good job of making a very unimportant man out of yourself, Kern. You might have been a big one. I've thought of that often and it has troubled me to see so much turn into so little. There's more fun and honesty in living than you know about. It has passed you by. You think Edward is evil? So are you. Evil in the way you let hate and suspicion feed upon your soul."

Shafter bowed his head slightly. "You may be right," he said, and left the room.

She stood still, hearing his feet crackle through the snow crust as he went toward the barn; she was very attentive to that, forgetting the presence of Garnett. The anger died out of her and her face lost its temper; her shoulders dropped.

"That's the girl," said Garnett. "You've hit him hard. I know how he looks when he's been beaten. I know the look on his face."

She had her back to Garnett. "Edward, as soon as Kern has driven away, get your team and cutter ready. We're going home."

He said: "Look at me."

She kept her position for a little while and when she did turn she was sorry to show him the feeling she knew he would see. He was a clever man with his eyes; he read what lay within people — that was his gift. He had, she realized, frequently read her mind or her wishes and had changed his mood to suit her, his manner to please her. In a way it was a versatility not quite honest, a skill that came of practice. She remembered then what Kern had said about him: "To other women who now think they share his interest exclusively."

"I'm sorry, Edward," she said.

He said: "You liked me yesterday. You don't like me now. Where was the change?"

She shook her head. "Never mind. Let's go."

"He made the change, didn't he? You believe what he said about me?"

"Let's not bother to go into it. A thing changes. People change."

"No," he said, "you believe him. And all those hard words you used on him meant nothing."

"Yes," she said, "I meant them."

He managed a thin smile. "You intended to hurt him, but you never intended to drive him off. You want him to come back. It is a very old way with a woman."

"You would know, wouldn't you?" she said quietly.

"It has been used on me more than once." He looked at her, withdrawing his smile. "I never have tried to cover up my weaknesses to you, Jo. I knew it was no good. If you had been just another woman with me, I would have used all the tricks in the book."

"You know the book very well."

"I don't deny it." He sighed and struggled with the pain pulsing through him. "When I saw you I knew I had come to something serious. You are the first woman with whom I have ever wanted to be honest. As soon as I realized that, I was afraid. I knew what was behind me. I knew you'd discover it sooner or later — as any woman will come to know about a man. That's why I told you to believe in me, whatever happened. I wanted you to know I meant to play the game right with you." He shrugged his shoulders, the weight of his thoughts fatally on him. "A sinner turned holy — and confronted with his sins."

"I believe you," she told him quietly.

"But now believing is not enough," he murmured. "There's too much behind me, and too little left in me."

"Yes," she said. "Let's go home."

He went back to the living room and got into his coat and left the house, soon bringing the cutter around. He helped her up and turned toward Bismarck through a lowering overcast which closed the horizons down. She looked for the shape of Shafter's sleigh in the distance and didn't see it.

"Edward," she said, "don't use your power as an officer over him now. Let all this die."

He gave a strange, almost irrational laugh which made her glance sharply at him. She said, "You're hurt, aren't you?"

"That's another thing about a woman. She goes through storm and then expects sunshine to erase the memory of storm. You misjudge me and you misjudge Shafter. Nothing will stop the way we feel. Nothing will stop me from getting at him."

"Edward," she said, "don't make yourself less than you are."

He shook his head and said nothing more until they reached the front of her house. She dropped out of the cutter and looked back at him a moment, sad for the way things had been, sorry that she had hurt him. He read that in her, too, with his eyes. He said: —

"I shan't see you again, I suppose."

"No."

He nodded. Then he said: "But you must understand something else about Shafter. I know him better than any other person. You believe he'll come back because — as you have already discovered — he's in love with you." He smiled in his bitter way. "But he won't come back. He never goes back to anything. Good-by, Jo."

XV

Boots and Saddles

ONE NIGHT the regiment lay crowded within the walls of Fort Lincoln; at tattoo on the following evening it camped in tents on a level plain three miles south of the fort. Winter was done and waiting was done. Terry's orders had come through and the Seventh stretched its legs in the open once more and smelled the old good odor of canvas and grass and campfire. There would be a period of preparation before Terry arrived from St. Paul to lead the expedition on its way.

The regiment was whole again, all its twelve companies lined up side by side on the plain, each with its company street and line of tents leading off the main regimental street. Across the regimental street stood the tent of the commander, now occupied by Major Reno. Beside the tent of the commanding officer sat the other tents of the adjutant and staff. Adjoining the cavalry troops were two companies of the Seventeenth Infantry and one of the Sixth Infantry; here also were three Gatling guns in charge of two infantry officers and thirty-two men — an innovation looked upon by the cavalry with mixed emotions. Still farther on lay the wagon park with its one hundred fifty wagons to carry the quartermaster and commissary supplies, near which camped a hundred and seventy-five civilian teamsters in their own clannish group. With the regiment as well was a small party of Ree scouts, Charley Reynolds, and two interpreters — Fred Girard and the Negro Isaiah Dorman. The scout detachment had been placed under the command of Lieutenant Charles Varnum.

Here it lay under the early May sunshine, a sprawling unit on the plain, the white tops of its tents softly shining, the year's early dust rising from its steady activity, its day hourly marked by the throaty summons of the trumpets, with despatch riders whirling in from Lincoln and Bismarck and slow freight caravans arriving to round out the regiment's supplies; with scout details trotting out for their daily sweeps westward and returning jaded at night, one day coated with dust and the next day freckled with the mud of a seasonal shower. Throughout the hours the companies drilled, the sharp calls of officers and noncoms flatting through the bland late-spring air and the horses wheeling and crowding and moving with the precision of long training, and metal gear singing its minor metal tunes, and saddle leather squealing, and carbines slapping on their slings. Throughout the hours, too, details filed away to the foot of a small ridge for target practice.

This was the shake-down of a regiment whose units had been long separated. Men sweated off the fat of winter and refreshed their memories of duties grown vague by disuse. Equipment was over-hauled, and replaced, guns tested and clothing mended or newly issued. Old men coached recruits and hazed them with the time-yellowed tricks of the service. New cavalry mounts were broken at the corrals and officers found bizarre flaws in old horses in order to secure younger stock for their commands. The pieces and parts of the regiment came together, stiffly from long lack of contact and then smoothly as they daily made union. At night campfires blazed on the earth, yellow dots against the velvet shadowing of the land, and men sang, or sat still, or argued, or wrote last letters home-ward, or thought of home and never wrote; and they sorted out their possessions and extra equipment and mementoes long prized and sent them back to barracks to await their return when the campaign was done. All sabers were boxed and stored and dress uni-forms put away. Threadbare trousers and battered campaign hats appeared, decorated by the frail blue and yellow flowers now color-ing the prairie.

New faces appeared with the returned companies — Lieutenants Godfrey and Hare of K, Godfrey with a huge nose and a stringy mustache and long goatee; Captain McDougal, transferred from E to command B; Lieutenant McIntosh with the strain of Indian blood in him, and Lieutenant Wallace with the long neck and serious manner; Benny Hodgson, a youngster loved by the com-mand for a sunny disposition; and Porter of I Company, and Captain Myles Keogh of I, a sharp-eyed, swarthy-skinned man with a pointed black imperial and indigo black mustache. It was Hines who described Keogh to Shafter. "There's three soldiers of fortune in this outfit. Nowlan and DeRudio and Keogh have served in Europe. Nowlan is a fine one and DeRudio is all right when he don't get excited and start talkin' Eyetalian at us. This Keogh, now, is the hardest of the lot, a martinet when he's sober and one that will throw the back of his hand at a trooper when he feels like it. We're goin' into this campaign in need of officers, Professor. We should have thirty-six or more and we've got but twenty-eight, and some of them are far from bein' the best in the world. For that matter, we could stand a few more men. Eight hundred to the regiment is not enough. It is Custer's idea that we can lick all the Sioux in the West. It is not mine."

"It looks like Reno in command instead of Custer," said Shafter.

Sergeant Hines gave him a look, shrugged his shoulders and turned away.

On May tenth the guardhouse trumpet cracked the afternoon with its sharp flourish for a general officer and Terry and his staff, and Custer, whirled out of the prairie and down the regimental street. It was as though an electrical shock passed through the command, stiffening it and exciting it. The presence of Terry meant the beginning of the campaign; and the presence of Custer meant that ease was over and long marches begun and sudden strains and unexpected shocks would come to the command. That night after retreat, the story of Custer was common knowledge in the camp, spoken of by officers in the presence of the sergeant major, and mentioned by him to the company sergeants, and in turn passed down the line. The regiment was a family with no secrets.

Hines said: "There Custer was in St. Paul, the President with a thumb on him and pushin' down for the things he'd said in Washington. And Sherman was out of patience with him, and Sheridan too. So he was a spanked boy watchin' his regiment go away and him not with it. Can you see the general pacin' up and down, cursin' the world because he wasn't out in front wavin' his big hat and sayin' 'Come on boys'?" Hines looked around him and grinned.

"So he writes this letter very humble to the President and Terry writes a nice letter to back him up, and Sherman likewise. Well, then, the President finally says back to Terry that if Terry thinks Custer will help on the campaign he'll let Custer go. But you know what Sherman wired Terry?" Hines's grin broadened into a laugh and he slapped the mess table with his hand. "Sherman wires Terry to tell Custer to be prudent, not to take any newspapermen along with him to write up his glorious deeds, and to quit makin' remarks about his superior officers in the future. So we got Custer back."

"Lickin' his wounds," said Sergeant McDermott. "He was spanked before the country and he knows it. The more he thinks of it, the worse it will hurt."

"That's a fact," said Hines.

"You know what he'll do to us now?"

"He'll take it out on us," said Hines. "Be ready to sweat."

"It is not the sweatin' I think of," said McDermott. "He will be devisin' ways to make the ones that spanked him look foolish. He will try to make a big man out of himself again, before the country. He will whip the Sioux, and then he'll be a hero once more. What I'm thinkin' is he'll ride this regiment into hell to do it."

"I guess he'll find hell enough out there to ride into," said Hines imperturbably. "There is no able-bodied Sioux left on the reservations. They're out west waitin' for us to come."

"A man in the Seventh," said McDermott glumly, "shouldn't be a family man."

"There's Terry to hold him down," said Hines.

"He'll do as he did before with Stanley. He'll listen to orders and march away and disobey 'em."

But Hines scratched his chin, long thinking. He shrugged his shoulders. "It may all be so. Still, I feel better with him around. I like to soldier under a man that is masterful at leadin'. Wherever we go, McDermott, he'll be at the front of us. We'll never have to look back to see if he's comin'."

"If he don't pull out and leave us to fight it alone," said McDermott. "Like he did Major Elliot at Washita."

"That," said Hines, "was a long time ago, and a thing full of argument. Let it be forgotten."

Shafter said: "You're an old horse smelling smoke, Hines."

"The truth," said Hines. "In spring my bones begin to ache with the memory of twenty-eight years of campaignin' and I sleep light and wake early and I think of a lot of lads I knew and a lot of fights we've had, and I want to be at it. I am a fool to think it, for the feelin' of bein' old has gotten at me lately. I guess this will be my last campaign."

It was as Hines knew, and as all the regiment suspected. The winter's ordeal had left Custer raw of nerve and pride; it had increased his terrific animal energy. His rough hand seized the regiment and shook it into redoubled activity. Officers' call was a repeated summons through the day and the drill period lengthened and men toiled late at special-duty chores. Inspections were repeated, company by company, with Custer's sharp eyes on everything. By day he was everywhere, whirling out of camp to the fort, the drill field or rifle range, or simply rushing headlong into the prairie to give himself a run; at retreat his nervous, staccato voice cracked across the plain; late after taps the guards saw his tent lights burning and his shadow pacing. There was no rest in him.

Crook, the grapevine rumors said, was well under way; and Gibbon was already as far as the Bighorn, having fought his way out of the West through the last winter storms. The May weather turned variable, one day warm and the next day sending down its riotous sheets of rain which turned the porous earth into spongy mud and set all the tents a-steaming. The *Far West* had already departed upriver with supplies, which would be left at a base designated by Custer. Terry had, meanwhile, made every effort to secure advance information of the Sioux whereabouts, and scouts drifted in fugitively with their information and drifted secretively out. The Rees, under Bloody Hand, arrived in camp on the fifteenth and pitched their tents. On the sixteenth general orders went out; the command would march the following morning. That night, on the eve of departure, the officers held a ball on the regimental street and all the ladies came out from Lincoln, and in the bland evening the

music of the regimental band swung them around and around while
the light of campfires glowed on colored dresses and faded fatigue
uniforms.

Shafter stood back, watching the couples — the cheerfulness upon
the men and the gaiety upon their women. This was the time, he
thought, when a woman looked upon a man with a sharpened tenderness, when she noticed the things upon a man's face with a mem-
orizing care, and stored in her mind the little things said, and
matched his carefree air and held back from him the hard anxiety
which lay like a lump in her heart. And this was the time when a
man felt the goodness and the excitement of soldiering and yet had
his own anxieties and tried to conceal them from the woman with
a greater buoyancy. This was the time when they laughed and
concealed harsher thoughts.

He moved back to his tent at tattoo and stretched out on his bunk.
McDermott was writing a letter by candlelight, making hard work
out of it. McDermott looked up at him, scowling. "If you're going
to soldier, Shafter, don't get married."

"Where's your family?"

"Iowa — Cedar Rapids." McDermott leaned back. "I've got a boy
who's three. Haven't seen him for eight months. I'll be glad when
this enlistment's up." He returned to his letter and struggled with
it and stopped again. "I suppose you've done your writing already."

"No," said Shafter.

"Better do it. I ain't been in the army ten years for nothing. I know
when a campaign's just a march and I know when it's going to be
a fight. This one's going to be a fight. I've seen it come all winter."

Shafter left the tent, moving down the company street into the
darkness. The band music floated through the windless air, the
swing and lift and melody of it carrying him back through his
memories, evoking scenes half forgotten and feelings long buried.
It shocked him to know suddenly how powerfully the music swayed
him, embittering him for things that had been and now were not,
making him sad out of reasons he could not understand, creating in
him an acute loneliness.

"Here," he said to himself, "you're thirty-two and past sentiment.

You've gotten rid of your dreams. That's what you wanted, wasn't it?"

He could not stop the outreaching of his thoughts, the strange swirl of his imagination. He remembered a lace fan lifted before a woman's face; and then the fan fell and he saw the sharp curve of her red mouth as she laughed at him, provocation in every soft curve of her cheeks, and the sound of her voice came over the great distance like a bell. The bell long since had turned silent, but the echo remained.

He remembered in sharp, stinging regret the kind of young man he had been; he recalled the wild flavor of his ambitions, the endless taste he had for life, the hopes and tempers and formless dreams which had buoyed him. Faith had been in that young Kern Shafter, and enthusiasm had made the world a fair place. He stopped walking; he put his hands behind his back and laced his fingers together, looking into the lush shadows of the night. Even now he caught the end of that hot vivid past, and suddenly said to himself: "When did I stop believing in things?" Somewhere along the line — and he knew when it was and how it was — he had flung himself upon the sharp point of disillusion, and it had opened him up and had drained out his faith; since that time he had walked as a bloodless man, turned stringy and colorless and heated only by a hatred.

But he saw that lace fan lift again over a woman's face and he heard her voice speaking to him, and then the fan dropped and the face was fair and smiling before him. It was another face — it was Josephine Russell's face and the smile was for him as long as it lasted. He watched it darken and die and he watched the glow of her eyes grow strange. He swung back on his heels; the music was still warm and beautiful in the night when he crawled into his blankets; and from the regimental street drifted the quick, stray phrases and laughter of the officers and their ladies.

Lieutenant Smith whirled his wife gallantly around, outward beyond the crowd. The music still played on but he broke away and took her arm and strolled across the slick prairie grass. "That makes me think of Saratoga," he said. "We had fun, old girl. Seems like a long time back. Just five years, though."

She said: "Do you know where I'd like to go again? Remember that little Connecticut town we passed through? All the houses painted white. The elms around them."

"We'll have our bills paid by fall," he said slowly. "Then I shall ask for leave." He stopped and turned her and looked down at her. "I regret all the things you've missed," he said, and kissed her.

She stepped back but she held both his arms. "This is the first time I've ever felt so afraid."

"It shouldn't be a long campaign. We are very well equipped, and we're going out in substantial numbers. This won't be another Fetterman affair. I think we'll have it done with by late August and be on the way home."

"I'm afraid," she whispered.

"Terry's a sound, safe man."

She shook her head, still clinging to him. It was a rare thing for her to be upset in this manner; both of them had a little ritual about these partings, which was to make them gay and very casual. But tonight she could not play the part, and his own feelings were strange in his chest. "I'm afraid," she said in a still lower, more breathless voice. "I've been that way all winter."

"You've stuck too long on the frontier."

"No," she said, "it isn't that." She pulled herself together and spoke with a pent-up feeling. "I wish the President had kept Custer away."

"Now — now," he said. "Anyhow, Custer will be under Terry's orders."

"If he sees a chance for a grand coup," she said, "he'll disobey his orders. I hate that man."

"Look here," he said gently, "we're in this regiment for another twenty years. You must not let your emotions shake you too much."

"Sometimes," she said, "I wish you were not in the army. I know it is your life and you want no other. But what have you gotten for all your faithfulness and service? You are beginning to turn gray. The hard usage of campaigning has done it to you. What do we have for it? A dozen silver spoons and a few cracked plates."

He was deeply disturbed and walked on without speaking. Presently she touched his arm and stopped. He saw a smile come uncertainly to her face. She murmured: "I won't send you off this way. Be good and take no unnecessary chances."

"I shall write you faithfully each night," he said. "We'll be in Connecticut this winter. Fresh apples, fresh vegetables. New clothes and old friends." He grinned at her and put his arms around her and kissed her once more; and so they stood in the darkness clinging to each other and reluctant to part while the long moments ran by.

In the four-o'clock darkness the drums of the infantry and the cavalry trumpets sounded the general and the glowing tops of the tent city collapsed as by the stroke of a single hand. Details moved on their crisscross errands, rolling and packing the canvas and stowing it away in supply wagons. Water details moved to the river and came back and orderlies rushed through the wan light of first daylight. Assembly blew and companies formed, each trooper's voice harking to roll call. Officers crisply shouted, swinging the companies into regimental line. The band was ahead and the colors swung by and Custer and his aides whirled up spectacularly. In the distance a bugler sounded "Forward" and at the same moment the band broke into tune. An ancient excitement rippled through Shafter, reviving the recollections of a hundred other marches in the past. After long waiting and long preparation, they were under way; over eight hundred troopers and infantrymen with scouts and guides and the long lumbering train of wagons rolling behind. The Seventh, in camp a collection of many men, now became a single-minded weapon, flexible, obedient and responsive. Ahead, Custer's huge campaign sombrero swung up in a wide gesture.

Shafter rode as right guide, the captain beside him. Moylan said: "We're parading through the fort. When we get beyond it we'll stop to let the wagon train catch up. There will be time for anybody so wishing to ride back and say so-long. Pass that word along, Hines." Then the captain looked at Shafter. "You got somebody to speak to?"

"No," said Shafter.

Moylan sat straight and blocky in the saddle—a man growing

old in his uniform. He had an excellent soldier's face, square and calm and shrewd; he was a good commander, his strictness tempered with practical wisdom. He saw many things he pretended not to see; but he always saw what needed to be seen. Lieutenant Smith rode half down the line. The second lieutenant, Varnum, had been detached with Hare to command the Ree scouts. These rode ahead of the regiment.

Somewhere between midnight and reveille it had briefly rained, so that all the grass stems were beaded with moisture. Morning's sun came up to lighten a faint fog and a courier galloped back from the head of the column at a headlong pace. As the troopers approached the walls of Lincoln they filed past Ree women gathered wailing and weeping to watch their men go. Moylan looked thoughtful when he heard it. "That's odd," he said. At Laundress Row the sergeants' families were likewise gathered and likewise crying. McDermott, reminded of his own wife and children, began to curse. Young Lovelace looked down upon the women and presently he found Mary there; she too had tears in her eyes.

The band struck up the regimental tune, "Garryowen," and so passed through the gate and marched across the parade. Along Officers' Row the families had assembled, and townspeople had come over from Bismarck for the departure. The infantry companies left in charge of the post were drawn up in rank to salute the passing column; a handful of troopers, on sick list or detached duty, marched beside their companions a little distance to say good-by. Thus the regiment passed through the main guard gate to the north and swung westward toward the ridge west of the post.

As A Company filed through the gate, Shafter saw more townspeople gathered and, looking over toward the little building of the commissary sergeant, he saw Josephine.

She didn't notice him at the moment. Her glance was on the column and she seemed to be scanning it very closely, her glance running through the stretched-out file with a hurried intentness. Presently she discovered him and her eyes stayed on him as he rode forward; he observed her face grow tighter than before and he saw her lips move. He lifted his hat and when he rode on he felt the effect of her glance. It seemed to remain with him, to follow him.

Half a mile onward the regiment halted to wait for the supply wagons to come forward; and the ranks broke, the officers and married men riding back to perform their own private farewells. Shafter stood beside his horse, watching them go; he got out his pipe and filled it and drew smoke heavily into his lungs. He squatted down on the hard earth, hard in thought, hearing the cross fire of talk of other troopers around him.

Bierss said: "Your last chance, Bill, on that gal you been goin' with. She'll have another soldier when you come back."

"I can get another gal."

"Them Sioux women ain't tame," said Bierss.

Frank Lovelace walked rapidly down the hill with the rest of the back-tracking men. He passed groups of people at the north gate, he heard them talking and laughing — and he saw a woman put both her hands on a trooper's shoulder, look long at him, and begin to weep. He moved across the parade's long length toward the south side, blindly pulled toward Mary. He hadn't talked to her for many weeks — not since the night of the quarrel — and he knew that the tears he had seen on her face were for her father who was also marching away. Or maybe they were for Purple. Still, he kept going; he couldn't help it. When he had gotten halfway across the parade he saw her come toward him. She was running.

He said, "Ah, Mary, don't run!" He raced toward her. She was speaking to him but he couldn't hear what she was saying. He stopped just in time to avoid striking her; her arms went around him and he felt the hard pounding of her heart and her tears ran hot along his cheeks when he kissed her.

She pulled back to look at him, showing him the terror in her eyes. "I didn't want you to go away like that, Frank!"

"I was coming to you," he said.

"It didn't mean anything," she said. "I'm sorry if you were angry. If you'd only turned back instead of walking away."

"I wanted to come back," he said. "I guess I was a big fool."

The trumpet was blowing from the hill, summoning them back.

The sound of it went hard through him; it made a pain in him. Her hands dug into his arms and she was trembling — and once more terror widened her eyes. "Frank — Frank — "

"I'll be back," he said.

"My father likes you. Frank — "

He kissed her again and turned, pulled by the music. Men were streaming over the parade and somebody called at him to come along. She clung to him, so that he had to lift her arms from him; and though he was very young, he did something that was as gallant as any mature man could ever do. He lifted her hand and kissed it, and he smiled and said again, "I'll be back," and trotted toward the north gate. After a few feet, he looked behind and noticed that she was walking after him. He called, "No, Mary." He shook his head and broke into a run. When he reached the north gate he again looked back and saw her standing in the center of the parade with her hand raised to him. The sight of her, so small and lonely on the parade ground's empty sweep, hit him in the heart.

Several officers had ridden down from the ridge to have a final moment with their families. Garnett came with them and went into bachelor's quarters to pick up a small notebook he had forgotten; when he came out of quarters he looked along Officers' Row and observed Mrs. Barrows standing before her house; her face turned toward him and he saw the care and the shadowing cast upon her features by her thinking. Then she looked away from him and he noticed the major coming across the parade toward her. Garnett climbed to his saddle and trotted briskly toward the north gate.

Lieutenant Smith had meanwhile dismounted before his wife, campaign hat in hand. He said: "I shall write you faithfully, by each courier. I really think we'll be back by August. Be a good girl, keep your hands busy and your mind out of mischief."

"What mischief is there to be found in an army post with all the healthy men gone?"

"Always one or two handsome beggars floating around."

"Pooh," she said, "I can't flirt with old men. That's all you're leaving me with."

They were light and foolish with each other. He said: "I shall come back with a mustache a foot long. One of the scratchy kind."

"I shall divorce you if you appear with mutton chops."

"It won't be divorce you'll be thinking of, when I show up."

"You're very egotistical."

The sound of the trumpet came again from the hill; and their smiling died. He took her to him and he said in a hard, grating voice: "I shall miss you like hell."

"Ah," she said, "be careful — oh, be careful!"

He held her as long as he dared and then wheeled and stepped up to his horse. He was again smiling, and looking down sharply at her until she brought a smile resolutely to her lips. "That's it," he said. "This winter, old girl, we're going to Connecticut. Goodby, my dear."

Shafter sat on the ground, looking down at the post, his thoughts wholly with Josephine. What stuck with him was the picture she made, her shoulders against the wall of the commissary sergeant's house, her eyes so carefully searching the column and at last stopping upon him. He said to himself: "She can have little interest in me," but her lips had said something to him across the distance. Very definitely she had spoken to him. Suddenly he realized he had to go back to her and discover if she had spoken to him, if she had anything to say to him. He rose and went into the saddle, dropping down the hill.

He came to the officers' club and skirted the post gardens. There were a lot of soldiers and people crowded around the gate and he didn't immediately see her and he thought she had perhaps returned to the ferry. Troopers had begun to come out of the fort, bound back to the column, and from his point of view he could see the long wagon train crawl around the west edge of the fort, now nearly caught up with the command; and from the main column came the sharp notes of the trumpet, summoning the stragglers. Threading the crowd, he saw her. She still stood by the house of the commissary sergeant and she had seen him and was watching him. He came before her and lifted his hat.

"Nice of you," he said, "to come here to watch us go."

"I suppose," she said, "you'll be away all summer."

"Never know. Nothing's certain."

She had nothing to add, and for his part he was caught in a silence which held him fast. Troopers streamed through the north gate. Captain Moylan passed, saying: "Time to go, Sergeant." Shafter watched her, with the clearest impression of her beauty and her strength. These were the things in her which most had appealed to him — these which gave her a capacity for laughter and teasing and gave her, too, a will which could be hard as iron.

"Good luck," he said.

"You're the one to need that, Kern. I should be wishing you the luck."

"Wish it, then," he said.

"If you think it worth remembering," she said, soft and calm, "I do wish you luck."

He stirred on his saddle. There was a question in his mind, and a wish and an uncertainty he wanted to be rid of; and he remembered how sweet her lips were and the vibrations of her voice when she was stirred. He was on the edge of dismounting and he had made a move toward it when Garnett rode up from the guard gate and saw him there. Garnett's voice hit him like a stone.

"Get back to your outfit, Sergeant."

Shafter saw her throw a glance toward Garnett, who swung from his horse and now stood by her. She looked at Garnett with an odd expression, and turned her smiling glance again to Shafter, still and sweet. He bowed his head at her, wheeled the horse and trotted to A Company.

Custer rushed by, lithe and magnificent on his horse, the feeling of motion and activity exciting the general. All down the line the sergeants were bawling at their men. A single word rippled through the column.

"Forward!"

The Seventh moved with a kind of elastic stretching; and the white-topped wagon trains made a sinuous half-mile trail behind. The ground sloped upgrade toward the little ridge west of the fort and one by one the companies came to the summit, tipped over and had a last backward look at Lincoln, lying under the sun-brightened morning haze. Shafter swung in his saddle to catch that picture, and Hines said. —

"Long time before we see it again."

They moved down the ridge into a rolling, broken land — headed toward the Heart River, the Bad Lands, the Powder and the Tongue and the Yellowstone and the Rosebud — to all that crisscross of strange names and colorful and mysterious names — to the mysterious depth of a land almost unknown to them. In that direction somewhere lay the Sioux. The band had ceased to play and the column tilted over the ridge in thoughtful silence. With the general rode his adjutant, his orderly and Charley Reynolds. With him too rode Marc Kellogg, representing the *New York Tribune,* one of those newspapermen whom Sherman had warned Custer not to take along.

From her place at the side of the commissary sergeant's house, Josephine Russell watched the regiment move up to the summit of the ridge and fall away. At that moment the sun brightened the haze and she noticed that a shadow was thrown upward by the column. The shadow strengthened into a mirage, so that she clearly saw the regiment marching through the sky and slowly fading in the sky.

She thought for a moment it was an illusion of her own; but then she heard people around her speak of it, half in excitement, half in wonder. One man near by shook his head and turned his eyes from it. "That's a sign. I'm damned glad I'm not along."

She swung back to the ferry, walking with her head lowered; she got to her horse and stepped to the saddle. "It might have been better," she thought. "But Edward came between us again. I expected too much. Now there's nothing left to expect." She thought she heard the far-off sound of the regimental band playing "Garryowen," and listened until she was certain it was only her imagination.

XVI

Westward March

THAT afternoon, the column marched thirteen miles and camped in a grassy bottom beside the Heart River. Water and wood details went immediately away and men took up clubs to clear the area of rattlesnakes. The horses were placed on picket down the middle of each street and the guards were pacing their rounds by the time the cook fires began to stain the shadows. Another detail went out to slaughter the beef issue from the herd of cattle driven with the column. At headquarters tent, Terry and Custer sat in close conference while pay call blew and the regiment filed by the paymaster.

Shafter said: "You going to walk down to the corner saloon now, Hines?"

"It is Terry's doin'," said Hines. "If the boys had gotten their pay last night in the fort we'd have a column of drunks this mornin'. Now it will keep till we get home."

Reveille blew at four on the following morning and the general sounded at five. By six the column was under way, a mile-long line sinuously following the contours of the land, with flankers to left and right and advance points far ahead, with the Ree scouts fading into the distance and creeping back as quietly in the late day. Rains came down in tempestuous squalls and they crossed the Sweetbriar in a slashing hail storm and crawled through bottom-land with the wagons hub-deep and double-teamed. Despatch riders arrived from Lincoln with the latest mail and later rode back. On the twenty-first they crossed the Big Muddy and moved through sharp showers and slept wet at night and rose sullen. The little creaks they came upon were bank-full from the steady downfall; the quick-bred mosquitoes swarmed thickly around them, driving the livestock frantic. Alkali patches began to appear and on the left forward horizon the Bad Lands showed as fairyland spires and grotesque, vari-colored minarets; at night burning lignite beds sent up their dull red columns, like signals of warning. They crossed the crooked loops of Davis Creek ten times in one day's march, moved through huge cottonwood groves and put the Little Missouri behind them. That day Terry sent Custer forward on scout but found no sign of Indians.

It rained again and grew cold and snow fell three inches deep. Wet buffalo chips smoldered without burning and horses grew hungry for want of good grass. Scouts came out of the broken land from Major Moore's detachment — who had been sent forward to establish a supply base — to report he had reached Stanley's Stockade and that the *Far West* waited there with supplies. The same despatches brought news from Gibbon to the effect that his Montana column was in motion down the Yellowstone. Terry sent back orders for Gibbon to halt and wait, and for the *Far West* to deliver one boat-load of supplies to the mouth of the Powder.

They followed the Beaver into rising, broken country, the column weaving around and about gullies and low masses of rusty sandstone. They forded Cabin Creek and traversed a barren country glittering with mica. Beyond O'Fallon's Creek they crossed a divide into the basin of the Powder and from the heights, in a short interval of sunlight, they saw far away the rugged, contorted bluffs of the Yellowstone. Thoroughly weary, and wet again from the intermittent rain, they camped on the Powder, which was at this point two hundred feet wide and two feet deep.

It was June 8, with the patient and thorough Terry growing unaccountably restless. Next morning he took Moylan's and Keogh's troops and rode down the Powder to the Yellowstone where the *Far West* waited and where also Major Brisbin of Gibbon's column waited. Terry left the two cavalry troops and proceeded up the river on the *Far West* to the Tongue where he had a conference with Gibbon. Then he came back on the boat to the Powder and returned with his two escort troops to the camp of the Seventh. That night Hines, having talked with the sergeant major, passed on the news.

"The base of supply will be at the mouth of the Powder. The *Far West* will move Major Moore and the supplies to there from

Stanley's Stockade. Meanwhile Gibbon's been ordered to go back up the Yellowstone to the Rosebud and wait until we march to him. The country over that way is full of Indians. Gibbon's outfit has been fightin' 'em in small details all the way along."

Now it was a game of hide and seek, with all the responsibility of making contact falling upon Terry's shoulders. Before him lay a rough area of land about one hundred miles square, bounded on the north by the Yellowstone, on the south by the fore edge of the Bighorns, on the west by the Bighorn and on the east — where he stood poised with the Seventh — by the Powder. In that area lay the main bodies of the Sioux, their tracks plain to his scouts, their smaller bands weaving rapidly from place to place as bait to confuse him and draw him off scent. Now, patiently, he set about a thorough scouting job to establish the whereabouts of the enemy's weight. Crook, somewhere around the Bighorns, acted as a fence on the south and Gibbon, camped at the mouth of the Rosebud, would bar the Sioux from westward retreat.

"The trouble is," said McDermott, "we're too slow and we're too few to make a good fence. If Crazy Horse or Gall or Two Moons or Red Cloud want to break out of this country, they can circle and be a hundred miles away before we get turned around. Now here's Terry tryin' to find where to hit. Meanwhile the Sioux scouts know where we are. We can be seen forty miles away. We ain't goin' to strike the Sioux by surprise."

"That," said Hines, "is what Terry's got Custer for. We'll just march here and there across the country until Terry's got it figured where they are. Then one night we'll set out under Custer and we'll go fast. We'll make a big jump and catch 'em before they see us."

On the tenth of June, Terry despatched Reno with six companies of cavalry and one Gatling gun to explore the upper part of the Powder. "You will go as far as the junction of the Little Powder," he told Reno. "Then go due west to the headwaters of the Mizpah Creek, cross and continue to the Pumpkin, and go down the Pumpkin to the Tongue. Then proceed down the Tongue to the Yellowstone where you will meet me. You will throw out smaller parties as you march, exploring the intervening ground. I wish it thoroughly

scouted, although I feel certain the hostiles are not in body this far
east. I think we shall find them beyond the Tongue. Do not, however, go beyond the Tongue."

Thus he intended thoroughly to convince himself of the emptiness of this smaller area before pushing ahead to where he believed
the action lay. Reno left early in the afternoon with his wing, A
Company included, and struck directly up the Powder. Faithful to
his orders, he turned west at the Little Powder, touched the headwaters of the Mizpah and moved on to Pumpkin Creek. He had his
feelers out all the way in the form of the Ree scouts led by Bloody
Hand; and each night they brought back the story of renewed trails
sweeping up from the southeast and going on toward the northwest,
on beyond the Tongue toward the Rosebud, toward the Bighorn.
Bloody Hand, to indicate the size of that far-away gathering,
reached down and cupped the clodded earth in his hands and let
it spill out. "That many," he said.

Reno had long service as an officer and a creditable Civil War
record; but now when he reached the Tongue he faced the problem
of an independent commander operating beyond the reach of his
superior officer. He had his strict orders not to go beyond the
Tongue, but his scouts all were in accord as to the presence of Sioux
over that way; and he judged his mission to be that of finding definite clues. Therefore, wrestling with the problem, he broke the
bonds of his orders and crossed the Tongue to the Rosebud, feeling
right and left constantly, and on the nineteenth he stopped near the
Yellowstone and sent a despatch to Terry of his whereabouts and
what he had discovered.

Terry meanwhile had been moving westward along the Yellowstone with the rest of the Seventh, keeping in contact with the
Montana column and with Moore by courier; and now slowly, as
news drifted in, he began to tie the ends of his expedition together.
Gibbon he held at the Rosebud. At the Tongue he met Reno's returning party and the three men, Terry and Custer and Reno, held
a conference. Terry listened to Reno's report and explanation of his
going beyond his orders without comment, being a mild and reserved officer. All he said was: "It is as I believed. The Sioux are

beyond. On the Rosebud and westward in the direction of the Bighorn. General — " indicating Custer — "you will move the Seventh on to the mouth of the Rosebud and join Gibbon. I shall take the *Far West* up there."

Custer and Reno left the general, Custer walking with a heavy, irritable silence that Reno immediately noticed; and for his part he had his dislike of Custer and now revealed it with a sour, caustic question: —

"I seem to gather from your manner that you disapprove of my stretching my instructions."

"When Terry gave you those orders," said Custer, "he already knew there was a concentration west of the Tongue. Therefore your march in that direction was a waste of six days' time."

"I judged the orders on their intent," said Reno stiffly. "I think I have an average intelligence."

"I do not question it," snapped Custer and walked away. He was in a bad frame of mind, his nervous energy goading him to an impetuous action he could not embrace because of Terry's restraining hand.

On June 20, the *Far West* landed Terry at the mouth of the Rosebud where Gibbon and his column waited. That same afternoon the Seventh arrived and a general meeting was held aboard the boat — Terry, Custer, Gibbon and Gibbon's second in command, Brisbin. Terry laid his big campaign map on the table and made his estimate of the situation.

"The Sioux are southwest of us, somewhere between the Rosebud and the Bighorn. General Gibbon's column will ascend the Bighorn. It will swing when it reaches the Little Bighorn and follow that stream. You will leave in the morning, Custer, with your regiment, and go up the Rosebud. The intent of this maneuver is that the two columns will act as anvil and sledge, with the Sioux between. We shall require a close consideration of the time. General Gibbon, at what time can you be at the mouth of the Little Bighorn?"

Gibbon took a long look at the map and made his calculations; at this stage of the game the element of time and distance grew vital and therefore he arrived at his estimation with a great deal of care.

"I shall," he said, "be at the Little Bighorn on the morning of the twenty-sixth."

"That is for your information, Custer," said Terry. "Your marches should be based upon Gibbon's arrival at that creek at the agreed time. Now," he went on, still speaking to Custer, "as you proceed up the Rosebud, you will explore right and left. When you reach Tullock's Creek you will send a man down that creek to meet Gibbon's scouts and thereby transmit such information as you have acquired to him. This country will no doubt be full of hostiles. Therefore you need a good scout to make it."

"Let me give him Herendeen," said Gibbon. "I'll talk to Herendeen."

Custer nodded absent-mindedly.

"At the upper reaches of the Rosebud," Terry said, "you will scout toward the Little Bighorn. But I wish you to constantly feel toward your left. I do not wish to hamper you with unnecessary orders, but you should adjust your marches so as to give Gibbon time to come along. On the morning of the twenty-sixth, therefore, you should be in some position southeast of the Sioux while Gibbon is somewhere northwest of them, the two of you closing in on either side. Do not rush the thing. Do not permit yourself to engage before Gibbon is up for support. Now, how are your supplies and how do you feel about your men? Do you need something added to the Seventh? Gibbon could give you Brisbin's battalion of cavalry."

Custer sat in glum thought, staring at the floor. "No," he said, "I'll need nothing more than I have. The Seventh is wholly able to take care of what it meets. The addition of outside cavalry would only interfere with our freedom of movement."

Terry considered him a thoughtful moment, knowing his man; and Gibbon and Brisbin studied him. Irritableness worked in Custer; an uncharacteristic gloom showed on him, as though the winter's injuries and humiliations, never healed, now freshly hurt him.

"Gibbon," said Terry, "give Custer part of your Crow scouts. Give him Bouyer and Girard. They know this country better than Reynolds. They can assist Reynolds." He stroked his smooth chin and had a commander's natural grave wondering; for he had made his explorations, formed his judgments and had arranged his maneuvers. Now the job was in the hands of his field officers. He sat still, checking all these things seriously in his mind. "Crook should be somewhere near us, and it would be a relief to have him in support. But I have heard nothing from him and have no idea at all where he is. Nor can I wait longer, for fear the Sioux will slip through us. You have a slightly farther distance to go, Gibbon, therefore put your troops in motion today for the Bighorn. Custer will leave first thing in the morning. That is all. I shall go with Gibbon's column and — " turning to Custer — "if all goes well, I shall meet you on the twenty-sixth."

Custer rose, saying, "I'll pass on the orders," and left the tent. Gibbon, Terry and Brisbin all watched him depart, their glances following his long shape, as it moved with impatient treading toward his own headquarters tent.

Officers' call ran through the Seventh, summoning them to Custer who sat in his portable easy chair, a lank figure in buckskin, with a scarlet flowing kerchief and a head of hair grown ragged. The sun had scorched his face scarlet, making his eyes a deeper blue. He sat still before his officers, with none of the electric energy showing in his talk or his muscles. He seemed to their sharp eyes unusually depressed.

"Gibbon marches up the Bighorn while we march up the Powder. We shall leave in the morning, light marching order. The wagon train stays. Each troop is assigned twelve mules which are to carry hardtack, coffee and sugar for fifteen days, bacon for twelve days. Use your strongest mule in each troop for extra ammunition, two thousand rounds per troop. You'll have to load extra forage on the mules also. Each trooper will carry one hundred rounds of carbine ammunition and eighteen rounds of revolver. And twelve pounds of oats."

The twenty-eight officers stood gravely before him, stained with a month's hard marching, their buckskins caked with old mud, their blue trousers faded out, their mustaches unkempt. They were a hard crew to look upon in the falling twilight; and they were

silent long after he had fallen silent, until at last he said in his always
touchy voice: —

"Are there any suggestions, gentlemen?"

It was Moylan who spoke. "That's not enough mules, General.
You'll break them down with the load you propose."

"Wagons are out of the question. Additional mules will slow us
too greatly."

French of M Company had a word. "Once your mules start to
lag you'll slow down anyhow."

Custer slapped the arms of his portable chair with a gesture of
open temper; his voice carried its rasp of anger. "Well, gentlemen,
carry what you please, but remember you are responsible for your
companies. The present arrangement of wings is abolished. Each
commander reports directly to me. The extra forage was only a
suggestion, but bear in mind we will follow the trail for fifteen
days unless we catch them before that time."

Captain McDougall said: "Are we to push on at will? I thought
I understood you to say we were operating in conjunction with
General Gibbon."

Custer was now moving back and forth along the ground, nervous
and wholly out of patience with his officers. "We shall follow the
Sioux, no matter how long it takes. We may not see the steamer
again." He swung on his adjutant. "Cooke, make out the orders so
troop commanders may have them tonight. Assign a sergeant and
six privates from each company to take charge of the pack train.
McDougall, your troop will guard the pack train. There is at present
an unequal distribution of officers among the companies. I shall
make temporary reassignments in order that each troop may be
properly officered. That's all."

He meant it to be all, but the officers lingered, not wholly satisfied.
McDougall said: "I don't think a few extra mules would be un-
wise, General."

Custer wheeled, his voice turned shrewish and sardonic: "Twelve
mules to a company. Take what you wish on them. Take nothing
if you are prepared to starve your troop. For that matter you'd better

take salt along. You may have to live on horsemeat before we're finished with this." Having said it, he whirled into his tent.

The officers turned and moved backward toward their companies in small groups. Godfrey moved beside Edgerly and quietly spoke his mind. "I have never seen him like that before."

"You must remember," said Edgerly, "he is smarting under the rebuke he received from the President. He is a very proud man."

Godfrey shook his head. "The smell of powder is usually a tonic to him — and the smell of powder is thick around here tonight. He is singularly depressed. In fact he has depressed me."

Darkness came and mess fires bloomed along the Yellowstone's bluff. Details moved back to the supply train to break out the extra rations and ammunition to be loaded on mule-back on the morrow; and off to one corner of the camp, the Indian scouts were in full voice with their own strange ceremony — the echoes of it sharp and mournful in this wild empty corner of the earth. In his tent, Lieutenant Smith was at the moment writing this letter to his wife: —

My dear: We leave in the morning on what seems to be the final part of the campaign. It will soon be over and then I shall look forward to the return — to leave this fall. I know how you feel when I am away. I have often thought of the hardness of it on you and I wish often that I were a more demonstrative man so that I could tell you how the sight of you and the nearness of you sometimes affects me. We are a sober lot tonight. The general is in an edgy frame of mind and there's not the usual racket along the company street. But that is as it always is before action. Be cheerful. There is no great prospect of danger here . . .

Lieutenant Porter stepped into Lieutenant Van Reilly's tent and found Harrington there; and stood by while these two made mutual wills. "My effects to you," said Harrington, "if I die and you survive. If you die and I survive, I shall take your things to your wife."

"Agreed," said Van Reilly. "Now in case we're both killed, let's have Porter do that chore."

"Agreed," said Porter. "And either of you is to look after my possessions and return them to my wife in case of my death. Is there a drink of hard liquor in this tent?"

Van Reilly found a bottle and measured it by candlelight. "One drink for tonight. One for tomorrow night. After that we shall not need it, being uplifted by victory, I sincerely trust."

In his tent, Custer was at the moment composing his nightly letter to Libby; and all along the regiment men made their casual disposition of their effects, or wrote final thoughtful messages home, or lay back and were silent, or played poker by candlelight, or walked abroad in the camp darkness. On the *Far West* a game of poker had started with Grant Marsh, Keogh, Tom Custer, Calhoun and Garnett playing; and on the bluff of the river Shafter stood alone, watching the steamboat's lights make their yellowed, wrinkled lanes across the water. The river was a steady washing tone in the night, and wind came down from the north, and somewhere southward a low moon shed a partial glow through the fog. The Crows and the Ree were steadily chanting out their strangely barbaric tune of farewell and warning — that beating rhythm a pulse of premonition all through the camp. One by one the lights of the regiment died and tattoo sounded softly. Shafter watched the black shadows thicken in the Yellowstone's canyon, and he looked backward and saw his life as an empty thing and found no clear answer for his future. His life marched to this point, void of hope or ambition, without sweet memories or faith — and tomorrow held nothing that made him anxious to be traveling toward it.

So the regiment settled down to sleep on the eve of its march. On that same night and at that same hour, one hundred miles southward, Crook's command lay with double guards around it and licked the wounds of a sharp defeat inflicted by Crazy Horse four days earlier. For the second time in five months Crook grew cautious and doubtful and now sent despatches back to Laramie — to be wired to Sheridan at Chicago — that he would not advance without additional re-enforcements. Of all this Terry knew nothing as he sat awake on the *Far West* and reviewed his plans.

XVII

Custer Pulls Away

A DAMP mist hung heavily over the water and the canyon, through which the cursing of the mule packers came in muffled explosions. The peremptory notes of assembly laid a rough hand upon the troopers, and the companies formed one by one on the rolling bench above the river. Custer swung to his horse and crossed the camp at a full gallop to join Terry, Gibbon and Brisbin who tarried behind their own column in order to see the Seventh away. Custer rounded in beside the three, his horse fiddling briskly. Down the bench rose Reno's shout of command, which placed the regiment in forward motion. There was no music to lead them on this parade; the band had been left at the Powder River base.

They came past the reviewing group, Reno saluting as he went by, each company commander swinging his head to the right and rendering a like salute. They moved on, company by company, stained by weather and a month's hard marching — dark and toughened and competent men made surly by early morning. There was none of a dress parade's flash or fancy display about them this day. Their clothes were ragged and their whiskers long, and they carried with them the bulky impedimenta of a field campaign — bedding roll lashed behind saddle cantle, haversacks, lariat and picket pins, nose bags and extra pouch of oats, carbine and revolver, extra bandoliers of ammunition, trenching tools, canteen — all these things attached to various quarters of man or horse, all slapping and clattering and shifting to the motion of the mount.

Terry watched them pass with a thoughtful eye. For the troops he had nothing but commendation. "You have a good regiment, Custer. I do not know of a better one in the service."

Custer showed a flash of his old spirit. He smiled, the constriction of it half closing his eyes and brightening them into audacity. "My regiment, General, has been the best in the army for ten years."

Terry smiled. Gibbon said nothing. Brisbin, a member of the Third Cavalry and a truculent man, gave Custer a sharply irritated glance and returned his eyes to the Seventh. It had always been a flashy regiment, more troublesome and more picturesque than any other, with ten years of campaigning to its credit, with its roll of honorable dead, with its actions and skirmishes and engagements a worthy list on its record. Its companies, never at full strength, had been further pulled down by details left at the Powder River base so that its eight hundred had diminished to seven hundred. But it had a strong core of old-time noncommissioned men and its captains were largely good, some seasoned and faithful like Moylan, some wild-tempered like Keogh, some stubborn and cool as was the white-haired Benteen who never forgot a hatred or a liking.

The companies were under-officered and Custer had made some changes of assignment. Moylan still had A Company, B was McDougall, C had been given to Tom Custer while Weir kept D. Algernon Smith had been taken from A to command E Company. F was Yates and G was led by Donald McIntosh, the officer with Indian blood. Benteen had H and I was commanded by Keogh and Godfrey led K. Custer's brother-in-law, Calhoun, rode in front of L. French retained M. There was also some shuffling of other officers to insure for each troop better leadership.

"The heart of a regiment," said Terry, "is faith in itself. I have every confidence in the Seventh."

The column went by. Sun began to break through the fog and the day promised to be fair and warm. Terry, laboring under natural weight of spirit, saw the sun as an omen and slightly nodded to himself, and then fixed a sharp blue eye on the pack train of 160 mules now passing under the escort of six troopers from each company, followed by McDougall's company as guard. The mules were improperly loaded and made a ragged, recalcitrant column. The general scowled at the sight of it.

"That's a poor shift for a supply train," he said with some degree of sharpness. "You're going to have trouble with it."

Custer flushed in embarrassed irritation and bit his lips. He looked straight before him. "We'll get it shaken down before the day's over."

"Better have been gotten in shape before you started," stated Terry. "Everything depends on the timetable we have set. Let nothing disturb that, even if you have to cut your worst mules out and let them go."

The last file passed and the better part of a half hour had gone by. Terry lifted a folded paper from his pocket and handed it to Custer. "This is the written statement of the instructions I gave you yesterday. I have left them purposely indefinite in certain things. I have too much faith in your judgment as a commander to impose fixed orders upon you."

Custer accepted the paper, gave it a careless glance and thrust it into his pocket. He was impatient to be away and his body communicated that feeling to the horse beneath him. It fiddled and danced in the spongy earth, carrying him around until he faced Terry.

Terry said: "I shall be with Gibbon and we shall be on the Little Bighorn the morning of the twenty-sixth. Be sure, when you reach the head of Tullock's Creek, to send Herendeen back along it to communicate with Gibbon. That will be a verification of your whereabouts. One last thing. I expect both columns to work in close conjunction. We cannot beat the Indians in detail, or surround them in detail. This movement depends entirely upon both columns striking at the same approximate time. Be sure to have your scouts always well ahead to establish contact with Gibbon at the first opportunity. I wish you luck."

Custer grasped Terry's hand and shook it with his swift impulsiveness, briefly accepted the hands of Gibbon and Brisbin, and whirled around. Just before he broke his horse into a gallop, Brisbin called after him: —

"Now Custer, don't be greedy. Wait for us."

Custer looked back, flushed and smiling. He flung up his hand, his horse springing up beneath him, and so making a figure of dash and gallantry in the day's growing sunlight. "I won't," he said. With that enigmatic answer he let his horse go, and rushed away toward the column's head.

A mile from the Yellowstone, Custer halted the command for a brief rest and divided the Indian scouts into two sections to cover each side of the Rosebud; after that he stood at the head of his horse and looked awhile into the haze slowly developing southward. Cooke was with him, waiting for anything the general might have to say, but Custer made no comment. Wrapped in an unusual kind of taciturnity, Custer presently mounted and swung up his hand for the forward march; and led the column over the Rosebud to the west bank.

From his saddle, Shafter watched the broken country unroll before him. The Rosebud lay at the bottom of a shallow canyon and the column, now without the impediment of wagons, took the most practicable course — sometimes following the edge of the water, sometimes traveling on a narrow benchland half up the side of the canyon, and sometimes rising to the top of the bluff. All this was a powder-gray, fine-grained land with grass and sage tufting it; all of it was a land scorched by summer's heat and scarified by severe winters. Now and then the command passed through willow growths. Otherwise there was no break in the rough rolling of the country.

A Company had a new officer. Smith had been put in command of E and Varnum was in charge of the scout detail; therefore Custer had assigned Garnett to A, and Garnett now rode at the foot of the troop. Shafter felt him as he would have felt a cold wind at the back of his neck; and all his thoughts of Garnett were cold and full of hate, shaking him out of his solemn, indifferent frame of mind.

Hines said: "Reminds me of the country around the Washita. It's gettin' hot. I never knew it to be any other way when the outfit went into a fight. Cold as hell or hot enough to give a man a stroke. Soldierin' is a funny life."

They bivouacked at noon, ate and lay idle in the warming drowse. The regiment now was definitely pointed into action, hourly penetrating deeper into the heart of Sioux country, and therefore men were more silent than usual, more withdrawn to their own thoughts — and more watchful. In the afternoon the regiment moved on, still following the Rosebud as it angled to the southwest; scouts returned with their news and sometimes this news came down the line, as overheard by some officer or enlisted man. Once Moylan spurred ahead, spoke to the adjutant and dropped back.

"Plenty of tracks ahead of us. The Sioux seem headed toward a general meeting on our forward right."

"Soldierin'," repeated Hines, "is a funny life. I knew I'd get sore bones out of this, but I wanted to come. Ten years from now I'll smoke a pipe and tell some youngster how Grandpaw fought the Sioux — and I'll lie like hell. It will seem wonderful to me, lookin' back at it. But right now my bones are sore."

"It ain't your bones," said Bierss.

Hines retorted: "My bottom's a damned sight tougher than yours, Cawpril. It has scrubbed leather a lot of years longer."

"You ain't had the fun I've had," said Bierss. "You never got run out of as many bedrooms. Ah, Sarge, you're a serious man. When you're dead you'll regret that."

"In heaven," said McDermott, "I wonder if a man could get chevrons put on his wings."

"If it takes as long to get a promotion in heaven as in this army," said Bierss, "you'll be fifty years a rookie."

"A good man's a good man, heaven or here," said McDermott virtuously. "Gabriel will have me runnin' a platoon inside of a week."

"All I want out of heaven," said Bierss, "is a bed and three meals and no work. And a woman who won't cry when I leave her."

"You'll be lookin' for a second-story window to jump through," said McDermott.

"No windows in heaven, you fool," put in Hines. "It is a city of glass. Everybody sees everybody. No dark corners and no walls."

"Good God," said Bierss, "can't a man have privacy anywhere?" He grinned at Shafter. "Professor, you've read books. What's heaven like?"

"A tunnel," said Shafter. "No light and no sound. You'll never know when you walk into it and you'll never reach the other end. In fact, Bierss, you'll never know you're there."

Bierss rummaged that conception through his mind for a quarter mile and made no headway. "I don't see that at all. It sounds like bein' buried underground forever."

"Who knows?" murmured Shafter.

"Professor," stated Bierss, "if that is what a book does for a man, then books are damned dangerous and I'm glad I never read one."

The column camped short of twilight, still on the Rosebud; and fires twinkled along the earth and guards threw a vigilant ring around camp. The Crow and the Rees slid mysteriously away and from afar presently came softly the repeated hoot of an owl, to be elsewhere echoed. An orderly summoned the officers to Custer's fire. He stood at the blaze with his officers ringed around it, and firelight played upon them somberly and brightly danced in their eyes. Cooke, the giant adjutant, stood near Custer, as did the mild and self-effacing Charley Reynolds.

"From now on," said Custer, "there will be no more bugle calls. Stable guards will waken the troops at 3 A.M. March will be resumed at five. I shall regulate the making and breaking of camp. Otherwise each commander is responsible for the actions of his company. You will observe proper interval between companies. Do not get ahead of the scouts and do not let the column stretch out. We must remain compact."

He spoke in a suppressed manner; he seemed jaded, he seemed half indifferent, half uncertain. None of the brusque and intolerant stridency so characteristic of him showed this night; and after his initial announcement he stared long in the fire and presently pulled himself out of a kind of reverie.

"Gentlemen, I have complete faith in this regiment and I have entire confidence in your loyalty and your entire support. I call on you particularly now to give me the best of your judgment and all of your talents."

He pushed his hands into his pockets and broke off, hard engaged in thought, his bony face tipped down, his thin long lips half hidden behind his mustache, his face in a shadowed, disillusioned repose. The ring of officers waited for him to continue, closely watching, carefully listening to this new tone, this somber reflection so unlike him. Silence weighted the circle. Benteen looked upon his commander with his ruddy, dogmatic face holding a steadfast reserve, an ingrained dislike; and Reno studied the man out of his dark-ringed eyes.

"We can," continued Custer, "expect to meet a thousand warriors or more. The trails are growing heavy, pointing ahead of us and west of us. It may be more than a thousand. It might be fifteen hundred. We came here to find Indians and we shall find them. We shall find them if I have to march this regiment all the way down to Nebraska or back to the Agencies. Let there be no misunderstanding as to our purpose. I have too much pride in the Seventh to go back empty-handed and I know you feel the same way. I ought to mention that General Terry offered me Brisbin's battalion of cavalry. I refused it. Frankly, I felt that there might be jealousy between the two groups and I wanted nothing to break the present knit spirit of our command." Then he paused and took on a moment's show of his old spirit. "Moreover, I am confident the Seventh can handle whatever it faces. If the hostiles can whip the Seventh, they can whip any re-enforcements we might have. That is all I have to say tonight, except you should be prepared for marches of between twenty-five and thirty miles a day."

The group slowly dissolved, walking in twos and threes back through the shadows toward the vague line of the troops lying like windrows along the earth. Godfrey and McIntosh and Wallace moved together toward the far end of camp, none of them speaking for a long spell. It was Wallace who broke the silence.

"You know, I think Custer is going to be killed."

"Why, what makes you believe that?" asked Godfrey.

"I have never seen him so disheartened before," said Wallace. "There is a shadow distinctly over him."

McIntosh made a troubled remark. "The general speaks of going as far as Nebraska if he must. I had the impression that Terry had definitely restricted us to a fifteen-day sortie."

"You know the general," said Godfrey, whereupon the three broke off, each going his own direction. Godfrey's troop was well along the camp and presently he passed a fire, around which he saw the interpreter Mitch Bouyer and three Crows squatting. Godfrey stopped and likewise squatted. One of the Indians looked at him and then spoke in Crow to Bouyer, who turned to Godfrey.

"Half Yellow Face wants to know if you've ever fought Sioux before."

"'Tell him I have," said Godfrey.

Bouyer passed it back to Half Yellow Face. The Indian asked another question which Bouyer relayed. "How many do you expect to find this time?"

"Oh, ten or fifteen hundred," said Godfrey. "What does he think?"

"He wants to know if you think you can whip that many?"

"I guess so."

Bouyer spoke for himself. "Well, I can tell you we're going to have a damned big fight and I ain't so sure. Neither are the Crows."

"How big a fight — how soon?" asked Godfrey.

"Soon," said Bouyer. "Don't expect the Sioux to retreat any more. They got their families with them. A big fight. All the fight you'll ever want."

The regiment was up at three and again in motion at five, with the troopers silent and stale. Within two miles they crossed the looping Rosebud three times and stopped once for watering. The day grew hot and the sun began to bite down for the first time during the long campaign and the porous earth changed from slick mud to dust by noon. The scouts, now working constantly ahead, reported back the mark of sign not over two days old. The long day wheeled on and the scanty foraging of the horses began to tell upon them; after thirty-three miles the regiment went into camp, ate and fell asleep. Once again at three it rose and at five was again marching.

Shafter said to Hines: "What's the date?"

Hines couldn't remember it and had to draw his roster book from his shirt pocket. "Twenty-fourth, but what's a day to you?"

"Birthday."

"Well," said Bierss, "tonight we'll bake a cake."

Captain Moylan, riding at his usual place beside Shafter, turned and said: "Good luck."

"Any kind of luck is all right."

The Crows sent back word of fresh sign and presently the column began to pass the round dead-grass spots where lodges had stood and the blackened char of old campfires. At noon the command halted for dinner — bacon and hardtack and coffee — and was hurried into the saddle by Custer. But after a brief forward march, he stopped the regiment at one o'clock. The Crows, vigilantly rummaging the distance, had sent back word of a camp freshly deserted at the forks of the Rosebud. Custer swung forward with two troops to investigate while the regiment rested. He was back in the middle of the afternoon and now began to throw his scouts in widening circles all around him. Seated cross-legged against the earth, Shafter knew that the trail had grown suddenly hot from the way the scouts ran in and out.

At five, Custer swung the command forward and now the trail passed into a valley whose short brown grass grew smooth and slick from a dry, stiff wind ruffling over it. The tracks of lodgepole travois scratched the ground everywhere and they came upon the skeleton frames of wickiups where a camp had been, and a sun-dance lodge. An officer left the column and moved to the lodge and rode back presently with a scalp lifted in his hand. Presently news came down the column: —

"White man's scalp hanging on that lodge. Cooke says it must have been one of Gibbon's troopers killed on the Yellowstone last month."

Custer seemed now to be pulled by the lively scent, for he moved the column steadily on through the last sunlight and into the blue-running dusk. The land tilted upward and the Rosebud made a shallow semicircle toward the southwest, fringed with willows. Beyond them, in the distance, lay a shallow knob.

Herendeen, who had been Gibbon's scout, now trotted up the line and reached Custer and spoke to him. "General, we're as close to the head of Tullock's Creek as we'll get. It's off there — " pointing to the right. "This is where I'm supposed to leave you and go down the creek to find Gibbon's scouts."

He waited for Custer's order on the subject and for whatever message Custer intended to convey to Gibbon. It was a night's ride down the creek, through the heart of Sioux-held ground and a risky prospect for a lone man. Gibbon had known this and had promised Herendeen extra pay for the venture. So now Herendeen waited for Custer's order to go, and rode silently beside the commander. Custer gave him a brief glance out of his deep set eyes, out of his bony, thought-hardened face; and then Custer put his glance into the forward blue distance and rode on without speaking. He had no answer for Herendeen and, after a half mile of this kind of traveling, Herendeen saw he was to be given no order. Being a man with a frontier touchiness, he wheeled away and dropped back along the column until he had reached his place. Apparently the general had changed his mind about sending back a messenger; it was just as well to Herendeen, who had no intention of risking his skin unless Custer definitely requested it.

At seven o'clock the command halted in sundown's last yellow flare of light and made camp with a dry, hard wind rolling the desert's smoke-fine dust at them. An orderly trotted through camp in lieu of officers' call and presently all officers stood in circle around Custer and Custer's headquarter's pennant. Benteen, whose mind always had an acid realism, stared at the flag with his unfavorable thought, at the two stars of a major general stitched on the pennant's field. This was what Custer had once been, in the Civil War, but no longer was; therefore in Benteen's critical opinion the commander had no right to the use of the two stars. It was a display of vanity that he held against Custer, adding it to his list of Custer's many other faults.

They stood stiff and spraddle-legged and dusty in the forming twilight, watching Custer's hawkish face swing around upon them; and, since all of them were in his hands and all their futures were at his disposal, they watched him closely, analyzing his unpredictable temper. The sourness and the gloominess had given way, but his buoyancy had not returned. He stood eager and straining in the windy evening, anxiously bedeviled by the nearness of the Indians, with all the consequent possibilities of a spectacular sweep against them; he was gnawed by the thought that he might miss them and lose that chance. All this was evident in the staccato manner of his talk.

"We have come seventy-five miles from the mouth of the Rose-bud. I have sent Varnum forward with the scouts. We're no more than thirty miles from the hostiles. I do not know yet which way they're running but I propose to find out."

Benteen's dry voice interrupted. "Are you sure they're running, General?"

Custer's voice had a special usage for Benteen; it was stiff and formal and brief. "If they were not running, we should have struck them before now."

"They know where we are," Benteen pointed out. "They know we're coming. It is my idea they may be picking their own spot to fight on."

"We'll see — we'll see," said Custer in his dismissing tone. "I propose to make a sudden jump at them. Troop commanders had better change your details on the pack train. May not get another chance. Look to your equipment. I suggest you water again tonight."

The pushing wind caught at the standard, whose end was plunged in the sandy earth, and suddenly knocked it over. Godfrey bent down and lifted it and jammed it into the ground again. It fell again, whereupon Godfrey patiently repeated the operation. All the officers watched this until Custer said: "Nothing more, gentlemen," and then they turned back to their various company streets, walking with a sprung-legged weariness. DeRudio said to Godfrey: "That was a bad sign."

Shafter lay back on his blankets, head pillowed on the McClellan saddle. Wind lifted the silt-fine sand from the ground and threw it against his face; the smell of dust was constant in his nostrils, and turned his throat dry. Night fell with its desert suddenness and the stars were very bright against the black bedding of the sky. Moylan had returned and spoke to Hines, who in turn spoke to Sergeant Easley. "Get six men and go relieve the troop's pack-train detail."

At nine o'clock, Lieutenant Varnum returned from his scout and reported to Custer who sat cross-legged in the darkness. Varnum crouched down to make his report.

"We went ten miles forward. Same kind of tracks as we've been crossing. We saw what looked like signal fires during the afternoon. They were off to the right."

Custer said: "The Crows tell me there's a high point on the divide between the Rosebud and the Little Bighorn where they used to go to steal Sioux horses. It is a lookout place called Crow Peak. It commands a view of the Little Bighorn valley. I want a responsible white man to go up there with the Crows tonight and have a look from there first thing in the morning and send word back to me. I'll be coming forward."

"I expect," said Varnum, "that means me."

"Take Reynolds and Bouyer with you, and whatever Indians you please."

Varnum had been in the saddle for many hours straight and was extremely weary. He got up and stamped his feet on the ground. "Daylight will be about four or a little after."

"Send back word as soon as practicable. What do your Crows say about the Sioux?"

"They guess a couple thousand. They counted the lodge marks at the last camp we passed."

Custer said: "These Rees are dead afraid of a Sioux. One Sioux is five to them. I doubt if the Crows have much more courage in that respect."

"I'd argue that, General. They're strong fighters."

"Send back word as soon as possible," repeated Custer and thus sent the dog-tired Varnum away. Cooke came up from the darkness and looked down from his great height. "Anything more, General?"

"No," said Custer. "Better roll in."

After Cooke had gone away, the general remained in his cross-legged attitude, solemnly thoughtful. The Rosebud, shallow and fickle, ran with a slight murmuring along the base of the low bluff before him. Behind him lay the regiment, soon asleep. He heard the sentries pacing, the occasional murmuring of their voices and the click of their guns. The wind had somewhat lessened but the scent of dust was strong, and the smell of horses and mules blew through the camp. He sat very still, his impulsive mind grasping the ends of his problem, and darting here and there, and jumping far ahead to the eventual scene which he knew he must make real — the scene of the Seventh smashing the Sioux in surprise attack. There was never any doubt in his mind as to the Seventh, never any doubt as to victory; the only thing which had ever worried him was his ability to catch up with the hostiles before they slipped from his grasp, before Terry's time limit expired, before Gibbon came up to join him.

He had a fighter's heart, this Custer, and a fighter's tremendous energy. He scorned the cautions which held other commanders back, he had a blind faith in the naked power of the sudden surprise rush and the naked power of a cavalry charge. On dash and surprise and swiftness he had made himself a general out of a boy lieutenant in four years and he could not change now. Nor wanted to change. Impatience and restlessness and a self-faith that never wavered were the stars that shone brightest before him, and moved him and made him.

So he sat, jealous of the chance before him and wanting neither Terry nor Gibbon to share it; and he thought of the ordeal through which he had passed during the winter — the humiliation put upon him by Grant, by Sherman, even by Sheridan, and all this he hated until the hatred squeezed out of him everything but the one dominating passion to strike and destroy the Sioux camp, and so recover his prestige. He had been a household name in his country, and still was; and once he whirled down upon the Sioux and scattered them to the winds not even the President would be able to stay the public applause or the public clamor for his advancement.

To himself he was a candid man. He knew what he wanted, and what he would do to get what he wanted — and never did he attempt to conceal it from himself. He had no hypocrisy in him, no political caution and none of that mellowness whereby a man might smooth himself a pathway through other men. The egotism which lies in the tissues of all men was thicker in him than in others; the hunger for applause which is a thirst in all men was a greater craving in him. The sense of drama which made quieter men silently wish they had the stature and the daring to play great parts was in George Armstrong Custer so vivid that it gave him the stature and the daring. He created the color which other men shrank from, even as they wanted it. He played his part straight as would a great actor and believed in himself and in his part until the two were one; in him was none of that critical self-reflection which caused others to draw short of appearing ridiculous. He was a simple man so hungry for greatness that he could ride roughshod over the personal feelings of other men and not be aware of it; he was so naïve in his judgments that even as he knew his enemies, he treated them in the manner of one who knows them to be entirely wrong and therefore to be treated charitably, indulged. He could be harsh and brutal for the sake of a soldierly ideal, but there was no gentle insight in him, no compassion, no deep sympathy. As inspiring a commander as he knew himself to be and as proud of his regiment as he was, he knew nothing of that man-to-man affection which tied a command together. One moment indulgent and the next instant full of fiery intolerance, he lacked any semblance of balance and was so blind to his own character that he needlessly broke army regulations out of a sense of complete virtue, and yet would instantly condemn and punish a subordinate officer for the slightest breach. All these things he was — an elemental complex of emotions and hungers and dreams never cooled, never disciplined, never refined by maturity; for he had never grown up.

He lay back, somewhere during the night, on his blankets and fell into that instant sleep for which he was famous. But the last thing on his mind had been a fear of losing the Sioux and the first thing to return to it when he woke near midnight was that same fear. He lay quiet for half an hour, thinking of it; and suddenly rose up and called to his orderly.

"Wake the company commanders and tell them to be ready to march at one o'clock."

XVIII

The Ordeal Begins

THE COMMAND struggled out of dead sleep and stumbled through the curdled blackness; and horses pitched a little and men cursed with bitter violence and sergeants' voices prodded the weary-drunk companies into formation. There was no talk as the Seventh moved forward. Horses sneezed and dust rose thick around the command; now and then an orderly ran down the column, and later ran back. They traveled with the Rosebud as it circled and slowly moved upgrade, and the land all around was a series of streaky black layers against which some heavier chunk of land thrust a deeper blackness. At three o'clock, this blackness began to move in muddy gray waves and at four light came, one dark tone moving into a tone less dark until a pearl dawn lay over the earth. A rippled order came back along the column, through the dense dry dust.

"Fall out for breakfast."

Shafter unsaddled and searched for the makings of a fire. Hines had dropped almost at once on his haunches and part of the command curled up and fell asleep again, wanting rest more than food. Shafter boiled his coffee and fried his bacon and put his hardtack in the bacon grease to soften it. He saw Captain Moylan standing near by and he beckoned him over and split his breakfast with his commander. Moylan squatted in the dust, his eyes bloodshot. The creek water had alkali in it, turning the coffee bad. Hines came over and sat down, groaning as he touched the ground. "This is soldierin' for you, Shafter. Don't stay in it as long as I'm stayin'. If I was thirty again — "

Shafter said: "I remember a night march from Chambers to Shaw Gap, during the war. It was worse, Hines."

"Much worse," said Moylan and grinned at Shafter. "There was a tougher commander along. He was in a hurry."

Hines looked at both of them and softly said: "So. Same outfit, hey?"

Garnett walked forward and stopped by the fire. He looked down at Moylan: "Any orders, Captain?"

"None that I know of," said Moylan. "Get off your feet, Garnett. It is a long day coming and nobody knows what's at the end of it."

Shafter looked up at Garnett and met the man's cool glance; he gave back the same arrogant stare and saw the flush of temper in Garnett's face. Presently the lieutenant moved away. Shafter heard Hines murmur: "There comes somebody," and turned his attention to the little hill ahead, down which a rider rode rapidly, rounding in before the head of the column. Shafter dropped back on his shoulder blades.

"Today's the day, Hines. Want to lay a bet?"

"What you bettin' on?"

"A fight," said Shafter. "I feel it in the middle of my belly."

Hines looked around him to the troopers scattered on the brown grass. "Some of those lads ain't heard the sound of bullets before."

Shafter lay idle, staring at the sky. One small cloud fluff sailed alone overhead and the sunlight had begun to brighten the blue arch. The day would be hot. "War," he murmured, "is a woman — beautiful when first kissed."

The mention of a woman brought the near-by Bierss upright from his prone position. "I'm a dumb one, Professor, but I get that."

"I don't," said Hines.

Bierss grinned at Shafter. "And you didn't get it out of no book."

Custer came down the camp, riding bareback. He stopped near Moylan. "Be ready to move at eight. Varnum sends word there is a concentration of hostiles to the west of the divide." He rode on. Shafter closed his eyes and fell instantly asleep. Presently he heard a trumpet blowing far away and somebody dug him urgently in the ribs and Bierss was saying: "Come on, rise and shine."

The regiment collected itself, slowly and with effort, and moved forward. From his place in the saddle, Shafter saw Custer and a small party riding on ahead. Dust began to steam up around the column again.

Custer galloped forward with Girard, one of the civilians lent him by Gibbon. Two miles on, he found Charley Reynolds waiting for him at the foot of Crow Peak. Reynolds led him up the slope toward a round knob from which the country fell away in its broken wrinkled outline. To the north, they could see the long cavalry file move forward in a smoky, serpentine line, gradually following the creek bed and sheltered from sight by the ridges to either side of the creek. Here, adjacent to Crow Peak, was the height of land which marked the head of the Rosebud's valley. To the west the land ran in small gullies and tangled ridges toward the Little Bighorn.

Varnum and Bouyer and Reynolds stood near the general; the Crows made a group of their own near by. Custer lifted his glasses on the valley to the west and gave it a careful scrutiny, a prolonged attention. He lowered his glasses. "I see nothing," he said in a disappointed tone.

"Look beyond the valley to the top of the bluffs," urged Varnum. "The Sioux horse herd is there. A big one."

Custer tried again, and shook his head. "I see nothing."

"Look for worms wiggling along the ground," said Varnum.

Custer took one more try with his glasses. Varnum waited in silence worn down by his steady riding and feeling the weight of his responsibility. Custer shook his head as he lowered his glasses. "No, I make out nothing."

Varnum showed his disappointment. "The Crow are quite certain of a big camp over there. We saw smoke rising on that plateau an hour ago. Dust smoke from horses. The Crow are also quite sure we have been seen by Sioux scouts."

"No," said Custer arbitrarily, "we haven't been seen. We've been riding under the rim of the valley."

"The Crow are sure we have been," stated Varnum. "They think the Sioux are off there in great numbers, waiting for us."

Charley Reynolds, always an extremely quiet man, now put in his advice. "You're going to have a big fight, General. A hell of a big fight."

"What do you base that on, Charley?" asked Custer.

Charley thought about it in his mild, thoughtful manner. "On my medicine," he said. "I have lived in the West a long while. I know what's up when I get a feelin'. I have seen enough tracks to convince me and enough dust to be certain." He pointed west and said seriously: "There are more Indians over there, General, than you ever saw in one place before."

One of the Crows gave a grunt and pointed to the northwest. Looking down from the knob, Custer and the rest of the party saw four Indians riding rapidly through a coulee toward the Rosebud. They had been somewhere near the crest of the divide, blended with the brown and gray soil; now they traveled away fast, their ponies breaking the dust.

"We've been spotted for certain," said Varnum.

"I doubt it," said Custer. "They couldn't see the regiment from there."

Charley Reynolds and Girard and Bouyer and Varnum gave the general a silent attention, forbearing to say more. Suddenly he turned off the knob, got to his horse and led the group downgrade. The head of the regiment had reached the foot of the ridge and now halted at his command. He said to his trumpeter orderly: "Officers' call," and sat on the ground, waiting for his officers to assemble. His buckskins were powdered with dust, his bright red kerchief silvered with it. Three days of hard sun had scorched his extremely fair skin. Beneath the flare of his great-brimmed hat, his bony features were soberly composed, his hawkish nose dipped and his eyes narrowly fixed upon the earth before him. He dug his fingers into the soil and lifted dust through them as he considered his problem with his restless will, his driving wishes. Presently he stood up to meet his officers.

They came forward on slow feet, all men worse for the wear, wanting sleep and suffering from a thirst the alkali water of the region could not slake. Dust and heat had gotten into all of them; even Major Reno's sallow cheeks were flushed; and Benteen's naturally florid complexion was scarlet. They stood jaded and lackluster around him.

"The camp," said Custer, "seems to be over that way," and motioned his arm westward. "The Crows are certain of it. I am not. The Crows likewise think we have been discovered. I am now inclined to agree. In any event, we move that way as soon as troops are in order. We will now break the command into three wings. Reno, you take M, A and G Companies. The scouts and guides will also be attached to you, and Doctors Porter and DeWolfe will follow your battalion. Hodgson will be your adjutant. Benteen, you will have your own company and also D and K. McDougall will remain as guard for the pack animals, and the arrangement of six men and a noncom from each troop to handle the animals will likewise remain as it is. Mathey will command that detail. I shall take C, E, F, I and L. Doctor Lord will go with me. You had better fill canteens and water the horses. We may not have time to do that later."

The officers went doggedly away, and presently watering details broke for the creek. A hot sun poured down from straight above and the air was thin and still. Custer stood alone by his horse, the old flame of haste burning in him, the old impatience nagging at him. He turned sharp to his adjutant who remained faithfully near by. "Cooke, ride through the command and take the report of the troop commanders when they're ready."

Shafter filled his canteen and brought his horse to water and watched it test the surface of the creek with its sensitive nose. It blew against the water, it smelled the water and expelled a breath and tried to skim the surface away, and lifted its head. The alkaline taste was too strong. Boots and saddles cracked the warming day, and at half-past twelve he was mounted again, moving forward.

The column rose with the divide, leaving the creek behind it, and now filed westward through the wings of a shallow pass. The horses were worn down and the command began to stretch out and a warning kept running back: "Close up — close up!" Moylan turned his head and beckoned at Garnett who rode near the foot of the troop. Garnett came up briskly to join Moylan. Shafter heard the captain speaking.

"I shall tell you this while we have time to speak of it. I do not give many commands, since my noncommissioned officers are all old hands at the business. But when I do sing out, I want quick answers. Half or better of the company has not been under fire. Therefore these men will shoot too fast and waste ammunition. You must constantly watch for this on the skirmish line. Keep the fire steady but hold down the hotheads. You must keep counseling these green men not to fire unless they have something to hit. You must also keep the company closed up. The Sioux always try to split a command into detail and chop up the pieces. Let nobody straggle or fall back on your wing. That is the main thing I want to tell you. Keep this company always together." He nodded, sending Garnett back.

Hines turned to McDermott and murmured: "You're top kick if I drop. Remember to get the duty roster out of my breast pocket."

There were three sergeants with the troop, Hines, McDermott and Shafter, the others having been detached for various duties; there were four corporals, and forty-one privates now riding two and two down the western slope of the broken hills. Ahead of them at a distance lay the half view of a valley stretching along the timber-fringed Little Bighorn, gray and dark olive and tawny in the hazy heat fog. Benteen suddenly swung out from the column's head and drew his three troops with him. Shafter heard Reno call out: —

"Where you going, Benteen?"

Benteen waved an arm at the rough hills to the south of him. "Goin' to scout that — and drive everything before me." He had, always, a dry voice and it was impossible to tell how much irony lay in it now. He shouted back and drew his own company after him, and Weir's and Godfrey's. These three rattled away.

A Company now was the head of the column; and suddenly Cooke dropped back from the general, who rode fifty yards ahead. Cooke reined around beside Reno. "The general," he said, "directs you take specific command of M, A and G."

"Is that all?" asked Reno.

"That is all he said," confirmed Cooke, and galloped forward.

The pitch of the hills steepened and the way wound between gray chunks of earth and clacked across a rocky underfooting. There was a little stream to the right of them dropping in liquid bubbling toward the Bighorn. Dust thickened and the horses grunted with the effort required to check their descent. Custer swung in his saddle and pointed at Reno, and then pointed across the creek; Reno at once crossed his column over. Now the two battalions marched side by side, Custer's to the one hand of the creek and Reno on the other. Meanwhile the pass widened as it descended and the ground before them showed the chopped tracks of fresh Indian travel. Moylan looked at those tracks with considerable thought.

The troopers moved through the dense dust, sweating and cursing, steeped in their own misery, gaunt from weariness and from thirst; but the pace quickened and a strange, lively feeling got into Shafter — the same warning of battle which had gone through him so many times before. The guides were ranging ahead, lifting up and down the little rolls of land which now and then shut out the valley before them.

Custer shouted at Reno and waved his hat in signal, whereupon Reno swung the column over the creek again, bringing the two battalions together. Suddenly they capped a ridge and saw a lone tepee standing in the valley before them. Custer flung up his hand, halting the command, and the Ree scouts went forward in stooped, lithe positions, like scurrying dogs closing in on a scent. Girard swung to the right, climbing a small ridge which gave him a view of the land beyond. Meanwhile the Rees, growing bold, reached the lodge. One of them entered — and came out, crying at Bouyer. Bouyer said to Custer: "A dead Sioux inside."

Girard shouted down from his vantage point on the ridge. "Injuns, runnin' down the valley!"

The Rees had set fire to the tepee. Custer spurred up the ridge beside Girard and had his look into the valley and turned and rushed down the ridge, yelling at the Ree chief, Bloody Hand: "Tell your people to follow them!"

Bloody Hand spoke back at the Ree. They stood still, saying nothing and not moving, and presently Bloody Hand shook his head at Custer. Custer cried out: "Forward," and started down the creek with the two columns racking after him. The little ridge which had blocked their view now petered out into the plain of the valley and gave them view of the creek as it looped toward the brush and willows which marked the course of the Bighorn. Dust in the valley showed where the fleeing Indians had been. The two columns pitched forward, men rolling in their saddles and sergeants shouting back. Cooke and Captain Keogh rode over from Custer's column and fell beside Reno, all of them at a canter. Cooke said: —

"The Indians are across the Little Bighorn, about two miles ahead of us, now. The general directs that you follow them as fast as you can and charge them. He will support you with the other battalion."

The Indian trail crossed the creek. Reno's battalion went splashing over the water and pointed at the Little Bighorn in its grove of trees. The valley continued beyond those trees, not visible to the troopers. Looking back, Shafter saw the column under Custer veer away in another direction, and presently slide behind a knoll of ground. In that direction the valley rose to a line of high bluffs.

Reno struck the Bighorn at a place where the trees were thinnest and yelled back, "Don't let the horses stop to drink!" Moylan turned to Shafter and repeated the command. Shafter dropped out of his file and stood with his mount belly-deep in the water. Corporal Bierss' animal came to a dead halt and thrust its muzzle eagerly down. Bierss sawed at the reins and cursed it, and then Shafter spurred near and gave it a hard kick with his toe and sent it on. But the little delay had broken the compactness of the line and troopers were tangled midstream, their animals half crazed by thirst. Shafter and McDermott ranged among them, kicking them on. A horse stumbled and went down and water sprayed up, wonderfully cool. Moylan's great voice bawled from the far bank and McIntosh of D and French of M were laying words about them like ax handles.

The column crossed, fought through the willows and came upon the broadened valley before them. To the right, across the stream, a bluff lifted and grew taller as it moved away until, two or three miles south, it was a ridge crowned by round-topped peaks; on the left the valley was held in by a low, slow-rising slope. Ahead of them, at a distance, a wooded bend of the river closed out the farther view of the valley; a mass of dust rose beyond those trees. At this moment Cooke came splashing across the ford and shouted at Reno. "Scout reports there's a hell of a lot of Indians under that dust smoke — beyond those trees."

"All right — all right," said Reno. He sat on his horse while troopers straggled out of the river. The companies had lost formation and officers were calling and sergeants swore their men into formation. Horses plunged, turned frantic by the excitement, and one horse took the bit in its mouth and raced a hundred yards away before the company checked it down.

"Take your time," said Reno. "There's enough ahead for all of us. Form up — form up!" He shouted at Cooke who now had wheeled back into the water on his return trip to Custer. "Where's Custer?"

Cooke turned in his saddle, shook his head, and pointed vaguely; and disappeared. The three companies had formed and now were in columns of fours. Men sat with hard-handed grip on the reins, dusty and water-splashed, reddened by the hard scorching of the sun, half exhausted and hungry. Reno called: "McIntosh, you're reserve. Varnum, take your scouts out on the left flank." He rose in his saddle to give the forward command, but changed his mind and turned to look at the valley. There was no Indian to be seen on it yet, but the whole floor showed the scarring of their ponies — and the distant dust column rose heavily behind the trees. Suddenly he spoke aside to his orderly. "Ride back to Custer. Tell him the Indians are in force in front of us." Now he rose in his stirrups again and shouted: —

"Left into line — guide center — gallop!"

The column broke like a fan, fours slanting out and coming into a broad troop front. The two advance companies formed a spaced skirmish line sweeping at a gallop down the valley, A to the left and M to the right, Reno, Hodgson, Moylan and French riding forward, and Garnett and DeRudio behind. G Company made a second line in the rear. Over to the left, skirting the edge of the footslopes, Varnum commanded his Ree scouts; with him were Reynolds and the two half-breed Jacksons, Girard, Herendeen, and the Negro Dorman.

XIX

Charge and Retreat

Ir was a two-mile run down the length of that valley toward the trees which barred their farther view. Dust thickened steadily behind the trees, and puffs of dust rolled forward around them and something flashed in the core of the dust — like lances glittering. Reno, out in the lead, turned in the saddle as he galloped and looked back anxiously toward the crossing of the river, looked for the support Custer had promised. The plain was empty. At the same time DeRudio shouted: "That's Custer waving his hat on the bluff!" Shafter, throwing his glance to the high bluffs to the right, across the river, thought he saw a single horseman on that far crest move slowly out of sight.

They were nearly abreast the trees which formed a screen; they swung to pass the trees and so continue down the valley. On the left, Varnum was cursing above the racketing roll of sound, above the thud and jingle and the heaving and the crying of men. "Goddammit, come back — come back!" His Rees had been watching the dust in the foreground and they had sighted the on-racing shape of Sioux; now they turned and fled. Bloody Hand, their leader, called and beckoned; but when he saw them run he flung up an arm and turned back to Varnum and the white scouts remaining. It left a gap in the left end of Reno's line. Suddenly Reno cried through the turmoil at McIntosh. His voice failed to carry but the gesture of his arm was enough. McIntosh spurred G Company forward into the line.

They skirted the timber and pushed by it. The dust storm was ahead of them, no more than two hundred yards away, and now the shadows within the dust leaped out of it and rushed on — Sioux warriors bending and swaying and crying. One wave of them wheeled and made for the left flank of Reno's line, meaning to turn it. Reno tossed up his arm and his mouth formed a phrase that was seen but scarcely heard: "Prepare to fight on foot!"

Horses went crazy in the sudden milling halt, in the sing of rifle fire, and for a moment the line was beyond control. One young trooper let out a screaming yell and plunged into the dust, his horse uncontrollable. Shafter watched him disappear, never again seeing him. Troopers dropped from their saddles, and in groups of threes flung their reins to a fourth trooper who wheeled and ran back with the mounts. The line became a crescent of kneeling men; the officers dropped behind to unmask the fire of their companies. Reno walked calmly to the rear of his command; he stood with his legs apart and his revolver drawn, taking careful aim and firing with deliberation.

The trees now were behind the command and the solid dust in front; and suddenly a wave of Sioux broke forward and curled around the left, where Varnum was posted with his guides. Firing rattled up from the troopers' thin ranks and Varnum's little group was in the thick of a swift, wicked melee. Sioux lead struck the earth hard by throwing up little streamers of dust, and men ducked and grunted at the sight of it. Hines knelt beside Shafter, sweat making straggling marks down the patched dust of his face; his complexion was purple but his lips were pulled apart as if he were grinning. "Professor," he said, "I wish I was thirty years younger."

The Sioux shots made a thin rain along the earth; their lead breathed hotly past. An arrow struck short and wavered snakelike on the dust. A man to the right of Shafter gave one soft grunt and settled forward on both knees. Hines turned his head in that direction. He called: "Cobb, you hit?" Hines had a grim stretch to his lips and he raised a hand to dash the sweat from his face; but the hand went halfway up, halted there and dropped. His head jerked from the impact of a bullet, his eyes rolled. He said, "Ah," and dropped dead.

Reno shouted, "Forward," and Moylan repeated it. Shafter reached to Hines's breast pocket and pulled out the roster book. He looked around him and saw other figures lying still; he saw McDermott shake his head. Wallace trotted toward Moylan and Reno. "Pressure's getting very strong. We're going to have our left flank caved in. Can't we send back to Custer for support?"

The Sioux were wheeling crisscross through the dust, charging and firing and rushing away. They made a greater and greater pressure, against which Reno's line slowly moved until it could move no more; men settled to their knees for better fire. Over on the left, Shafter watched Sioux suddenly appear out of the wrinkled high ground and sweep behind the cavalry line. To the right, where the river lay, he saw the cloudy shapes of Indians darting through the willows. Reno saw it too and stood still to think of his position. Wallace had trotted toward Varnum's position; now he came back with Billy Jackson, one of the half-breed guides.

"You want to go back and find Custer?" asked Reno.

The dust had rolled over them and beyond them; there was no view of the valley in any direction. Billy Jackson saw all this and shook his head. "They've cut us off. No man could get through."

The horseholders, a hundred feet behind the line, were firing into the smoky haze, now being attacked from the side. Reno said to McIntosh: "Pull out your company and go guard the horses."

McIntosh and Wallace both signaled G Company out of the skirmish line. Firing began to strike at them from other angles, left and right. Young Lovelace cursed his gun and reached for a knife to dig a stuck shell from the chamber. Shafter stood up to look for McDermott, whereupon Bierss grinned at him. "Damn you and your black tunnel. It bothers me."

Shafter called at a youngster wildly firing: "Take your time — take your time! You're hitting nothing!" He saw Garnett standing a yard behind the line, as tall as if he were on parade. The lieutenant had his revolver half lifted and his eyes strained into the dust mist, waiting for a target. Whiskers darkened his sallow face; his mouth was trap-tight. Shafter moved back in time to see George Busby drop. Donovan raised a crimson face and called at Shafter. "We can't hold this place. Somebody better tell Reno that while there's time."

Reno knew it and Reno had made up his mind and had given his orders. Moylan was shouting those orders through the steady slam of gunfire. "Drop back to the timber!"

The line rose, ragged and broken, and slowly retreated, followed by the bold and confident Sioux who charged closer and closer to the cavalry guns. They were sweeping down in greater numbers on the left, and their lead came out of the river willows. Under this cross-whip of fire some of the green troopers began to break and run for the timber; the voices of the officers struck them and seized them and settled them to an orderly withdrawal. Pace by pace, the line gave way and presently got to the protecting edge of the brush and timber and stepped inside it.

As soon as they left the open ground they lost contact with each other; the battalion lost unity and runners began to crease through the brush, seeking the major for his orders. Reno had taken stand in a little clearing in the middle of the timber. He had his adjutant Hodgson with him, and his trumpeter; he listened to the firing slash its way through the loose brush and strike the tree trunks and ricochet on in whining tangents. He ducked as one of these sounds came close, and swore at himself. He said to his trumpeter: "Get the horseholders up here in this clearing."

A runner sifted through the undergrowth. "Captain French says the Sioux are massing on the other side of the Bighorn and mean to make a crossing and cut us off!"

"Tell French to swing his company against the river side," said Reno. Then he turned to Hodgson. "Go see where A and G have got themselves placed."

Shafter crouched at the edge of the timber and watched the Sioux shapes lace the thickening dust before him. They raced forward through it, firing at the timber, and wheeled and faded away; they were curling around the grove, drawing a tighter ring about the command. The woods reverberated with the steady echoes of the troopers' firing and he heard men crying questions through the thicket. The men of A Company were spaced so far apart in the brush that he saw only the nearest files. Donovan was on his left, coolly waiting, coolly firing. Bierss knelt at his right. Bierss was a heavy man and had dripped his sweat all the way up the Rosebud, but now Bierss had no moisture left in him and gave Shafter a glance of pure misery. "Pretty soon I got to crawl to the river for a drink, Professor." Shafter passed him his canteen.

The pressure increased against the grove. Shafter had the feeling that the troopers on his left flank had drifted toward the center of the area. There was no longer any resemblance of order. Cut off from their commands, the men grew afraid.

"Bierss," he said, "how much ammunition have you left?"

"Fifty rounds. Where the hell you suppose Custer is? He was goin' to support us."

Shafter got up and broke through the brush to his left. He found Lovelace and Ryan and Corporal Mudd; after a ten-yard gap he discovered O'Dale. He said: "You seen McDermott?"

"No," said O'Dale. "I ain't seen anybody. Where's the rest of the outfit? I'm all alone here."

A bullet touched a willow and went on with the sound of a hard-plucked banjo string. He pushed farther on to make contact with the lost fragments of his company; he parted the brush before him, at the same time hearing carbine fire strengthen behind him. That would be the Sioux crossing the river. He lifted his voice, calling: "McDermott!" Suddenly, knocking the thicket aside with the barrel of his carbine, he came face to face with a Sioux, all naked save for a breech clout. The Sioux took a backward pace and flung up his carbine. Shafter had that one instant in which to see black shock dilate the man's lids, to see a reaction stretch the red man's face broad. He fired and heard his bullet tear through the Sioux's chest, and for the briefest moment he watched the Sioux fall and turn and die.

Deeper in the trees he heard Garnett shouting: "Moylan, where are you?" He turned back, not knowing the Sioux were filtering into the woods and that in a little while the battalion would be completely surrounded and completely trapped. He passed O'Dale and then struck off toward the heart of the timber and had gone fifty feet when he met Moylan.

"We can't stay here, Captain. We'll be out of ammunition in fifteen minutes."

"Reno's debating a retreat," said Moylan. "The Indians have crossed the river and broken our flank there."

"They're coming in on this side, too."

"I'll go tell Reno that. Pull the company back toward the center."

Shafter retraced his path to O'Dale. "Give way to the middle of the timber." He went along the line again repeating it, and reached Bierss. "Swing to your right and tell the lads to collect in the center clearing." Then he turned to the left once more, seeking to find the other flank of A Company, lost somewhere in the thicket. He passed the dead Indian and drove his shoulder through the small willows, listening to the steady crackle of gunfire. Dust came into the woods from the plain and presently he caught a smell that was something else than dust — the taint of leaves burning. Directly after that he heard the dry rustle of flames. The Sioux had fired the grove.

He found three A troopers together in an isolated spot and sent them back; now crouched and running, he moved twenty feet and came upon Doctor Porter, kneeling over Charley Reynolds. "Fall back, Doctor," said Shafter. "Toward the center."

"Give me a hand with Charley," said the doctor and turned to Reynolds. He put a hand on Reynolds' chest and shook his head. "No, never mind," he said and got up. The Negro Dorman lay dead ten feet away with a little ring of cartridges around him — and a trooper from M was near at hand, also dead. Shafter ran across a clearer patch of ground with the doctor behind him; when he reached the middle clearing he saw the remnants of the battalion gathering from the edges of the grove, and the horseholders standing ready. Reno waited by his horse, his feet apart and his face flushed and dark; he was an anxious, uncertain man with a terrible decision riding his shoulders.

He said: "Where's McIntosh — where's DeRudio?"

Shafter moved down A Company's half-assembled ranks. He said, "Bierss, have you seen McDermott?" Bierss shook his head, too tired to answer. Heat lay through the trees in smothering pressure and the flung-up dust grew heavy and the smell of smoke increased. Carbine fire rattled all through the timber and men straggled forward, so spent that they dragged the butts of their guns on the ground. Lead from the Sioux guns whipped the clearing. Moylan and Wallace and French waited — and grew tired of waiting. French said: "This position is becoming untenable, Reno."

The Ree leader, Bloody Hand, swung up to his pony and murmured, "Better go — better go."

Reno cast a strained eye around a command grown thinner from casualties and from strays still lost in the grove. The weight of his decision grew so great that it deadlocked his mind. But suddenly he said, "We'll charge back up the valley and cross the river to the bluffs." He swung to his saddle, close by the waiting Bloody Hand. Moylan and French were calling to their troops and men rushed toward the horseholders and the confusion grew into half panic. McIntosh plunged breathless from the woods, his hat gone and his dark face pinched.

"Column of fours!" roared Moylan.

"My troop's not collected!" said McIntosh.

French shouted at him, "We can't wait, Tosh. You go first, Moylan. I'll follow. Bring up the rear, Tosh!"

Reno had swung his horse around; and at that instant a Sioux bullet made its sightless track across the clearing and punched its way through Bloody Hand's brain, showering blood on the near-by Reno. The major flung up a hand to his face, so badly shaken that he jumped from the saddle and said, "Wait!" The loose-formed column began to break apart under the pressure of bullets singing and sighing all around. The smell of smoke came to the horses and fright grew among them. Reno shook his head and clawed his way to the saddle. He yelled, "Forward!" and set his horse to a gallop.

The column, not yet untangled, followed in loose disorder — all the officers laboring to get the battalion in some sort of shape. They were in full motion when they came out of the timber into the valley, into the rolling clouds of dust raked up by the Sioux who had now swept around the grove and set up their sharp fire at the column's head. Horses slammed together under excitement and troopers, venting strange needs, began to yell full voice. Reno and Hodgson led the way, Reno swaying hatless in his saddle. Moylan galloped beside Shafter, now and then looking back at his troop.

When the head of the column had gotten a hundred yards from the grove, Shafter glanced behind him and saw M Company directly following; but beyond M Company, G came in scattered, straggling bunches.

Wallace tore forward, overtaking Reno. He yelled: "For God's sakes men, don't run! Don't let them whip us!"

Reno turned his head and harked out a savage answer. "I am in command here, sir!"

Dust rolled heavier and heavier and suddenly the Sioux darted in, riding parallel to the column. They made dark, shining figures on their horses; they flung up their carbines, took bobbing aim, and fired. They made sudden dead-on runs at the column until their horses scraped against the running mounts of the troopers and presently the column, pouring forward at a full run, was engaged in a deadly, hand-to-hand wrestling.

Shafter jammed his carbine into its boot and now used his revolver point-blank. He saw his targets waver and he turned to watch an Indian fall and noticed Lovelace locked in a Sioux's tight grasp — the Sioux seeking to unhorse the lad. Shafter wheeled and blew a hole in the Sioux's flank and gave a sudden push to Lovelace, who was three quarters out of his saddle. But the Sioux were racing up in greater numbers, pressing in with a daring that came from sure knowledge of their victory; and the close fire struck home and troopers fell screaming and riderless horses bolted away. Shafter saw Lieutenant McIntosh running alone beside the column with two Indians boxing him. He swung over, but was too late. McIntosh flung up both hands and his head bobbed down. Shafter watched him disappear beneath the hoofs of the oncoming Indians. Far back he noticed a little isolated band of troopers drop out of sight as the Sioux cut across and blocked their escape.

It seemed an endless, hopeless run down the valley. The battalion was a skeleton, its identity half buried in the smothering, close-riding Sioux; the horses ran in the loose gate of near-exhaustion. Shafter galloped beside Bierss who rolled like a drunk in the saddle. Bierss' face had a stoniness on it, an unrecognizing blankness. Shafter cried: "Sit up, Bierss! Hang on!"

"Ah," murmured Bierss. "A long day — a long day."

Reno had swung the column toward the river, apparently meaning to cross. This maneuver brought them close by the bordering
willows and thus they ran with the bright flash of the water
beckoning them at the foot of a bank which ran sheerly up and
down, too high to jump. Across the river stood the wrinkled hard
slopes of bluffs whose rough-crowned tops promised safety.

One trooper wheeled from the column, came to the edge of the
bank and made his desperate fifteen-foot leap. Horse and rider
struck in a great spray and afterwards the horse struggled on alone,
the rider never coming to the surface. Garnett, so far at the foot of
A Company, now put spurs to his horse and drew forward until
he rode abreast Reno, and he cried out, "Here's a ford," and rushed
down a crack in the bluff.

The battalion followed that narrow cut to the edge of water. The
leading horses, crazed by thirst, slackened and tore the reins free
from the troopers' tight grasp. They stopped belly-deep in the stream
and made a barricade which spread back and blocked the small pathway down the bluff; the men of the battalion, coming on in desperate
haste, fanned out and took to the river from whatever point they
found themselves. Carbine fire began to whip at the troopers in the
water.

Shafter had crossed the river when he saw Donovan's horse drop,
sending Donovan to the ground. Donovan got up and shouted as
troopers fled by him toward the rising slopes of the bluff. Donovan
lifted his pistol and took his stand, firing back across the river,
blood-flushed but cool. Shafter ran beside him and kicked one foot
out of his near stirrup. Donovan put his foot in the stirrup and
lifted himself behind Shafter, whose horse now dropped to a slow
and weary walk.

"There goes Benny Hodgson!" shouted Donovan.

Hodgson had fallen midstream, waist-deep. He got to his feet
and staggered forward. A passing trooper paused long enough for the
boy lieutenant to seize a stirrup and in this manner he was towed
out of the river, turning around and around, dragging his limp feet.
He was on the gravel shore when a second bullet dropped him. For

a moment the trooper paused and was on the impulse of dismounting; then he saw Hodgson to be dead and rushed at the slope.

Halfway up that hard, bitter incline, Shafter saw Doctor DeWolfe die, struck by a bullet from the heights. Troopers dotted the trail, some racing far ahead, some still coming over the water; they slashed the last grain of energy out of their half-dead horses, they scrambled afoot; they stopped to fire, they plugged on, one weary yard at a time; they collapsed and sat in momentary agony, and got up and went on again. They fell and lay still.

Not far from the summit Shafter saw Garnett reel in his horse, make a futile grab to save himself, and fall shoulder first. He was crawling upgrade on his belly when Shafter passed him and he turned his head hopefully and looked up, about to ask for help; but when he saw Shafter he closed his mouth and groaned and resumed his painful inching progress.

Shafter reached the crest and found Reno with half a dozen troopers already arrived. Reno stood hatless, watching his broken battalion come up with a gray, dazed expression on his face. He kept saying: "Spread out and cover the others." Donovan dropped off and Shafter dismounted and fell to his stomach on the edge of the crest, bringing his carbine into play. For a moment he lay wholly still, his heart painfully pumping, his throat parched dry and his chest aflame. He felt himself half groggy and for a moment he had to squeeze down on the carbine to keep himself from fainting.

One by one troopers reached the crest and fell in their tracks. Moylan arrived and French came up, both going to Reno. "We had better arrange a defense here," said Moylan. "The Sioux will re-form and attack."

Far down, near the water's edge, Shafter saw the Sioux rush toward dark figures on the ground, bend and describe a swift motion, and rise and run on. Garnett lay flat on the ground, three hundred feet below, apparently dead; but presently Garnett raised his head slightly and looked up to the crest — and lowered his head again, turned still. Across the river, back in the valley out of which the battalion had made its way, the Sioux were swinging and racing toward the grove; they were streaming around the grove to the valley's lower end, beyond sight.

"They're not following up their attack," said Moylan.

"I'm damned glad of that," said French. "We're out of ammunition."

He heard someone yell, "Here comes Benteen," and he looked to his left, eastward along the bumpy spine of the bluffs. Benteen's three companies moved briskly forward and Benteen jumped from his saddle. He said: "Where's Custer?"

"I'll be damned if I know," said Reno. "He was to have supported me. We got down there and took one hell of a beating. Where's McDougall and the pack train?"

"Coming," said Benteen.

"Send somebody back to him. Tell him to cut out one ammunition mule and get it here as soon as possible."

The Sioux made a long, cloudy line on the plain, racing away, and Moylan murmured: "I don't understand that." Then, in the following half silence, all of them heard one far-away volley westward.

"There's Custer," said Benteen. "In a fight."

Troopers continued to struggle up the slope, their eyes glazed by exertion; and now other troopers, partly rested, moved back down from the summit to rescue the wounded stragglers. Shafter heard the officers talking near by, but he paid no attention. He had his eyes pinned to Garnett's motionless shape. He watched the man, and a steady hatred held him still. Bierss crawled beside him and groaned and lay full length. "Professor," he murmured, "it was bad."

"We're here," said Shafter.

"A lot of us ain't," said Bierss. "There's Hines and McDermott — "

"But we're here," said Shafter roughly. He laid aside his carbine and slid down the slope. A stray Sioux bullet struck near him and in the thin heated silence the crack of it sounded on and on. He got to Garnett and crouched. "You alive?"

Garnett slowly turned his head on the dust. He looked at Shafter's feet, murmuring, "You got any water?"

"No," said Shafter. He hooked Garnett around the shoulders with his arms and sat him upright. He braced the man against his legs and heaved again, pulling Garnett up. He balanced him a moment, doubting his own strength; then he crouched and in one sharp effort he got Garnett on his shoulder and went up the hill. His feet ground into the soft, rocky underfooting and slid back. A bullet struck short and ricocheted with a liquid whining; elsewhere a carbine flatted an answer. He said at the extreme end of his lungs, "You dog, I shouldn't be doing this." Fifty feet from the summit, Donovan came down and gave him a hand.

At five o'clock, a dust-red sun flamed low on the western horizon and from the west now and then came the pulse of gunfire, so faint that some men heard it and others were uncertain. It was the worried and impatient ones who heard it; it was the exhausted who neither heard it nor cared. The valley below was almost empty of Sioux but in the rocky crevices of the two higher points surrounding this peak Indians lay and intermittently fired. Benteen, salty and cool under disaster, moved briskly around the rim of the peak, posting the companies while the jaded Reno moved aimlessly from point to point, unafraid but dazed by what he had undergone and what he feared he must yet endure. The walking wounded toiled painfully up the stiff slope; details were bringing up those critically injured, while Doctor Porter moved among them, making such shifts as he could.

McDougall's B Company had arrived with the pack train and extra ammunition. Captain Weir, one of Custer's nearest friends, stood arguing with Reno, half pleading, half in ill-covered anger. "We should be moving out to support Custer. He is very definitely engaged at the lower end of the valley."

"So were we very definitely engaged," said Reno, irritably. "My orders were to attack and that I would be supported. I attacked. I was not supported. I had no orders at all to support Custer. It is only by God's miracle we survived to reach this hill."

"He may be in extreme trouble," said Weir.

"He may be," said Reno. "And so are we. Take a look around you, Weir. Does this look like a battalion presently fit for service?"

"Definite orders or not," said Weir stubbornly, "you have your judgment to exercise. I should think judgment would indicate supporting the wing now in need of help. My God, there are a thousand or two thousand Sioux down there fighting him."

"I'm better aware of it than you are," said Reno, dryly. "I have just come out of all that. My judgment is first to protect my own battalion. We shall be attacked again."

Weir went stamping angrily away and Shafter saw him move over to his lieutenant, Edgerly. The two remained in considerable conversation, after which Weir mounted his horse and came back toward Reno. He dismounted and said something to Reno, and then got on his horse and moved out to the north alone. Within five minutes Edgerly pulled D Company into formation and followed Weir. In that direction the faint volleying sounded again.

Benteen came up to Reno. "Where's Weir going?"

"Damned if I know."

"You're in charge here, aren't you?" said Benteen acidly. "I'd suggest you pull him back."

"No," said Reno, temporarily resolute. "We'll move out and see if we can support Custer, wherever he is."

The troops drearily assembled. Blankets were opened and the wounded placed upon them, four men to a blanket. In the harsh, swimming sunlight of late afternoon the battalion started west along the rough summit of the bluffs. A mile onward they got to a high peak and saw the lower end of the valley, all hazy with the churning of Sioux horses, and on a lower peak they discovered Sioux madly circling into sight and riding down out of sight again. Beyond that lower peak was a hidden extension of the valley; and from it came one last volley, followed only by the popping of an occasional gun.

Weir was ahead and now Weir stopped, his troopers dismounting. The crooked ravines before Weir suddenly disgorged Sioux and within five minutes he was in a bitter fight, gradually retreating until he came upon the main command. "Now, dammit," cried Reno to Weir, "you see what it's like!"

Indians erupted over the lower peak and slashed forward; they struck up from the long slopes to the north; they clambered forward on the rocky outcrop of the sheer bluff to the south. The battalion, thus abruptly faced with fire from three sides, slowly

jockeyed itself into position. D took the force of the attack while
the remnants of A and G painfully moved backward with the
wounded. Presently M replaced D and then Godfrey dismounted K
and made a screen for the rest of the command; thus beyond six
o'clock Reno's battalion, exhausted by a steady twenty-four–hour
march and half destroyed by an afternoon's fighting, reached its
original peak and flung itself into defensive position. Benteen
paced back and forth, maneuvering the companies in a rough circle
to defend the knob; there was a shallow depression in the middle
area of the knob and here he posted the pack horses and made a
breastworks of the packs, behind which he placed the wounded.

"Wallace," he said, "put G here," and indicated the place with
his arm.

Wallace said wearily: "There are just three men left in G."

"Very well. Place those three here."

The sun was low and the light had changed. Now at this hour, the
Sioux poured back, clambering up the bluff, sidling along the
ravines and rock barriers, boiling across the river. From the two
adjoining higher peaks the Sioux fire began to break, plunging
down upon the exposed circle. That leaden rain splashed up the
dust and furrowed the sandy earth, biting into men and animals
and packs.

"God damn that sun," panted Bierss. "Why don't it set?"

Shafter lay flat, watching the distant rocks, waiting for a fair
shot. Donovan died silently beside him; a crazed horse rocketed
around the circle and stepped on his outstretched legs and charged
down the slope, and tripped itself on its dropped reins and went
end over end in a small avalanche of shale all the way to the river.
There was no letup while daylight lasted; that pelting storm played
cruelly and fatally upon them all as they crouched and dismally
took punishment. The command was a half-unconscious body,
quivering to each added lash but unable to strike back. At eight
o'clock the sun fell and the shadows came mercifully to end the
gunfire; in the twilight and in the onset of peace, Shafter stirred
out of his position like a man drugged and heard a trooper crying
among the wounded.

XX

Farewell to Glory

Now MEN who had been wounded and who had said nothing of it began to move toward the center of the area where Doctor Porter steadily worked and voices began to lift, shaken by agony. "Who's got some water?" The officers stirred around, taking check of their companies. Moylan said to Shafter: "We have got to dig in tonight. They'll be at us when daylight comes. We've got to throw up breastworks. Where's Garnett?"

"Over there," said Shafter.

"Alive?"

"I don't know," said Shafter.

He got his bacon and hardtack out of his haversack and sat down to his first meal since the night before; but he had no water and his mouth was too dry to dissolve the hardtack and therefore he chewed on the raw bacon for its moisture, and presently grew thirstier. The groaning of the wounded got steadily worse and one of these men had a question that never left his tongue: "Where's Custer? Why don't he come?"

Somebody, anonymous in the darkness, flung back an answer: "He's pulled out and left us, like he did Major Elliot at Washita."

Moylan spoke up, coolly. "Let that go, boy."

Pickets were sent down-slope and presently stragglers, trapped in the grove or the river's willows during the valley fight, began to creep in. Shafter listened to their hard breathing and the sudden grunt that came out of them when they sat down. He moved along A Company's line. "Start digging. Dig yourself a hole. Make yourself a shelter."

"What with, Sarge?" asked O'Dale.

"A knife or a spoon if you've got nothing else." He came to Bierss and found the corporal sound asleep. He stood a little while, hating to break that exhausted slumber; he nudged Bierss with his foot and then he had to reach down and shake the corporal. "Bierss — dig yourself in."

"The blacker the tunnel the better," murmured Bierss. "What you meant was just to rest and forget, wasn't it, Professor? Sounds better now than it did before."

The call for water from the wounded was a thing that rubbed Shafter's nerves raw; it was worse than anything that had gone before. Some of A Company's men were over there in Doctor Porter's compound; he thought he heard Lovelace and stepped over and found the boy. Lovelace had a hole in his leg above the knee, and he was trying to endure it without complaining, but his voice shook when he spoke. "Jesus, I hope this thing don't get so bad they have to cut it off. You got a drink, Sarge?"

Shafter unhooked Lovelace's canteen; he collected a dozen canteens and searched for Moylan in the shadows. "I'm going down to the river."

"The valley is crawling with Sioux," said Moylan. "Hear all those owls hooting?"

"I can hoot as well," said Shafter. "Remember when we crawled through the rebel lines?"

"The rebels weren't as smart as these Sioux."

"Where do you think Custer is, Myles?"

Moylan thought about it a long while and let his voice fall to a murmur. "Maybe he broke through and went on to meet Terry, but I don't think so. I think he's dead. I think they're all dead."

"So he waved his big hat and went out to meet his beloved."

"I don't mind that so much," said Moylan. "But he took more than two hundred men with him. Terry's all we've got to hope for now, and he'd better come soon. There's three thousand Sioux in that damned valley and they'll all be at us first thing morning comes."

Shafter dropped down the slope, softly calling to the pickets. He tried to make a quiet trip of it, but the loose shale crumbled beneath his boots and rolled away. Half-descended, he stopped and listened into the night; at the lower end of the valley he saw Sioux campfires burning and he heard strange rhythms and strange echoes drift forward. He crouched in the muddy darkness for ten minutes and then proceeded with greater caution until he got to the softer ground at the bottom of the bluff; and went directly to the water's edge. He flattened on his belly and drank sparingly and drew back to feel that cold wetness spring through him like an acid injected into his veins; it was the sharpest possible sensation through every part of his body. He put his arms into the water when he drank again; he ducked his head under and drew back once more, licking his tongue against his dripping mouth.

He filled the canteens and crouched still. There was a sibilance in the willows, and a slight steamy echo from the river as it flowed past, these sounds sharpening his feeling of danger. He swung his head to orient one sound or another and he watched the shadows pulse around him. He thought: "This is the last drink for God knows how long," and regretted leaving the river; and drank again, until he felt slightly sick. Gathering up the canteens he turned back to the bluff.

The canteens weighted him down and they made a small racket which betrayed his position. A third of the distance up the bluff he sat down, suddenly so weak that he doubted if he could carry the load. Somewhere now he definitely heard a body gritting along the near-by surface of the bluff, and in a little while a voice said: "They're up this ravine. Come on." He sat still and let the party go on ahead of him. He wanted to call to them for help, but the night was too still to take the risk.

He grew less cautious, once they were ahead of him, and now tackled the slope again, each foot of advance using up his wind; his leg muscles ached and he seemed to have a hole in him through which his strength poured like sand. Presently he sat down, feeling the dogged beating of his heart. "When I was twenty, this would have been easy." It was harder to rise and the steepness of the slope dragged at him and pulled him back. Dried out as he was, he began to sweat. He thought: "If I stop again I'll throw away some of the canteens, so I had better keep going." Beyond the halfway point he had ceased to think of the Sioux creeping around him and he no longer troubled to walk quietly. He created a racket in the night, plugging one foot before him, making strange sounds with his mouth, shoving himself on. A picket's voice came at him: —

"Who's that?"

"Give me a push," said Shafter.

"You got water?"

"Not for you," said Shafter.

"To hell with you then," said the picket.

Shafter churned the rubble under him; the whole weight of the bluff bore against him and pushed him. His lungs had a spongy, bubbling ferment in them and his pulse slugged at his temples, his neck, his wrists. He was a man on the edge of collapse, indecently listening to his own weakness. When he came to the summit he stumbled and fell, flinging the canteens into the darkness. The liquid sound of them brought men at him on the run; he heard them searching the ground for the canteens. He rolled over, suddenly furious. He got up and struck a bent shadow. He panted, "Leave those alone!"

Bierss called at him from a short distance. "You want help there, Sarge?"

He got his canteens together and walked over to Doctor Porter's stockade, where the wounded lay. Doctor Porter crouched beside a man, a stub end of a candle lighting his work. "A little water," said Shafter.

Porter paused a moment and gave the canteens the sharpest kind of stare; his own thirst tortured him and he showed the struggle on his face. Then he called quietly into the darkness. "Toomey, come here and dole out this water. None for you, Toomey, and none for any who is able-bodied."

Shafter kept his own canteen. He saw Lovelace near by and he bent and propped up the boy and gave him a small drink and watched inexpressible relief slash sharp lines on Lovelace's face. He stood up, oppressed by the sound of misery around him, and by the smell of misery. Men lay under the feeble circle of the candlelight, they were shadows beyond the candlelight. He heard them calling: "Toomey — for God's sakes bring me a drink!" Porter suddenly leaned back from his patient and gave the man a long look.

"Nothing more for you until we can get you in a better place."

"You don't have to tell me that way, Porter."

Shafter looked around, recognizing Garnett's voice. He stood undecided in his tracks, hearing Porter answer. "I haven't told you anything, Garnett," he said, and moved on to the next man. Shafter bent, seeing Garnett's pale face grow rough with the knowledge of his own dying. Garnett's eyes were wide and his pupils were big; he stared up at Shafter.

"Light's bad," he whispered. "That's you, Kern?"

Shafter unscrewed his canteen top. "Take a drink."

"You're wasting it. I'll be dead in a little while."

"A man's got a right to die with a drink in him," said Shafter. He stared down, not even now able to feel sympathy. His hatred was as rank as it ever had been; this was a man he despised, a man whose memory he would always carry like the scar of a wound treacherously inflicted. It even rankled him that Garnett should refuse water in order that the living might have it; none of that charity or goodness had ever been in Garnett.

Garnett sighed. "Give me the drink, then," he said.

Shafter slid the flat of his hand behind Garnett's head and lifted it; he listened to the greedy sucking sound of Garnett's lips on the canteen. He pulled the canteen away. "That's enough to die on."

Garnett moved his head, side to side. He murmured: "I think the bullet smashed my spine. I can feel nothing from the hips down."

"This time," said Shafter, "you couldn't duck."

Garnett said: "I was never afraid of anything and you damned well know it." Garnett stared at him with a kind of malicious satisfaction. "You're waiting for me to cry for mercy — or pity. You're alive and I'm dying, and you're pleased as hell and you think I'm going to go out on my hands and knees, crawling and afraid. You're wasting your time. I'm not sorry for a thing I've ever done."

"It is a good thing to know you'll never ruin another woman."

A shadow came upon Garnett's face. He lay still and thought about that. "Why," he said finally, "it was a game with me. The only game that ever interested me. A man and a woman. A man in pursuit of a woman. But you've got the wrong view of that, too, Kern. I am a kind of a specialist in women and I guess I ought to know what lies in them as well as anybody. Now that I look back I doubt if I ever ruined any woman. I doubt if I ever made a woman do something she hadn't made up her mind to do. Do you understand that, Kern?"

"No," said Shafter.

Garnett had a dying man's patience and now slowly brought his thoughts to bear upon the thing he wanted to say. "A man is supposed to be the hunter and the woman the hunted. Who started that idea? A man did. A man always figures himself the one who does the chasing and the winning. I have looked into the eyes of many a woman and I have said to myself: 'I can make her want me.' But that was really a delusion. It is women who really make the conquests. They get what they want, Kern, but the blame goes to the men. That's the way a woman holds a man — laying the blame on him. She surrenders but she captures. I was smart enough to know that. I played the game just as women wanted it played. But I never let myself get captured."

"You believe that?" said Shafter. "Would you do it all over?"

"I'd do every bit of it over," said Garnett.

"You're better dead," said Shafter.

"You're thinking of Alice," murmured Garnett. "A dead man doesn't have to be a gentleman, Kern, so I'll tell you something about her. She was my kind, not yours. You think I took her away from you. I had damned little to do with it. She was after me and I played the game. She knew you and I were friends. She broke up that friendship without the least scruple. But after she got me, she didn't want me. She was looking for fresh meat. She was a beautiful woman, Kern, and she had no trouble at all in making me want her. I had my illusions about her, as you did. I thought the whole world was in her eyes, as you did. Then afterwards I discovered the coldness behind her beauty. She cured me of my illusions. I have never respected another woman. Is that candle going out? It's getting dark."

"No," said Kern. "It is still burning."

"Then I'm the one going out," murmured Garnett softly. "What a hell of a mess today's been. Where's Custer?"

"Nobody knows."

"I wish you luck for tomorrow," said Garnett.

Shafter had no answer for that. He watched Garnett with an impersonal attention; he watched the man's face lose its sharpness one line at a time, its definiteness one degree upon another, until presently Garnett was a spirit quietly withdrawing, half free but not wholly free of his body. Nothing, he thought, stopped Garnett from immediately ceasing to breathe except the mortal fear of the last long jump into space and blackness. Garnett held on, dreading the step.

"In pain?" asked Shafter.

"No."

"The easy way," said Shafter, "is to just shut your eyes and die."

"Kern," said Garnett, "do me one favor. See that I'm buried deep enough to keep the coyotes from digging me up." Then the faint malicious tone came back. "If you are alive to do it."

"Anybody you want a letter written to?"

"Don't be hypocritical, Kern. How could you compose a letter of soldierly regret concerning me?"

"I could say you were dead, nothing more. Have you got anybody who might care enough to hear it?"

"You always were a fellow who hated to change," murmured Garnett. "You would burn your bridge rather than go back over it." He was silent for so long that Shafter thought he had died; then his head moved on the ground. He looked up into the night, at the far stars winking. "The earth is my pillow, the earth is my mistress. The earth is a woman and, like all women, stronger than any man can be. Men are the vessels God made to carry illusions. Women are the realists; they are the strength of the race. They love, they hate, they bear. They pray and they sin. But they are stronger than love or sin. If I had it to do over again — " He ceased to speak, coming upon his final convictions and knowing them and struggling with them. "I should not do the same things. That's what you're waiting to hear, Kern — the cry of a man afraid."

"I am disappointed in you," said Shafter.

"The last woman was the one I wanted and could not have because of what I had been before I met her. That is something you didn't know about me. I was more of a man of honor in her presence than you supposed."

"Josephine?" said Shafter.

"Josephine," whispered Garnett and died.

Doctor Porter moved past, dropping his question. "How's Garnett?"

"Finished."

"Fortunate," said Porter and knelt down with his candle beside another man. Shafter got up and moved on his stiff, dead legs toward the northern edge of the defense circle. He passed Moylan, standing solitary in the dark. He said, "Here's a drink, Myles," and handed over the canteen. The captain accepted the canteen. He shook it and judged its contents and for a long moment he struggled with his thirst, and handed it back unopened. "Spread it thin among the boys," he said.

"Garnett's dead," said Shafter.

"Poor soul," said Moylan. "Feel sorry for him?"

"No."

"You had better catch a wink. Tomorrow's a bad thing to think of."

Shafter found Bierss lying on his back. Bierss had scooped himself a hollow spot the size of his body and had tossed the dirt up as a breastwork and now he slept in the depression with the dirt for a pillow. Shafter settled down, feeling the dullness of his body throughout. He thought: "I've got to dig my own shelter," and dreaded the chore. He was sore of muscle and dried out and his lungs burned from exertion and dust; he was tired in a way he had never been tired — made stupid and indifferent by it. His mind moved slowly and his will had little effect, but exhaustion had put a kind of poison in him which would not let him sleep. He lay still, feeling the heat die out of the earth and the air. Some of the wounded mercifully slept but for others the agony went on and their groaning made him grit his teeth and turn on the ground; over there in the improvised hospital men were going through a hell that would leave its scratches on them forever. This was the glory of battle — this was the end of the band playing and the bright pennants flying and all the dreams of gallantry and personal triumph; a man dreamed of glory and it came to this. A lithe figure in a buckskin suit and a flowing red tie stood up in his stirrups and flung his great hat impetuously over his head and the regiment went into battle line, the voices of men shouting out their power and their excitement, and afterwards the smoke and heat and dust folded over them and death struck and long later in the aftermath's stillness men lay physically and spiritually smashed and thought only of water and rest and peace.

Yet Garnett was right. Men were vessels to carry the dreams of the race — the bright visions of gallantry and courage and daring which made the life stream fresh and quick, the steadfast visions of honor and loyalty, and the great flame of faith.

The good and the bad died for those visions, never wholly realizing why they fought; the good and the bad lived to enjoy the peace which came of nights like these, never fully understanding how their peace was secured for them.

The name of this little battle in a remote western valley would fade as time went on until few people knew of it or the reason for it. But even if they forgot it, it would still be a part of that red thread which ran continuously through the fabric of the country. Battles of the past had stained the thread, and this battle now would add its scarlet color, and other battles yet to come. Some of these battles were just and some were unjust, some were necessary struggles of survival, some need never have been fought; but there was never any way of knowing.

A man was faithful and he fought, and had his hopes of betterment; and somewhere else a man stopped his plow and looked upon the long furrows with his mind fertile with ambition; a river packet steamed down the Ohio with its cargo of two hundred people asleep while the pilot smoked his stogy in the wheelhouse and watched the dark river bend; a jockey at Saratoga sat on his horse at the barrier and wickedly waited for his break; a man in some New York tenement room sat before his table and wrote his pamphlet inciting the oppressed to rise against the barons of coal and steel; a boy and a girl walked through moonlight under the hickory trees of Indiana and knew nothing except each other's presence; a married woman stood in a room and looked across it, beyond the crowd and beyond her husband to her lover, and met his glance and knew what it meant. The just and the unjust, the faithful and the crooked, the pure and the sinful — all were one, breathing a common air and pacing a common earth, the most pure with his temptations and the most dissolute with his moments of grandeur. All were one, walking forward through the sunlight and the dark, each with his end but each a part of the life stream which came out of time and went on into time.

This was his country and this was his part and his place. He thought of Hines dead and Bierss alive; one an upright man and one a lewd scoundrel. But each had taken his place in the ranks of men and each had been faithful, one with his duties discharged and one yet to suffer before his grace was achieved. Tonight the camp lay at fitful rest and each of the living nourished his memories, his wishes and his hatreds but all were waiting together for tomorrow — and again would stand together. Their lot was a common one; the commonness of it made all of them good.

He thought: "I've got nothing but a spoon and a knife to work with." He rose to a sitting position and found his haversack and got out his knife and began to dig the sandy-powdered soil. He worked mechanically, his muscles reluctantly answering his will. This was the bitter end of a day now twenty hours old and pieces of that day worked through his mind as strange and vivid pictures telescoped together. He remembered many mixed sounds, and the shock of cold water at the first ford went sharp through him; he recalled the way Cooke had turned at the ford and had gone away, his Dundreary whiskers flowing to the breeze of his gallop; he remembered the terrified face of young Adkins, whose horse had bolted straight into the dust and toward the Sioux. He thought: "I shouted at him to fall off the saddle, but he didn't hear." He scooped the loose earth into a mound and recollected Bloody Hand's sudden shudder in the saddle and the violent blood splashing against Reno's face. He could not recall when he had last seen McDermott. He tried

to recollect McDermott on the firing line; he tried to follow Mc-
Dermott from that point. "Dead and scalped," he concluded.

Reno came tramping around the circle and stopped near Moylan.
Shafter heard the major speak with an exhausted incoherence. "How
in God's name can a man possibly sleep?"

"Who's asleep?"

"Benteen," said the major. "Sound asleep."

At midnight or beyond, Shafter had a shallow depression scooped
out. He thought, "There'll be hell around here at daylight. They've
got positions higher up and they'll scorch us." But he had done all
he could and now settled in his depression, uncomfortably lying on
his cartridge belt; he made some attempt to adjust himself, and
fell asleep.

XXI

Bugles in the Afternoon

HE WOKE with a sudden upfling of his body from the ground, startled by the sound of a single shot. Day trembled through morning's twilight and the peaks to either side of this one now came into view; below him a mist moved thinly over the Little Bighorn. Benteen strode past, sharp of voice and full of vigor. "Keep under cover, boys. The music's starting again."

A second shot arrived, slitting the dust behind Shafter, the echoes of it rolling on and on through morning's stilled air. Bierss grunted to himself and pointed westward to the adjacent peak, whose heights commanded this knob on which they lay. "Comin' from there, but I don't see a damned thing."

Moylan came forward and sat down by Shafter. He said: "You take the left wing of the company, I'll take the right."

"Myles," said Shafter, "don't expose yourself."

"I am too old to duck," said Moylan. He crossed his legs tailor fashion and stared a long while at the hill from which the fire now came more strongly. Lead arrived, breaking up dust and forming a thin haze on the knoll. "Boys," called Moylan, "watch those rocks and wait till you see something to shoot at. We have got all day." Far below, fresh waves of Sioux came up the valley and flung themselves at the river willows and made the water crossing; they dismounted and began to work their way forward on the slope, climbing in crisscross fashion and dropping behind the rough furrows of earth, the frequent slabs of rock. The sun rose, the first touch of it reminding Shafter of his thirst and his hunger. This day would be hot.

"Give me your carbine," said Moylan and took it from Shafter and braced his elbows on his knees and snugged the gun to his cheek. He waited a long while, holding the muzzle dead on one spot; the gun roared and the recoil slightly swayed him. His mouth creased. He returned the carbine to Shafter, nodding.

Bierss said: "For God's sakes, Cap'n, get down."

"Kern," said Moylan, "I wrote a letter a month ago to General Summers. You remember him?"

"Yes."

"He's close to Sherman. I told him to open a case that had been shut too long."

Shafter said, "You ought to let dead things alone. They'll never touch it."

"I did Summers a good turn once when he was a young captain. He owes me a turn and I told him I wanted it. A word from him to Sherman will be enough. A word from Sherman will do all of it. That would be a good thing."

"Once," said Shafter, "it would have mattered. Now, I don't care."

"Yes," said the captain, "you do. Otherwise what brought you back to the uniform?"

"I could think of nothing else to do."

"So you did the thing which was in your mind, my boy. You came back. You'll be soldiering until you're mustered out an old man, or until you're buried on the battlefield."

Shafter turned in his hole and smiled at the captain. "A bunk to sleep in, a payday for a little whisky and a little poker — that's enough, Myles."

"We shall see," said the captain and moved away, strolling as though he were on Lincoln's parade ground with no care in his mind.

Company A held the east segment of the circle, facing the higher peak, from which Sioux fire now strengthened. H and K lay overlooking the ford to the south and M guarded the west, taking the fire from the peak which stood as a high point in that direction. To the north, where the ridge ran gradually downward into flat land, B and D and the pitiful remnant of G had been placed. It was from this direction Reno and Benteen expected attack.

The sun came full up. At nine o'clock the firing had grown to an outright engagement and the Sioux had apparently begun an encircling movement. A constant, down-plunging leaden rain came from the two peaks to north and south. Along the lower rocks, between the south rim and the ford, the brown Sioux bodies made a spotty, shifting pattern against the gray earth. Reno came over to look down that way and spoke his judgment.

"They wish to draw our attention. The main attack is shaping to the north."

Over there the land fell gently, slashed by frequent gullies into which the Sioux filtered in quick sallies; a great party moved around the base of the southern peak, made a wide sweep and rushed forward into the gullies. Benteen, vigilant and calm, came up to Reno.

"If they get any nearer, they'll swamp us with a sudden charge. We've got to attack."

"You'll lose every man you take out there," said Reno.

"We have got to drive at them," repeated Benteen.

Reno said irritably: "If you can get a party together you have my assent to it."

The firing never let up. Horses began to drop in the center of the area and the smell of powder lay acrid in the air. Bierss snugged himself into his shallow pit, fired and loaded and fired again until the barrel of his Springfield was too hot to grasp. Moylan sat behind his section of the company, loading guns and passing them to his troopers with his calm counsel. "Take your time. Wait until you see the sweat on their bellies."

Shafter had gone to the left of the troop line; he stood here watching the earth around him show dimpled jets of dust. Behind him Benteen's voice made a strong, steady call and troopers were gathering themselves for a rush. The Indian line, now drawing about the knoll from all sides, brought a heavier gunfire to bear. It grew into fury, echoes all blended into one rolling, crackling racket. Shafter watched A Company's thin line wilt on the ground; he watched men die and he saw them flinch and roll helplessly aside and turn wild glances upon him. Bierss moved a little in his hole, as if settling for a better aim; the corporal's gun steadied on the near-by peak and the corporal's body lifted and fell to his breathing. Shafter turned his head for a brief while to watch Reno trot toward the other side of the area. "Benteen," said Reno, "I'll take this." Swinging his glance back again, Shafter noticed Bierss' gun tipped idle over the dust parapet. Bierss had flattened himself full length and seemed to be taking a short rest.

"Bierss," said Shafter, "look alive."

Trooper O'Dale looked about and shook his head. Shafter stepped forward until he saw that Bierss had a bullet through his brain.

Reno's voice came back through the hark and the snarl of gunfire. "Forward!" Shafter swung and ran after him as the major jumped forward with his revolver, leading his troopers downgrade toward the nearest gully. Shafter came abreast of the line and ran with it. He remembered the way Bierss had relished his worldly pleasures, but he remembered, too, how Bierss had marched and endured and fought and had grinned through all his misery.

The skirmish line rushed on toward the gully, firing as it ran. Reno had no hat and his lank hair jiggled down over his forehead; he kept discharging his revolver at the gully and he kept shouting: "Forward — jump 'em!" Men whimpered a little and paused and sat slowly down and were left behind. Twenty yards from the gully, Shafter watched Sioux spring out of it and run backward toward the next lower gully. The slope of the plain boiled with dust and his heart began to slug in his ribs again from the run. Reno had stopped and turned. "That does it," he said, his eyes round and black-ringed. "Back to the top." The line swung, trotting upgrade, pushed now by the danger to the rear. Bullets whipped by and scraped up flinty showers of earth. Shafter breathed from the bottom of his lungs, he heard men from the higher parapet call him forward. He reached the top and half turned to look behind him, and at that moment he was struck hard in the body and he dropped to his hands and knees and was puzzled at his fall. He started to rise again, and saw Lieutenant Edgerly striding toward him. He reached out for Edgerly's hand, but his own arm grew too heavy and fell back. For the smallest interval of time there was a roar in his head like the breaking of surf; after that all sound ceased.

The sortie had driven the Sioux back from the near coulee and the firing slackened and men began to reach out for the wounded. A pair of D troopers carried Shafter to the pack barricade before

Porter, who worked on his knees, his sleeves rolled up and his long hands blood-stained. He gave Shafter a single, hard look and said to the troopers, "Take his shirt off," and returned to his immediate job.

Moylan came up a little later and found Porter working on Shafter. Moylan said: "Where's he hit?"

"Near the kidney," said the doctor and leaned back to dash the sweat from his nose.

"What's that on his face?"

"He hit a rock when he fell."

"Porter," said Moylan, "how much does a man have to suffer to earn salvation?"

Porter shook his head and returned to his labors. He rolled back Shafter's eyelids and peered down and sat a moment, making up his mind; and got up and turned to the next man.

At noon, half a dozen desperate troopers ran the gantlet to the river and came back with water. The sun moved on, blistering the earth with its heat, and the wounded began to stir under it and cry out when they could no longer be still. At two o'clock, the Sioux fire grew brisk and for half an hour the command fought doggedly; in the following lull the officers held a conference.

"Custer must have gone on to Terry," said Weir.

"Terry," said Godfrey, "was due at the mouth of the Little Bighorn this morning. He should be here."

Moylan shook his head. "If he's anywhere around this valley he's in one hell of a fight, same as we are."

Captain French made a short roundabout gesture with his hand. "Time can't be held much longer. We're being cut to ribbons. We have got to move to one of those two higher points tonight."

"We have got to get water tonight," added McDougall.

Reno said dourly: "We have got to have help, or we won't last tonight."

"By God, sir," said Benteen brusquely, "we'll last."

He had fallen asleep and now he was awake, and he had slept so hard that his body was numb below the hips. He looked at the sun crawling half down the sky; it had been straight overhead when he last saw it. "How could I have slept for three hours?" he wondered. He rocked his head from side to side and recognized the barricade of packs and discovered men lying in a row beyond him, some still and some groaning. Then he knew he had been hit and he tried to move his legs and had no luck. Pain began to move through him; it trickled like water and seemed to have no source.

Toomey, Doctor Porter's orderly, was near by. He said: "What's the matter with me, Toomey?"

"You got a hole in your guts," said Toomey.

Shock sickened him and a bitter fright yelled through him; but that was only temporary. The wave of vitality passed, and left him dull. He thought: "I must be dying."

The pain began to take on the rhythm of his pulse, slow and steady, and in a little while he was a mass of flame. "Four days ago," he thought, "we were at the mouth of the Rosebud and Custer led us. Twenty-four hours ago we were coming over the pass. Then we sighted the lone tepee." It was far back; it might have been a month ago. He remembered how the troop had looked when it marched away from the Yellowstone and he visualized the men he knew to be dead, and then he visualized the troop without these men. "My God," he said, "we're not enough to mount a guard."

He watched the sun slide west and he heard the firing come in fitful volleys. A bullet occasionally struck the barricade of packs with a sharp thump, and now and then a bullet bounced from the earth and screamed through the thin hot air like a suddenly burst piano wire. Moylan came over and looked down. "How are you, Kern?"

"All right."

"Terry ought to be up to relieve us pretty soon."

"I hope he's got a better hill than we have."

"The Indians have quit massing against us," said Moylan. He watched Shafter a moment in an extraordinarily sharp way — the way of a man who looks upon death; and then Moylan went away.

There were fewer and fewer exchanges of firing. The men at the parapets began to rise, dusty and parched, and to move around with the looseness of physical exhaustion. The smell of the wounded hung in the air, faintly sweet, faintly foul; the dead man next to him had begun to swell in the belly. Details formed and moved the horses downgrade toward the river, and he heard Reno talking to Benteen.

"They've gone back toward the foot of the valley."

"They wouldn't be leaving us unless they were threatened elsewhere," said Benteen. "That will be Terry or Custer."

A detail returned with water for the wounded. Moylan came over to give Shafter a drink, and sprinkled some of it on Shafter's face. There was smoke in the air.

"Sioux burning the grass in the valley," said Moylan. Godfrey called to him and he went back toward the south rim of the peak.

"Look there," said Godfrey.

The Sioux had broken camp at the lower end of the valley and now were passing up the same area across which Reno's troop had charged. The column was as wide as the valley itself and it stretched on and on, braves and squaws and travois and horse herd. All the officers and men lined the brow of the hill to watch it pass and swing south into the broken land.

"A mile wide and three miles long," said Benteen, estimating the column. "Fully three thousand warriors in that party. That's what we ran into."

The sun had begun to set, its long rays flashing on Indian lance and gun; the murmur of that vast band — the sound of voices and the rattle of gear — came up the slope like the faint babble of geese in the distant sky. Benteen said suddenly: "There are white men in that outfit."

"White men's clothes," said Godfrey; and then all of them heard the notes of a cavalry trumpet — a pure blast without orderly meaning — come from the column.

"Clothes and trumpet," said Moylan. "There's your answer. Stripped from dead troopers."

"I wish," said Weir in a groaning voice, "Custer would come."

Moylan and the other officers only looked at him.

Night came down, the stars bright and immense in the sky. Moylan brought Shafter a cup of coffee and said: "You want some bacon, Kern?"

"No," said Shafter, "I'm not hungry, but I could drink a gallon of water."

He turned on his side, but a great bomb of pain exploded in his belly and sent out its waves of agony. He stretched his arms and dug his fingers into the ground and slowly sweated and felt sick. A wind came up and cooled him slightly; and thus partly relieved, he fell asleep. When he awoke the wind still blew but he was increasingly hot and he called softly for Toomey and got another drink; and lay listening to the little sounds in the camp, to the pacing of the sentries and the snoring of exhausted men and the suppressed sighing and gritted suspirations of the wounded around him. He saw light break through the east and when day came he was a thousand years old, with strange thoughts in his head; and he had made his exploration into the sub-world which the living and healthy never see, and heat burned throughout him; then he fell asleep a second time.

When he awoke again the sun had started up and he saw a column of riders come over the hill's crest, General Terry in the lead. Terry got down and reached out and shook Reno's hand and Benteen's hand. There were tears in Terry's eyes.

"General," said Reno, "where is Custer?"

"Custer," said Terry, and nodded to the west, "is three miles down there, dead."

"Where's his battalion?"

"Dead," said Terry. His voice broke and he bent his head, wrestling with his self-control. "All of them, every man and every beast. A terrible blunder — a terrible, tragic, unnecessary blunder."

The group of officers stood around him in stunned silence; their own ordeal had taken much capacity of feeling out of them, yet this was a shock that all felt, this complete extinction of five companies, all their officers and all their men who had ridden away the previous afternoon. Reno lifted a hand and surreptitiously wiped moisture from his eyes. Weir, who had loved Custer, flung up a hand and turned aside. Terry looked around him and saw the remnant of Reno's command and the brutal evidence of its ordeal.

"What are your casualties?"

"I have got thirty dead and forty wounded. There are others missing." Reno passed a hand over his face, at the end of his physical resources. "I do not entirely know."

Terry stood still, looking into space, a sad and weary and troubled man whose campaign, so carefully planned, so thoughtfully and painfully arranged, had turned into greatest disaster. This regiment which had marched up the Rosebud in high hope, its colors flying and its commander dreaming of gallantry, now lay as a broken thing on the dry hot earth, more than 250 of its men dead and another sixty wounded. The regiment had come upon the Sioux at the high flood of their power, upon the greatest concentration of strength ever seen upon the plains. Uncaptured and undefeated, that Sioux power now slowly moved away while Terry with his battered command could not follow.

He knew, as he stood so gravely here upon the scene of defeat, how that defeat had come about. His trap, designed to snap shut, had been prematurely set off by the impetuous disregard of General Custer of his orders; wanting glory and blindly believing in himself and his regiment, Custer had not waited; the power of waiting was not in him. More than that the expected help of Crook had not come. With a command greater than Terry's, Crook dallied on the upper Powder, cautiously sealing himself in with double-strength pickets, made afraid by his defeat and calling for help. Of this Terry then knew nothing; it only mattered that the campaign had failed.

He turned to his adjutant and said slowly: "Send a man back to the *Far West* and tell Marsh to push the boat upstream as far as he dares. We shall be bringing on the wounded, who must be taken to Lincoln. Remind him to have plenty of wood aboard and to arrange the lower deck as a hospital. We must have details out at once to bury the dead. Waste no time. We have got to pull out."

From his place behind the packs, Shafter saw the command's sudden activity with a disinterested eye. Fever thinned his blood and lifted him so that sometimes he seemed weightless above the ground. The talk of men moved around him and left no impression. He saw Moylan bend down and he heard Moylan speak, and nodded in return. He saw the dead carried away and never quite understood why. Later he was lifted into a blanket litter slung from poles, two mules fore and aft on the poles; with this motion cradling and easing him he slept and woke and saw the sky bright, and slept again, later to wake and find the sky black. He heard Lovelace's voice somewhere near him and Lovelace was saying: "I'll be back. I'll be back." Three days later he was on the *Far West* and only vaguely was aware of it; there was a different smell and a different motion — and the sight of the sky disappeared. From time to time he heard a whistle blowing and always he heard the murmur of men — their sighing and their suppressed words. Some of the words came from him.

On the third of July, the *Far West* blew its whistle for the landing at Fort Lincoln and, with its jack staff black-draped and its flag at half-mast, touched shore. A runner went out immediately with the news and in the middle of the night officers reluctantly walked toward Officers' Row to notify the wives of the dead. The wounded were carried to the post infirmary. In Bismarck, a telegrapher sat at his key to flash the news east, and at midnight exactly someone rapped on the door of the Russell house. Josephine had heard the boat's whistle. Now, moved by the intimations of fear, she rose and dressed and hurried to the post.

XXII

"It Was Written in the Book"

THERE was space around and above and below him; he swept through it, back and forth, as though in a giant swing. At times he rose directly upward and fell down and down yet never touched earth. Occasionally, great storms swept this space and he was whirled end over end with the screaming tumult of the storm filling his ears; then calmness would come and he floated without motion or sound or feeling. There were moments when he drifted near consciousness and heard voices, and recognized his own voice among them, and felt the touch of the bed and sometimes the cold pressure of a hand on his face. Sensations of fire and suffocation ·made him turn and protest; and after that he lost these sensations and floated into complete blackness and knew nothing. When he returned to near-consciousness he always knew he had been away, and his mind always tried to distinguish the real from the unreal but never quite succeeded.

On those occasions when he came out of blackness and approached the border of awareness he seemed always to ask himself: "How long has it been?" and his mind strained to answer the problem. Now it was but a moment he had been away, now it was a hundred years. Time was something that would not stay fixed; it had nothing definite about it, nothing real. It was a distance between two points — but the points were forever moving, so that the distance was never the same. He walked back and forth between those points time after time with his watch in his hand. It always took him fifty-seven minutes, no matter how near each other the points were, no matter how far apart they were. Then he changed his way of calculation. He dug deep holes and buried posts and laid rocks against them so they could not move, so they would always be exactly in the same places. Now he walked back and forth between them and found he could make the trip sometimes in one minute, sometimes in six hours. But there was no difference between the minute and the six hours. His mind strained onward toward truth, reaching out and out and almost grasping a thought but never quite touching it. It excited him and he put all his will into it. He said: "There is no such thing as time," and felt a great wave of peace roll cool and wonderful through him. He would never have to worry about time any more.

He stood again by one of the posts he had planted deep in the ground and he looked around him. Where was north? Where was down and where was up? Distance marched away, but it had no ending. It began where he stood, but the place on which he stood was nothing; it did not exist — and space marched out from nowhere through nowhere, to nowhere. There were no boundaries. When he walked away from the post he walked into emptiness, and emptiness was all around him and it made no difference which way he traveled, for there was no such thing as direction.

Then he returned to the post and he said, "But this is somewhere — this is solid. I am here. This is here." He reached out and touched the post to feel its solidness, and discovered the post was an illusion, for his hand passed through the squareness and the definiteness of it and there was no squareness, no definiteness, no post. It did not exist. It was only something he had wanted to be there. It was only a wish, a dream. Suddenly he swept his hand back to his chest, to feel his own solidness, and his hand passed through his chest, and he looked down at his hand, and it was not there. He was not there. He was a shadow in shadows. He was less than that — he was emptiness floating in emptiness. "No," he said, "that can't be true. I think and I feel — and I see." But what did he see and what was it he felt? He sought for his answer, patiently and stubbornly. He was alone, a bodiless thing in a space that had no beginning, no form and no end. He was a voice that had no sound, he was a wish, a dream, a spark of being. His mind worked at it, pushing at the thought and pressing it narrower and narrower. He was a spirit. Where came that spirit and what gave it power and what was its form, its meaning or its purpose? He was still now, he was motionless in the motionless void around him; but somewhere in the void was a presence waiting for his answer. "What am I?" he asked. Then he said: "I am something."

He awoke as he had wakened thousands of other times; consciousness arrived softly and he opened his eyes and saw the walls around
him, the stove in the room, the iron frame at the foot of his bed, the
gray blanket folded there, and the orderly looking down at him.
Josephine sat beside the bed.

"Hello, Kern," she said.

"What time is it?"

The orderly gave him an odd glance and pulled out his watch.
"Nine in the morning."

"What morning?"

"Saturday morning. July 6."

"This Fort Lincoln?"

"Yes."

Shafter lay with his head turned, watching these two, Josephine
and the orderly. They were solid figures silhouetted against the daylight streaming through the hospital windows, their voices made full
sounds, and Josephine's lips were red and real and there was a
strange moist shining in her eyes. He said, "Bend forward," and put
out his hand. It had weight and the weight was hard for him to
manage, but he touched her cheek, and felt its smoothness and its
reality. He murmured, "A very odd thing," and then, as though this
one gesture had worn him out, he fell asleep.

He came awake again somewhere during the night and felt the
hollow, exhausted peace within his body. His lips were rough when
he touched them with his tongue and a great lassitude made it impossible for him to move. But he was thinking of the strange things
which had been in his mind and now he tried to bring them back,
grasp their meaning and their dark importance. They would not
come; it were as if, close to the margin of death, a gate had drawn
aside to permit him a glimpse of another world. But he had cheated
death and the gate had slammed shut and some power was even now
at work, erasing within him the half-revealed secrets which did not
belong to him as long as he was in this world. "A man could not
endure living," he thought, "if he saw both sides of the fence." He
slept into the middle of the following day and woke and was fed.

Josephine came in for a short time and sat at his bed. She watched him, darkly and without a smile; it was the way he knew her best, her pride making her strong, her will giving her force.

"Garnett's dead," he said.

"I know." Then she added, "Why do you think of that before you think of other things?"

"He spoke your name." He thought of that a moment, and added: "Of all the women he knew, you were the one he remembered."

"Did he ask you to tell me anything?"

"No."

"Why are you speaking of him now?"

"A woman should know when a man dies with her memory in him."

"And the memory of other women."

"No," said Shafter, "he wasn't thinking of the others."

"Do you want me to thank you for telling me all this?"

"I'm only doing a chore."

She watched him and he held his eyes on her, wondering what emotions lay behind her self-control. He wanted some sign from her, but she gave him none. She had closed up on him entirely so that he no longer saw in her eyes or on her lips, nor heard in the cadence of her voice, the telltale warmness of her heart. He felt irritated at it, at her, and at himself.

She said: "Better sleep," and went away.

A little later he saw Mary Mulrane pass him. He watched her stop at a far bed and bend over; he raised himself a little and thought he recognized Lovelace in the bed. When Mary returned he stopped her. He said: "How's Frank?"

She was happy, he saw; and she had been crying. "He's all right," she said. "The doctor says he's all right. If I knew about my father — "

"Your father," said Shafter, "was stationed at the Powder River base. He's safe."

She looked at him and was tempted to speak of something; and struggled with it, and spoke. "What happened to Jack Purple?"

"He died with his troop." He looked at her and felt free to give her some advice. "Mary," he said, "don't waste a tear on him. Your boy is better."

"Oh," she said, "I know that. I always knew that. I am just sorry — I'm sorry for all of them."

Major Barrows and his wife called that afternoon. They talked a little while, the major inquiring about his officer companions, those living and those dead. Mrs. Barrows sat by, scarcely speaking, but attentive, and presently the major murmured, "Stay a moment, Margaret. I want to speak to Doctor Jordan." He gave his wife a sharp glance and strolled down the room.

Mrs. Barrows said: "It was terrible for all of you, wasn't it?"

"It was a hard fight," he said.

She pressed her lips together and sat in silence, looking at him in a rather desperate way. She turned her head to notice that her husband was at the far end of the room and now she swung her glance back to Shafter, suddenly grown strained and harassed. "Sergeant," she murmured, "how did Edward Garnett die?"

He knew then how it was with her. He said to himself: "So he got her, too." She loved the man and was tortured now. He thought of what he was to say very carefully, and said it: "We were halfway up the hill when he was hit. He got to the top and lasted until that night. But he wasn't in much pain. He knew he was dying and it didn't matter to him."

She absorbed his words. She sat still, waiting for him to continue, her eyes begging him to add something she seemed in an actual agony to hear. Presently she drew a long sigh and spoke in a tone scarcely above a whisper. "Were you with him when he died?"

"Yes."

"Did he speak of me at all?"

This was what she wanted to hear, so urgently that she had stripped herself of her honor before him. It meant life or death to her.

"Yes," he said, "he called your name when he died."

Feeling rushed across her face and filled her eyes. She drew a ragged breath and her hands came together and whitened with pressure. She started to speak to him but found no voice. She bowed

her head, struggling with her composure, and in a little while the
major returned from the far end of the room. Shafter noticed the
way his eyes surreptitiously touched his wife. Then the major said
quietly: "We mustn't wear him out, Margaret."

She stood up, very cool again. She said: "God be with you,
Sergeant," and for the first time she smiled.

Major Barrows had started away, but now came back and looked
down at Shafter. "Sergeant," he said, "how could it have happened?
How could it have been possible?"

Shafter murmured: "I've been thinking of it. General Terry split
his forces into two sections, to approach from different sides of the
Sioux. That turned out to be a mistake. Then Custer split his regiment into three pieces — and that was a mistake. He was to have
waited for Gibbon to come up. He was to have sent a scout through
to check with Gibbon. He didn't send the scout through, and he
didn't wait. Both mistakes. We had counted on Crook, but Crook
never came. Add all those things together."

Barrows said: "If Terry had held his command together, if Custer had waited — "

"We still would have been beaten, I think. There were too many
Sioux."

"A tragedy of errors," sighed Barrows and shook his head.

Shafter looked at the major. He looked at the major's wife. What
he said was for both of them. "Men do the best they can. That's all
they can do. This thing was written in the book. The hand that
writes in the book is one over which we have no control."

"It is as good an answer as any," said Barrows and led his wife
away.

The wind blew rough and dry across the parade as the major
and his wife stepped from the hospital. The major took her arm and
looked at her with a consideration that was odd in him. "Turn
your face from it, Margaret."

"I'm not that fragile."

"This land is hard on precious things," he said.

She gave him a startled glance. "Why, Joseph, I haven't heard
you say that for so long — "

"I know," he murmured. "I know."

Shafter lay in a still and wonderful ease while his mind turned the case of Mrs. Barrows patiently over and over. She had been a woman racked with terrible emotions, with feelings so urgent that she had bared herself to him; and then in one phrase he had restored within her some faith, some flame, some spiritual loveliness more necessary to her than her loyalty to her husband. Maybe she had been lonely most of her days, the grace and romance of life slowly shriveling until Garnett had come along to see her need and to prey upon it. Perhaps she had feared or suspected it was a cheap thing with him, nothing more than a conquest in return for all her passionate giving, and so she had come to him, to Shafter, for one word which would restore her faith. Well, he had given her the thing she wanted to hear. He had supplied Garnett's memory with a dignity the man himself did not possess.

But he thought of other women Garnett had captured by his charm and it occurred to him that all of these women had seen in Garnett something which he was not. How had they seen it then? He puzzled over it until he remembered Mrs. Barrows' eyes. It was a dream they sought to make real. These women all had hungered for the music, the color and the vivid richness of living; it was a cry in them, to be important, to fill the empty tissues of existence with those full and beautiful experiences for which the human spirit was created. They had come to Garnett, crowded of heart and body, and had made their surrender in hopes of a like return. That was their fulfillment — to love and to be loved.

He remembered the stillness on Josephine's face, the stillness upon her lips; and he slept.

The hospital orderly brought him a letter the next morning. "Came last week," said the orderly. "War Department."

It was from the adjutant general. It said: —

By order of the General of the Armies, please be informed that your record has been reviewed and certain findings set aside. This is your authority to request re-instatement, as first lieutenant of

cavalry, United States Army. If you wish to act upon this authority, make application through the adjutant, Seventh Cavalry, submit
to physical examination and return papers to this office for approval.

Moylan, he thought, had done that. When Josephine came that
afternoon he showed the letter to her and watched her eyes move
back and forth over the writing. She had an intent, interested expression on her face, and her lips stirred and she looked at him with a
lively expression playing behind her reserve.

"Are you going to accept it?"

"Yes."

"Many things have happened to you, Kern. Some of them have
been harsh. Or were you a wild young man?"

"It was a woman with whom I was in love," he said. "Garnett
was my best friend in those days."

"He took her from you, Kern?"

"Or she went to him. Who knows about those things? In any
event, the world fell down. She had come down behind the lines
to see me. This was in the Shenandoah Valley, in a little town.
When I got away to go to the town to meet her I found Garnett
with her. The hotel room," he added irrelevantly, "had rosebud
wallpaper. I drew my sword on him and we fought all the way
downstairs and out through the door. I slashed him and he fell.
He was senior to me as an officer and naturally preferred charges.
Neither of us could explain the cause of the quarrel and therefore
it stood as insubordination on my part. I was dismissed from the
army, enlisted under another name and served the rest of the war as
a private."

She listened to him with an absorbed attention. She said swiftly:
"You saw her again. You told me that once. When you saw her,
Kern, did you have any great feeling about her? Did you hate her
greatly, or still want her greatly?"

"I saw her in Fargo, on my last mail trip. It was all gone —
everything. You can't restore faith. I was very young and love is a
terrible thing when you're young."

"But not when you're a mature man, Kern?"

He shrugged his shoulders.

She said: "I can understand why you hated Garnett. You still do, don't you?"

"No," he said. "It would be difficult for me to hate any man, living or dead, who rode down that valley with me."

"But he changed your life for you."

"Maybe I did my own changing. I lay no blame on anybody for what I am."

She spoke out of a dark, cold distance. "He always walked between you and other people. Whenever he did that, you were never the same. He destroyed your faith. You have never had it since. Not in anything or anybody."

"Could I have a drink of water?"

She poured out of a jug into a glass. She started to hand it to him, then bent and slipped an arm under his head and lifted him and held it. Her hand was warm and firm on his back, her eyes intently searched him, her lips stern. He dropped back, hearing sharpness in her voice.

"You're so thin, Kern."

"I'll be standing retreat one month from now," he said. "In this regiment."

"At least," she said, as though to herself, "you have faith left in one thing, in your kind of men. That's all. For all other things, you are an empty man. Garnett and that woman killed so much in you. They left you a bare, bleached skeleton."

"Why, Josephine," he said. "He's dead and she's two thousand miles away."

"Are they?" she said and rose. She looked down at him in a way he well remembered, hating him bitterly for his lack of trust in her, injured by his unspoken judgment. It was the same look she had given him when he had faced her in the kitchen of the Benson house. "I don't think so, Kern. Whatever he touched he ruined for you. You don't forget and you don't change your mind." The anger in her was real. Her feeling in the matter was a growing storm. "Perhaps," she said, "he destroyed many things for me, too."

Mrs. Custer came to see him, and Algernon Smith's wife. They sat by him, forlorn women now, each made aimless by a Sioux bullet. Mrs. Smith took his hand and silently held it, asking for comfort rather than giving it. He listened to the pacing of the sentry on the baked earth and he heard the echoes strike hollow through the emptied garrison. He had his recollections of Hines and McDermott and of Bierss. There was a woman over at the Point of whom Bierss had often spoken; she was a woman to whom any soldier could go, but she had been fond of Bierss. He thought: "I'll go over there and tell her about Bierss." He slept soundly the night through and woke and was restless throughout the morning and spent a long afternoon. He ate supper and watched the lights go out and irritably composed himself for the night.

When Josephine came the next afternoon she gave him a keen look. "You're better," she said. "You're cranky. Now I shan't have to come as often."

"When did you first come?"

"The night the boat brought you down. It was twelve o'clock at night. Who shaved you this morning?"

"The orderly."

"He left a mustache on you. Don't grow a mustache, Kern."

He had his head on the edge of the pillow, uncomfortably turned to look at her. She watched him a moment, and bent forward to lift his head and replace the pillow. She drew back her arm, but held her position, looking straight down upon his face; feeling roughened the smoothness of her lips.

"I can't reach up," he said.

"Do you want to?"

"Yes."

"Do you always want your own way? Do you always expect people to come back after you've knocked them down?"

"When you hate a man," he said, "your eyes turn dead black."

"It isn't hate," she whispered. "But I've got too much to give you to even let myself start — if I can't be sure you have something for me."

"Remember the last time I kissed you?"

"Yes."

"Was it a very mild thing, Josephine?"

Her lips were near and all her fragrance came to him; he saw her lips move and become heavy, he watched her eyes darken. She made a little gesture and put herself on the edge of the bed and lowered her face to him, and her warmth and her weight came impulsive and fully meant against him. She drew her mouth away, whispering into his ear. "Will you keep me close, will you never tire, will you never be less than you are now?" She waited for no answer, knowing him well; and came to him again. It was like a tall fire springing up through the black sky, touching heaven; and by its light the land around lay full and mysterious and wonderful.

THE END